Acclaim for Christina Courtenay

'The Queen of Time Slip
A romantic and compellin
Sandy

'A brilliantly written time
and romance into a compelling and vividly imagined story'
Nicola Cornick

'Christina Courtenay is guaranteed to carry me off to another place and time in a way that no other author succeeds in doing'
Sue Moorcroft

'A wonderful dual timeline story with captivating characters and full of vivid historical detail bringing the Viking world alive, I didn't want it to end!'
Clare Marchant

'Seals Christina Courtenay's crown as the Queen of Viking Romance. This sweeping tale . . . will leave you wanting more'
Catherine Miller

'An absorbing story, fast-paced and vividly imagined, which really brought the Viking world to life'
Pamela Hartshorne

'A love story and an adventure, all rolled up inside a huge amount of intricately detailed, well-researched history. Thoroughly enjoyable'
Kathleen McGurl

'Prepare to be swept along in this treasure of an adventure! With a smart, courageous heroine and hunky, honourable hero at the helm, what's not to like?'
Kate Ryder

'Christina Courtenay's particular talent is to entice you into her world and capture you'
Alison Morton

'I was totally captivated by this story of love and adventure which had me racing through the pages . . . I was drawn into the Viking world so easily which felt authentic and real'
Sue Fortin

'Brought the 9th century world alive to me and made me desperate to read more about it'
Gill Stewart

Christina Courtenay is an award-winning author of historical romance and time slip/dual time stories. She started writing so that she could be a stay-at-home mum to her two daughters, but didn't get published until daughter number one left home aged twenty-one, so that didn't quite go to plan!

Since then, however, she's made up for it by having eighteen novels published and winning the RNA's Romantic Novel of the Year Award for Best Historical Romantic Novel twice with *Highland Storms* (2012) and *The Gilded Fan* (2014), and once for Best Fantasy Romantic Novel with *Echoes of the Runes* (2021).

Christina is half Swedish and grew up in that country. She has also lived in Japan and Switzerland, but is now based in Herefordshire, close to the Welsh border. She's a keen amateur genealogist and loves history and archaeology (the armchair variety).

To find out more, visit **christinacourtenay.com**, find her on Facebook **/Christinacourtenayauthor** or follow her on X **@PiaCCourtenay** or Instagram **@christinacourtenayauthor**

By Christina Courtenay

Standalones
Trade Winds
Highland Storms
Monsoon Mists
The Scarlet Kimono
The Gilded Fan
The Jade Lioness
The Silent Touch of Shadows
The Secret Kiss of Darkness
The Soft Whisper of Dreams
The Velvet Cloak of Moonlight
Hidden in the Mists
Shadows in the Ashes
Shadows in the Spring

The Runes novels
Echoes of the Runes
The Runes of Destiny
Whispers of the Runes
Tempted by the Runes
Promises of the Runes
Legacy of the Runes

SHADOWS IN THE SPRING

CHRISTINA COURTENAY

First published in 2025 by Headline Review
An imprint of Headline Publishing Group Limited

1

Cataloguing in Publication Data is available from the British Library

B format ISBN 978 1 0354 1866 4

Typeset in 11/14 pt Minion Pro by Jouve (UK), Milton Keynes

Printed and bound in Great Britain by Clays Ltd, Elcograf S.p.A.

Headline's policy is to use papers that are natural, renewable and recyclable products and made from wood grown in well-managed forests and other controlled sources. The logging and manufacturing processes are expected to conform to the environmental regulations of the country of origin.

Headline Publishing Group Limited
An Hachette UK Company
Carmelite House
50 Victoria Embankment
London EC4Y 0DZ

The authorised representative in the EEA is Hachette Ireland, 8 Castlecourt Centre, Dublin 15, D15 XTP3, Ireland (email: info@hbgi.ie)

www.headline.co.uk
www.hachette.co.uk

To Lina Langlee, my wonderful agent –
thank you for everything you do!

Prologue

Germania Barbaricum (north-east France), mid May AD *80*

The jolting of the cart over a particularly large bump in the track woke Gisel. Her head felt as if someone had speared her skull with a knife and her gaze was unfocused. Only a sliver of light filtered in under the material that covered the wagon where she lay trussed like a fowl ready for the roasting spit. Everything was dim, and she wasn't sure whether it was reality or merely a bad dream.

Then she remembered.

The ambush. The uneven fight. Blood. Gut-wrenching screams. Grabbing hands, and then the harsh commands in the Roman language. She had feared for her chastity and her life, but they had caught her easily when she tried to run. Someone had thumped her on the head with a hard object and she'd passed out. When she came to, her hands were tied behind her back and she was being thrown into this stinking cart. The smell that permeated its planks hinted at past use for manure and animal transport.

Now *she* was the animal, as a captured slave would be treated no better than cattle. The goddess Nerthus help her.

She tried to move her head and saw that she wasn't alone. A

couple of legionaries sat at the back of the cart, their spears pointing skyward as they kept guard. They had removed their helmets, but still had swords and large daggers strapped to their belts. On her other side were the remnants of the group she'd been travelling with, all ruthlessly secured like her.

And in the corner, the one man she wouldn't have minded if they'd killed: Eberulf, his dark blue gaze fixed on her, intense and penetrating.

She shuddered and closed her eyes. It would seem that even in captivity, she couldn't escape him.

Chapter One

Iceni lands (north-east Norfolk), late May AD 80

Duro couldn't believe he was actually riding at last across the flat landscape of his ancestral tribe, the Iceni. It wasn't completely level, but gently rolling in parts, and the sky appeared endless, especially by the coast. It seemed unreal that he was finally here. He had dreamed about it for so long, he didn't trust his senses when they told him he wasn't asleep. He shivered in the bracing wind, but he didn't mind the cold. After so many years living under the hot Campanian sun in Pompeii, he relished the cool air caressing his face. Had longed for it during unbearable, stifling nights in the gladiator barracks room he'd shared with his friend Raedwald. Even the drizzle of fine raindrops couldn't dampen his spirits.

He was almost home.

Soon, the settlement came into view. Lazy drifts of smoke rose into the air, trickling through the tall, conical thatched roofs of the collection of roundhouses. His horse broke into a canter, as if it knew they were nearly at the end of their journey, and they headed along a rough track towards the enclosure. A ditch and a wattle fence encircled the cluster of buildings, vegetable plots and animal pens. There were sounds of activity, and familiar cooking scents wafted on the breeze towards him. He took a deep breath and smiled when he recognised it for what it was – the smell of home.

The main gate stood open, and chickens scratched around in the dirt, clucking quietly to themselves. They scattered with affronted squawks as he rode into the settlement, and a couple of dogs came running, barking to alert the inhabitants to his presence. Someone had already spotted him, and raised voices carried through the still air of the late afternoon. He wasn't surprised to find a group of people waiting for him outside the largest of the roundhouses, whose double doors faced the sunrise each morning.

As he dismounted, he scanned the men standing before him, their expressions ranging from wary to outright hostile. Dressed in baggy woollen trousers and colourful long-sleeved tunics, there were about a dozen of them, ranging in age from callow youth to middle age. Two were past their prime, but intimidating nonetheless. All the adults sported moustaches and longish hair. The one standing in the middle looked familiar, and Duro fixed his gaze on him and smiled.

'Commios?' he guessed, seeing some of his own features reflected in the face before him. He received only a scowl in return until a woman gasped and rushed out from behind the men. Her multicoloured tunic flapped around her spare frame, and long grey plaits whirled as she threw herself at him.

'Durobelinos, by all the gods! Is it really you?'

'Maerica!' He caught her around the waist and swung her in a circle, laughing. She was older, and somehow faded and frail, but he'd recognise her anywhere. She'd been his mother's best friend and had often helped to look after Duro and his siblings. Although she'd frequently scolded him for his wild ways, she had always been kind. Probably kinder than he'd deserved, as he had been a little tearaway, getting into one scrape after another.

'Durobelinos? My . . . brother?' Commios had taken a tentative step forward and was peering at him as if he couldn't believe his eyes. 'I . . . We thought you long dead.'

Duro put the old lady down gently and turned back to the others, who had now been joined by several more women and a few curious children. 'No, as you can see, I am alive and well. I've spent many years as a Roman slave, but I am a freedman at last. I have come to see how you all fare.'

He glanced at the plain bronze ring on his left hand, a mark of his supposed status. Only citizens and freedmen were allowed to wear rings, and his had been on his finger long enough to show a glimpse of the white skin underneath where it wasn't tanned. Anyone seeing that would assume he'd been free for years. There was no need for them to know that he hadn't been granted manumission, but had escaped captivity. His owner – the gladiator master Marcus Antonius Varro – was likely dead and buried under mountains of burning ash and pumice, and there was no one else who could dispute Duro's right to freedom. The last time he had seen the man, he'd been holed up in his quarters at the gladiator barracks in Pompeii, refusing to leave. Varro had proclaimed himself convinced that the earthquakes would soon stop, and by time he realised the nearby mountain was exploding, it would have been too late to leave.

'And to take over as chieftain?'

Duro raised his brows at his brother's belligerent question, which jolted him out of his thoughts. It would seem his homecoming wasn't welcomed by everyone, but then he hadn't expected it to be easy. 'Not necessarily,' he said, keeping his tone even. 'But I do now own the land you are farming and inhabiting.'

He had paid the relatively cheap sum of three thousand silver *denarii* for the large tract of land just a few weeks ago. He'd signed a contract in the shape of two wax tablets bound together and sealed with the witnesses' signets so that they couldn't be tampered with. A record of the land purchase had also been entered into the Roman archives at Venta Icenorum, the *civitas*, or administrative centre, for this region of the Britannic province, situated half a day's ride south of here. He'd had to go there several times, but didn't begrudge the effort, as he was keen to have everything legally watertight. Following the unsuccessful Boudican revolt some twenty years ago, much of the Iceni territory was now under Roman control. It was supremely satisfying to have bought back even a fraction. Duro was determined to purchase even more in future if circumstances permitted.

'What do you mean?' One of the other men moved forward to stand next to Commios. 'This is our land. We pay rent to the Romans fair and square.'

As punishment for taking part in Queen Boudica's rebellion, Iceni tribesmen had had ownership of their ancestral lands taken away from them by the Roman conquerors. Upon his return to these shores, Duro had learned that they had been allowed to go back and live there, on condition that they pay rent and taxes to their overlords. He would guess that had irked them no end, but they'd have had no choice in the matter. It was that or move elsewhere.

'You did, but now they have sold it to me outright, so apart from the taxes we are all burdened with, you won't be paying them in future,' he told them. Everyone was taxed in various ways by the Roman administration; there was no avoiding that whether you were a landowner or not.

His statement was greeted with a glare of downright mistrust from his brother, and silence from everyone else. Despite only having seen twenty-four winters, Commios appeared to be the designated chieftain of this settlement. Presumably that was on account of his lineage – their family was kin to the former Iceni kings. His resentment of someone barging in was understandable, especially since Duro, being the eldest, had the right to demand to take over. Never mind the fact that the land was his by purchase. That was not his intention, though. At least, not immediately. He'd come prepared to tread softly.

He held up his hands in a peace gesture. 'Look, I am not here to take charge. I only sought to relieve you all of the burden of the Roman yoke. Wouldn't you rather the land was owned by one of us than by the usurpers? I'm not expecting anyone to pay me rent, but I would be grateful for a place to stay and a portion of the produce. I will, of course, do my fair share of the work while I'm here.'

'What do you mean, while you're here? You're not staying, then?' Was that relief in Commios's voice? It saddened Duro that his little brother wasn't as happy to see him alive as he himself was to find at least one relative intact.

To the Iceni, family was everything. They lived in kinship groups of extended families, where ties of blood were strong and children were greatly valued. Despite the lukewarm welcome, Duro was ecstatic to be reunited with what was left of his kin. He was never severing their connection again if he could help it. Commios would just have to adapt to his presence in their lives. He would have some time to get used to it, as Duro was only here for a brief visit for now.

'Not immediately, no,' he replied. 'I have had many years to think about the fate that befell our family. I seek revenge. I was forced to watch when that Roman cur disrespected our mother and sister, and I remember him well.' Disrespect was an understatement, but the others all knew what he meant and there was no point spelling it out. 'I heard his name and I know which legion he was part of. I have sworn an oath to the gods that if he is still alive, I will find him and make him pay for his misdeeds.' He paused to take a deep breath, tamping down the emotions swirling inside him as they always did when he thought about what had happened. 'I don't suppose you have any news of our sister, Rufilia?'

Although their mother had been killed in front of him, his sister was still alive last he saw. She'd been taken into slavery, just like him.

'No. She's probably dead,' Commios replied, a fleeting expression of sadness flashing in his eyes. 'She must have become a slave, and if she'd managed to escape, she would have returned to us. No one has seen or heard from her since that time, so we lost hope.'

'Right.' Duro wasn't surprised, but it was still unwelcome news. He surveyed the assembled males once more, looking for another familiar face without success. 'And our younger brother? What became of him?'

Maerica entered the conversation, grabbing his arm as if to make up for his brother's less than enthusiastic welcome and boorish behaviour. 'Last we heard, Caratius was a cavalryman in the Legio Secunda Augusta. He came home once to visit when they were on the march nearby. Seemed happy enough with his lot.' She shrugged, as if it was unfathomable how anyone from their tribe could fight on the enemy's behalf.

Duro understood, though. Caratius would have only been three during the time of the rebellion, and when he grew up, the Roman army offered opportunities. At home, he would always have been in Commios's shadow, whereas a soldier was well paid and looked after by the Roman state. It was a chance to be on the winning side, rather than bogged down in defeat and resentment. The Iceni were known for their great horsemanship, so his brother would be well suited to life in a cavalry unit.

'The Legio Secunda? Hmm.' That was the legion he sought, but for a different reason. The man who had violated and killed his mother, then raped his sister and taken her prisoner, had belonged to a vexillation – or small detachment – of the Legio Secunda. They'd been present to help out the main force that defeated Queen Boudica, the Legio XX Valeria Victrix. It was strange that his brother had ended up in the same legion as Duro's nemesis, but Caratius couldn't have known that. He hadn't been anywhere near the battlefield and would have no memories of that time.

He turned to Maerica and resolutely changed the subject. 'Would you happen to have any of your famous stew in the pot? I'm fair famished after my long journey.'

He hadn't come all that far today, but he didn't tell them that. He'd only travelled from the domains of his friend and former fellow gladiator Raedwald, to the east, out by the coast. Since their return from Pompeii, he and Raedwald had been busy setting up a trading business. He'd also helped the man and his wife, Aemilia, get settled into their new home. All was well with them now, and their burgeoning business was thriving. He had felt he could safely leave them to see to his own affairs for a while.

'Of course! What am I thinking?' Maerica tugged on his sleeve. 'Come inside, do, and I'll serve you in a trice.'

'Thank you.' He smiled at her. It was nice that someone was happy to see him. Hopefully he'd win the others over gradually, and Commios would simmer down once he realised Duro wasn't here to oust him from his position as chief. He just had to persuade him that was the truth.

Chapter Two

Brussels, Belgium, late May, present day

Mackenna Jackson tugged her suitcase into the large hotel foyer. She knew it was somewhere in the centre of Brussels, part of one of the luxury hotel chains, but she didn't care which one. It looked like all the other umpteen hotels she'd stayed in during the last six months, and the name and location were irrelevant. They were beginning to blur into one. She would be extremely grateful when she could go back home to the UK and live in the same place for a while.

She had met her boyfriend, Bryan 'Blue' Daniels, during a party held by the record company she'd worked for as a temporary receptionist. It was a clichéd meet-cute, but there was instant attraction between them and they'd started dating. Mac felt the whole thing was a bit surreal, as Blue was the lead singer in the famous band Valhalla Storm. She was Cinderella to his Prince Charming, drawn into a whole new world where shopping at Harrods and eating at the finest restaurants was nothing out of the ordinary. Money slipped through Blue's fingers like water, and although Mac tried to curb his excesses, he just laughed and carried on regardless.

When he'd asked her to give up her job and travel with the band on their upcoming tour, she hadn't hesitated. It had seemed like the opportunity of a lifetime, and the glamorous lifestyle beckoned. Unfortunately, the reality was much less exciting. Long, boring days of travel, a lot of waiting around in hotel rooms, and endless parties with groupies and other hangers-on. Even the concerts, which she'd once felt so privileged to watch from the side of the stage, became samey. Something to be endured, not enjoyed. Not that she would ever tell Blue that. He was inordinately proud of Valhalla Storm, and rightly so. If you didn't have to hear the songs on repeat, they were fabulous.

A bodyguard stationed by the lifts nodded to her. They had all become her friends during their travels and she always felt safe when they were around. 'Hey, Mac, you're back! I heard the news – so sorry for your loss.'

'Thank you, Jimmy.'

She swallowed down the lump in her throat. She'd had to fly home to attend her beloved aunt Sandra's funeral, and it had been a difficult time. Aged only sixty-one, Sandra should have had many more years to enjoy life, but she'd been diagnosed with a savage type of cancer. Things had progressed quickly after that, and Mac couldn't believe she was gone. It was like a bad dream, but now she just wanted to put it all behind her and start the grieving process.

'Let's get you a key card. I bet you want nothing more than to crash, am I right?' Jimmy ushered her over to the reception desk and swiftly procured a card to Blue's room. Mackenna hadn't been with them when they checked in, as they had recently arrived from Amsterdam, their previous stop on the tour.

'Thanks, you're the best.'

Tired beyond belief, she took the lift to the top floor, where the band members all had a suite each. She had managed to get away a day early and couldn't wait to see Blue again. To be enveloped in his arms and let go of all the tension roiling through her. He'd make her feel good and help her to forget her sorrow for a while.

Stepping out of the lift, wheeling her case behind her, she was hit by a wall of music coming from one of the suites, whose door stood wide open. The bass thumped so loudly she could feel it vibrating in her stomach, and she sighed. There wouldn't be much rest around here until the party tailed off. That could be any time between now – nearly midnight – and dawn.

She guessed Blue was in the thick of it – he loved to party and never missed an evening of fun – and she decided to leave him to it. Heading for his room, which thankfully wasn't the loud one, she slotted in the key card and pushed open the door, stepping into a lavish sitting room. Immediately, she heard giggling coming from the adjoining bedroom. Leaving her suitcase, she walked over to peer in through the door, stopping dead at the sight before her.

It was yet another ultimate cliché, and presumably every rock star's dream. Blue was lying in the middle of the giant bed with a blonde woman on either side of him. Despite having different facial features, they were eerily similar. Both were in possession of very large, very fake boobs, and their naked bodies had clearly been spray-tanned recently, judging by the somewhat unnatural colour of their skin. They were pretty, though, it had to be said. Mackenna could see why Blue might have had a hard time resisting them. And yet he should have done. Had sworn he would never want anyone but her.

Yeah, so much for that.

'Oh Blue, you're so perfect. I'm gonna lick every inch of your gorgeous body,' one of the blondes murmured in a thick French accent, while her clone was already busy doing just that.

Blue chuckled, clearly having the time of his life, until he looked up and caught sight of Mackenna. His eyes went comically wide and he struggled to sit up, flailing against the onslaught of the blonde bombshells. 'Mac! Baby! You're back already? Didn't you say . . .?'

'That I was arriving tomorrow? Yes, but I managed to get an earlier flight. Guess I shouldn't have bothered. Enjoy the rest of your evening. And the rest of your life.'

She turned away from the awful scene in front of her, unable to watch for even a second longer. The lump in her throat had grown to epic proportions and would not be contained any longer. Tears spilled over and ran down her cheeks, and she swiped at them impatiently. Honestly, had she really been naïve enough to think she'd be enough for a rock star? That this would last? Yes, she'd been told by her friends that she was beautiful, smart and fun to be with, but he could have anyone he wanted. Anyone in the world. Supermodels. Blonde clones. Why would he want to tie himself to one woman? That wasn't very rock 'n' roll, was it?

God, she'd been such fool. It was time to return to reality.

Grabbing her suitcase, she marched out of the room and slammed the door shut. She turned to head for the lift and ran smack into a hard chest. When she looked up, she realised it belonged to Jonah Miller, the band's songwriter and lead guitarist. Taller and broader than Blue, with a shock of golden hair, he was objectively as handsome as her former boyfriend, just more rugged. Because Blue had the sort of pretty-boy face that looked fantastic in every photo, he was invariably the one who was complimented on his looks. Mackenna had always thought this unfair, but Jonah himself seemed content to remain in the background.

'Whoa there! Mac? What's wrong?' Jonah grabbed her upper arms to steady her. Looking from her tear-stained face to the door she'd come out of and back again, he put two and two together. He swore softly. 'I don't bloody well believe it. I'm going to kill that arsehole, I really am,' he hissed through gritted teeth. 'I'm so sorry.'

'Don't be. It's not your fault. I should have known better. And I'd rather have found out now than another six months down the line.' A slightly hysterical giggle erupted from her mouth. 'He was trying to talk me into marrying him last week. Thank God I didn't take him seriously!'

Jonah's ice-blue eyes went dark and his brows came down in a fierce scowl as he swore again. The door behind them was flung open and Blue came tearing out wearing only his jeans with the fly half unbuttoned. His hair was standing on end and his eyes were glazed from one too many drinks, or possibly something else. But the fact that he was under the influence didn't excuse his behaviour. Mackenna could see that he wasn't far enough gone not to know exactly what he'd been doing. He just hadn't thought he'd get caught.

'Babe! Come back,' he begged. 'It didn't mean anything, I swear!' He gave her puppy-dog eyes but she found herself immune. 'They're leaving now. Seriously, I was just—'

Mackenna cut him off. 'I don't care. It meant something to *me*,' she snarled. 'Go back and finish what you started. We're over.' She glanced up at Jonah. 'Thanks for . . . everything. You guys have been great and I've loved getting to know you. Good luck with the rest of the tour.'

'*Mac-kennaaa*,' Blue whined, as if she was the one acting like a difficult toddler and not him. She ignored him and headed for the lifts.

'Please can you text me to let me know you got home safely?' Jonah called out, earning himself a muttered 'What the fuck, man?' from Blue.

'OK, I will.' Mackenna had all the band members' mobile numbers in case of emergencies, but she'd never used them. Jonah was sweet to be concerned about her, though, so she figured she owed it to him. And they had actually become good friends during the tour, when he'd discovered that she was half Swedish. He had a secret obsession with Vikings – hence the name of the band, which was his idea – and thought it was cool that it was part of her heritage. Mac, in turn, was impressed with his knowledge and the fact that he actually liked reading. Blue never read anything more serious than song lyrics, and had scathingly called Mac and Jonah 'book nerds'. Neither of them had cared.

The last thing she heard as she walked into the lift was Jonah practically growling at Blue, 'You're a complete and utter moron, you know that? A spoiled brat who doesn't know a good thing when it smacks you in the face. Christ! You didn't deserve her and I'm glad she found out what you're like. In fact, I'm sick and tired of you, your ego and your immature antics. As soon as this tour is over, I quit!'

Mackenna didn't hear Blue's reply, but she could imagine he wasn't best pleased. Valhalla Storm would be nothing without Jonah, as all the best songs had been written by him. He helped produce their unique sound too, while Blue did nothing but vocals and lolling around looking hot. Good luck to him trying to keep the rest of the band together if they had to find a new guitarist and songwriter. The drummer, Owen, would probably walk too, out of solidarity with Jonah, as they were best mates. The thought of how devastated this loss would make Blue cheered her up no end, but she still couldn't stop the tears.

It had been a really shitty week.

Chapter Three

Iceni lands (north-east Norfolk), late May AD *80*

'So you were a gladiator? For seven years? How on earth did you survive that long? I've heard tell most of them only last a fight or two.' Maerica's mouth hung open in awe as she handed Duro a steaming bowl of stew.

He accepted it with thanks and breathed in the familiar smell, which brought back so many memories. How he'd missed this. The simple home-cooked foods of his childhood served in a plain bowl – none of that fancy Samian ware they'd used in Pompeii. Cooked with butter rather than olive oil, and served with beer, not wine. No unnecessary spices and strange ingredients either. Best of all, he could eat whatever he fancied now, although he always made sure not to overdo it. As a gladiator, he'd been on a strict diet – usually consisting mainly of cereals and pulses – to complement the daily training. It was only when he and Raedwald had been out and about in the town of Pompeii that they'd been able to partake of other dishes.

Sitting by the fire inside a cosy roundhouse with his family and tribe members around him. Talking, laughing, sharing the ups and downs of rural life. Something inside him loosened, as if the tight hold he'd had on his emotions ever since his capture at the age of eight could finally be set free. He exhaled and allowed his body to relax.

'I did my best to win every fight and I trained hard,' he told Maerica. He knew the others were listening as well, but they hadn't spoken to him directly yet, so he pretended not to notice them. 'Also, I had a very good friend, Raedwald. We sparred with each other and made sure we were both in the best shape for every bout. We made a pact as soon as we met to try and escape or buy our freedom, and we worked towards that goal with fierce determination.' He shrugged. 'And here we are. Or rather, here I am. He's bought his own lands to the east of here, where he's settling with his wife.'

Maerica's eyes lit up. 'Do you have a wife too? This place could do with more little ones.' She threw a meaningful glance at Commios, who studiously ignored her. Duro gathered his brother hadn't taken a wife yet, although he was certainly old enough and should have done. Or perhaps he'd had one and lost her? That was a mystery for another day, though, and he wouldn't pry.

He shook his head. 'No, I've not found one yet.'

'Well, there are a couple of girls of marriageable age here – Bellicia and Mina.' Maerica nodded towards two young women who'd been casting him interested glances. They looked to be around twenty winters, which he recalled was the usual age for women to marry here. This differed significantly from Roman custom, where girls as young as twelve could be wedded, although consummation of the marriage would not be for some years after that.

'Bellicia is the eldest daughter of Belcatus, and Mina is his niece by marriage,' Maerica continued, as if that was a point in their favour.

Duro had gathered that Belcatus was the oldest man in this

settlement. As they were all a kin group of extended families, he was some sort of relative of his and second in command here to Commios. He had probably led the inhabitants until Commios became old enough to take over, but the older man didn't seem to resent not being the chieftain now.

'I'm not interested in wedding anyone here, Maerica,' Duro told her firmly. 'As I said, I shall be on my way soon. For years, the need for revenge has festered inside me. It is something I have to do, else I'll never rest easy. If the man who hurt my loved ones is still alive, he has to suffer as they did and pay for his crimes. I believe the gods will be with me, and I have asked for their assistance with my quest.'

The old woman sighed. 'Perhaps you'll think differently when you return. The girls might not have found husbands by then.'

'We will see.'

Duro had no intention of taking either of those two to wife. They were comely enough, but seemed giggly and very immature. He was used to more experienced women who knew what they wanted and acted boldly. He'd bedded quite a few during his time in Pompeii, as some of the Roman matrons sought out gladiators for bed sport. It had been preferable to paying for such encounters, and in its own way it was an indirect revenge on the men of the race who had captured and enslaved him. Not that he had ever wanted a Roman woman as his wife. No, he'd like someone who would be content to live a simple life like this with him. Unlike Raedwald, who had bought a Roman villa complex, Duro was determined to stick to his roots. Roundhouses had been good enough for his forebears; they would do just fine for him as well.

Bellicia must have taken his reply as encouragement, as she came to serve him some beer with a flirtatious smile. He pretended not to see, and did not return it. That made her pout, but she didn't give up. A short time later, she sat down next to him on the hewn log that served as a bench near the fire.

'Will you tell us what it was like over there in the Roman lands?' She fixed big hazel eyes on him, and he could have sworn she fluttered her eyelashes on purpose.

'It was very hot a lot of the time,' he replied evenly, moving away slightly so that he didn't brush against her. 'If I hadn't been a slave, it wouldn't have been so bad. The houses are well built, the food is plentiful and tasty – albeit strange – and there were perks like the communal baths.'

'Baths? We've heard about those. Didn't you say they'd built some in Camulodunum, Father?' Bellicia said.

Belcatus nodded and entered the conversation for the first time. 'Yes. Haven't tried them myself, but a cousin of mine seemed quite taken with the practice.'

'It is very relaxing,' Duro told them. 'There is hot and cold water, attendants who cover you with scented oil and then scrape it off, together with any dirt, and others who will rub your sore muscles with fragrant balm. Each bath house can hold lots of people at once, making it a social activity as well.'

Bellicia wrinkled her nose, making it look like a dried-up grape. 'That doesn't sound at all appealing to me.'

'You'll just have to try it some time. You might change your mind.'

'Did you have to fight with lions?' a little boy piped up, his eyes alight with curiosity.

Duro laughed. 'No, never. I was the kind of gladiator who fought other men, not animals. We wore special armour and each of us had different types of weapons. The aim was to battle someone unlike yourself, thereby making it more interesting for the audience.' And more gory, but he didn't add that as there was no point frightening the child.

'But you have seen a lion? They exist?' the little boy persisted. His mother tried to shush him, as if he was being impertinent, but

Duro didn't mind. He would have been the same at that age, thirsting for knowledge.

'I have and they do. You'd be surprised at the variety of animals the Romans kill in their arenas.' He went on to describe some of them, although they didn't have names in his native Brythonic language. The little boy – and everyone else – hung on his every word.

This must be what it was like to be an itinerant bard, he thought, keeping his audience spellbound. He remembered evenings sitting around this very hearth as a child, listening to epic tales of long-dead heroes and their incredible deeds. They'd been told in rhyming verse or sung to the accompaniment of a lyre, the boastful stories conjuring vivid images in the listeners' minds.

'Are you sure you are telling the truth? It all sounds unlikely to me,' Commios sneered.

Duro gave him a tight smile. 'I can always arrange for you to go and fight there yourself, then you'll see that I'm not lying.'

Commios sent him yet another glare. 'No, thank you. One gladiator in the family is more than enough.'

'Yes, well, it's not as if I had much of a choice,' Duro replied with asperity, glowering right back. Did his brother think he'd enjoyed his time away from home? That couldn't be further from the truth. 'I was eight when I left these shores,' he continued through clenched teeth. 'You're lucky you were too young to be with Mother near the battlefield or you would have been a slave too. Sold like an animal. Forced to do whatever your master asked of you, whether you wished it or not. Looked down upon. Beaten. Given a name not your own at your owner's whim. Told to fight other men to the death merely to entertain people with more blood thirst than sense. It wasn't exactly a joyful experience.'

He stood up abruptly, taking a couple of breaths to calm down. His brother was annoying him, but he didn't want to fight. 'If there is somewhere I can bed down for the night, I think I'll retire now.' He looked to Maerica, who indicated a bench at the back of the roundhouse, her eyes full of compassion and understanding.

'That one is free. Sleep well, dear boy. I can't tell you how pleased I am to have you home.' She patted him on the cheek, as if he was a child. He let her, because it was nice that someone appreciated his presence.

Unlike some others.

Camulodunum, southern Britannia, early June AD *80*

Duro stayed for two weeks, but after that he couldn't delay any further. He was itching to start looking for the man he sought. Until he had fulfilled his quest for revenge, he couldn't begin his new life. Old wounds needed to be healed before there could be a future.

Besides, he couldn't take another moment of Commios's sullen behaviour. His little brother hadn't warmed to him and, no matter what Duro did, refused to trust him. It was unfortunate, as Commios might be the only close living relative he had left, but it was what it was. He didn't have time to change matters right now.

Commios was also vehemently anti-Roman, and appeared to take Duro's more prosaic attitude towards them as a personal insult. He complained bitterly of what he perceived as the conquerors' transgressions, and the ignominy of having to submit to their rules. Apart from the fact that he no longer had to pay them rent, there were numerous taxes levied to pay for the Roman administration and all the soldiers needed to keep the Britons under control. The Romans claimed they were there to protect them, but Commios didn't buy that. All taxes were supposed to be paid in coin, but in reality the locals paid with grain.

'I'm convinced they always cheat us,' Duro heard his brother snarl at Belcatus when the subject came up around the fire one evening. 'That last tax collector brought his own measure, and although we had the correct amount ready, he claimed we were short. I'd say his measure held much more than he said it did. We were swindled.'

As he hadn't been present, Duro couldn't refute this, and therefore kept his mouth shut. He thought it highly likely his brother was right, but no matter how aggrieved Commios was, he would never win an argument with the Roman authorities. It was pointless trying, although next time the tax collector came round, Duro hoped to be present. He'd make sure their grain was sold first to someone honest, then the taxes could be paid in coin.

If necessary, he had sufficient wealth to cover any costs himself, but he'd prefer to keep that a secret. Before leaving, he carefully hid most of the gold and silver he'd brought in one of the smaller huts – one used for lambs in spring. Digging a hole in the floor, he buried the strongbox he'd purchased to keep all the earnings from his time as a gladiator. When covered with animal dung and some wisps of straw, no one would ever guess what was hidden underneath.

In search of information, he headed to Camulodunum first. Until Queen Boudica's rebellion, it had been the largest and most important town – or *colonia*, as the Romans called them – in the new province of Britannia, and the base of the Twentieth Legion. They'd constructed a large fortress, which Duro vaguely remembered seeing as a young boy, as well as an impressive temple dedicated to the conquering Emperor Claudius. The Iceni and their allies had hated everything these monuments stood for, and it had become the first target of the uprising. Young as he was, Duro had been present, although he'd been kept away from the actual fighting when Boudica and her troops attacked the fortress and the temple, slaughtering everyone inside and burning it all to the ground. If he closed his eyes, he could still see the flames licking the buildings and the smoke rising into the sky. The acrid smell of burning had lingered on everyone's clothes for days afterwards.

As he neared the place now, after a day's ride, he noticed that it had been completely rebuilt. Passing through the gates, he could see there were new town walls, at least eight feet thick and taller than the height of four men by the look of it, with a huge defensive ditch outside. Watchtowers had been placed at intervals, as well as quite a few gates. The main one had temples on either side of it, and led straight onto the Decumanus Maximus, the main street running east to west. Knowing something of Roman town construction by now, Duro guessed there was also a north-to-south road, and smaller streets laid out in a grid pattern. It seemed to be the way the Romans always operated when building new settlements.

The hated Temple of Claudius had also been rebuilt, or so he'd been told. To him, as it had been to his parents and their generation, it would always be a symbol of Roman authority. He would never be able to look at it without remembering the oppression it represented. He knew that tensions were still rife in places. There was simmering resentment among the native Britons that broke out in open revolt from time to time. Still, he was pragmatic enough to know that the Romans were here to stay now, and there was no point fighting their superior forces. They would prevail one way or another. The best thing to do was to work within the system to further his own ends, as he and Raedwald had done in Pompeii. And he would, just as soon as he had finished this quest.

The street was paved, and the shorter gable ends of the rectangular dwellings and shops that lined it faced the road. Large shuttered windows displayed the wares made in the workshops inside. Most of these buildings were half-timbered, whitewashed and single-storeyed. A few had red roof tiles, others thatch. Trade was flourishing, and the local eateries, *thermopolia*, and *cauponae*, taverns, were doing good business. There were throngs of people crowding the walkways either side, some spilling out onto the street itself from time to time. It reminded him of Pompeii. A brief flash of sadness speared through him as he remembered all the lives that had been lost in the volcanic eruption. Such a waste, and he would be for ever grateful to have been spared by the gods.

He guided his horse to the house of a man Belcatus had grudgingly recommended: one Toutius, a comb maker, who welcomed him cautiously. He was ushered into the family's best room, which sported painted walls and a flagstone floor, showing that their business was doing well.

'You are related to Belcatus, you say? Then come in, come in. My wife will find you a place to bed down for the night.' Toutius shouted for a slave boy to take Duro's horse to the back of the property and see to its care.

'Thank you, I am much obliged. I won't trespass on your hospitality long. I'm just here to try to find some information on the possible whereabouts of my siblings. We were separated following the rebellion, and I have only just returned to these shores.' He didn't say whence, as Toutius had no need to know that.

'Ah, I see. Well then, I would suggest you take yourself off to the nearest *caupona* – the owners of most of them seem to relish gossip, and they hear much.'

'That was exactly my thought. Please tell your good wife that she need not provide me with victuals. I'll fend for myself.'

He set out almost immediately and visited several such establishments. At first, he merely listened to the conversations going on around him. From the Roman citizens present, he heard a lot of complaints – about the cold, harsh weather in Britannia, the overabundance of rain and lack of sunshine, and the generally barbaric conditions. Some also discussed the locals, as if there weren't any present who could easily overhear them.

'This crude provincial outpost was in dire need of organisation and some culture, I tell you,' one man averred loudly. 'They are forever squabbling among themselves without resolving anything. Our system of government and superior roads and buildings were definitely needed here. Not to mention art, literacy and some basic cleanliness.'

Duro gritted his teeth and forbore from correcting the man. He'd listened to these types of derogatory comments for years about anyone the Romans considered a barbarian. They simply couldn't conceive of others as being equal to themselves, and their way of life was always considered superior. He wasn't here to argue, though. It was information he sought.

In each of the taverns, he surreptitiously enquired about the whereabouts of the Legio Secunda. Luck was with him when he struck up a conversation with a rather inebriated former Roman legionary who seemed not to mind talking to a native Briton. He was an older man, a veteran who had just been given a plot of land outside Camulodunum to settle on, he said.

They chatted of mundane things first, before Duro steered the conversation towards the Roman military presence in Britannia, which was considerable. 'What legion were you with?' he asked. 'I've heard tell there are a few different ones in this province.'

'Oh aye, there used to be four, but only three are left permanently now. I was with the Twentieth, the Valeria Victrix. We helped put down the rebellion some twenty years ago, but things have calmed down in these parts. Most of the trouble is in the north and west at present. The Legio Secunda Augusta and the Legio Nona Hispana are sorting it out.' He waved a hand as if he had complete faith in their ability to quell any resistance.

A quick mental calculation told Duro that with three legions present, there must be some fifteen thousand legionaries in Britannia. Plus whatever auxiliary troops they had – probably an equal number – so a total of thirty thousand well-trained and disciplined men. There was no way the natives could stand against an army of that size. Just as he'd thought, they were here to stay.

'Any idea where the Legio Secunda are usually based?' he asked casually.

'The Secunda? The ones who aren't on their way north with the new governor, Gnaeus Julius Agricola, are at Isca now.' The man seemed to have been high-ranking enough to know what he was talking about.

'Isca?' Duro questioned. He hadn't heard that name before.

'It's a fortress out west, just past the border between the Silures and the Dobunni. Those damned Silures are still a thorn in our side and won't settle down, so we were forced to build a fort to keep them in check.'

'I see. Well, I thank you for telling me. My brother is serving in the cavalry of that legion and I haven't seen him for some years. I need to speak to him about some family matters. Can I buy you another cup of wine?'

'Yes, please. And good luck to you. Shouldn't be hard to find him,' the Roman slurred.

Duro hoped he was right, although it wasn't Caratius he was most interested in finding, but a certain Aulus Julius Felix, usually known as just Julius Felix. The man's *cognomen*, or last name, meant 'favourable' or 'auspicious', a fact Duro had heard him boast of to his comrades at the time when Duro was taken captive. He very much hoped to change that to Infelix – unhappy and extremely unlucky indeed.

And now he knew the whereabouts of the man's legion, he would see about making that happen as soon as possible.

Chapter Four

Bath, late May, present day

Mac: *Hey. I made it back to my aunt's flat in Bath.*
Jonah: *Thanks for letting me know. Was worried about you. Bath? I thought you lived in London?*
Mac: *I didn't get a chance to tell anyone, but Aunt Sandra left me everything she owned in her will, so I've decided to live here now. Was sick of London anyway and there's a uni here where I can continue my studies.*
Jonah: *Oh right – cool! Glad you had a place to go back to. Good luck with the studies. I'll look you up when this endless bloody tour is over.* ☹
Mac: *Things still tense? Sorry if I made everything awkward. Didn't mean to.*
Jonah: *No! Not your fault. Was a long time coming. B is an arse and I can't put up with his diva shit any longer. Either we're a band who work together or he can take his own show on the road. Told him I'm quitting and I meant it. Enough is enough.*
Mac: *Sorry to hear that but totally understand.*
Jonah: *Thanks. You take care now. J x*
Mac: *You too. M x*

Mackenna put her mobile down on the kitchen counter and sighed. Jonah was a great guy and he deserved better than to deal with the likes of Blue. Hopefully he had made enough money from their successes that he could take some time off and decide what he wanted to do next. Perhaps he'd start another band. He was the talent behind Valhalla Storm and everyone knew it. The others were just along for the ride.

She would never have been disloyal enough to think that way when she was Blue's girlfriend, but with hindsight she could see everything more clearly. Either way, it was no longer her business. She doubted Jonah had meant it when he said he would look her up. Why would he come all the way to Bath just to see his ex-bandmate's ex-girlfriend? That made no sense. She was grateful that he'd wanted to know she'd got home OK. That meant a lot. And she would be fine. One day.

Looking around Sandra's kitchen, she knew she had her work cut out for her. The flat was a spacious ground-floor in one of the old sandstone-built terraced houses Bath was so famous for. Situated not too far from the centre of town, it was apparently worth quite a lot, but Mackenna wasn't selling, even though that would have made more sense economically. Her aunt had entrusted it to her and it held a lot of memories she wasn't ready to let go of. Not that it was officially hers quite yet. Probate and legal stuff took ages, but since Sandra had given her keys to come and go as she pleased, the lawyer had said she could move in any time. And there was no problem with the will – it couldn't be contested on any grounds – so she was free to start changing the place to how she wanted it. As for the contents – furniture and knick-knacks and so on – Sandra had already given her written permission for all or any of it to be sold, and for Mac to keep the proceeds.

There was no mortgage to pay, but the freehold of the building was owned jointly with the people who lived in the other flats, so there were still costs involved. She would need to rent out one of the rooms to keep up with the expenses. There were two bedrooms, both with en suite bathrooms, so it shouldn't be too difficult to find a tenant. First, however, she needed to do some redecorating. Everything looked old and tired, and in dire need of a coat of paint.

'Well, that shouldn't be too hard,' she told herself, and pulled out a roll of rubbish sacks and a couple of boxes from the supplies she'd bought yesterday. Time to tackle the drawers and cupboards full of old papers and knick-knacks.

She was aiming for minimalist, whereas her aunt had been a borderline hoarder. As a stallholder in one of the indoor antiques markets in town, Sandra had bought whatever caught her eye. Anything that didn't fit on her stall ended up at the flat. When she became ill, she had sold her business to a colleague, and most of the proceeds had gone towards paying off the mortgage on the flat in order to leave it to Mac unencumbered. She was grateful for that, and for the fact that she didn't have to deal with the stall either. Although she'd occasionally helped out with it, she didn't know how to run a business and wasn't knowledgeable about antiques. Leaving her in charge would have been a disaster.

The charity shops around here were about to have a windfall, although Mac would try to sell some of the stuff on eBay first. Sadly, being property-rich but cash-poor, with only her student loan to live off, she had to be pragmatic. She'd keep anything of sentimental value, but everything else would have to go.

'I hope you don't mind, Sandra,' she murmured. 'It's not that I'm ungrateful, but needs must. And I promise I won't sell anything you really treasured.'

She had three months before her university course started again in September, and she would need to have everything ready by then so that she could focus on her studies full-time. She'd done one year of a modern languages BA course already, studying French and Spanish remotely while travelling with Blue and the band. Now she had transferred her credits to Bath University, and she'd be able to go to lectures in person and really concentrate on her second year. She told herself that what had happened was a good thing. The itinerant life with a rock band was not conducive to learning anything properly, even if it gave her the opportunity to use her language skills in person.

'Blue did me a favour,' she muttered.

If she said it often enough, perhaps she'd even believe it eventually. For now, his betrayal still hurt.

Jonah threw his phone onto the huge king-size bed in the bland hotel room. As always, the sounds of partying came floating through the wall on one side, but he wasn't in the mood. It had been exciting at first – the touring, the adoring fans and groupies, the accolades, the magazine coverage – but it had grown old very quickly. Now he longed to escape from the whole circus. It seemed to be less about the music than about image, and music was his only reason for doing this in the first place.

He wondered how Mac was getting on. He'd been on the verge of texting her again today but didn't want to come across as creepy or stalkerish. She hadn't been *his* girlfriend and he had no right to be a part of her life.

He wished he had.

From the first moment he'd seen her, he'd been captivated. She was Blue's usual type when it came to looks – blonde, tall and willowy, with curves in all the right places – but he'd found himself instantly attracted as well. In Jonah's opinion, she was unique and stood out because she was a lot more natural than the girls who normally hung out with the band. She hadn't flirted or flattered to capture anyone's attention, just been herself. And he'd soon discovered that she had a great sense of humour and a very down-to-earth attitude to life that appealed to him immensely. It didn't hurt that she was effortlessly beautiful, even when hung-over and tired. Her most arresting features were her large aquamarine eyes, and a curtain of dead-straight blonde hair that was silky-smooth and came all the way down past her bottom. He'd wanted to touch it so badly, smooth his palm down the soft length and wrap it round his fist as he kissed her . . .

Yeah, that was never going to happen.

They'd been friends, sure, and often chatted about various shared interests – mainly his love of the Vikings and fascination with history in general. It was a subject she knew quite a lot about too, being part Scandinavian. It was nerdy, it had to be said, but they'd both enjoyed the discussions, which helped pass the time during long, boring journeys. The physical attraction, however, was all on his side. She'd been so into Blue, Jonah doubted she'd noticed anyone else even when they were right next to her. And now? Now she was probably regretting ever getting involved with anyone connected with Valhalla Storm and the world of music. Besides, if she was into pretty boys, she wouldn't be interested in someone like him. He was a bit rough around the edges, not magazine-cover material like Blue. Girls threw themselves at Jonah as well, but he'd never deluded himself that they wanted him for anything other than his fame and money. He'd learned that lesson early on.

Mac wasn't like that. From the very beginning, she'd seemed genuine and totally uninterested in being in the spotlight. Jonah had never seen her spending Blue's money unnecessarily, and she'd had to be actively persuaded to buy a glamorous dress for an awards event they'd all attended together. Mostly she wore casual clothes: torn jeans and little T-shirts that left a tantalising sliver of her toned stomach bare. And those jeans were usually tight, showcasing . . .

'Shit!' Jonah slumped down onto the bed and covered his eyes with his forearm. He didn't want to think about Mac in jeans or that gorgeous dress.

He needed to stop thinking about her altogether. End of story.

His phone rang and he glanced at the screen. It was Harriet Pierce, their PR guru, and he debated letting it go to voicemail. That would only put off the inevitable, though, as Harriet was nothing if not persistent.

'Yeah?' He knew he sounded rude, but he didn't care. He'd already informed everyone in their management and PR teams that he'd be leaving the band once the tour was over. They'd not been best pleased. Each and every one of them had tried to talk him out of it, but he was holding firm to his decision. It was time to go his own way.

'Jonah, how are you doing?' She sounded chipper as always. Her positivity and enthusiasm were what gained them lots of publicity, so he shouldn't complain, but sometimes it grated no end. Like now.

So they were doing small talk first, were they? He sighed, not in the mood for another lecture about all the opportunities he was losing out on, which was sure to follow the pleasantries. 'Fine. You?'

'Good, good. Listen, I just wondered if anyone in the band would be able to get in touch with Blue's ex-girlfriend? I, er, don't want to ask him, for obvious reasons.'

'Mackenna? Why?' Had Blue done something else stupid? Trash-talked her in the press to cover up the fact that the break-up was entirely his fault? He clenched his fist as anger surged inside him.

Harriet's next words calmed him. 'The cover design, remember? You all agreed to use those photos of her for the next album, so we need her sign-off. Wasn't it you who said her hair from behind went perfectly with the title, *Blonde Revolution*?'

'Oh. Yes.'

He'd almost forgotten that they were due to release their final album soon. He wasn't looking forward to it the way he had in the past. Promoting it would be a pain and would entail spending a lot more time with Blue than he'd like. Still, he was proud of the songs – most of which he'd written – and they should earn him a tidy sum. If he didn't help promote it, he'd be shooting himself in the foot. The band's break-up might shift more copies too, as it would be front-page news. A contract was binding, though, and all the work that had gone into the making of those songs couldn't be wasted.

As for the photo of Mac – yes, he'd been the one pushing for it when Blue insisted on using one of the song titles as the album name as well. Jonah had written 'Blond Revolution' with Mac in mind – although she and Blue didn't know that, of course – so it had seemed fitting. They'd talked her into a photo session with a well-known photographer, and the resulting pictures were stunning, as he'd known they would be.

Blue himself had bleach-blond hair and assumed the song was about him. That had made Jonah laugh and tell Blue he'd written it about himself; he had blonde hair too, even if it was more of a golden hue. It made no difference. The egotistical singer still seemed to believe the song referred to him. Or possibly one of the many women he spent time with. To Jonah, they were interchangeable. All except Mac.

'So can you help?' Harriet's voice brought him back to the present.

'Right. Sure. I can get in touch with her. Shall I give her your number?'

'Please. That would be fab, thanks.'

Something occurred to him. 'She will be paid for this, won't she?'

'Um, I'm not sure.' Harriet cleared her throat. 'I thought she agreed to do it as a favour to the band. And you guys paid for the photographer.'

'For fuck's sake, Harriet!' Jonah's anger roared back to life. 'That would be taking advantage. If we'd used a model, she would have been paid for her time. You need to give Mac the going rate.'

'What? You can't be serious!' Harriet sounded appalled.

'Dead serious. Talk to the legal team and make it happen, or I won't do a single more thing for this band. And I won't get Mac to sign off on using those photos for the cover either. You'll have to come up with some other idea.' That would take time they didn't have, as he well knew. Harriet was no doubt aware of it too.

'Fine. I'll see what they say. Have her call me soon, OK?' She sounded terse now. Too bad.

'I will. And you'd better have some good news for her by then.'

He hung up without saying goodbye, knowing full well that made him as much of a diva as Blue, but he didn't care. If it took acting like a bastard to get his way in this, he'd do it. For Mac's sake, he'd stand his ground.

And it gave him the perfect excuse to talk to her again.

Chapter Five

Southern Britannia, early June AD *80*

The Romans had created a network of wide, mostly straight, surfaced and well-drained roads called *viae* across the southern parts of Britannia, and they were constantly adding more. All such roads were built to a certain standard in terms of the materials used and their measurements. They were mostly intended for the legions marching from one place to another, allowing them to move swiftly to wherever they were needed, but anyone was permitted to use them. Duro took advantage of this road network in order to reach his destination faster.

He headed south towards Londinium first, but skirted round this busy port. It was now the capital of the Roman province of Britannia following the sacking of Camulodunum. He turned west along a road he was told ended at Calleva Atrebatum. This had originally been the centre of the Atrebates tribe, whose king had submitted to Emperor Claudius right at the beginning of the Roman conquest. The area was now relatively peaceful, and without the need for constant military supervision. Hence he didn't come across any troops along this stretch. Not that it mattered – they had no reason to pay attention to a lone traveller such as himself.

Calleva was a place where quite a few roads converged. Rather than sleeping out in the open as he'd done recently, he spent the night in a *mansio*. This was a type of guest house, built by the central government, to be used by people travelling on official business. They were large buildings, with decent beds, stabling for horses, good food, and often with their own bath houses attached. Duro felt in dire need of a proper wash. He was used to bathing at least every few days. Even though he knew he wasn't eligible to stay in the *mansio*, a bribe persuaded the doorman to turn a blind eye to the fact that he had nothing to do with Roman officialdom. Silver talked everywhere, a fact he often made use of.

'If you take the north-westerly road out of here towards Corinium and Glevum, someone there should be able to direct you to Isca,' a fellow traveller informed him when he enquired about the fastest route the following morning.

'Thank you kindly.' It seemed straightforward enough and he didn't anticipate any problems, just the tedium of endless days on horseback. He hadn't ridden since he was a child, but the lessons he'd learned then stood him in good stead. The members of his tribe had always been keen horsemen and skilled charioteers, and they began to teach their children at an early age.

He went to collect his mount and strapped on the saddlebags before swinging up into the saddle. Calleva was obviously thriving, as it boasted not only the usual temples, baths and forum complex, but also an amphitheatre, which he had glimpsed on his way into the centre. These were all built in the Roman style, imposing edifices with red-tiled roofs.

He joined the stream of traffic along the main road, fighting his way through the throng of people on foot, in carts and on horseback. The din of voices as craftsmen cried their wares mixed with animal noises and general chatter. Smoke hung in the air from the many hearths in homes and workshops. The enticing aromas emanating from the eateries and street-food sellers combined with the stench of rubbish and animal excrement.

He reached the forum complex, the heart and most important part of any Roman town. This comprised an open square surrounded on three sides by commercial buildings behind a covered portico, with a basilica forming the fourth. The square was used as a marketplace, and some towns also had an indoor one, a *macellum.* On this particular day, there was some sort of auction going on. Duro paused briefly to watch. His stomach muscles clenched when he realised the commodity being sold was slaves. They were being dragged up onto a raised platform, naked and in chains, or with their hands and necks tied with rope.

'Taranis curse them!' he hissed under his breath, hoping the Celtic god of thunder would come down and strike the slave traders dead.

He felt bile in his throat as he remembered how it had felt to stand up there, gawked at by strangers and occasionally prodded. He had been a mere child, and not as sought-after as a full-grown man, but there had still been some interest in him. The memories were ones he normally tried to suppress, but here they rose to the surface, nearly choking him as the vile sensations came rushing back.

Taking a deep breath, he prepared to turn away from the horrible spectacle, but something caught his eye. He watched as a young woman was manhandled up onto the platform, resisting all the way. She was stunningly beautiful, her thigh-length white-blonde hair shining with gold and silver highlights in the sun. Her body was perfectly proportioned, exactly the shape a man would want, but what immediately caught his interest was her proud bearing. The dignity with which she held her head high and the glares she threw at those around her, despite being nude and captive.

'A Germana,' he murmured, mesmerised by the sight of her.

She snarled something at the man tugging on her arm. This was not a woman cowed by her predicament. The emotions flickering across her face struck a chord inside Duro and he knew what was running through her mind. He'd been there, in that exact position – powerless and vulnerable, as well as defiant, angry and resentful. Definitely not yet reconciled to the fate of being someone's slave. Someone's possession. Judging by her flashing eyes and scowling countenance, she was strong-willed and suffering from a deep sense of injustice. He reckoned it would take years before she accepted her fate, unless she was beaten into submission.

No! He couldn't bear to think of anyone harming her.

He'd occasionally seen Germanic women in Pompeii – usually slave girls trailing after a mistress – and had always dreamed of marrying one of them. Raedwald had poked fun at his imaginings, but to him those women had seemed like perfection in feminine form. They were known for being fierce and unafraid, as well as stunning, capable and hard-working. What more could a man want?

And they were the complete opposite of the dark-haired Roman matrons he'd bedded during his time in Pompeii. Although logically he knew it had nothing to do with hair colour, he never wanted to lie with a woman with black or brown hair again so long as he lived. Although he'd enjoyed their bodies, they represented the hated masters who had owned him. And even though they'd sought him out, they still saw him as a slave, someone they had power over and looked down upon. It reminded him of the bad times before he became a gladiator and had more say in his day-to-day activities.

'Hold her tight,' someone ordered, while the Germanic woman continued to struggle as potential buyers came up to squeeze her breasts and backside. She was hissing imprecations and curses in her own language, which was similar enough to his own that he got the gist of it.

She was clearly furious as well as embarrassed, and who could blame her?

Duro dismounted and moved closer to the auction platform, his gaze never leaving the woman. At one point their eyes met and she stilled as if she could sense his empathy. He wanted to shout out encouragement, tell her she was magnificent and that all this would soon be over. But that wasn't true. The auction was only the first step on the road to degradation, and probably not the worst. As if she had reached the same conclusion, her shoulders slumped and she turned her gaze elsewhere, leaving him feeling bereft.

He should have departed, but he was compelled to find out her eventual fate and stood rooted to the spot. He couldn't have left if his life depended on it. It was none of his business, but his mind was spinning with ideas of helping her. Rescuing her. Buying her, and . . . then what? Logic urged him to let it go. He was on a quest for revenge. He didn't have time to rescue damsels in distress, no matter how appealing or deserving they might be.

Still, he stayed to watch until a middle-aged Roman man bought her for eight hundred *sestertii*, the equivalent of two hundred silver *denarii*. He also purchased another Germanus for a thousand *sestertii*, an adult male who looked as if he probably came from the same tribe. Interestingly enough, the woman shied away from him when he tried to shield her. Duro surmised that there was some bad blood between the two, especially when the man sent her a glare. They were led away to a waiting cart, where the new owner had them dress in basic loincloths and tunics before tying them up again and loading them into the back.

With a sigh, Duro was preparing to be on his way at last

when he heard the Roman exchange a few final words with the auctioneer.

'I'll have her cowed by the end of this evening,' the man boasted. 'I've broken in fillies like her before and I know just how to do it. It'll be a pleasure taming a woman that headstrong. The more she resists, the better. She'll soon realise it's not worth the pain, but I hope she holds out for a good long while.'

The two men chuckled, obviously in perfect accord, while Duro had to stifle the urge to kill the pair of them on the spot. Bile rose in his throat once more at the callous words. By Teutatis, he'd like to see how they would fare if the tables were turned.

The Roman had an entourage of servants and a driver for the cart, while he himself mounted a horse. The group set off in the same direction as the one Duro had intended to take, and he came to a decision – he was going to rescue that woman, one way or another. He could buy her off the new owner, offering so much gold and silver the man couldn't refuse. Or if that didn't work, he would use persuasion of a more violent kind. But first he had to catch him alone, away from civilisation.

To that end, he encouraged his horse into a slow walk, following in the wake of the Roman and his servants. His quest could wait a little while longer.

Gisel burned with humiliation. Her whole body felt scalded and tainted by all those people who had eyed her naked form and pawed her everywhere. She was sure she was still blushing. No one should have seen her in her natural state other than her rightful husband. *No one!*

The spectators hadn't cared about her distress. In fact, they'd relished the spectacle and egged on the men who had manhandled her, which made it worse. All except that one man whose gaze had been compassionate. For a moment, she'd had the impression he was about to save her, but why would he? They didn't know each other and she had no idea why he'd even sympathised with her. It had been there in his eyes, a mixture of sadness and understanding; she was sure she wasn't mistaken about that. And yet, in the end, he had done nothing more than watch like all the others.

Now here she was, trussed up like a chicken yet again. She tugged at the ropes that bound her wrists, relieved that at least they were in front of her this time and not behind her back. The man who had tied the knots had done a good job, though, and there was no way of loosening them. She sighed and leaned back against the side of the cart, staring up at the sky. Was her family missing her? Had they figured out what had happened yet? And who to blame for it all. She glanced briefly at the man sitting next to her, sending him her fiercest glare.

This was all Eberulf's fault, curse him. She hated him with the heat of a thousand suns.

'Don't look at me like that,' he growled, as if he'd heard her thoughts. 'You have no one to blame but yourself for this predicament. If you'd accepted my honourable proposal, I wouldn't have had to snatch you from your village and we wouldn't have been riding during the hours of darkness.'

She shuddered at the memory. Venturing out last thing at night to use the privy, she'd had a blanket thrown over her head the moment she stepped out of the stinking latrine. At first, she hadn't known what was happening or who her captors were, but she'd soon found out. Eberulf had tossed her across his horse and ridden off into the night, stopping after a while to make her sit up in front of him. She'd struggled and cursed him every way she knew how, but it had been in vain. He had been adamant that she was going to marry him, and nothing would dissuade him. Until they came across a Roman patrol who thought they were *all* fair game . . .

'You shouldn't have been so proud and stubborn,' he added now.

'And you should have taken no for an answer,' she retorted. 'I had my reasons for refusing your suit, and my father agreed with me.'

'Your father is an old fool,' Eberulf sneered. 'And whatever you had heard about me was grossly exaggerated.'

She snorted. 'I think not. Otherwise, why would you have snatched me under cover of darkness? Your tribe's reputation for underhand dealings, alternately spying for the Romans and working against them, preceded you. Even if only half the rumours were true, it would have been enough to make me say no.'

'You don't know what you're talking about. We did what we had to do. What was best for our people. We all walk a fine line with the Romans these days.'

'Well, it's not as though it matters now, is it? We'll never see our homes again, either of us.'

'I'll find a way, and when I do, I'm taking you with me. As my wife.'

For the love of all the gods, did he never give up? She ground her teeth and suppressed the urge to headbutt him, a move her brother had taught her when they were younger. 'Over my dead body,' she hissed. 'I'd rather marry a Roman than you, you despicable swine.'

And she meant it, but she'd prefer to choose the man in question. She very much feared she had no options whatsoever now, and her wishes wouldn't come into it.

She was a slave, and one way or another, her new master would break her. Unless she could escape first . . .

Chapter Six

Bath, early June, present day

The doorbell rang, and Mackenna put down the paintbrush and wiped her hands on her old leggings. Looking through the peephole, she almost jumped back at the sight of Jonah standing outside. She unlocked the door and blinked at him.

'Hello, what on earth are you doing here?' she blurted out, ignoring the squirming feeling in her stomach that told her she was very pleased to see him.

'Nice to see you too,' he deadpanned, one dimple appearing as he smiled at her. Something like nervous tension flickered in his eyes, but she must have imagined it, as it disappeared in the next moment and he was back to his usual laid-back self. 'Can I come in?'

'Oh! Sure. I mean, of course. How have you been? Sorry, I wasn't expecting to see you in Bath of all places and . . .' She realised she was rambling and stepped aside so that he could enter the flat. 'Um, how did you even find me?'

'Harriet,' he said, walking past her and stopping as if he didn't want to go further without being invited. 'Your address was on the contract.'

'Oh, right.' That made sense, although she wasn't sure why Harriet would show the contract to him. Not that she minded. Far from it. 'Er, can I offer you some coffee? Tea? A beer?'

'Tea would be great, thanks.'

He followed her into the kitchen, which now sported freshly painted pale-grey cupboard doors and primrose-coloured walls. The woodwork was pure white around the huge windows and the French doors opening onto a small terrace. The whole look gave a clean and sunny impression that Mackenna was very proud of. She'd left the original white and grey marble tops alone as they were only a little bit worn and cracked in places. Finishing it all off were newly sanded and varnished floorboards covered with a long rag rug in grey and yellow stripes. It had been a present from her Swedish mother, who lived in Stockholm. She made the rugs herself on an old floor loom she'd inherited from her own mother, and had promised to teach Mackenna how to use it one of these days.

'Wow, this is fab!' Jonah took it all in, then went over to look out of the French doors. 'And you have the perfect spot to sit out on a summer evening, right?'

'Yes. Or it will be once I can afford to buy some patio furniture.' She'd had to throw away Sandra's rickety old set, as it was rotten to the core. It shouldn't have been left outside all winter, but her aunt must have been too ill to notice or care.

Jonah was still looking around. 'You've painted all this yourself?'

'Yes, I can't afford professionals, so I did it. Took quite a lot of effort, but I think it was worth it.' She was pleased with what she'd achieved so far, but there was still a long way to go with the other rooms.

'Definitely. Mind if I have a quick peek at the rest of the place?'

'Um, go ahead.' She busied herself with making tea while hoping she had remembered to at least straighten her duvet this morning. The other rooms were tidy, now that she had got rid of the clutter. The decor she had envisaged was beginning to take shape, and she loved the new minimalist modern look mixed with antiques she had going on.

'Impressive,' was Jonah's verdict when he came back into the kitchen. She handed him his tea. 'Thanks. You're settling in OK?'

'Yep. Love it. And I have the whole summer to finish painting the other rooms before my course starts.' Although she fully intended to do it as fast as possible so she could have some free time too.

She gripped her own mug and gestured for them to move into the sitting room, where she sank onto an old chaise longue. Jonah settled in an armchair nearby and she couldn't stop staring at him. What was he doing here? He was big and tanned and gorgeous, filling out ripped faded jeans and a white T-shirt very nicely. Tattoos in the sinuous Viking Urnes style snaked and spiralled down his arms, ending in swirls across his wrists. She'd actually contemplated getting something similar but smaller herself as she liked them so much. She must look into that soon.

She had never allowed herself to notice exactly how attractive he was before. That would have been wrong, but now there was nothing to stop her drinking in the sight. It felt strange to have him in her space. A mega rock star who didn't really belong in a place like this. Yet at the same time, it was right somehow. She'd missed him and the other band members – well, apart from Blue. Missed the camaraderie, teasing and joking around. The friendships, especially the one with Jonah. The truth was, she had no friends here in Bath yet, though she'd told herself that would change once lectures began.

'So what brings you here?' she dared to ask at last. He'd said he was going to look her up, but she hadn't believed he really meant it.

'Well, you probably weren't aware of it, but I actually own a property not far from here. About half an hour away.' He gestured in a vaguely north-easterly direction. 'I'm planning on settling there for the foreseeable future. Going to hole up and write some new songs. I'm hoping to sell them to other people, make some money that way. Perhaps collaborate with a few bands, that kind of thing. I'm tired of being in the limelight myself. It's exhausting. I just want to concentrate on the music.'

'Oh, that sounds perfect!' And she meant it. She could see him doing that. Staying in the background, but still creating the beautiful sounds he was so good at. 'How long have you had a place here?'

He shrugged. 'A couple of years. I bought it when we were last back in the UK for a longer spell. My business manager had advised me to invest in property, so I figured I might as well have a couple of different options. I've always liked this area. My grandparents were from around here as well, although they're gone now. You know I have a flat in London too, don't you?'

'Yes. Didn't we go there for a party once when I first started dating Blue? A gorgeous warehouse conversion with exposed brickwork and massive windows overlooking the Thames?'

'That's right.' They both winced at the mention of Blue's name, but they needed to get that elephant out of the room. It wasn't like he'd died or anything. 'Anyway, I thought it would be neighbourly to come and say hello.'

'I see. Well, thank you. I appreciate it.' She smiled at him. She really did, more than he would ever know. His kindness, despite the way his bandmate had behaved, was touching. And very Jonah. He'd always been the quiet one, the voice of reason, and the one who took care of the others whenever necessary. The strong but silent type.

Mackenna found that she liked that about him immensely. Among other things.

'There was another matter.' He smiled and pulled an envelope out of his back pocket. 'I brought you the payment for being our cover model. I figured I might as well deliver it in person, as I was coming down here anyway.'

'What?' She took the envelope and opened it, gasping when she saw a cheque for a huge sum of money. 'This can't be right. Harriet said I'd be paid the going rate for a photo shoot if I signed the contract giving you guys permission to use the pics. I'm not exactly a supermodel, am I?'

His smile widened. 'Oh, I would disagree with that. Those photos were amazing!' When she opened her mouth to protest again, he held up a hand. 'No, please, you've earned this. After she spoke to you, Harriet researched the current rate for models appearing on album covers and this is it. I swear. It's only right that you should be paid properly.'

Mackenna was speechless. This cheque was way too generous, she was sure of it, but she didn't know how she could possibly prove that. And if the band wanted to somehow compensate her for the asinine behaviour of their lead singer, as she suspected was the case here, who was she to refuse? She'd already signed an NDA and would never talk to the press about her time with Blue, so they didn't have to bribe her. But there was no denying she needed this money badly. It would allow her to stay afloat until she had a regular income from a paying tenant.

'I don't know what to say other than thank you. You're the best!' On impulse, she got up and went over to throw her arms around Jonah in a fierce hug. To her surprise, he hugged her back and kissed her cheek.

'You're more than welcome. Now, how about having a late lunch or coffee with me? Preferably somewhere quiet where I won't be hassled too much. That is, if I'm not disturbing you? Do you have to get on with painting?'

He was still holding on to her and she had to make a conscious effort to step out of his embrace. 'Not urgently, and I'd love to, thank you.' She thought for a moment. 'How about the Pump Room for afternoon tea?'

He spluttered out a laugh. 'Afternoon tea? What are you, seventy?' he teased.

Her cheeks heated up. 'Yeah, yeah, I know it's a bit fuddy-duddy, but hear me out. First of all, you have to book in advance, so not anyone can just wander in off the street, and second, it's usually pretty empty there this time of day. We'd be arriving between the lunch rush and teatime. I know because I used to go there with my aunt and we always timed it that way as it was so peaceful.' She had to swallow as she was immediately swamped with memories of Sandra, but she pushed them to the back of her mind for now. 'Maybe it's a bad idea. It does sound rather lame, huh?'

'No! Actually, it sounds perfect. And what's not to like about scones, right?' His smile reassured her.

'OK, if you're sure? I, er, had better clean up a bit though.' She regarded her paint-spattered leggings and oversized T-shirt ruefully. 'I doubt they'll let me in looking like this.'

Jonah laughed. 'Go shower and change. I can wait. I've got some emails I need to reply to anyway, so take your time. And I'll book a table.' He waved her towards the bedroom while taking out his phone.

'I'll try to be quick.'

And she would need to get the butterflies in her stomach under control too. She was going out for afternoon tea with Jonah Miller. It seemed unreal, but she was very much looking forward to it. Perhaps a little too much.

Jonah glanced down at the woman walking by his side along the busy streets of Bath. It was a warm day in early June and she was wearing a flirty little sundress that was distracting as hell. It was a halter-neck and also quite short. The hem fluttered above mid thigh, showing off legs that were long and shapely, even though she was just wearing Roman sandals rather than heels. Her beautiful hair hung over one shoulder in a long, slightly messy plait. He pushed his hands into his pockets. It would have been wonderful to thread his fingers with hers, but he reminded himself again that she had only just come out of a relationship. One that had ended very badly. No way was she ready to start another one. Especially not with Blue's former bandmate.

'So what is it you're going to study again?' he asked, keeping his face hidden under the brim of his baseball cap as much as possible. He wore dark sunglasses too – so clichéd – but he really didn't want to be recognised and accosted by fans today. It didn't happen to him as often as it did to Blue, but there was still the odd moment when he got mobbed. People were like flocks of sheep sometimes – if they saw someone asking for a selfie, they immediately wanted in on the act, whether they knew who he was or not.

'Modern languages. French and Spanish,' she replied.

'Oh yes, I remember you helping us out in Madrid when that receptionist was being a pain in the arse.' Blue had bragged that his girlfriend spoke the language fluently, as if it was his own personal achievement. Jonah had wanted to punch the guy to wipe the smug expression off his face, but he wasn't normally violent and had refrained.

She laughed, a lovely sound that hit him right in the chest. Jesus, what was it about this woman that got to him to such an extent? He just had the feeling she belonged with him somehow. It was an almost visceral knowledge, soul-deep, one he didn't understand but couldn't fight against. Why, he had no idea.

'I'd forgotten about that. She really was a pain, wasn't she. Not very understanding when it came to rock-star tantrums.' She threw him a teasing glance.

He held up his hands. 'Hey! I've never thrown a tantrum in my life. My mum said I was the calmest baby she'd ever seen. Even took me to the doctor to ask why I wasn't more lively, in case I needed vitamins or something.'

She grinned. 'I was the opposite. Always getting into trouble. A good thing I grew up in a little town in Sweden where I could run wild.'

'You did? You never told me that.' They'd never discussed anything really personal before. He'd always kept the conversation on other topics when chatting with her in order not to annoy his bandmate. Discussing Vikings was one thing, but not their life stories.

'Well, as you know, my mother is Swedish. She and my dad divorced when I was three. After that I lived with her most of the time but spent summers with him and his new family here in the UK.'

'You don't sound Swedish at all, but you speak the language, right?'

'Yes, I'm totally bilingual.'

'Impressive. And was it OK being here with your dad and stepfamily? I mean, did you get on with them?' He was curious and wanted to know all about her now. Any tiny detail she cared to share.

She shrugged. 'Mostly. My younger half-sister resented my presence, but I didn't let it get to me. She's the type who wants all the attention all the time. Total drama queen. And when I wasn't there, she was the typical spoiled only child. Her maternal grandparents were very rich and she inherited a trust fund from them when she turned twenty-one. That's why my dad's sister bequeathed everything she owned to me, I think. Evened things out a little, you know?'

Jonah saw the sadness lurking in her eyes and guessed this had caused problems between the siblings. 'Well, that makes sense. Fair is fair.'

'Exactly, but Savannah didn't see it that way. She had expected to receive half, even though it should have all gone to my dad really. I mean, he was kind of first in line. He doesn't need it, though. He's got his own company and is pretty well off.' She took a deep breath. 'Anyway, it's all water under the bridge. And speaking of bridges, isn't this one gorgeous?'

He decided not to comment on the abrupt change of subject. They were just crossing Pulteney Bridge and stopped on the other side to look down on the River Avon. It cascaded down a couple of man-made steps, or weirs, at this point, before flowing on downriver. The bridge itself was lined with tiny buildings on either side. Shops and cafés so small you couldn't fit many people in each.

'Yes, I love this place. My grandparents used to bring me every summer. We went to the Pump Room at least once, and picnicked in the park down there.' He indicated the gardens fronting onto the riverside, an area you had to pay to access these days.

'Sounds idyllic. I was here quite a lot too. Whenever Savannah and I fought too much, Dad would send me to stay with Sandra. Just think, we could have met as children.'

'Maybe we did.' He certainly felt as though he'd known her for a long time. *Several lifetimes.* He frowned at that strange thought, and studied her face. Turned up to his with a half-smile on her lips, it seemed so familiar. *Beloved.* He shook himself mentally. What on earth was the matter with him? They were friends, that was all. For now. He pulled himself together. 'Come on, I'm starving.'

They walked the short distance to the famous Pump Room, where he'd made a reservation while he waited for her to get changed back at her flat. Sure enough, not many of the tables were occupied.

'Oh good, we get the place almost to ourselves,' he murmured. Even so, he made sure to sit down with his back to the door before taking off his hat and sunglasses.

A waitress came to take their order, and they decided on the full works, including a glass of champagne.

'This feels very decadent. Cheers!' Mackenna tapped her glass to his as soon as they'd been served, and took a sip of the bubbling beverage. 'The rest isn't very rock 'n' roll, though. Are you sure your street cred can handle being seen here, taking tea like some old fogey?' she joked. 'It's not exactly your usual kind of haunt.'

'Hey, watch it! I'm only a few years older than you, I think.' He pretended to scowl at her, but couldn't stop his mouth from twitching with amusement. 'Maybe my usual haunts include old-fashioned places. Besides, I've never cared much about how others see me. I don't mind doing stuff like this on occasion, and you know I'm a secret history buff. If that makes me uncool or boring, so be it.'

'Actually, I'm the same,' she confessed. 'I like following traditions. Anything old or historical appeals to me and I'm not ashamed to admit it.' They shared a look of mutual accord.

Mackenna looked around the room, taking in the lavish decor and huge windows, and the glimpse of the Roman baths outside. 'I love this place. And I can never resist a visit to the baths when I have the time.'

'I can relate. Although I love reading about the Vikings, the Romans were awesome too. I remember being brought here by my grandparents and I was fascinated. Maybe we can go together sometime soon?'

But right now, he preferred to look at her. Those aquamarine eyes were luminous in the afternoon sun shining in through the windows. Her hair shimmered, despite being so blonde it was almost white. It was as though there were silver and gold threads running through the strands. She also had tiny flecks of paint on one cheek that he longed to wipe off. And a luscious mouth he'd dreamed of more than once . . .

'Aren't you going to have some of the famous mineral water?' She twinkled those ocean eyes at him and nudged him with her shoulder. 'It's medicinal, and you might need a pick-me-up after all those months of touring.'

He shuddered in exaggerated fashion. 'No, thanks. I tried it once and felt queasy for the rest of the day. Besides, the only thing I need in order to recover is to be left alone. Not have people around me all day, every day, telling me where to go, what to do, what to say to reporters. It's such a relief to be allowed to do whatever I want.'

Her gaze turned wary. 'Perhaps you should have come here on your own. I don't want to intrude on your downtime.'

He gave in to the urge and grabbed her small hand, plaiting their fingers. 'I didn't mean *you*. Of course I don't mind spending time with you. I wouldn't have asked you otherwise. And so far you haven't told me what to do a single time.' He grinned at her to show that he was joking.

She relaxed and squeezed his hand before slowly untangling herself and fiddling with the large linen napkin she'd placed on her lap. 'I never will, I promise.'

Something flashed on her finger, and he nodded towards it. 'Nice ring. Looks old.'

'What? Oh this, yes. I found it in my aunt's jewellery box when I was clearing it out. Mostly she had worthless old costume pieces, as she liked anything that glittered, but this looked valuable, so I kept it. I took it to a jeweller and he said the setting is definitely pure gold. The gemstone is an amethyst with an engraving on it. He called it intaglio. That's where the design is cut into the flat background of the stone, making a little hollow. Apparently it's a copy of the kind of rings the Romans liked. Maybe Victorian?'

She removed it from her finger and handed it to him. 'Hold it up towards the light. You'll see it's a woman. Probably Venus or one of the other goddesses.'

He did as she suggested and saw the skilful depiction of a Roman lady in a long dress that draped around her in graceful folds. So tiny and yet so perfect. A frisson shot down his back. He felt as if he'd seen this gemstone before, but that couldn't be right. He'd never even been to a museum to look at Roman stuff, except for the one here in Bath. Was that where he'd come across a similar gem?

'What a lucky find,' he commented. 'And I guess it's something to remember your aunt by.'

'Exactly.' She beamed at him and put the ring back on. 'I decided I'd always wear it in her honour.'

Their food arrived just then, and they dug in to the bountiful spread, artfully arranged on a tiered stand. Tiny sandwiches, scones with clotted cream and jam, and dainty pastries, together with a large pot of tea. They'd both chosen Ceylon tea, showing that their tastes aligned in that respect. He wondered if they did in other ways, but didn't ask. For now, he was content to just spend time with her and enjoy the meal.

Once they were done, he walked her back to her flat and gave her a hug, probably lingering a little too long. He couldn't stop himself from inhaling the scent of her skin, her hair and a subtle whiff of perfume, and stored it in his mind.

'Maybe we could hang out sometime? You know, now that we're almost neighbours,' he suggested, attempting to sound casual.

'Sure, any time.'

'How about tomorrow?' he blurted, before he could think it through, then cringed inwardly. What was he doing hassling her like this? She probably had other stuff to do.

'Tomorrow?' She looked surprised, and no wonder. They'd been friends for months while on tour, but never this close. She must be asking herself why he was taking a sudden interest in her.

'I wouldn't mind going to the Roman baths again, now that you've reminded me. It's been so long. And I don't know anyone else around here who'd go with me. Anyone who'd even be interested, to be honest.' It was the only excuse he could come up with on the spot.

She hesitated, then smiled. 'OK, but can we make it late afternoon? That way I'll get some painting done first.'

'No problem. I'll come pick you up at four. How does that sound? And I'll book the tickets.'

'Perfect, thank you. See you tomorrow then.'

As she disappeared inside, he wanted to smack himself, but at the same time he was smiling. He'd scored another date with her and it was a step in the right direction. He'd just have to play it cool again tomorrow and see where it might lead.

Chapter Seven

Southern Britannia, early June AD 80

Darkness had fallen, or at least the half-dusk of a summer's evening. It didn't really get fully dark this time of year, but it was shadowy enough for Duro not to be seen by the Roman or the entourage of slaves the man was travelling with. Duro had been watching them for a while now as they went about their duties, setting up camp and erecting a luxurious leather tent in a clearing not far from the road. While their master waited impatiently, seated on a stool with a cup of wine in his hand, they put up the tent poles and fetched the heavy stitched-together goatskin panels that made up the walls. Guy ropes were fastened to the corners and secured with wooden pegs.

Once the outer part was assembled, the slaves prepared the interior. They assembled a camp bed, carted in a chair and a table and laid rugs on the ground. A brazier and a half-dozen oil lamps completed the preparations. Someone else had started a fire outside and was cooking something in a pot suspended over the flames on a tripod. Another slave returned from a nearby stream with two buckets of water, while others were seeing to the horses.

Everyone appeared to be tiptoeing around their master,

flinching every time he raised his voice to give an order. His expression was one of perpetual disgust and dissatisfaction. It would seem he meted out swift punishment to anyone who didn't do his bidding fast enough. One unlucky young man had his ears boxed for spilling a tiny drop of wine when refilling the man's cup. Another was sporting bruises, while a third winced when he moved, as if he'd been flogged recently. Duro's jaw tightened. He recognised the signs of a cruel master all too well. He'd had one himself, a long time ago, before a gladiator trainer saved him and his lot improved. This one needed to be taught a lesson.

Once all was ready, the man – whose slaves were calling him Primus – stalked into the tent and asked for the two new slaves to be brought. The blonde woman and her companion had been sitting in the back of the cart, after a brief outing to relieve their bladders, and no one had paid them much attention. Now they were dragged into the tent, reluctantly on the part of the woman, while the man walked with his head held high. The flap closed behind them.

Duro wasn't sure what to do. He'd planned to ride into the camp and ask to speak to Primus. He'd hoped to catch him in a good mood after he'd had his supper and some wine, then he might be more willing to sell the female slave. With the way the man had been behaving, though, there seemed little chance of him being amenable. And why had he ordered the two slaves into his tent?

A premonition of danger had him reaching for his sword, a short Roman *gladius* with a lethal point and sharpened blade. As a civilian, he wasn't allowed to carry a sword in public – or even own one, since he was of the defeated Iceni tribe – but he refused to travel anywhere unarmed. To keep his weapon from being seen, he'd fashioned a type of baldric that allowed the sword to rest in between his shoulder blades, where he could keep it hidden under a cloak.

Watching the scene for a while longer, he decided to wait for the slaves to emerge again, but when he heard screaming coming from inside the tent, he changed his mind. Having tied his horse to a tree earlier, he'd crept closer on foot and had been peeking out from behind an extra-thick tree trunk. Now he charged across the clearing, brandishing his sword as he went, startling the slaves, who were going about their business. He ignored them and wrenched the tent flap aside.

The scene that greeted him made his blood run cold.

The woman was lying on the bed, held down by two male slaves, while Primus ripped her tunic in half, baring her naked form. She fought like an animal possessed, but she didn't stand a chance. Primus's henchmen gripped one of her wrists each and clamped down her thrashing legs with their other hand. No matter how much she bucked and squirmed, even going so far as to bite one of them on the arm, they didn't let go.

Fury coursed through Duro as his mind returned to the past. Suddenly he was eight winters old again, being held fast by a laughing Roman legionary while the man's superior raped first his older sister, then his mother, who'd also been forced to watch her daughter being violated.

'I, Aulus Julius Felix, of the Legio Secunda Augusta, am your master in every way, Iceni bitch!' the man had snarled once he was done. He'd pulled out his sword and slashed Duro's mother deeply across her abdomen. 'I hope you die slowly. Go join your ancestors, knowing I'm taking your daughter as my slave and sending your son to be a drudge among my people. He'll never be a proud warrior like your husband. There will be no one to avenge you, ever.'

The last thing Duro had seen, before he'd been pulled away, was Julius Felix spitting on his mother, and her returning the favour. Despite being mortally wounded, her fighting spirit never left her, and he heard her shout after him, 'Stay strong, my boy, and don't let them win!'

He'd strived to always follow her advice, even if he wasn't prepared to do battle with the Romans the conventional way. It was better to beat them by stealth and cunning. Sometimes, however, like right now, the only thing that worked was violence.

Primus began to pull up the front of his tunic. The expressions of his two slaves remained carefully blank, as if they didn't relish what they were doing but had learned long ago not to question his actions. As for the male Germanus, he stood to one side with a smirk on his face, which turned to confusion when Duro rushed inside.

That did it. The swine was enjoying the sight of his fellow tribeswoman being raped, was he? He'd pay for that.

Without uttering a sound, Duro charged towards the newly enslaved man and knocked him down with a powerful punch to the chin. The Germanus fell head-first into a table that held a washbasin and ewer, sending water flying everywhere. He lay motionless, knocked out cold. Excellent! One fewer to deal with. The others looked up, surprise registering on their faces, but he didn't give them a chance to react. He raised his sword and attacked.

'What in the name of all the gods . . .?' Primus backed away, fumbling to snatch a long knife off a nearby chair where he'd left his unbuckled belt and weapons. 'Get him!' he ordered the slaves, but they vacillated, clearly unsure whether to let go of the woman.

One of them did so, and immediately received a kick in the gut from the leg he'd released. With one arm and leg free, she was able to fight her remaining captor more efficiently, and Duro turned his attention to Primus and the other man.

'Get out of here unless you want to die,' he told the slave. 'Take everyone and leave, because I can guarantee you won't have a master from this night onwards.'

The man nodded and ran out, despite Primus shrieking after

him, 'Don't you dare! You'll pay for this, I swear it! A thorough whipping, and I'll have your tongue cut out as well.'

'No, you won't,' Duro hissed. 'You're not going to be alive long enough to order any such thing. Come on, you coward. Fight someone your own size who isn't being held down.'

He brandished his sword and Primus blanched, taking a step back. His eyes were still sparking with defiance, but there was fear lurking in their depths too. 'You don't fight fair. That sword is twice the length of my dagger.'

'Fine. We can do it your way.' Sheathing his sword, Duro pulled a knife out of a sheath attached to his belt. 'Better? Now try to attack me, you scurvy dog.'

With one eye on the woman, who was now fighting off the second slave in earnest, Duro decided not to prolong the fight. He allowed Primus to advance on him and almost get in a jab or two, but as soon as there was an opening in the man's defences, he stuck his dagger into Primus's heart in one swift stroke. With a look of astonishment, as if he couldn't believe his life would end in this way, the coward sank into a heap. The light went out of his eyes, and he was gone.

Duro had absolutely no compunction about killing him. Primus was scum. Roman scum at that. The entitled type he'd put up with for far too long as a youngster. He was well aware that slaves were property. A master had a right to do whatever he wanted with them, but the thought of him raping this beautiful creature – or any woman, for that matter – had been more than he could stomach.

He gazed over at the second servant, whose mouth had fallen open at the sight of his master's lifeless body. He was so distracted, the woman managed to kick him in his private parts, and he doubled over with a howl of anguish. Duro marched over and grabbed him by the back of his tunic, shoving him towards the door.

'Get out and leave this place,' he snarled. 'You never saw what happened here, and we have no idea you were ever a slave. Take your freedom and run far away while you have the chance.'

The man nodded and scurried out of the tent as if Cerberus himself was after him.

Out of the corner of his eye, Duro caught movement. When he turned around, it was to see the Germanus raising Primus's dagger, which he must have grabbed off the floor. He'd used it to cut the ropes that had bound his wrists and now advanced on Duro, who judged him to be a much trickier opponent armed, as he was clearly a trained warrior. Like most Britons and northern barbarians, he was taller than the average Roman, but still shorter than Duro, whose height had made a gladiator master select him all those years ago.

He didn't doubt he could beat the slave, and prepared himself for the attack. Just as the Germanus lifted the blade, however, the woman appeared behind him so fast she was a blur of motion. In her hand was the earthenware ewer, which she brought crashing down on the back of the man's skull, and he crumpled to the ground once more, dead to the world. Good. Duro would like to wring his neck for the apparent enjoyment he'd derived from seeing the woman helpless. It was sick and twisted, and deserved the very worst punishment, but one death was enough. The foreigner could stay here until he woke, hopefully with a very sore head.

The woman stood over the prone man for a moment, muttering something in her own language. Duro caught the words 'treacherous swine', but not much more. She was breathing heavily, while holding the front of her tunic together with one hand. Her entire body was shaking with the shock of what had so nearly happened. She must be on the verge of tears, but somehow she was holding them at bay. When she looked up and stared at him, her eyes were wild, like those of a cornered animal. She was probably wondering if he was going to attack her next. And who could blame her?

He held up his hands, palms towards her. 'Shh, calm down. I won't hurt you, I swear. I'm here to save you. Take you away from that cur.' He nodded in the direction of Primus's corpse. 'Come with me and I'll take care of you, I promise.'

When she remained silent, he tried again in his own language. 'Do you not speak Latin? Can you understand me now? My tongue is similar to yours, is it not?'

Although her tribe was clearly of Germanic origins, she'd spoken a language related to his Brythonic, so he guessed perhaps they had settled somewhere within Gaul a long time ago.

She took a deep breath, relaxing a fraction when he didn't make any threatening moves or come any closer. 'Yes,' she said at last, raising her chin a notch. 'I understand both, but Latin is easier than your strange dialect.'

That made him smile. She had courage, that was for certain, but he had to make her understand that he didn't pose a threat. Communication was the first step. 'Good. Then we'd best be on our way. I'll find something for you to wear until I can buy you new clothing.'

Striding over to a chest sitting in one corner of the tent, he flipped open the lid and rummaged among the many fine tunics inside. He pulled a couple out and held them up. 'What do you think – will either of these do for now?'

Primus hadn't been a tall man, only stout, but the clothes would still be huge on her. They were better than nothing, though, as he definitely didn't want her walking around naked. As it was, the image of her on the sale platform in all her glory was imprinted on his mind. For now, he had to forget that and earn her trust.

'This one,' he decided for her, and threw a shapeless green

tunic in her direction. It was less ostentatious than the other, and wouldn't draw attention to her. 'If it's too big, that's all to the good. It gets cold at night.'

She caught it one-handed, still holding her ripped garment together with the other. 'Thank you,' she whispered, but her gaze was suspicious, mistrustful. 'Can you . . . may I have some privacy, please?'

'Of course.' He swivelled round and stared at the tent wall. In case she decided to either bolt or stick a dagger in his back, he kept himself ready, ears attuned to the slightest sound, but she did neither.

'I'm dressed,' she informed him, and he turned back to face her.

He looked her up and down and had to stifle a grin. She was adorable in a tunic that swamped her feminine shape. The sleeves would have been three-quarter length on Primus, but reached to her wrists. The lower hem of the garment almost touched her ankles.

'That should keep you warm at least,' he commented drily. 'But let's see if he has a cloak we can take as well.' Another search through the chest produced an exceedingly fine one made of wool lined with linen. It was pale blue and perfectly matched her eyes, but he didn't mention that. 'Here, put that on, then we can bury the body.'

'B-bury it? Why?'

'If no one finds him, I can't be accused of murder.'

'You fought him honourably,' she pointed out, although the words sounded as though she'd had to drag them out of herself against her will. Duro gathered she was reluctant to think well of him. That was only prudent, since she didn't know him.

'I did, but who is going to believe you if you tell them? You were his slave, about to be violated by him. And I doubt your companion will sing my praises.' He glanced at the man who was still prone on the ground.

She sneered. 'He's not my anything. Eberulf is an ass.'

The vehemence in her voice made him raise his brows at her, but she turned away as if she couldn't bear to speak of it.

'Agreed. And he's a coward, like your late master. I won't let him harm you again.' When she sent him a sceptical glance, he thought it best to change the subject. She'd soon learn that he meant what he said. 'What is your name? I'm Duro.'

'Gisel.'

'Very well. Wait here one moment,' he told her. 'Please,' he added, so as not to sound too autocratic. 'If Eberulf wakes up, hit him again. And can you tie him up with something?'

'Will do.'

He saw her pick up what was left of the ropes. They wouldn't hold the man for ever, but hopefully long enough to keep him from following Duro and Gisel when they left.

Peering through the tent flap, he was relieved to find that everyone in Primus's entourage had fled. Most of his belongings were gone too, apart from the cart. He ducked outside and went to look in the back of it. As he'd thought, some implements and supplies had been left behind. He pulled out a spade, and on the way back to the tent, he grabbed one of the buckets of water he'd seen someone fetch earlier. The fleeing servants hadn't thought to take that with them, thankfully. He sloshed some of it on the fire before carrying the rest inside, where he poured it over the brazier.

'Can you blow out the lamps, please?' he asked the woman.

She nodded and went around extinguishing them, leaving the tent more or less in darkness, although he'd left the flap open.

'Can you lift his legs if I carry his upper body? If not, I'll try to sling him over my shoulder.'

He could easily carry the man on his own, but he wanted Gisel where he could see her. If she helped him, she'd be right by his side. When she nodded again, he went over to Primus and picked him up under his armpits. She took hold of his ankles and straightened up.

'Where to?'

'There's a wooded area nearby. Let's bury him there.'

Somehow he managed to carry the spade as well as the dead weight of the man, and together they brought him a good way into the forest.

'You can sit there and wait if you wish.' He pointed at a fallen tree trunk, and Gisel sank down onto it, panting slightly.

The moon was quite bright, and Duro made short work of digging a shallow grave. He rolled Primus into it, face-down and without bothering to remove the ring the Roman wore on one finger. He'd brought the man's dagger, not wanting the Germanus to have a weapon if he woke sooner than expected, and threw it into the grave. He'd also gathered up the fancy leather belt and money pouch Primus had discarded earlier, which went the same way. Perhaps the man would need these items in the next life. Duro didn't much care, but he wasn't a thief. After shovelling dirt onto the body, he manhandled a couple of large boulders over the top to keep wild animals from digging up the corpse. Finally he scattered moss, leaves and twigs around the area to try to hide the burial place as best he could. He doubted anyone would come looking for Primus here, but you never knew. Either way, there was nothing linking him to the dead man. Nothing other than Gisel, but the only people who would know that were the long-gone servants and Eberulf, the Germanus.

'Time to go.' He stretched out a hand to Gisel, whose head was drooping.

She startled, and leaned back, sending him another deeply suspicious look. 'Wh-where are we going?'

'On a quest, and then I'm taking you home. But first we need to clear away all signs of Primus and his entourage.'

They returned to the camp and found Eberulf stirring with a moan inside the tent. Duro raised his eyebrows at Gisel, and she took the hint. With her mouth set in a grim line, she stalked inside and knocked the man out cold again, using a broken-off table leg this time. Duro picked him up and carried him outside, propping him against the nearest tree.

'Help me pack everything away, please,' he said. 'It's best if there's no trace of anyone having stayed here.'

Together they set about clearing the site, packing up the tent and anything else left behind, and loading everything into the cart. The servants had left the mule harnessed to it, and Duro led the animal back to the road. Once there, he smacked it on the rump and watched as it disappeared round a bend. Hopefully it would keep going for a bit, and whoever found it would never know where Primus had stopped for the night.

He led Gisel towards the place where he'd tethered his horse. When he looked back, the only thing left in the clearing was the unconscious Eberulf.

Gisel gazed at the broad back of the stranger who had saved her from being raped. Duro. A strong name for a strong man. And not quite a stranger. She'd recognised him as the man in the crowd at the slave auction who had sent her a look of empathy. He hadn't helped her then, so why was he here now? And what did he want in return for rescuing her from Primus? A slave he hadn't had to pay for?

So far, he'd not demanded anything of her other than help with mundane tasks, but she was sure it was only a question of time. Men all wanted the same thing. They merely went about it in different ways. She couldn't deny that he'd treated her with kindness and consideration, and not in any way like his chattel. He could easily have carried on where Primus had left off. With his superior strength, she wouldn't have been able to fight him off even without others helping him. All he'd done, though, was put her on the back of his horse and tell her to hold on tight so she wouldn't fall off. She was a good horsewoman and preferred to grip with her thighs, just hovering her fingers near his waist in case the horse stumbled. She was reluctant to touch him, in case that set him off somehow.

Now they were riding along a straight Roman road in the moonlight, and she had no idea where they were going.

A quest, he'd said. What did that even mean? It sounded like something out of the tales itinerant bards told around the fire of an evening. Duro did have the look of one of the heroes of such yarns, she had to admit. He was too good-looking by half, with dark golden curls flowing over his shoulders, intense blue eyes and an unbelievable physique, and he was obviously sure of himself. Where had he come from? He had appeared out of nowhere just when she needed him most, as if sent by the gods, but she had no clue why.

He slowed his horse and turned into a small clearing. 'We'll stop here and get a few hours' rest,' he decreed.

Gisel's insides churned. Was this when he'd exact his payment? She swallowed hard, but had no choice but to wait and see. At least if she had to belong to anyone, he was better than Primus. For one thing, he didn't seem inclined to violence against women. She'd seen his expression when knocking out Eberulf. He had clearly been disgusted at her tribesman's enjoyment of her predicament. And that was something she'd never forget or forgive either. *May the gods curse him!*

'I don't have a tent, but I have blankets, and you can roll yourself into your cloak.' Duro had dismounted with a leap that was more graceful than such a large man ought to be capable of. He took hold of his horse's bridle to keep it steady while she jumped off in turn. 'I'll just tether him over there.' He nodded towards a sturdy tree.

Gisel waited until he returned with two rolled-up blankets and a couple of saddlebags. She could have tried to run, but what would be the point? With his much longer legs she'd be caught in moments. And then he might be angry and punish her. Better to stay meek for now and await an opportunity.

'Can you unfold them, please?' He thrust the blankets at her. While she did as he asked, he pulled something out of one of the bags. 'I take it you weren't fed earlier. Would you like some bread and cheese? It's a little stale, but better than nothing, right? And I have beer to wash it down with.'

Sitting down cross-legged on one of the blankets, he held out the food and drink. She hesitated, then sank down next to him and accepted his offering. 'Thank you.' Her stomach growled its approval. She was so hungry it felt as if her insides were hollow. She ate quickly, while he only took a few sips of the beer, letting her have the rest.

'We'll buy more tomorrow,' he said. 'Do you think you'll be able to sleep now?'

His voice was gentle, as if he understood that the shock of what had happened earlier was beginning to sink in. Her limbs trembled involuntarily from time to time, and she couldn't seem to get her brain to stop thinking about it, replaying the scene over and over again.

'I don't know.'

'Wrap yourself up and lie down. If you don't mind, I'll hold you. I won't let anything bad happen, you have my oath. Trust me?'

He stared into her eyes, and something in the depths of his made her nod her head.

'Swear you won't run away, please. I don't want to have to chase you, but I will if I must. You won't be safe on your own,' he added. Gisel believed him.

In truth, it would be more dangerous to try to escape him than to stay. Who knew what dangers awaited a lone female in this strange land? She'd heard her captors mention that they were in Britannia, which was far from her homeland. That explained the day-long sea crossing she'd had to endure. She had no way of returning, and chances were she'd be taken captive and sold yet again if she tried.

'I swear by all the gods not to try to run from you,' she said, her voice only quivering a tiny bit.

He smiled. 'Then lie down and let us rest. We have a long ride ahead of us tomorrow.'

She did as she was told, and he wrapped a well-muscled arm around her middle, drawing her back against his front. There were blankets and cloaks around both of them, but she could still feel how solid he was. How his large body dwarfed hers, but also cocooned it in a protective manner.

For the first time in weeks, she felt safe. With that strange thought running through her mind, she slipped into oblivion.

Chapter Eight

Bath, early June, present day

'This whole building is amazing, isn't it!' Mackenna looked around the entrance hall to the Roman baths. She had forgotten what it was like, as it had been years since she'd last visited. The reception area was set among the grandeur of Corinthian pillars and a vaulted roof with ornate plaster mouldings. She loved it.

'Yes, but that's nothing compared to the baths themselves,' Jonah commented, ushering her towards a door.

They emerged onto a balcony walkway that ran around the bath complex. It looked down at the main swimming pool from above. Opposite them were statues of Roman emperors and other dignitaries, staring haughtily across the open space. The pool itself was a murky green in the sunlight, surrounded by another walkway, this one colonnaded with large pillars. Everything was hewn out of the golden sandstone so common in this city, and it was breathtakingly beautiful.

'I always find it hard to believe that this has been here for two thousand years,' Mackenna said. 'The Romans were incredible engineers.'

'Yep, very impressive,' Jonah agreed.

They walked all the way around and took some touristy photos, including selfies with the statues in the background. When they received a few furtive looks, Mac was reminded that she was with a famous person.

'I promise I won't post these photos anywhere,' she whispered. 'They're just for me.'

Jonah was wearing a baseball cap and dark sunglasses again, but she saw his eyebrows rise. 'Hadn't crossed my mind,' he said quietly. 'I trust you.'

It sounded heartfelt, and his faith in her made a warm feeling spread through her chest. She turned away to hide the blush that was no doubt staining her cheeks. 'Well, good,' she said.

They made their way down a set of stairs to the exhibition explaining all about the baths. There they learned that the exact date of construction wasn't known, but that the first buildings had certainly been finished by AD 76. As well as the baths, there had been a temple here to worship a local goddess, Sul, or Sulis as the Romans called her. She was the spirit of the sacred spring around which the baths and temple complex was built, but as was their custom, the newcomers associated her with one of their own deities and named her Sulis Minerva. Mackenna marvelled at the remains of the temple pediment, featuring the carved head of a man, or god, with long hair and a beard and moustache. She tilted her head to get a better look at him.

'I feel like I've seen him somewhere before,' she murmured.

Images flashed through her mind. Distant memories that remained elusive but hovered on the edges of her consciousness. *The pediment intact, on top of a set of pillars, with steep stairs leading up to them. The shadowy interior of a temple, the murmuring of voices and the scent of incense drifting through the air . . .* She drew in a deep breath and tried to concentrate on the here and now, ignoring her overactive imagination.

Jonah was frowning, his nostrils flaring as if he too could smell the sweet smoke. 'Yes, and me. Weird.' He shook his head. 'We probably saw it in a history book at school.'

'Yes, perhaps.' But that didn't account for the sounds and fragrance. 'Is it me, or does it smell funny in here?'

'No, I noticed it too. Maybe something they do on purpose to make the experience of visiting more authentic?'

'Ah, of course. That makes sense.'

Yet as they carried on and took in the other exhibits, Mackenna became more and more confused. The amphorae and red Samian ware dishes also seemed awfully familiar, and she itched to pick them up. It was as if she'd handled them frequently and her fingers knew inherently what it would be like to touch them – the clay surface of the amphorae rough, while the Samian ware was smooth and cool. In one display cabinet there was a large round dish with a sort of spout on one side.

'Oh look, a *mortarium*,' she exclaimed. 'My friend had one just like it.' She stopped dead as she realised what she'd said.

Jonah, who'd been right behind her, ran into her back and had to steady himself by putting his hands on her shoulders. 'What was that?' He leaned forward to peer at the exhibit, causing her to become flustered at his nearness.

'Er, nothing. I've read about those.' She gestured to the dish. 'Roman women used them for cooking, cutting everything up into small pieces and crushing it before it was eaten. Kind of like with a pestle and mortar.'

'Oh yeah? Why?' Jonah frowned at the *mortarium* as if it had offended him somehow.

'Because some of the vegetables were tough and stringy, so it made it easier to eat and digest them. Or so I've read.' She hadn't, actually, so how she knew this was a mystery. Unless she'd absorbed such facts without realising?

'I see. Sounds gross.' He grabbed her hand and tugged her towards the next cabinet. 'Come and look at the treasure they found here. Leather bags full of coins. Wouldn't it be awesome to dig up something like that? Much better than old bits of pottery.'

'Definitely.' She stared at the reconstruction of a leather pouch stuffed with silver. Again she had the uncanny sensation that she'd held something like that in her hands. She still remembered the weight of it, and the clinking of metal as the coins rubbed together. What the hell was wrong with her?

They continued touring the exhibition, admiring mosaics, stones with inscriptions in Latin, the bronze head of the goddess Sulis Minerva that must have once stood inside the nearby temple, and lots of other Roman artefacts: combs and little statuettes and other votive offerings. Finally they came to the so-called curse tablets – small pieces of lead with inscriptions on them that had been rolled up and cast into the sacred spring, the supplications on them for the goddess's ears only.

Mackenna thought she heard Jonah murmur, 'I did that.'

She raised her eyebrows at him. 'What do you mean, you did that?'

'Huh?' He had a faraway look in his eyes, his expression totally blank for a second. Then he blinked, as if he realised where he was. 'No, I said I would totally do that,' he mumbled, his cheeks turning pink. 'You know, if I wanted to curse someone. How cool is that?'

There was something he wasn't telling her, but she let it go. 'Mm, me too.' She smiled. 'Maybe I'd put a hex on a certain part of Blue's anatomy.'

His eyes lit up. 'You definitely should. A shame they don't sell the bits of lead any longer. I'd damn well buy one for you.'

Laughing, they made their way out into the sunshine.

* * *

Jonah hadn't been joking. Not entirely.

If he could curse Blue and any part of him so the guy would get his comeuppance, he would. Although in a way, he ought to thank him for making Mackenna break up with him as it gave Jonah a chance with her. Not that he thought she was ready for that yet. They were getting to know each other as proper friends, but this wasn't a date. Although he was extremely drawn to her, he wasn't sure his attraction was reciprocated. She was a bit hesitant around him, as if she wasn't quite sure of his motives for seeking her out. And who could blame her?

Baby steps, he reminded himself. He had to let her heal first from the nasty break-up. Finding your partner in bed with someone else must be one of the worst ways of ending a relationship. Double that, as in the case of Blue and the blonde clones, and it made for a very traumatic event indeed.

'Oh, I love this! I so wish I could jump in right this minute. The weather is really warm today.'

Mac was fanning her face with an exhibition brochure and enthusing about the large swimming pool, whose still surface reflected its surroundings in the sunlight. The water was green and cloudy now, due to the amount of algae flourishing in it. The signs told them this would not have been the case in Roman times. Back then, the bath complex had a roof to keep out the sun's rays and thereby prevent the growth of the algae. Looking up, Jonah could imagine it. Impressive and, from what he'd gathered in the exhibition, something extraordinary the native Britons had never seen. They'd have been awestruck.

'Yes, it's very tempting, especially on a hot day.' He flapped his T-shirt away from his body to cool down a little. It really was almost unbearably warm. Just like it would have been two thousand years ago. In fact, that would have been worse, the air humid and moist in the enclosed space.

'It must have been fun to come here and be pampered.' Mac waved a hand to encompass the complex, and her Roman-style ring flashed in the sunlight. Jonah wondered how many other ladies visiting this place had worn the same kind of jewellery. Probably quite a few of them.

In his mind's eye, he pictured the baths as they'd been back then. *Mostly naked men and women splashing and swimming lengths in the pool, while others sat around in groups in the various alcoves placed at intervals along the edges of the walkway that ran all the way round the pool. There was laughter, gossip and whispers. Shrieks and grunts from the nearby gym where men were exercising. The odour of sweat mixed with the delicate scents from the fragrant oils used for massage and cleansing, as well as the faint whiff of sulphur from the sacred spring itself* . . . He moved towards the shallow steps into the pool to join them, but was halted by someone tugging on his arm.

'Jonah!' Mac hissed at him, gazing around furtively, eyes wide. 'You can't go in there. It's not allowed. And you've got shoes on, for goodness' sake!'

He looked down and saw his sneaker-clad foot hovering just above the surface of the water. Swiftly he pulled it back and pivoted, again running into Mac so that he had to encircle her waist with his hands in order not to pull them both into the pool.

'Whoops! Sorry. Got a bit carried away there.' He smiled at her to show that he hadn't been serious about going in, but he saw the doubt in her eyes. It had been a close-run thing and they both knew it. What on earth had got into him?

'Yes, well, please don't get us thrown out of here. I haven't finished looking yet.' She held out her mobile. 'Can you take a photo of me here, please? I want to send it to my mum. I'll sit by the edge.' She sank down onto the warm sandstone and leaned against a pillar.

'Sure.' He framed her in the picture and told her to smile. 'Actually, let's do one where you look all serious and dreamy, staring off into the distance. Yes, like that. Now throw your hair over one shoulder. It's so gorgeous, we need to showcase it. Try to catch the breeze a bit.' To his delight, she was wearing it loose today, and as usual he'd been itching to run his fingers through the silky tresses.

She did as she was told, although she sent him another funny look when he handed back her phone. 'You like my hair?'

He gave her a lopsided smile and shrugged, aiming for a nonchalance he didn't feel. 'Who doesn't? It's beautiful. People must tell you that all the time, right?'

'Occasionally, yes, but it's nothing special apart from being long.' She wrinkled her nose. 'It's dead straight.'

'You're wrong. It's definitely special. Why else do you think we wanted you on our album cover?' *And why else am I so obsessed with it and you?* 'Trust me, it's dead gorgeous.'

Her cheeks turned a dusky pink. 'Thank you, that's . . . very kind of you to say.'

He wasn't being kind in the least, but he refrained from telling her that. It was still too soon.

When they had seen everything there was to see, they wandered through the narrow lanes in the centre of town and bought ice creams to cool down. Jonah tried to draw out his time with her as much as possible, but they garnered some attention from a couple of fans who spotted him, and he became uncomfortable with the scrutiny. After allowing them to take some selfies with him, he walked Mackenna back to her flat. Once again he gave her a long hug goodbye, but this time he knew he couldn't push for any more dates. Or non-dates, as the case might be. He had to give her space, and he wanted her to take the next step if she was interested in seeing him.

'If you ever need anything, I'm around,' he told her. 'Just give me a call or text me, OK?'

'Sure. You too, if I can help you with anything.' She laughed a little self-consciously. 'Not that I have much to offer a rock star who can probably pay to have anything he wants done for him.'

He let go of her and playfully pushed her shoulder. 'Hey! I'm just a normal guy. I don't have staff and I manage everything on my own. Well, except taxes and investments and stuff. And contracts. Those are boring as hell to read.' He made a face, and as he'd hoped, it made her laugh and relax.

'I'm sure. Well, good luck with the songwriting. Can't wait to hear the results. And thank you for today. I had a great time, and the baths were just stunning, weren't they?'

Yes, and so are you, he wanted to say, but he made himself turn and walk away. It was too soon to confess any such thing, and he wasn't sure the right time would ever come.

Chapter Nine

Southern Britannia, early June AD 80

Duro had slept fitfully, afraid his travel companion would go back on her word and bolt during the night. Thankfully, she was still there when dawn broke, curled up peacefully in his arms. There was such perfection about the sensation of having her there, he took a moment to revel in it. He knew he'd done the right thing. The gods had meant for him to find her and rescue her. It was as though their immortal souls had met before in previous lives, and now they'd come together again. Inevitable. Predestined. He didn't doubt she belonged in his future. Now all he had to do was persuade her of this.

That would not be an easy task.

Without waking her, he went to fetch the leftover bread and cheese from his saddlebags, then made his ablutions in a nearby brook. There, he also filled a leather container with cool fresh water, as they'd finished the beer last night. Then he brought his horse over to drink its fill before tethering it once more near a patch of grass. It should be enough to keep it going until their next stop.

Gisel was blinking awake when he returned. She sat up a little too quickly, as he saw her sway before steadying herself with one hand. He sank down next to her, but not too close. He sensed that she was still wary, and rightly so. It would take time to win her trust, but he was in no hurry.

'The bread is very dry now, I'm afraid, but we can wash it down with water.' He held out a share to her, as well as a piece of hard cheese.

'Thank you, master,' she muttered, the last word sounding as though it had been wrung out of her by force.

He shook his head. 'Duro. I'm not your master. We're travelling companions from now on, nothing more.'

'But you said you were taking me home,' she reminded him, raising her chin as if in challenge. 'After we go on some quest. That doesn't make it seem like I have a choice.' The look she threw him was suspicious in the extreme.

'I should have chosen my words more carefully,' he admitted. 'Let me rephrase. Gisel, would you like to accompany me on a quest for vengeance, and then back to my home to see if you'd want to live there?'

'Live there? As your slave or concubine?' Her eyes flashed with clear disdain for either of those options. Duro admired her spirit, but pretended not to notice her belligerence.

'Neither. Out of your own free will as part of our tribe. If you agree to give it a try for, say, a few months, then I'll swear an oath to take you back to your own family if you find you dislike it.'

Again suspicion lurked in the depths of her turquoise eyes. 'Why would you want me to do that? Of course I'm going to want to go to my own home.'

He smiled at her. 'Let's just say I hope to persuade you otherwise.'

She huffed, but relaxed a fraction. After a moment's hesitation, she said, 'Very well. It's not as though I would fare better travelling on my own. Where are we heading?'

Duro wondered whether he should tell her, but decided that complete honesty between them was the only thing that would work henceforth. She had been manhandled and probably duped enough. She deserved nothing but the truth from now on.

'Ultimately we are going to a Roman encampment by the name of Isca. It's apparently somewhere to the west of here. I've never been there before because it didn't exist when I last lived on these shores.' At her puzzled glance, he explained, 'I've spent many years as a gladiator in Campania, in the land of the Romans proper, not too far from their greatest city, Rome. Do you know where that is?'

'Yes, I've heard tell of Rome. It's far south-east of my homelands,' she replied promptly.

'And where is that? Raetia? Germania?'

'The Romans call it Germania Superior. My tribe are the Treveri.' She told him the name in her own language, and Duro nodded, recognising it. 'I grew up in a small settlement not far from the Rhenus river, and although the area is part of the Roman Empire, my father mostly followed the old ways. He and the rest of my kin are proud of our Germanic origins. We usually went to the nearest town on market day, but other than that we didn't have much contact with the Romans.'

'I thought so. You have the look of a Germana. Anyway, as I was saying, much has changed here since I was a child, so we are both travelling into the unknown. Still, these straight roads should help ensure we don't get lost. I'd been told that if I stayed on the one Primus was travelling on first, I would have eventually reached Glevum, and someone there could have directed me the rest of the way to Isca. However, he turned towards the south-west, and last night I decided to continue that detour.'

She had finished her breakfast, and took a couple of sips of water when he passed her the skin. Wiping her mouth with the back of her hand, she frowned. 'Why? Is your quest not urgent?'

'The vengeance I seek is long overdue and well deserved, but I think it would be wise to have the gods on my side. I've been told that there is a very special sacred spring not too far from here, dedicated to the goddess Sul. The Romans call her Sulis Minerva. Minerva is one of their own goddesses, a powerful being of wisdom and justice, as far as I understand it, who can hopefully aid me in my quest. Even if the native goddess residing in the spring has nothing to do with the Roman one, she'll still be mighty, so adding a plea to Sul can't hurt. I propose to go there first to ask for assistance and protection. Yesterday we were about halfway to a place named Durocornovium when Primus changed direction. If we continue south-west from here, we'll arrive at the spring of Sul eventually. I believe it's referred to as the *aquae calidae* – the hot waters. There is supposed to be another straight road that we can pick up closer to it. What do you say? Are you game?'

She shrugged. 'Do I have a choice?'

They both knew she didn't.

Gisel was confused. She'd never met a man like Duro, who appeared to hold the upper hand in every way yet was still asking her opinion. Either it was a trick, or he was all about in the head. He couldn't possibly be that nice for real.

She was absently holding on to his waist, her hands having gone there of their own accord this time. For some reason, she wasn't as averse to touching him this morning. She couldn't claim that he was repugnant in any way. Quite the opposite: he was male temptation personified. She contemplated the broad shoulders and honed physique of the man sitting in front of her. He had been a gladiator, he'd said, and she could well believe it. Raw power emanated from him, and yet she felt safe in a way she never had before in her life.

He could have forced her to go in front of him, where she would have had to sit with his arms around her to stop her falling off. That thought didn't appeal. Or rather, it did, but she didn't want it to. She was too aware of him as it was; the sheer size of him, his strength, and his scent teasing her nostrils whenever the horse moved. He smelled clean, and of man, in a good way. And he shone like the sun – golden in every way, from his gilded curls to his sun-kissed skin and the bronze ring he wore that glinted in the light.

She shouldn't be impressed, but she was.

Still, it could all be a ruse to lull her into a false sense of security before he pounced. She only had his word for it that she wasn't his possession. Just because he hadn't molested her last night didn't mean he wouldn't eventually. No, she would be on her guard until he showed his true colours.

Gisel wasn't a fool.

They were riding through an open landscape that was alternately hilly and flat, with the occasional river or stream gushing by and quite a few agricultural settlements. Mostly these consisted of isolated farmsteads enclosed by fields and woodland. The majority of the buildings were native roundhouses, but dwellings in the Roman rectangular style cropped up as well. Really dense patches of forest were rare, and it was beautiful and peaceful out here in the countryside, but she was still traumatised from the past few weeks and jumped at the slightest sound.

Duro must have noticed. 'Don't worry, I have my sword to hand,' he said, glancing at her over his shoulder. 'I won't let anyone take you again.' His blue gaze was reassuring, and she relaxed a tiny bit, although she couldn't help but scan their surroundings, despite his words. He was but one man, and who was to say they wouldn't be attacked by a whole horde?

'I thought weapons weren't allowed,' she commented. 'They

aren't where I come from.' She'd seen him strap the sword to his back before they departed that morning.

He grinned mischievously. 'They're not, but no one will know I have one unless you inform them. Are you going to tell on me to the authorities?'

She shook her head. No chance of that. They both knew she'd be putting herself in danger if she tried to speak to the Romans in charge here.

The road they were on was clearly an ancient track, its surface dry and not too rutted. Relatively wide, it was not as straight and even-surfaced as a Roman one, but it was bustling with activity. They definitely weren't the only travellers out and about. Both two- and four-wheeled carts and wagons trundled along pulled by mules or oxen. They passed people on horseback and on foot, and occasionally a faster rider overtook them in turn.

'Probably messengers carrying important missives from one Roman fort to another,' Duro told her when he moved to one side onto the verge to make way for one such.

A larger settlement came into view. There appeared to be some sort of market going on, competing with the workshops that opened onto the roadside on either side. Gisel guessed they were all taking advantage of passing trade to sell their goods. The craftsmen and stalls had various things on offer: food, leather goods, combs and cloth. Duro dismounted, lifting her off to stand beside him. Rooting around in one of his saddlebags, he retrieved a small dagger in a sheath, which he held out to her.

'Here, you should have this for protection, but stay close to me.'

She took it slowly, pulling it out of the leather casing. The bone handle was elaborately carved, and the blade was honed to lethal sharpness. Sending him a taunting look, she asked, 'Aren't you afraid I'll stick it in your back when we continue our ride?'

He smiled, a knowing glint in his eyes as if he was calling her bluff. 'We both know you are a beautiful woman alone in a strange land, with no idea where you are and no mean's of protecting yourself. Even if you rob me of all the silver and gold I carry, you won't be able to buy yourself safety. There will always be men who'll want your body, no matter how much you try to bribe them. They'll take your payment, then you. Is that what you want?'

He thinks I'm beautiful? She cursed herself for a fool. That was not the most important thing about what he'd said. Much as she hated to admit it, he spoke the truth, and for now she was at his mercy. She huffed, but didn't reply. What was the point?

He held out his hand. 'Shall we go in search of some decent clothing for you? I hate to say it, but at the moment you look more like a scarecrow than an elegant lady.'

Her gaze dropped to her oversized garments and she could only agree. 'Very well.'

She placed her hand in his, and to her surprise he plaited their fingers together, which sent a jolt up her arm. His palm against hers was warm and callused, his fingers also rough, but she liked it and didn't pull away. Instead, she followed him to a booth where a woman was hawking linen shifts and woollen tunics in all the colours of the rainbow. They weren't newly made, and the gods only knew where she had obtained them, but at least they looked clean. After letting the woman hold them up to gauge Gisel's approximate size, Duro purchased two shifts and two long-sleeved tunics in the Britannic style. One was green, the other pale blue, and the material was very fine.

'We'd better have one with short sleeves as well,' he decreed, and allowed her to select a light pink one that appealed to her. It had decorative bands along the neckline and hem, and was as lovely as any garment she'd owned at home. 'Oh, and a cloak, if you please. Something warm, even though it's summer now. It's good to have at night.'

The woman produced a thick woollen mantle in a deeper green, lined with linen to make it less scratchy on the skin. 'Will this do?'

Duro looked at Gisel. 'What say you?'

She was flustered at being asked her opinion, as if she was his wife or relative, and felt her cheeks heating up, but she nodded agreement. It would do very nicely indeed.

'Thank you,' she murmured as they moved away from the stall and headed towards a leather worker.

'My pleasure,' Duro replied, and sounded as if he meant it. Gisel still couldn't fathom him out. He was a complete enigma.

After buying her a comb, a belt and a pouch to hang off it, he led her into a wooded area nearby and turned his back so that she could change into her new clothes. She added the knife and pouch to the belt and cinched it tight around her waist. When she was done, he nodded approvingly.

'Much better. You can pass for my Iceni wife. Just make sure you wear your hair in two plaits, please, like my kinswomen. Now, let's burn your former master's tunic and cloak, lest someone find them and connect them with us. Not that I think anyone will mourn him, but the Roman authorities may take issue with one of their countrymen being robbed and killed.'

Gisel wanted to burn the garments for other reasons, as the mere thought of Primus made her skin crawl. She watched with approval as her last connection with that pig disappeared in flames. Hopefully he was having a horrible time of it in the underworld. It was what he deserved.

'Good riddance,' Duro muttered as they shared a look of satisfaction at a job well done.

Something sparked between them, other than the embers of the burning clothes, and Gisel drew in a sharp breath. In that moment it was as if they were in accord in every way, but she couldn't let herself be fooled. To all intents and purposes, he owned her, even though he'd claimed they were equals. He had total control over her as long as she was vulnerable to attack from others and had no choice but to remain with him. Only time would tell if he could be trusted.

Though a foolish part of her was beginning to hope that he could.

Chapter Ten

Bath, June, present day

A week went by with no more visits or messages from Jonah, and Mackenna told herself she shouldn't have expected there to be. He'd merely been kind, checking up on her and taking her on an outing. OK, two outings, but who was counting? Now he was probably busy with his songwriting. Or maybe he'd gone to London to see friends. He had a life, one that didn't include her, and it was none of her business what he was up to. She had no claim on him or his time. The fact that a tiny part of her was disappointed that he hadn't at least texted her was something she tried to ignore. That was just silly. And there was no way she'd message him, despite what he'd said. She was sure it had been nothing more than a platitude.

She threw herself into the decorating, singing along to a loud rock song being belted out through her iPod speakers. Out of the corner of her eye she saw her phone move as it vibrated with an incoming message, and she stopped what she was doing. Wiping her hands on her messy leggings, she picked it up, and her heart gave a little jump of joy as Jonah's name flashed up on the screen.

Jonah: *Going stir crazy staying indoors. Zero song inspiration. Want to go do something fun?*

She typed out her reply with shaking fingers, which she told herself was ridiculous. They were friends, nothing more, and he was bored. Presumably he didn't know anyone else in Bath yet either. It made sense for them to hang out occasionally, if that was what he wanted.

Mac: *Sure. Like what?*
Jonah: *Stand-up paddleboarding on River Avon.*
Mac: *What???*
Jonah: *Can you swim?*
Mac: *Yes, like a fish.*
Jonah: *Excellent! That's all you need. Instructors will do the rest I'm told. Up for it?*
Mac: *OK, bring it on.*
Jonah: 😜 *Great! Wear swimwear and gym-type clothes that dry quickly. Pick you up at 2. J x*

Mac put the phone down and hurried to clean her paintbrushes and put them away. She had time for a quick shower to wash off the paint splatter she knew covered her from head to toe, but only if she was quick. A frisson of anxiety shot through her. She'd never been paddleboarding before and was afraid she'd make a fool of herself. It looked easy enough, but was it? She knew how to ski and surely it couldn't be harder than that.

She'd soon find out.

Jonah was punctual, waiting in a black SUV outside her house at exactly two o'clock. She opened the passenger door and jumped in, throwing the bag she'd brought into the back seat.

'Hi,' she said, a little breathlessly, and felt her cheeks heat up when he smiled at her.

'Hey yourself. Thanks for coming with me. Did you bring a towel?'

'Yes, of course.' She laughed. 'There's no way I'm going to survive this without falling into the river at least once.'

He gave her a lopsided grin. 'Yeah, me too, but it's really hot today, so I bet it will feel refreshing.'

He put the car in gear and pulled away from the kerb, heading south and then west along the river. Mac fiddled with the hem of the tank top she wore over her bikini. She'd paired this with Lycra cycling shorts that clung to her curves, and regretted that decision now. Perhaps she should have worn something loose, but then again, if she fell in, any clothing would stick to her.

'Have you done this before?' she asked, glancing at Jonah's profile.

He was looking very handsome today, his golden-blond hair messy and his chin sporting a bit of stubble, as if he hadn't shaved for a few days. He was in board shorts and a T-shirt with the sleeves cut off. It emphasised his muscular arms, shoulders and chest, and showcased those spectacular Viking-style tattoos that suited him so well. She had to look away so as not to be caught staring.

Why had she never noticed before how attractive he was? Had she really been that blinded by Blue? A part of her knew that wasn't quite true. She simply hadn't *allowed* herself to notice Jonah, because that would have felt like a betrayal of her boyfriend.

'No,' he said, in answer to her question, 'but someone told me it's fun and I'm always game to try new things. You scared?' He sent her a teasing look, his blue eyes twinkling.

Mac scoffed. 'Of course not! I mean, what's the worst that can happen? We get wet.'

'Mm.' He turned his gaze back to the road, his hands tightening on the steering wheel for a moment. 'Anyway, I understand the instructors are great, and they'll be with us the whole time. It'll be fine.'

They followed the curve of the river on the other side, opposite and below the centre of town, and arrived at the paddleboarding place. They parked and went inside an office, where they met their instructor, Rick.

'I'm afraid it's just the two of you this afternoon,' he said. 'Normally we take groups of up to ten, but the other people cancelled at the last minute. Someone got sick apparently. Anyway, we'll have fun, I promise.'

'No worries.' Jonah took the thin, high-quality life vest Rick handed him and put it on, while Mac did the same.

'Have you ever done this before?' Rick enquired.

They both shook their heads.

'OK, no problem. No experience necessary. You might want to lose the sunglasses, though,' he added. 'And leave your phones locked in the glove compartment of your car. I'll be taking lots of photos, so you won't miss out. Most mobiles don't like going for a swim in the river.' He laughed at his own joke.

Jonah took both their phones back to the car, and must have left his sunglasses there too. He came back wearing just his baseball cap, but back to front for a change, showing his face. Rick did a sort of double-take, but wisely didn't comment on having such a famous client, even though he'd clearly recognised him. Instead, he led them outside and told them where they could leave their bags with the towels and spare sets of clothing. Then they went down to the river's edge and the waiting boards.

'Right. We've got two hours, and this is what we're going to do . . .' Rick launched into a brief spiel about safety and the basics of paddleboarding.

They started off on their knees, navigating out onto the river. Mac wobbled a bit before steadying herself and her nerves.

'You'll soon build up your confidence,' Rick assured them. 'We'll have you standing up in no time.'

That was perhaps an exaggeration, but it didn't take as long as Mac had feared. And once on her feet, she loved it. They were heading up the river towards Pulteney Bridge, where Rick said they'd turn around and go back. Seeing Bath from this unusual angle was lovely – the view of the old buildings gleaming a dull gold in the sunlight was both peaceful and stunning. They passed swans, ducks and other water fowl, which sent them mistrustful glares and scooted out of the way. Meanwhile, Rick was giving them step-by-step instructions, and occasionally taking pictures. He didn't talk all the time, though, giving Mac and Jonah a chance to chat and enjoy each other's company.

'Woo-hoo! This is awesome.' Jonah smiled at her, wobbling a bit on his board but paddling with strong strokes. His biceps bulged every time he put the paddle in the water, the tattoos expanding and contracting, making it seem as though the Viking-style animals were alive and moving. Mac almost fell off her own board while watching him. She recovered just in time and turned away to hide her hot cheeks.

'Yes, it's great fun,' she agreed. 'Thanks for suggesting it. I never would have thought to try this on my own.'

'Good thing you have me to corrupt you, then.' He shot her a mischievous look that had her entire body heating up. Not that he'd meant it the way her warped mind suggested, she was sure. Although she realised she wouldn't mind being corrupted by Jonah in any way he chose.

We're just friends, she reminded herself. Why would he want his bandmate's leftovers? No way.

She pushed these thoughts to the back of her mind, and instead admired the view some more. It really was gorgeous here, but . . . hang on. Where had the buildings gone? As she blinked into the sunlight, the sandstone town had disappeared.

As if through a haze, she could see water meadows, jetties, and people loading goods into various boats and vessels. A huge white building with a red-tiled roof seemed to tower over the few other dwellings nearby. All one- or two-storey, and not blocking the view of the many hills surrounding the valley. Apart from those, the landscape was bare. Pristine almost. Some sheep and cattle mooched around, grazing lazily, and the swans and ducks were still there. But the people all wore strange clothing and the words that drifted across the water were not in a language she'd ever heard. Or had she? It seemed familiar somehow . . .

Lost in thought, she'd steered too close to Jonah's board, and despite the shouted warning from Rick, she bumped into him. The next thing she knew, she'd gone head-first into the frigid river, trying not to swallow a mouthful of water. She came up with a little scream, spluttering and wiping the moisture out of her eyes.

'Shit, that's cold!' She glanced towards the riverbank, which now appeared to have gone back to normal, chock-full of sandstone buildings as usual. What on earth had just happened? Why had she had such a strange vision? But she didn't have time to think about it now, as Jonah was right behind her.

'You're telling me. Thanks for the dunking, Miss Jackson. I'm going to get you for that!' He grabbed her round the waist from behind and pulled her under briefly. She came up spluttering again, but giggling at the same time and trying to splash him in the face.

'Cut it out!' she hissed. 'Rick's going to freak.'

The instructor was nearby, watching them with raised eyebrows but not commenting as yet.

'Then I'll have to get you back more later,' Jonah promised with a chuckle.

He was so close, his body warm against her back despite the chilly water, and when he spoke, his mouth brushed her ear. A shiver ran through her, all the way down to her toes. Had he done that on purpose? She swivelled round, blinking at him, but his expression was innocent, giving nothing away, and then he let go of her.

'Come on, babe. No time for splashing about in the river. We've got paddling to do,' he declared, heaving himself onto his board effortlessly.

Babe? She decided he'd probably called her that out of habit. With the number of women that always surrounded the band, the guys probably called everyone that as they wouldn't remember so many names. Mac told herself she wasn't special. She scrambled up onto her own board with much less grace, but with calm instructions from Rick, she managed to get back on her feet. The instructor handed her the paddle, which she'd completely forgotten about. Her cheeks flamed at the thought that she'd lost all sense when Jonah had her in his arms like that. Rick must think her a complete moron. She vowed to concentrate on the paddling from now on, and not the stunning scenery, which included Jonah's now thoroughly wet body.

An almost impossible task.

Jonah cursed silently. He hadn't been able to resist holding Mackenna in his arms for a brief moment, but she'd looked so startled, he wasn't sure it was a good thing. She hadn't pushed him away, so he didn't know if she was appalled or confused. Or whether she'd liked it.

Aarghh! He should keep his hands to himself, but she was so gorgeous today. He had to get himself under control, or he'd need to fall in the river again on purpose to cool off.

Rick was giving him knowing looks, but didn't comment. Hopefully the guy thought Mac was his girlfriend and therefore off limits. He had better not be ogling her, the caveman part of his brain added before he reined it in. He thought about the photos Rick had taken. They'd been assured that they'd all be sent to them and not shared or stored elsewhere. Jonah hoped that was true, or else he'd have to get his solicitors to sue the paddleboarding company. Not because he minded having his picture in the press, but he felt supremely protective of Mac. She'd been gossiped about enough because of that twat Blue.

The speculation had been endless for a couple of weeks, when the newshounds got wind of the break-up. The pair of them had been so photogenic, they'd been the darlings of the media for a while. Blue, being the show-off he was, had relished every moment, but Jonah had noticed Mac cringing quite a few times. She wasn't comfortable in the limelight, and if this outing today landed her back there, he would never forgive himself. He'd only wanted to spend time with her and have some fun. Cheer her up. And despite having vowed to let her be the one to take the next step, he'd been unable to stop himself from texting her.

He'd needed cheering up as well, truth be told. He had been feeling down ever since he made the decision to quit Valhalla Storm. It was the end of an era, and the future loomed before him, full of possibilities but also terrifying. What if no one wanted any of his songs? Or to collaborate or work with him? Sure, he had enough money for another five lifetimes, but without music in it somehow, that meant nothing.

It didn't help that everyone had been hounding him, trying to make him change his mind. The barrage of texts and phone calls had been relentless, making him doubt himself at times. Deep down, he knew it was the right decision, but when both the band's manager and several of the PR people had muttered about him being selfish, it had really got to him. He was in effect taking away part of their livelihood, but it wasn't his problem. He needed to look out for his own well-being first and foremost. And there were other bands they could work with. Valhalla Storm wasn't the only one. They'd survive.

He took a deep breath and concentrated on the here and now. It was a beautiful day and he was having an adventure with a stunning woman. He was going to enjoy the hell out of it.

They succeeded in paddling themselves up to just below Pulteney Bridge, close to the weir, then back downstream again. Mac loved every minute, and told herself it had nothing to do with the company. Or not much. But she knew she was fooling herself. Jonah in playful mode, happy and laughing, wasn't something she'd seen a lot of during the time she'd spent with the band. He had always remained in the background, quiet and unassuming. Although he'd let loose a few times during the wild parties, she had never seen him glowing the way he was today. It made her all warm and fuzzy inside.

He deserved to be happy, and she had a feeling people like Blue had dragged him down, pushing him into the shadows when he should have been shining in his own right.

After they finished their session, they dried off and changed into fresh clothes. She put on another bikini, but with cut-off jeans shorts and a different tank top, while Jonah wore a similar outfit to his previous one.

'You hungry?' he asked, as they headed for the car.

'Starving, actually.' The exercise, as well as spending several hours in the baking-hot sun, had given her an appetite, and her stomach grumbled for emphasis.

Jonah laughed. 'Good thing I brought a picnic then. Let's find a park somewhere and eat.'

'You did? Wow, you've thought of everything.' Mac was impressed. The guy was seriously organised, having booked the paddling beforehand too.

'I aim to please. Hop in.' He threw their wet things into the boot and got in the driver's seat. As soon as Mac was strapped in, they took off. He threw her a glance as he drove, frowning slightly. 'You don't think he'll send those pics to the tabloids, do you?'

Mac had wondered the same thing, but shook her head. 'No, he must know that would cost him his job. If the company can't keep client photos secure, they'll soon be out of business.'

He nodded. 'Yeah. I'm counting on that. I wouldn't want you to have to suffer for being seen with me.'

She stared at him. 'Suffer? Oh, you mean they'd make up stories about us? I don't care. I got used to that. I don't think even a tiny percentage of what they printed about me and Blue was the truth. I won't look at any of it, I promise.' Impulsively she grabbed his hand, which was on the gear knob, and squeezed it. 'Don't worry about it.'

He turned his hand to enclose her fingers with his and squeezed back. 'OK, thanks. That makes me feel better.' When he let go again, she felt bereft, but told herself not to be so silly.

They ended up in a park on the outskirts of town, and Jonah wore his sunglasses and the baseball cap the right way round. Still, he was a big guy and not exactly inconspicuous. Mac privately thought he probably drew the eye even without anyone knowing he was famous, but she didn't mention it. They found a secluded spot in the shade of some massive trees, and he produced a blanket and the cool bag he'd brought. They settled down and he opened the bag and took out an array of items.

'We've got cheese and tomato, tuna mayo, and ham sandwiches,' he told her, placing various packages on the blanket between them. 'Grapes, strawberries, clotted cream and shortbread biscuits.

There's carrot cake for dessert as well, and some chocolate. To drink, you have a choice of water, beer or a soft drink. I wasn't sure what kind of wine you like, so I didn't bring any. Sorry.'

'Sorry? Are you mad? You've got an absolute feast right here! Thank you, it all looks amazing.' She couldn't believe he'd prepared all this. It was incredibly thoughtful.

'Well, dig in. I'm starving too, and my mum told me a gentleman never starts eating before a lady.' He grinned at her and gestured to the food.

'A gentleman, huh? The kind who dunks people in the river, by any chance?' She opened the packet of cheese sandwiches and helped herself, before holding it out to him.

He nodded. 'Exactly. And I owe you more than that. Just you wait.'

She shivered, but not in fright.

They ate in silence after that, but it was companionable and not at all strained. Mac hadn't been this relaxed in ages, and loved every minute. After a while, Jonah's phone buzzed and he took it out of his pocket, then put it back with a frown without opening whatever message had arrived.

'Everything OK?' Mac asked, concerned by the expression on his face. There had been a fleeting look of frustration mixed with guilt that she didn't understand.

He took off his hat and fiddled with it before running his fingers through his hair and putting it on again. 'Yes. Just Blue hassling me. Again. He's been blowing up my phone trying to make me stay in the band.' He sighed. 'I don't think he realises that the more he argues, the less likely I am to change my mind. After all, he's one of the main reasons I'm leaving.'

She hesitated, but couldn't help asking, 'Not because of what he did to me, right?'

'No. Well, sort of. That was just the last straw. I'd had enough of his antics, you know, and what happened that night showed me how completely toxic he is. I don't want to be around him any more. Seriously, don't worry about it. He'll get over it.' He chuckled. 'Not much can dent his ego.'

'True.' She had to admit that Blue's self-belief would no doubt remain intact.

Jonah changed the subject, and she didn't probe further. It wasn't any of her business and she didn't want to spoil the outing by talking about her ex. Chatting about the paddleboarding, and how they should do it again soon, they finished the sandwiches and moved on to the cake, followed by fruit.

'Here, you should dip your strawberries in the clotted cream. It's fab.' Jonah pushed a berry into the pot of cream, scooping up a large glob, then held it to her lips. She opened her mouth and bit into it, making a noise of approval that had his eyes widening for an instant. 'You like that, huh?' he murmured, staring at her mouth.

'Mm, so good. Your turn.' She did the same for him, and almost lost herself in watching his lips close around the ripe fruit. It was incredibly tempting to lean over and lick off the juice that stained his mouth, but she restrained herself.

As she turned away, an image came into her mind of being fed a different type of berries by him. *His handsome face leaning over hers, his fingers lightly brushing her mouth as she accepted the offering. Blue eyes staring intently into hers, a callused thumb smearing the juice off her bottom lip. Golden hair hanging down in curling waves across his shoulders, his stubble glinting in the sunlight . . .* She blinked, and swallowed the mouthful she'd forgotten she was chewing. Long hair? That wasn't Jonah. His was longish on top and often hung over his eyes, but it was buzzed short around the bottom. So why had she pictured him like a knight of old? Weird.

Clearing her throat, she picked up another strawberry, but ate it by herself this time. He did the same.

'So the songwriting isn't going too well?' she asked, needing to send her mind in a different direction.

'Not for the last few days, but I think I've just had an idea.' He was smiling when she dared another look at him. 'I'll let you know how it goes.'

'Please do.'

If he at least texted her about his work, they wouldn't lose contact completely. And she was sure now that she wanted to stay in touch with him any way she could.

She was falling for him. Dammit.

Chapter Eleven

Southern Britannia, June AD *80*

They spent one more night sleeping in the open, and this time Duro managed to relax enough to get some rest. Gisel had been calm the previous day, and he doubted she would try to run away from him now. She was intelligent enough to see the dangers she would face on her own, and as long as he didn't scare her away, he reckoned she would stay.

He already knew he wanted her to remain with him for ever.

To that end, he would need to woo her carefully. As he was the first to wake up again, he pondered how to go about it while washing himself and combing out his hair. Not that he was vain, but looking scruffy and unkempt wouldn't help his cause. He'd been told he wasn't unattractive to the opposite sex, and had been pursued by quite a few lovelorn female supporters when he was a gladiator. He could only hope he would have the same effect on Gisel as well, even though he no longer had fame on his side.

In a hedgerow nearby he spied some wild strawberries, and the sight made him smile. As a child, he'd picked them with his mother and siblings, threading them onto a long piece of grass in a colourful row. On impulse, he did the same now, and brought his bounty back to Gisel, who was stirring at last. When she raised herself on one elbow, rubbing sleep out of her eyes with one hand, he sank down onto the blanket next to her and leaned over.

'Look what I found. They're early this year,' he said, showing off the grass straw.

He proffered a ripe berry, holding it up to her mouth, and she blinked in surprise. Allowing his fingers to brush her lips lightly as she accepted his offering, he saw her frown as if he'd thoroughly confused her. He gazed intently into her ocean-coloured eyes, while he caught a droplet of berry juice off her lower lip with his thumb. She shivered, goosebumps forming on her arms. His hair fell forward, shielding them both from the sun. The moment felt intimate, as if time was standing still, holding its breath. It would have been easy to bend down even further and kiss her, but he refrained.

She wasn't ready for that yet.

'Good?' he asked, sitting back to give her space. 'Here, have the rest. I've already had my fill.' That was a lie, but she didn't need to know that.

He'd bought fresh bread and some dried meat the day before, and he rose to fetch the provisions while she finished off the berries. She chewed slowly, as if savouring the flavour, and he swallowed hard. He would have liked to share the taste of them on her tongue, but it could wait. There would be other opportunities, he hoped. For now, they'd eat some breakfast and be on their way.

When they had finished their meal, he remembered another purchase from the market. From his saddlebag he retrieved a small ceramic pot. The contents were protected by an oiled cloth tied around the rim with string, which he undid.

'I bought this yesterday.' He held it out to her. 'It's to soothe your rope burn.'

He'd noticed that her wrists were rubbed raw in places from

having been tied together for a long period. Her ankles and neck also showed signs of having been abused, although they were in a better state of healing.

'What is it?' She took the jar and sniffed the contents cautiously.

'Bear's grease and dock leaves, I was told. I remember my mother used something similar on me when I was little. I hope it helps.'

'Um, thank you.' Her cheeks had turned pink, as if his kindness embarrassed her and she wasn't sure how to react.

He merely shrugged, as if it was nothing, and started to roll up the blankets, giving her time to smooth the ointment onto her skin. He would make sure nothing ever marred it again.

They rode through one of the few areas of truly dense forest, with ancient trees that reached far into the sky. Although they weren't the pine and spruce she was used to, it made Gisel feel at home, as it reminded her of the enormous tracts of woodland surrounding her father's settlement. At the same time, she was unsettled by the deep thickets that could hide potential dangers. Shadows danced among the trees, sometimes making her heart beat too fast when she imagined someone in hiding, waiting to jump out at them. It was a relief when, soon after setting off, they came upon the Roman road Duro had been told about.

It appeared to be a work in progress, with some unfinished sections, and a couple of times they passed groups of men working on parts of it.

'Roman soldiers,' Duro whispered. 'I've heard it's part of their duties to build roads.'

They looked like ordinary labourers, one arm slipped out from the necks of their tunics to give them more freedom to move. Men on horseback circled them from time to time, keeping an eye on proceedings, making sure no one was slacking off.

'Cavalry,' he told her. 'One of my brothers is in a Roman

cavalry unit. I suppose that means he doesn't have to do this kind of hard labour. I'm glad.'

On the finished sections of road, it was easy going. Once, as they were taking a short break, a unit of soldiers marched past. Their long spears were like a lethal forest, pointing to the sky, and their sheathed swords swung as they walked. The din of hobnailed boots striking the surface of the road repeatedly in time was loud enough to drown out the birdsong. The strange leather aprons they wore hanging from their belts added to the clamour, as the metal decorations adorning them clinked with each step. Gisel shrank back behind Duro until they had passed, the sight of the men bringing back bad memories.

'Are we on the right track for the springs of Sulis Minerva?' Duro asked a foreman of one of the working parties sometime later, and the man nodded.

'Aye, carry on exactly as you are and you'll be there before nightfall.' One of the soldiers taking an unsanctioned break caught his attention. 'Oi, you, get on with it!' he snarled, promptly forgetting about Gisel and Duro.

They weren't the only travellers today, not by a long chalk. Most of the people they met gave a casual greeting but didn't engage with them further. And Duro didn't initiate any conversations either. Gisel was grateful, as some of the men's eyes lingered on her a little too long for her liking. One time she thought she heard Duro literally growl while sending a particularly offensive man a steely glare, but she couldn't be sure. Either way, the man swiftly turned his ogling gaze elsewhere.

It was a long day in the saddle – or on the horse's rump in her case – and she was relieved when they finally descended a steep hill into a beautiful deep valley with a broad river flowing down from the north. Upstream, they found a wooden bridge that allowed them to cross over before the waterway began to curve towards the west. A sprawling settlement was nestled in the bend, including an extraordinary white building close to the river. It was several storeys high and surrounded by smaller ones to make a compound of sorts. A temple complex, perhaps? The buildings there all had red-tiled roofs, whereas the ones in the rest of the settlement were thatch or shingle. The sight was unexpected, as well as impressive, and certainly made a statement.

'There, that must be it.' Duro turned to her with a smile. 'We'll find somewhere to sleep for the night that isn't on the ground. Sound tempting?'

She nodded, trying not to show just how much the thought appealed.

'It doesn't look like an ordinary Roman town,' Duro commented, as they came closer. The descent gave them a good view.

'How so?' Until she was brought to Britannia, Gisel had only ever seen the town she used to visit with her father on market day. Here her focus had been less on her surroundings and more on survival.

'It's not laid out in a grid pattern. Most of them are, almost obsessively so,' he told her. 'I suppose it makes it easy for them to plan where everything is to be built, and to find their way around wherever they are. There are certain buildings they consider necessary, and they almost always include them.' He shrugged. 'Perhaps this settlement was already here in one form or another when they took over, and they haven't bothered to change it. After all, it's not attached to a fort or meant for governing this part of the countryside, as far as I know. It's merely for anyone seeking advice or help from the goddess, or looking to be healed by the waters.'

'Healed? Is there magic in the spring?' The thought intrigued her.

'I don't know, but I was told it is most unusual. Very hot, and apparently good for anyone who is ailing. Some people drink it to purge their insides. Others swear it cures diseases of the skin. Why, are you feeling ill?' He sent her a teasing smile that made her insides flutter.

She tried to ignore the sensation. 'No, not at all. I was merely curious.'

'Well, you will see for yourself tomorrow when we visit the temple.'

There were no town walls, and they were soon riding along a fairly wide street lined with timber-framed wattle-and-daub houses. Most were shops or workshops, presumably with living quarters towards the back, and a few had yards or gardens in between them. The townspeople appeared to consist mainly of native Britons, judging by their clothing. Most of the men wore the characteristic baggy trousers and short tunic Duro had on, rather than Roman-style garments. But there were also plenty of visitors who were clearly off-duty soldiers.

Duro headed for a large Roman building. Gisel gathered it was a guest house of sorts, although he whispered that it was meant to be for officials only. She watched in silence while he bribed someone to give them a cot to share then saw to the horse's comfort in a stable. Inside, they were led to a small, plain room with a single bed. She looked at it with misgivings, but didn't give any outward sign of the trepidation that rose inside her. They'd spent two nights together now, and he'd done nothing but hold her against him. Could she trust him to do the same here?

'Come, let us go in search of victuals,' he said, after he'd found a loose floorboard under which to hide his sword and a pouch that clinked as if filled with coin. 'We'll see if there are any *thermopolia* here, or at the very least a *popina*.'

Gisel frowned. 'I have heard bad things about taverns like that,' she muttered.

Although her father had always stayed away from such establishments, she'd listened to the tales of those who frequented them. According to them, *popinae* were the kind of places where a man could go to find both food and a willing wench. Drinking, fighting and gambling were common there, and a respectable woman probably shouldn't set foot in such a place.

Not that she was respectable now. She was a slave, or had been one at least. No decent man would want her, even if she did manage to make it back to her homeland. She was damaged goods. A lowering thought, but no point thinking about that now.

Duro grabbed her hand and threw her a smile. 'Don't worry. I will make sure you are not importuned. And if anyone asks, you are the wife of Marcus Antonius Durobelinus – me.'

'Wife?' She stopped to stare at him.

'Why not? You'll be safer that way. Most men would think twice about bothering another man's spouse. And if you'd have me, I would marry you right now,' he added casually, as if they were talking about the weather or something else commonplace.

Gisel followed him in a daze, barely aware of their intertwined fingers. This man's mercurial utterings confused and amazed her in equal measures. Why would he want to marry her? He knew nothing about her family or her social standing. When he'd come across her, she'd been someone else's property, no better than an animal. He'd only known her for a matter of two days, and he had her at his mercy. There was no need for him to marry her in order to have her in every way. He could simply force her to do whatever he wished.

Yet he hadn't. Why not?

'This will have to do. I'm starving.'

'What?' His words brought her out of her reverie, and she took in her surroundings.

He had bypassed the many sellers of street food – bread, sausages, pastries and the like – and stopped in front of a noisy tavern, where customers spilled out onto the pavement outside. Gisel took in the long counter adorned with tiles and containing deep earthenware pots she knew were called *dolia*, along with flagons, presumably containing wine or beer, and a selection of smaller jars with sauces and spices. The walls behind the counter were decorated with paintings depicting what might be various classical myths, none of which she recognised. One featured a god with an overlarge phallus that had her eyes widening. She looked away to hide the blush that was spreading across her cheeks. That was the sort of thing she had been afraid to see, but at the same time she was fascinated and had to stop herself from looking again.

Mouth-watering cooking smells hung in the air, and she remembered how hungry she was. If Duro said it was safe to go in, she'd trust him. As he was by far the biggest man here, she doubted anyone would dare to molest her while in his company.

'What would you like?' he asked, manoeuvring her to stand in front of him, shielding her with his body from the throng around them. 'There's lamb stew, beef broth or fish of some sort.'

'Lamb, please.' She realised belatedly that this would be the most expensive item on the limited menu, but Duro didn't bat an eyelid. He ordered two portions, plus bread.

'Do you prefer wine or the local beer?'

He had one hand on Gisel's shoulder, as if it was the most natural thing in the world, and she tried to ignore the heat of his palm through the material of her clothing. She had an almost irresistible urge to lean back against him and allow him to envelop her in the safety of his protection.

'Um, beer?' She liked wine well enough, but she was used to drinking beer every day and it made her feel more at home.

'A flagon of beer as well, then, please, with two beakers.'

'Coming right up.'

'While I was in Pompeii, I missed the pale-yellow beer of my homeland,' he confided as they took their bowls of food and the beer to a table that fortuitously became empty just as they walked further into the tavern. It was cramped, and Duro had to move his chair back in order to squeeze in, but it was better than trying to stand up to eat. 'It must be the same as the type your tribe makes, right, from malted barley? The Romans call it *cervesa* and they do have something similar, but the taste was never quite the same as here.' He took a long swig and sighed with contentment.

Gisel was more interested in eating and attacked her food with the spoon he handed her. He must have had an extra one in his pouch, as she hadn't heard him ask for one.

Duro chuckled. 'I see I'm going to have to feed you more regularly. You were famished, eh?' He dug into his own food with gusto. 'Mm, this isn't bad. A bit too Roman, though. I prefer it plainer, but I suppose they're trying to cater to the soldiers who come here for the sacred spring.'

'It's the best thing I've eaten in weeks,' Gisel muttered, her cheeks once again suffused with colour. She was embarrassed at the way she'd thrown herself at the food. Where had her manners gone?

'I have no doubt,' he replied drily. 'From now on, I'll see to it you never go hungry again. I know what that is like.'

She stared at him across the table. His expression was serious, as if he'd given her a vow. Then the rest of what he'd said registered. 'You've been starved?'

'Yes. I don't know if you've heard of the massive rebellion in these lands some twenty years ago, led by Queen Boudica?'

She nodded. 'I have. The bards told many tales of her bravery. But ultimately she lost, did she not?'

'Unfortunately, yes. My family belonged to the same tribe as her, the Iceni, and my father, Ivonercus, was killed in the final battle against the Romans. I was there with my mother and sister, waiting on the fringes. In the aftermath, Mother tried to flee with us and fought off some of the legionaries.' His mouth quirked up in a sad smile, but there was pride in his eyes. 'She was a formidable fighter in her own right, and had only stayed away from the battle in order to protect us children. I'd seen eight winters, my sister Rufilia fourteen. There was nowhere to run, however, and we became surrounded. A Roman by the name of Aulus Julius Felix had us captured and brought into a hut of some sort. There he proceeded to rape my sister while Mother and I were forced to watch. Then he raped and killed my mother as well.' A muscle in his jaw ticked and his grip on his spoon tightened. 'He declared Rufilia his personal slave henceforth, while I was sent off to be sold. I was taken to Rome, and let's just say I was a lot scrawnier when I arrived than when I left these shores. So yes, I know what it is to be starving.'

He bent his head to finish his stew, before taking another large drink of beer.

Gisel had forgotten her own food while listening to his tale. He didn't merely empathise with her plight; he understood it on a fundamental level as someone who had been through the same thing. He knew exactly what she'd experienced because he had been there himself. And as a mere child, aged only eight. Her heart clenched at the thought of that poor little boy. Yet somehow he'd not only survived, but thrived and become the powerful man he was today.

'How . . . how did you escape?' she whispered.

'I had help from the gods and a good friend named Raedwald. We plotted for years, secretly amassing coin to help us buy a boat. We were going to row away from Pompeii one dark night and hoped no one would follow us. If challenged, we'd use some of the coin to buy our freedom. In the end, the nearby mountain erupted with such force it obliterated the entire town. We were able to get away before the worst of it, and as far as I know, no one is any the wiser. I very much doubt our former master survived, as he stubbornly insisted on staying in his quarters. He didn't think the earthquakes were anything but a minor inconvenience. More fool him.'

'Indeed.' Gisel was impressed despite herself. Duro was made of stern stuff, a survivor and a resourceful man. She wouldn't want to get on the wrong side of him. Something he'd said earlier niggled at her, and then she remembered. 'How come you have a Roman name?' she ventured to ask, picking up her spoon to finish her rapidly cooling stew, but chewing more slowly.

He'd mentioned a so-called *tria nomina* – three names that signified Roman citizenship, as far as she was aware, but he was a Briton and an escaped slave.

'I'm a freedman now.' He shrugged. 'I went to register with the local censor and told him I had been granted manumission. With my former master dead and all Pompeiian records destroyed, who can prove otherwise? If we're being pedantic, my name ought to be Marcus Antonius Drusus, which is what they called me when I was a gladiator, but I'd rather have the name I was given at birth.'

'And what about me? If I'm to pretend to be your wife, what is my name?'

'What were you called before you were taken captive?'

'My father's name is Rautio.' Just saying his name gave her a pang of longing for home, but she suppressed it. 'So I was Gisela Rautia for official purposes.'

'Then we will ignore the fact that you were ever enslaved and refer to you as Gisela Rautia, the wife of Marcus Antonius Durobelinus. There is nothing suspect about your country of origin. And obviously you're a freedwoman, as your tribe is part of the Empire. That is important, else our children won't be Roman citizens.'

Children? Gisel almost choked on her latest mouthful of stew. She hadn't even contemplated a proper marriage with this man, let alone offspring, but she refrained from commenting on that for now.

'Very well.' It would take some getting used to, but she could see the sense in pretending while they were travelling. 'This quest of yours, what does it entail?'

'My aim is to give Aulus Julius Felix a very nasty surprise, if he is still alive and provided I can locate him. He owes me a blood debt, and I'm determined not to rest until it is paid.' Duro dunked his bread in what was left of the gravy in his bowl. 'The man foolishly bragged about himself, telling us not only his full name, but that he was a legionary in the Legio Secunda. That legion is currently stationed at Isca. He was a young man then, and the usual term of service for a legionary is twenty-five years, so unless he's died, he should be there.'

'I see.' Gisel drank some of her beer and looked him in the eye. 'Then it will be my honour to assist you in any way I can, as you helped me. People like that are scum and do not deserve to live.'

A smile spread over Duro's features, and he lifted his beaker to clink against hers. 'Thank you. I'll be glad to have your help. May the gods be with us.'

Chapter Twelve

Bath, June, present day

After their lovely day out, Mac had sort of expected to hear from Jonah again soon, but she had only received one text message, which read: *Working on new song. It's about strawberries! J x*, then nothing more for the rest of the week. She was genuinely puzzled. It had felt as though there was a lot of chemistry between them. A tug of something starting to happen. He'd been happy and carefree – apart from when the text from Blue arrived – showing her his true self, and she'd thought he had been trying to flirt with her a little. Had she imagined it? She must have done.

'It's not like you're an expert on guys,' she muttered to herself, slapping paint onto the walls with angry brushstrokes.

He was probably just being kind. That was who he was – a genuinely nice guy. She was the one who'd been reading something else into his actions, the attraction one-sided, while he had simply tried to cheer her up by taking her mind off recent events with a fun new activity.

'God, I'm such an idiot!' she shouted, frustrated with herself.

She had things to do. There was no time to moon over a rock star who had done his duty and was now getting on with his own life.

Left over from her clear-out was a bag of smaller items that she needed to take to an expert for a proper valuation before selling them. She'd saved these when going through her aunt's things, and as far as she could make out, the objects were genuine antiques. A couple of Moorcroft vases, some military medals, a few porcelain figurines and possibly a Regency fan, together with a pair of kidskin gloves. She shed a few tears as she bundled the items into bubble wrap. It pained her to part with anything that had belonged to Sandra, but she couldn't keep it all. The man who had bought Sandra's stall at the antique market, Henry, would be the best person to ask. Mac decided to go and see him straight away.

She still couldn't believe her lovely aunt was gone. Most of the time it felt surreal, but every now and then she was speared by a sharp grief that made her almost breathless. Was she being hasty in getting rid of these things? No, Sandra had been eminently practical and not at all sentimental, and would have been the first to tell her it was OK to sell. And although the cheque Jonah had brought was a godsend, Mackenna couldn't afford to be too nostalgic. With bills to pay now, every penny was needed. Besides, she had kept any items that had memories of Sandra attached to them, like the antique ring she now wore. Her aunt would always be in her heart and never forgotten.

After cleaning herself up, she headed out into the sultry heat of the June afternoon. The antique market was situated up near the Assembly Rooms, a venue that had been in use since the Georgian period. The pavements were thronged with tourists. Mac had to weave in and out of groups of people chatting in a multitude of languages. Bath was a popular destination – and rightly so – and she felt privileged to be living in such an amazing place permanently. Soon she'd start to make friends and a new life for herself here. She was looking forward to that. Being on tour with a rock band had been exhilarating for a while, a fairy-tale interlude, but it wasn't a normal way of life. At least not for someone like her. She was just an ordinary person, a student at Bath Uni. Who needed rock stars to be happy? Not her.

As she walked along, the sun scorched the top of her head and she began to feel a little dizzy, wishing she'd thought to wear a hat. She noticed that her vision was flickering around the edges, the way it always did when she was about to get a migraine. It was a most peculiar and uncomfortable sensation, but she knew it was only the beginning.

'Shit! Not now,' she mumbled, putting up a hand to massage her scalp. She needed aspirin or ibuprofen stat, but hadn't thought to bring any. *Dammit!*

She took a deep breath and slowed her steps as the buildings around her began to oscillate, the way hot air did during a heat-wave. *The scene around her appeared to be wavering, undulating, then changing. The sandstone buildings disappeared and were replaced with strange dwellings. They were made out of some sort of render – wattle and daub was the term her brain supplied, although she had no idea how she'd know that – and almost all the roofs were thatched. The houses seemed to be lined up with their gable ends facing the road. Most had a large opening that could be closed with shutters, and inside she glimpsed all manner of goods for sale: leather belts and pouches, unusual jewellery, daggers, and food of various kinds. Lined up on a red cloth in the nearest shop were intaglio rings like the one she was wearing, and they flashed in the sunlight, as did hers when she automatically held up her hand to compare it.*

Blinking rapidly, Mac could only stare at the scene before her.

She recoiled as the stench of humanity and waste mixed in with cooking smells hit her, and began to notice what was going on all around. Strangely dressed people were milling about, and various animals added to the chaos – mules, chickens, mangy-looking dogs and a couple of cows. There were merchants shouting for business, chatter, laughter, insults and a cacophony of other noises. No one paid her any attention, and although she was observing the scene, it was as if she wasn't a part of it.

She shook her head and took another huge breath. What on earth was wrong with her? Why did she keep seeing these weird things? Closing her eyes briefly, she stopped to lean on a nearby building. When she put out a hand to support herself against the surface, it was smooth and hot to the touch. Opening her eyes, she realised it was an ordinary sandstone wall in present-day Bath.

Everything else had been an illusion. A figment of her imagination. But it had been so real.

'Maybe I have heatstroke,' she murmured, shaking her head to see if it was OK. The dizziness was gone and she didn't have a headache, despite the migraine warning signs. 'Or I've breathed in too many paint fumes.' Yes, that had to be it. She'd take it easy for the rest of the day and not do any more painting until tomorrow. Open all the windows wide to let in fresh air. That should do the trick.

Hurrying on, she huffed her way up the hill to the antique centre. It was situated in an old building, with stalls on three floors. The moment you entered, it was like stepping back in time. Old-fashioned glass counters and display cabinets of dark wood housed a plethora of antiques and vintage items, each more fascinating than the next. Furniture, jewellery and watches, militaria, old dolls, art, coins and silver were just a few of the things on offer. Mac had always loved spending time there and had often helped Sandra with her stall in between browsing the others. That meant she'd got to know some of the other stallholders, and a couple of them waved at her now as she made her way to the second floor.

Henry was an eccentric man in his early fifties who dressed like a Victorian gentleman when manning the stall. A colourful silk waistcoat – today it was a deep burgundy – cravat and white shirt with puffy sleeves perfectly complemented the enormous twirly moustache he had going on. It was cheesy, but fun, and Mac liked him immensely. He'd been very supportive after Sandra's death, and she was pleased that he was the one to take over her stall. He lit up now as he saw her approaching, and she smiled in return.

'Mackenna, my dear, how lovely of you to stop by! To what do I owe this honour?'

She explained why she'd come, and together they went through the items she'd brought. Henry ended up buying them all from her, which saved her both time and effort. She knew he'd never cheat her on the prices, and he in turn was pleased to have some new stock. Folding up the now empty bag, she said goodbye after promising to come back soon for another visit.

As she headed downstairs, someone called her name, and she stopped and looked around. In a corner full of antique furniture, she spotted Jonah standing with a pretty brunette. It was the woman who was waving at her, while Jonah himself looked supremely uncomfortable. Mac's heart sank.

Of course he hadn't been sitting at home pining for her. He was a good-looking guy and a rock star, and he'd never lack for female company. She was the idiot who'd read more into their recent interactions than he'd intended. How could she have been so stupid? Feeling extremely foolish, she walked over to the couple, wondering how the woman knew who she was. Mackenna had definitely never met her before.

'Hiya. Out shopping?' she asked, directing the question at Jonah, since she wasn't acquainted with his companion.

'Just browsing,' he said, frowning slightly. 'Um, this is Rachel, who seems to know you already?' He looked from Mac to Rachel and back again, seemingly puzzled.

'Not exactly, but who doesn't know Blue's former girlfriend?' Rachel gave her a little finger wave and a huge fake smile. 'It's so lovely to meet you in person.'

'Er, thank you?' Mac was all at sea, having no idea who this woman was or why she'd be pleased to meet Blue's ex. And was it her imagination, or had Rachel emphasised the word 'former' as if that made her happy? How catty.

'What a coincidence, meeting you here,' Rachel continued, ignoring Mac's discomfort. 'I'd only just run into Jonah and we were going to go for a coffee and catch-up, weren't we, babe? You should join us.' She threaded her arm through his and leaned her head on his shoulder. Mac noticed that he took a step to the side, as if trying to avoid this gesture, but the woman was tenacious and clung on tightly, leaving him no room to manoeuvre.

'I'm sure Mackenna has better things to do,' he said. 'And I should really—'

Rachel cut him off. 'Of course. We won't disturb you, Mackenna. Have a lovely rest of the afternoon! Sooo great to meet you.' That last sentence was palpably insincere, and the smile she threw Mac triumphant.

She tugged a somewhat reluctant Jonah towards the door, and he went with her, after one scowling look over his shoulder at Mac, who stood rooted to the spot.

Could they have made it any clearer that she was de trop?

Anger swirled inside her as she headed for the exit on the other side of the building, and she walked home at a cracking pace.

She really was the world's biggest fool.

'Let go of me!' The command came out as a growl, and startled Rachel into doing as he asked.

'Sor-*ree*! Didn't realise you were so sensitive.' She pouted but didn't protest when he ushered her into a small alley off the main street. He figured they were less likely to be seen there, and he really didn't want anyone taking photos of the two of them together.

Rachel was an ex-girlfriend, although they hadn't been together for long. He had realised very quickly that she was the jealous and clingy type, something he couldn't abide. She'd also been inordinately proud of having landed a rock star, as she'd put it. It didn't take a genius to figure out that she was in love not with him, but with his fame and fortune. He had ditched her as soon as possible, but she hadn't taken it well. For weeks afterwards, she'd bombarded him with messages and phone calls, begging him to take her back. She had even cornered him before a concert, having blagged her way in by telling one of the newer bodyguards that she was his current girlfriend. The man had believed her when she showed him lots of photos she'd taken of them as a couple.

It had got to the point where Jonah had contemplated a restraining order, but in the end, he simply bought a new phone and changed his number. He also gave strict instructions for Rachel to be barred from any event he attended, and the hotels the group stayed at. Finally she got the message. That was a year ago. He hadn't seen her until today.

'What are you doing here?' he asked, making sure he didn't stand too close to her. Having her hands on him again had made him cringe, and he had no wish to repeat the experience. The only reason he'd followed her out the door was to get her away from Mac. If Rachel caught wind of his friendship with Blue's ex, she'd be sure to use that knowledge somehow. Probably latch on to Mac and try to inveigle herself into her life in the hope of seeing Jonah more often. After he'd broken up with her, she had sold her sob story to a tabloid, but fortunately the gossip soon died down when he didn't comment or react in any way. He didn't want Mac exposed to any more of that sort of thing. She'd had enough already after her break-up with Blue.

The expression on Mac's face as he'd shut down Rachel's suggestion that she join them for coffee and chat – surprise and hurt that had been quickly masked – bothered him, but he'd explain it to her later. For now, the main thing was to separate the two women as quickly as possible. Also, he'd had no intention of going anywhere with his ex, especially not a coffee shop or tearoom where anyone could see them. He had no idea why Rachel had asked Mac to come with them, but presumably she'd thought he would find it harder to say no if he was with two women rather than just Rachel. Or perhaps she'd known Mackenna would refuse, thinking she was a third wheel, and had issued the invitation merely to be bitchy. Who knew?

'I'm in Bath visiting friends,' Rachel explained now. She smiled and batted her eyelashes at him. Did she seriously think he'd fall for that?

'And you just happened to walk into the same shop as me?' He crossed his arms over his chest, regarding her sceptically.

She shrugged. 'I saw on social media that you were here, so I've been keeping an eye out in case I ran into you. Today was my lucky day.'

Unlucky for him, but he didn't say that out loud. 'I haven't posted anything about being in Bath.' In fact, he hadn't posted anything at all since the end of the tour. He found social media a chore and had better things to do.

'Oh, not you, your fans. Didn't you take some selfies with a few of them the other day? I saw Pulteney Bridge in the background.' Rachel sounded as proud as if she was Sherlock Holmes and had solved a particularly knotty case.

Unease crawled up his spine. If she had been keeping such a close eye on what his fans posted, that meant she was still stalking him, although not as overtly. It gave him the creeps.

'Well, I guess I'll have to stop allowing people to take selfies with me from now on.'

Her gaze turned speculative. 'That was over a week ago, and you're still here. Does that mean you live in this area now?'

'No. I'm also staying with friends nearby,' he lied.

'And looking at furniture? Not very likely.'

Jonah ground his teeth together. That was an astute observation, but he wasn't going to acknowledge that she was right. 'Like I said, browsing. Thought I saw a piece my mum might like. She's into old stuff.'

'Uh-huh. Sure.' She smiled in a knowing way that irritated him no end. 'Don't worry, I'll keep your secret.'

'There is no secret to keep.' He couldn't keep the exasperation out of his voice. 'You know I live in London.' That was where they'd met. Fortunately, she didn't know where exactly his current flat was, as he'd bought a new one soon after their relationship ended. 'Now please leave. I'd appreciate it if you never approach me again, or I'll have to take drastic measures.'

'Aww, don't be like that. We were good together. You know we were! Come on, give me a chance to show you. Please?' She made puppy-dog eyes at him, a look calculated to soften the hardest of hearts. Perhaps it worked on others, but unfortunately for her, his was made of stone today.

When she reached out to grab his arm again, he retreated and fixed her with a death glare. '*Do* not *touch me!* Can you please get it into your head that I want nothing to do with you. We broke up. I *will* file for a restraining order if I have to. Sue you for harassment too. Please go away and leave me the hell alone! I mean it.'

Her face fell and tears glistened in her eyes, but it didn't move him. She needed to learn to take no for an answer, and he'd made it very clear he didn't want her around. He had tried to be nice about it at first, because he wasn't a mean person, but when that didn't succeed, he'd had to be tougher. Now he had no choice but to get the law involved if she didn't stop.

He suddenly noticed that she'd had one hand behind her back during their entire conversation, and warning bells sounded in his mind. 'What are you hiding?'

'Huh? Nothing.' Her expression turned wary. She was the one to take a step back this time, but he was blocking the entrance to the alleyway and she had nowhere to go as it was a dead end.

He lunged for her and pulled her arm out. She was clutching her mobile and struggled against him when he tugged it out of her hand. 'Give me that,' he hissed.

'No! It's mine. You have no right to take it!' She jumped to try and reach, but he was much taller and she had no chance of succeeding.

A quick glance showed him that a recording was in progress, and he swore under his breath. The screen was unlocked, and he sidestepped her attempts to take back her phone while he deleted the file. He checked the rest of her apps to make sure she hadn't taken any photos or videos as well before handing the device back to her.

'Get out of here before I call the cops,' he snarled. 'This is your final warning.'

'OK, fine! You're an absolute bastard, Jonah Miller, and I'm going to let all your fans know,' she shouted back. Her face had gone from tearful to furious in a nanosecond, but Jonah merely stared her down, not giving her the reaction she obviously craved.

'Go ahead. See if they'll believe you,' was all he said.

With a noise like an angry kitten, she turned to stomp off, while he breathed a sigh of relief. Now all he had to do was get home without her following him.

Chapter Thirteen

The Spring of Sulis Minerva, southern Britannia, June AD *80*

Back at the *mansio*, Duro told Gisel to lie down on the narrow bed, facing the wall. She sent him a suspicious glance, but did as he asked. He hoped that meant she was beginning to trust him. It was still early days, though, and he sensed she wasn't ready for any wooing yet. He lay down behind her and wrapped his big body around her smaller one protectively, with one arm round her waist. They fitted together perfectly, and he felt a calm spread through him, as if he was exactly where he should be. She remained stiff for a while, but eventually fell asleep, becoming pliant in his arms. Duro smiled and closed his eyes.

The following morning, they ate a quick breakfast, then got ready to go to the sacred spring and the temple complex.

'I'll bring drying sheets, and we'll need a change of clothes,' he told Gisel.

She stopped in the middle of combing and braiding her long hair. 'Why? Are we going in the spring? I thought that was only for people who needed healing.'

'There is a bath house adjoining it. We might as well take the opportunity to enjoy some time there after we make our requests to the goddess, don't you think? Have you ever been to a Roman bath? It's delightful.'

'No. I'd never been further than the nearest town before Eberulf . . .' She broke off and shook her head, as if it was something she didn't want to talk about.

'Before Eberulf what?' He'd finished putting his own change of clothing inside a linen drying sheet and waited for her to explain.

She sighed. 'The other slave who was in the tent when you, um, dealt with my former master. He came to my village to ask for my hand in marriage, but I refused him.' She lifted her chin. 'Father agreed with me. Although unquestionably Germanic, Eberulf isn't a Treveri, like us, but from the Vangiones, a tribe that lives across the Rhenus river to the east in Germania Barbaricum. They are supposedly allies of Rome, but they're a bit suspect. They appear to change their allegiance on a whim whenever it suits them. I don't know if you heard about the Batavian rebellion ten years ago?' Duro nodded, so she continued, 'Well, some Treveri took part in that – although not my father – and when they were defeated, they fled into Barbaricum and the Vangiones took them in, thereby going against the Romans and us. So you see why Father wasn't sure he could be trusted.'

'Yes, I would be wary as well if I were him. How did you meet Eberulf?'

'We came across him in town on market day. He claimed to have taken one look at me and decided he wanted me for his wife. Apparently he'd made enquiries and found out where I was from, then came to propose. As I said, he was refused – politely, of course. He didn't take it well and left in a huff. I thought that was the end of the matter, but then later that night, he and his men snatched me when I visited the privy. Eberulf said he wasn't taking no for an answer and that I'd be his wife one way or another. The utter pig!' Her hands clenched on the strands of hair she was holding.

'So he is your husband?' Duro wanted to curse out loud. That was a complication he hadn't reckoned with.

'No! Absolutely not.' A hollow little laugh escaped her. 'The Romans saved me from that fate at least. A group of them attacked Eberulf's abduction party halfway back to his settlement and took us all captive. I think they were suspicious of anyone who was out riding at night. It was the only good thing about it.' She looked away. 'I'm afraid he still thinks of me as his, though. If he's managed to free himself from the restraints we left him in, he'll try to find me. The man is obsessed, although I've no idea why.'

Duro did, but he wasn't going to enlighten her right then. He too had taken one look at her and wanted her, although not merely for her beauty. That had only been a small part of the instant attraction he'd felt – he wasn't that shallow. Besides, he would never try to force her into a relationship the way Eberulf had done. He would woo her slowly, and hopefully win her trust and affection eventually. For now, he was relieved that he wouldn't have to challenge or kill another man in order to have her. One fewer obstacle in his way.

'We'll deal with that if it happens. I take it you know how to defend yourself and wield a knife?'

In his tribe, most girls had been taught basic fighting techniques. They were brought up to eventually be equal partners in a marriage, husband and wife supporting each other in their daily endeavours and in any conflicts that might arise. This was very unlike the way Roman women were treated by their husbands, from what he had observed. They were guarded and looked after as if they were fragile and incompetent, and had no say in any important matters. It seemed the wrong way to go about things, in his opinion, and he had no intention of emulating it.

'Yes, but I never had a chance when Eberulf abducted me, as he and his men took me by surprise and overpowered me. There were simply too many of them.' She carried on with her braiding, although he could see that her hands were shaking. Reliving those memories was clearly painful, and she must have felt so helpless and afraid.

He put a hand over one of hers and gave it a squeeze. 'Don't worry, I won't let him take you again. This time he's alone and has no power. No men to do his bidding. He might not even be free to search for you. Someone could have found him tied up and taken him as a slave again. Either way, he'll have to go through me to get to you.' He gave her a lopsided smile. 'And I'm bigger.'

That made her laugh, as he'd intended, and some of the tension ebbed from her. But the next moment she frowned again. 'What if he tells someone about me being an escaped slave? And our former master's fate?'

'Why would he? He'd have to admit to being a slave himself. The transaction will have been recorded by the seller at Calleva with both your names noted. Besides, Eberulf was unconscious when I fought Primus, and later when we took the Roman away for burial. He didn't actually see anything, so there's nothing to tell. No, if he does intend to take you back, he'll keep a low profile. I doubt he's stupid enough to speak to the Roman authorities. We'll just have to keep an eye out.'

She nodded. 'Yes, you're right. That makes sense.'

Soon afterwards, they set off for the sacred spring, and once again he took her hand and twined his fingers with hers. It wasn't how men normally treated their wives, but he craved the connection and couldn't resist. She didn't protest, which pleased him.

The temple complex was surrounded by a high wall, and they went through a gate on the eastern side to enter it. In front of them was the temple building itself, fairly small in circumference, yet tall and impressive. It was set on top of a podium with a very steep flight of stairs at the front. There were four huge pillars with a triangular pediment above them. In the centre of this was the carved head of a man with hair like long snakes, and a big moustache. It was set inside a circle of leaves that was held up by two winged creatures standing on top of two globes. Duro had no idea what it meant and couldn't care less. He was only here for the goddess.

In front of the temple was a paved courtyard with a sacrificial altar near its centre. He knew that the Romans usually held their religious rituals outdoors, sacrificing animals at such altars and then having a *haruspex* – an augur of some sort – look at the animals' entrails in order to search for omens and predict the future. He had watched a few such proceedings in Pompeii, but as he had his own native gods to pray to, he'd merely been a spectator.

To their left was a huge building that he guessed was the baths.

'That's the tallest building I've ever seen,' Gisel marvelled, craning her neck to look up towards the roof.

Duro had seen taller, but it was still impressive. Simple, yet beautifully made, with white walls that gleamed in the sunlight. The sacred spring itself appeared to be situated in a corner of the courtyard, next to the bath house, with one side abutting the building's outside wall. It was a many-sided pool, open to the sky and surrounded on the other sides by upright stone slabs that formed a wall to enclose it.

A man dressed in formal Roman garments, including a *toga*, approached them. He had a haughty expression, as if they were somehow beneath him since they were clearly local Britons, but he had to allow them entrance anyway. Duro didn't know why the man felt himself to be superior, but the entire temple complex was clearly a statement of imperial Roman authority. It was meant to show their power, and they'd spared no expense in their efforts.

He almost snorted out loud. The spring had been here long before the Romans arrived, and the goddess Sul didn't belong solely to them. She would choose with care those she honoured with her assistance. No matter what this upstart of a man believed, Duro was sure she would listen to a heartfelt plea and see that justice was served.

'Welcome,' the man said grudgingly. 'Have you come to make an offering in the Fons Sulis, the sacred spring?'

Duro nodded. 'Yes. We would like to purchase some lead sheets to write on, please.'

'You wish to curse someone? Very well. Wait here and I will bring them to you. You'll need my guidance when making your offering. No one is allowed near the spring unsupervised.'

That was ridiculous, but Duro knew better than to protest. As long as he could have access to the pool that served as a portal to the goddess, he didn't care.

He turned to Gisel. 'Can you write?' he asked. 'If not, I'd be happy to do it for you.'

'I can write my name, but not much else, and I'm very slow, so I'd be grateful for your help,' she replied. 'My father taught me. I'm faster at reading.'

He guessed that like many other people, she had learned enough to be able to read the type of basic information that was often displayed on walls by the Romans: announcements, advertisements and price lists. As she hadn't lived in a town of the Empire, she wouldn't have needed to know more than that.

Still, Duro was impressed that she could do either. Most Romans were at least semi-literate, but native tribespeople usually weren't, except for those in positions of leadership. He surmised that Gisel's father must have been fairly important if he'd had his daughter taught her letters.

The man returned with two pieces of lead and two styli. Duro paid for them with Roman coins and took them over to a nearby bench.

'I'll do mine first,' he told Gisel. 'In the meantime, consider carefully what you'd like yours to say.'

He placed the sheet on the bench and picked up a stylus. There was no need for him to think about his own message, as he was very clear about what he needed to write.

DUROBELINOS TO THE GODDESS SULIS MINERVA, I OFFER A GOLD *AUREUS* THAT YOU MAY ASSIST IN MY REVENGE AGAINST AULUS JULIUS FELIX OF THE LEGIO II AUGUSTA. MAY HE BE ACCURSED IN BLOOD AND SUFFER FOR ALL TIME.

He quickly scratched the letters into the lead. To stave off boredom in the evenings at the gladiator barracks, he and Raedwald had paid someone to teach them reading and writing. He had even become proficient in the cursive style commonly used by administrators when sending messages to each other. It was faster, so he used it now, then rolled the lead up into the shape of a small cylinder and set it aside before turning to Gisel.

'Are you ready?' He picked up the second sheet and waited.

She hesitated. 'What did you write?' He told her, and she bit her lip. 'I have nothing to offer the goddess, so perhaps I shouldn't do this. She'll not listen without an offering.'

'I will give you a gold coin.' He fished one out of his leather pouch. It featured the head of the emperor Vespasian, who had died just before Duro left Pompeii. Very few of the new emperor Titus's coins had reached these shores as yet. 'Is that enough?'

'More than. Thank you. I will pay you back somehow.'

He took her hand and placed the coin on her palm, closing her fingers over it. 'No need. Consider this a gift, especially if you are cursing the person I think you are.'

'Oh yes.' She cleared her throat. 'Please write the following: "Gisel to the goddess Sulis Minerva, I offer a gold coin. May the hands of the worthless man Eberulf fall off and rot if he ever touches me again. Be he accursed for eternity."'

Duro did as he was bid, feeling greatly satisfied that she really didn't want anything to do with her erstwhile suitor. He'd have paid more than an *aureus* to be assured of that.

'Here, roll it up, then we'll make our offerings.' He handed her the lead piece and waved to the supercilious attendant.

'Are you ready? Then follow me, please.' Nose in the air, the man preceded them through a small gate into the sacred spring area. 'You may cast your *defixiones* and other offerings here.' He pointed to a specific area of the water, although Duro didn't think the exact location mattered.

They threw in the lead tablets and gold coins, both with their eyes closed, and in Duro's case at least repeating his plea silently to the goddess. He knew that justice was on his side and trusted that she would agree. As if to confirm this, he thought he saw a shadow pass through the water, just underneath the surface, as if the deity herself had swum past to acknowledge their gifts. He took it as a good omen.

'Thank you,' he said to the officious man as they were ushered out. He didn't receive a reply. 'Right then, Gisel, let's bathe.'

She bit her lip and eyed a group of people making their way towards the entrance to the baths. 'Are you sure we should? It seems a bit strange bathing with so many other people.'

A steady stream of visitors to the bath complex had been arriving while they made their offerings to the goddess. Duro had been told that Romans from all over the southern part of the province – especially soldiers on sick leave – flocked to the *aquae calidae*. It was obviously a popular destination. He could understand Gisel's reluctance, though. Members of his own tribe would be sceptical as well, since they considered washing their face and hands every morning, plus a more thorough wash with a cloth every few days, sufficient.

'Trust me, you'll love it,' he assured her. 'It really is enjoyable.'

The look on her face told him plainly that she didn't believe him, but she followed him nonetheless.

'Why are the Romans so obsessed with bathing anyway?' she muttered.

Duro shrugged. 'It's part of their culture. I've heard them call us "unwashed barbarians", so it must indicate refinement to them. Mostly it's their way of socialising. You'll see. There will be groups of people chatting, gaming and even discussing business in an informal and relaxed manner. It's how they interact best.'

'Fine. Let's go then.'

Duro paid for a lead admission token for them each, then stopped inside the main doors when Gisel pulled on his sleeve. As she'd never been to a Roman bath before, she had to ask him what to do and expect. It was embarrassing, but it would have been worse had she stumbled inside without a clue.

'There will be a changing room first,' he explained. 'Leave your clothes there in a hamper and bribe an attendant to keep an eye on your belongings, or trust me, they won't be there when you return.'

'What, all my clothes?' She'd never appeared nude in front of anyone in her life until recently, and she definitely wasn't keen to repeat that experience.

'You can leave your undertunic on if you prefer, but be prepared – others may not be as delicate.'

She swallowed hard. 'Very well.'

'After that, you will proceed into the *tepidarium*, which is pleasantly warm. You will find benches to sit on and a *labrum* basin to wash yourself in. I put a cloth for that purpose inside your drying sheet. I suggest you go and sit in the *laconium* for a while after that. It's a very hot room where you will sweat off any dirt from your body. There should be attendants outside who offer to massage you with oils before scraping everything off with a strigil. I'll give you enough coins for that, as it's a wonderfully relaxing experience. Normally you would enter the *caldarium* thereafter, where there would be a small pool of hot water. I'm guessing that the large swimming pool will be just as warm here, so you may as well come and meet me there, before finishing with a plunge into the freezing-cold pool in the *frigidarium* afterwards.'

'M-meet you? We are bathing together?'

His mouth quirked into a wry smile. 'Mm-hmm. Unless you don't dare?'

She scowled at him. It wasn't a question of courage. Surely it wasn't seemly. 'Is that what everyone else does?'

'Most people, yes.'

He said it with a straight face, but Gisel wasn't sure if he was teasing. She reckoned she'd soon find out by following the other women who were entering the baths. 'I'll think about it,' she muttered.

'Fair enough. Here are the coins you'll need.' He gave her a handful of bronze and copper *asses* and *dupondii*. 'If it's not enough, send someone to find me.'

She began the ritual he'd outlined, stepping into the changing room first. There was a strong smell of damp, mould and human bodies, making her wrinkle her nose and try to take shallow breaths. An attendant agreed to watch her belongings for a fee, and she undressed while throwing surreptitious glances at the other women present. None looked as self-conscious as she felt herself, and she tried to suppress her misgivings. She wasn't brave enough to go without the short-sleeved linen undertunic, even though she was surrounded by a lot of nudity.

The first room was indeed quite warm, but not overly so. Groups of women sat around on the benches that surrounded the walls, gossiping and laughing. Most were Roman, judging by their hairstyles and the fact that they were wearing face paint. Gisel had never even tried to outline her eyes with black – it wasn't the done thing in her tribe – but it seemed to be expected of Roman ladies. Unlike her, they also wore their tresses bound up with some sort of bands, and not hanging down in plaits.

She ignored their curious looks and went to wash herself in the marble basin as instructed by Duro. There was a hollow feeling in her chest. She felt left out and very much alone, missing her friends back in her homeland. Here she was a stranger and knew no one. She was even regarded with suspicion, or perhaps she was imagining that. Either way, it would have been much nicer to go through this experience with someone, rather than on her own.

There was no point staying any longer in there, and she quickly proceeded to the *laconium*. It was like stepping into a furnace, the heat almost smacking her in the face. The floor scorched the soles of her feet and she ended up half running, half skipping across to the nearest bench. She noticed that the other people present were sensibly wearing wooden sandals for protection. If she ever went to a Roman bath again, she'd want some too. She made sure to sit on her drying sheet in order to avoid burning her backside on the bench.

For a while, she sat still and endured, the sweat pouring down her back and in between her breasts. She found it unbearable and soon decided she'd had enough.

'May I help you, lady?' An attendant materialised by her side the moment she stepped out of the hot room.

Gisel jumped. 'Excuse me?'

'I'm happy to give you a massage for a small fee. The oil is included in the price and I have several fragrances for you to choose from.' The woman indicated a basket that contained tiny stoppered greenish-blue glass vials.

'Oh. Yes, please.'

'Then follow me.'

After sniffing a couple of the scents on offer, Gisel settled on one that smelled of lavender and bergamot. She was instructed to take off her tunic and lie on a bench, face-down. After a moment's hesitation, she did as she was told. There were others in here having massages too, and they were all naked. The attendant smoothed oil into her skin with long, languid strokes that relaxed and soothed, then kneaded her muscles with strong hands. Gisel had to admit that Duro had been right – it was wonderful. Thankfully the marks on her wrists and ankles had faded, in large part due to the bear's grease she'd been applying. The attendant didn't comment on them, and Gisel hoped no one else could see that she had so recently been someone's slave.

'I'll just scrape this off now,' the attendant murmured. She picked up a strigil, an implement Gisel had seen before but had never used, and wiped it on a cloth. Scraping it against Gisel's body, she removed most of the oil and probably a good amount of skin as well. It felt strange, but not unpleasant.

'Shall I pluck your legs and armpits?' the attendant asked.

'What? Oh. Um, yes, please.'

Gisel had never considered it necessary to remove any of the hair from her body, as no one would see it other than herself. Besides, she was blonde and not particularly hirsute. But she had heard tell that Roman women were obsessed with eliminating all body hair, and thought she ought to try it at least this once. She soon regretted this decision, gritting her teeth and swearing silently at the pain, but it was too late to back out.

At last the torture was over with, and she thanked the attendant and paid the fee with the last of her coins. Apart from the plucking, it had been a marvellous experience. Her entire body was limp and relaxed after the massage, and her skin glowed, clean and sweet-smelling. She put her tunic back on and followed a group of women out through a door that led to the pool she'd glimpsed.

This area was the most magnificent part, and slightly overwhelming. The large rectangular pool, the so-called *natatio*, was inside a timber-roofed hall, with a row of glazed and iron-framed windows set high up to allow daylight to illuminate the space. A wide walkway, paved with smooth white stone slabs, surrounded it, separated from the water by pillars and arches. There were alcoves with benches set at intervals in the outer walls of the hall. These had smaller windows with shutters open to let in light and the fresh summer breeze. Groups of bathers sat in each one, laughing, gossiping, discussing business or playing board games, and a few were even eating. Gisel noticed attendants scurrying around selling all manner of snacks, making her stomach grumble at the enticing aromas.

All the walls were plastered and painted white, but with the occasional pattern added in different colours. There had been mosaic floors in the other rooms, but here there was only paving. The people who were currently in the water were splashing and shouting, and the entire chamber was as noisy as a chieftain's feast. There was steam swirling around in lazy drifts, and the air was warm and thick with humidity, condensation running down some of the walls. She could feel the moisture in her lungs as she inhaled the mingled scents of perfumed oils and the peculiar smell of the water.

She stood to one side at first, observing the bathers. Duro had been right: there were quite a few naked ones, both men and women. Other unclothed people wandered past her, sending her interested glances, but she ignored them. She was looking for one man in particular, and her breath stuck in her throat as she caught sight of him. His golden head, slightly darkened by being wet but still unmistakable, ploughed through the water as he swam with powerful strokes in her direction. When he was only a few feet away, he emerged, shoving his long hair back over his head and smiling at her.

'You came.' He was watching her cautiously, as if he was afraid she would bolt.

She almost did when she noticed that he had not a stitch of clothing on his sculpted body. Her reply died on her tongue and she could only manage a nod.

'Well, are you joining me?' He swept out a hand in invitation, giving her a smile that almost made her knees buckle. By Belenos, but the man was too handsome for his own good.

'Y-yes.' Judging by the fact that he was standing up and the water came to about halfway up his chest, she knew she'd be able to reach the bottom. There were some stone steps at the side of the pool, and she descended slowly. Once her toes touched the base, she noticed that it was lined with metal, most likely lead, a favourite with Roman builders, or so she'd heard. The water was wonderfully warm, but too clear for her liking. She could see every part of Duro. Every. Single. Part. *Dear gods!*

Her cheeks flamed as she averted her gaze. She shouldn't have looked.

She heard him chuckle, but decided to ignore him. 'I'm going to swim,' she declared.

'Good. Me too.'

At first, he followed alongside her. Since she wasn't going as fast as him, however, he soon tired of that and took off with longer strokes, his muscular arms slicing through the water. She almost swallowed some of it while watching him, then told herself to concentrate on her own efforts. It was difficult to find a straight path through all the other bathers, and she eventually came to a stop at one end to catch her breath.

'Well, well, what have we here? You're a tasty morsel and no mistake.'

She looked up to find a middle-aged man ogling her chest, which she belatedly realised was on display in the now wet linen tunic. She crossed her arms over her breasts and turned her face away, ignoring him.

'Don't be like that,' the man protested, reaching for her elbow. 'I'm willing to pay well for an hour of your time once we are finished here, my beauty. I bet you taste as sweet as you look, eh?'

'Go away,' she hissed, managing to evade his grasp at the last moment.

His expression darkened. 'I said I'd pay you well. Above the going rate, in fact. No need to be difficult, you little *quandrantaria*.'

She gasped out loud at the insult – the man had just called her a 'five-*quadrans* whore'. As a *quadrans* was worth no more than a quarter of an *as*, the amount was minuscule and definitely not complimentary. How dare he?

'I'm not interested and I'm not for sale,' she snarled at him. 'Please leave me alone.'

'Now see here . . .' The man surged forward, but at the same time Gisel was pulled back, out of his way and into a hard chest. One she thankfully recognised. A strong arm wrapped around her waist.

'Are you importuning my wife, by any chance?' Duro's voice was silky smooth, but with a lethal undertone that even a fool would notice.

The man in front of them froze. 'W-wife?' he stammered, his gaze flitting between Gisel and Duro.

'Yes. She is clearly of high status, any oaf can see that. She's wearing a tunic for the sake of modesty. Would she be doing that if she was available to all and sundry?' Duro's arm pulled her even tighter against him. 'Apologies, my sweet, I shouldn't have left you at the mercy of the riff-raff here.' She felt his warm lips connect with the skin of her neck, just where it joined her shoulder. A full-body shiver went through her.

'She . . . she's not wearing a ring or . . . or anything,' the man stammered, his cheeks now mottled red with embarrassment. 'How was I to know she was married?'

'Most people here aren't,' Duro countered, even though he himself was still wearing his bronze ring.

The man harrumphed and scuttled backwards, stumbling on someone along the way. He muttered an apology, but it was barely audible, and Duro growled, 'Pig! I hope the goddess doesn't see fit to heal whatever ails him. With a bit of luck, his manhood will rot and fall off.'

Gisel snorted a giggle and turned to raise her eyebrows at him. 'How uncouth.'

'Not half as uncouth as him. Who does he think he is? Accosting females without ascertaining whether they belong to anyone.' His blue eyes flashed azure lightning as he glared after the man one last time. 'Did he hurt you?'

'No.'

His arm was still encircling her waist, and he raised the other one to hold her more securely. Her front was now plastered to his from chest to knee. With only the wet linen of her tunic between them, she could feel all the lean, hard planes of his body. His skin was even hotter than the pool water, while hers was covered in goosebumps, even though she wasn't cold in the slightest. The two of them were moulded together, and she had an unaccountable urge to climb him and wrap her legs around his middle. She splashed some water onto her blazing cheeks with one hand.

'Duro . . .' she whispered, intending to protest against the closeness. The words didn't want to come, though, because in truth, she loved the sensation of having him so near.

'Yes? Do you not like me holding you like this?' His voice was deeper than usual, gravelly, yet smooth in a way that sent another shiver through her. 'Tell me what you want, Gisel. I'm yours to command.' He bent forward and placed another kiss on her throat, under her ear this time.

'I . . . You shouldn't do that,' she protested half-heartedly.

'Then I won't, unless you wish it,' he whispered back. 'But I trust you will let me know if or when I can. Because I want to. Never doubt that.'

He let her go, and she felt bereft. 'Swim with me for a length or two, please,' he begged. 'I cannot leave the pool in the state I'm in. I need to calm down first.'

A quick glance at his lower half showed her why, and she had to duck under the water to cool her cheeks again. Not that it did much good, as the water was so warm. When she came up for air, he was waiting for her with one eyebrow raised and his arms crossed over his chest. His biceps bulged, and she wanted to hide again, but instead she followed him as he turned to swim at a more leisurely pace.

The image of him in all his glory would stay with her for eternity. And dear goddess, but how was she supposed to resist a man like that?

She'd have to be made of stone.

Chapter Fourteen

Near Bath, June, present day

Mackenna carried on with her painting project, and finished one room after another in the flat. Anger at herself and her silly assumptions fuelled long sessions every day. She tried to forget the humiliation of realising that she was no one special to Jonah. That she had, in fact, imagined that there was a spark between them. It was embarrassing to contemplate that she'd thought so for even a moment.

He'd tried to call a couple of times but hadn't left a voicemail. When she didn't ring him back, he had sent a text saying only: *Sorry about Rachel. She has no social awareness. I'll explain next time I see you. J x*

Mac didn't want or need any explanations. She had eyes in her head and no intention of bothering him further. He had Rachel to hang out with now, so he wouldn't be bored. She doubted she'd hear from him again.

So absorbed was she in her DIY tasks, she forgot to watch the news or even check her phone most of the time. Her mother rang a couple of times to make sure she was still alive, and her father left a voicemail, but she ignored that. After the funeral, he'd tried to talk her into giving Savannah at least a part of the inheritance from Sandra, but she'd flatly refused.

'Why should I, Dad?' she'd argued vehemently. 'Savannah has had everything handed to her on a plate since she was born, while I've always worked for what I have. This is *my* inheritance.'

'I gave you an allowance and I paid your mother child support,' he'd protested. 'It's not as if I neglected you. Plus, you spent summers here with us.'

'That child support was the absolute minimum you could get away with, and the allowance was what – fifty pounds a month? Which you stopped paying as soon as I turned eighteen. As for staying with you guys, yes, very uncomfortable it was too. You know Savannah resented me and made my life hell whenever you and Kate weren't around. Never once was she told off for that. You didn't even believe me until I recorded her a couple of times.'

He had cleared his throat, his cheeks going ruddy. 'I'm sorry about that. It was . . . unfortunate. You know Kate is very protective of our daughter.'

'As you should have been of me! No, I'm sorry, Dad, but Sandra wanted to balance things out a little and Savannah doesn't need any part of this inheritance. If she's blown through her trust fund already, that's her problem, not mine. She can get a job like us ordinary mortals.'

She'd rung off in a huff and refused to speak to him since. He had no right to demand anything of her. Kate ruled the roost in their household, and until he learned to stand up to his wife and younger daughter, Mackenna didn't want anything more to do with them. The lawyer had told her everything was legally correct and no one could contest the will. The flat and everything in it was hers and hers alone, as Sandra had wanted. Savannah was merely pushing the issue for the sake of it, because she liked to cause dissent between Mackenna and her father.

Sadly, as on this occasion, she very often succeeded.

Finally finished, Mackenna put away her paints, cleaned the brushes and rollers, and took a very long shower, scrubbing herself from top to toe. Her fridge was bare and it was time to venture out and do some much-needed grocery shopping. Free of paint stains at last, she grabbed her purse, mobile and keys and stepped out into the warm sunlight.

Only to stop dead in her tracks.

There was a throng of people outside on the pavement, most of them with cameras that clicked loudly as she blinked at them in surprise. A veritable wall of voices shouted at her, and at first she couldn't make out what they were saying. She was too stunned to register actual words, but slowly they began to penetrate her brain until she could make sense of them.

'Are you going to get back together with Blue now that he's put you on his album cover?'

'Was the break-up just a publicity stunt to get Valhalla Storm more PR coverage?'

'Did you really walk in on him having a threesome with a couple of supermodels?'

'Is he coming to see you soon?'

'Did you know he spent last weekend with Ashley Kenton, the actress?'

The questions rained down on her thick and fast. She gaped at the journalists as she tried to understand what was happening. Although she'd been through similar media assaults a couple of times with Blue, this time it was completely overwhelming because she was the sole focus. She put up an arm to shield her face from their scrutiny, then decided that wasn't protection enough. It was evident they weren't going to let her pass without answering them. They would continue to pester her until they had what they wanted – a soundbite. But she had nothing. She couldn't tell them anything without violating the NDA, and she didn't want to anyway. In this case, retreat was the better part of valour, as her aunt would have said.

'No comment,' she muttered, before yanking open the door and fleeing inside again.

Once she had locked the door of her flat behind her, she sank down with her back against it and her head between her knees, hyperventilating until she got herself under control.

'What the hell was that?' she whispered. What was going on?

Digging her phone out of the pocket of her jeans shorts, she googled 'Valhalla Storm' and 'new album cover'. The screen immediately filled with images of her. Well, her from behind, anyway. The photo shoot they'd done had focused on her hair because of the album title, *Blonde Revolution*, and her face could only be seen in part profile. Mostly the image concentrated on her long, gleaming tresses, cleverly highlighted from above and set against an indigo background that complemented the gold and silver strands perfectly. The journalists hadn't had to search very hard to find out who the woman on the cover was. There had been lots of photos of her in the press during the time when she'd dated Blue, and she had often worn her hair down because he liked it that way. To her, it had the added advantage of acting as a curtain shielding her from the worst of the paparazzi. Now it had been the clue that led everyone to her door.

What should she do? She needed food, and she couldn't stay holed up in here until they lost interest and decided to go home. The band members had told her horror stories of journalists camping outside their gates for days if there was a particularly juicy story going round. They wouldn't give up at the first hurdle.

She stared at her phone, hoping for inspiration. There was no one here in Bath who could help her, as she didn't know anyone yet. Her dad lived two hours away, in Buckinghamshire. Could she patch things up with him long enough for him to come and fetch her? But then she'd be lectured about the inheritance again, if not by him then certainly by his wife.

She could order takeaway, but she'd still have to open her door, and the poor delivery person would be subjected to the melee outside. That wouldn't be right.

Jonah. Her treacherous mind turned to the one person, apart from her mother, who had shown any interest in her well-being recently. She was extremely reluctant to contact him again after the awkward meeting at the antiques centre, but he *had* said to call him if she needed anything. She believed he'd meant it, as a friend. Well, how much needier could she get? And he of all people would understand what she was dealing with. He'd know what to do.

With trembling fingers, she looked up his contact details and hit 'call'. He picked up almost immediately, throwing her off balance for a second. 'Hello? Mackenna, is everything OK?'

He sounded genuinely concerned, and she had to swallow down a lump in her throat. 'N-no. I don't know what to do,' she said, sounding hoarse and close to tears.

'What's going on? Are you hurt?' His voice had a panicked note to it, as if he was afraid for her.

'No, nothing like that. It's just . . . there's, like, an army of journalists outside my place with cameras and microphones. They shouted all kinds of questions at me, as if they had every right to the answers. I was going to go out and buy some food, I've got nothing at home, but I can't and I . . . How do I get past them, Jonah? Or get rid of them? Should I call the police? Or your PR people and ask what to say? No one warned me the album was out today and—'

'Fuck! I'm going to kill Harriet. What's she playing at? Hang on. I'm coming to get you.'

'What? No! You don't have to do that. I just needed some advice. I mean, you've been there, right? I'm sure this has happened to you. How do you normally deal with it?'

He sighed. 'I either have someone deliver food and sit tight, or I run away. In this case, I think you need to leave for at least a few days, until they get tired of waiting.'

'But where am I going to go?' She supposed she could fly to Sweden to visit her mum, but she hadn't planned on spending money on plane tickets this summer, despite the unexpected cheque from the record company.

'You're coming to stay with me,' Jonah said firmly. Before she could protest, he added, 'I won't take no for an answer. They won't find you here. I have great security, and high walls surrounding my place. Really, I insist. Now go and pack a few things and I'll arrange transport. I'll call you back in a sec.'

He hung up before she could say another word, and she stared at the phone in her hand. 'Shit, that wasn't what I was angling for.'

Did he think she was trying to inveigle herself into his life? Cling to the last vestiges of her brush with fame? That would be pathetic. And what about Rachel? Or any other woman he was seeing at the moment? They wouldn't be best pleased, but she had no other option at the moment. And once she was at his house, she could leave from there and go somewhere else.

Yes, as long as he could get her out of her flat and away from the journalists, she could come up with a better plan.

Jonah swore out loud as he cut the connection to Mac. Damn the press. Why would they hound her when all she'd done was pose for a couple of photos? But he should have guessed they'd put two and two together, and the story of her and Blue's break-up had been juicy gossip for a few weeks. Damn Harriet too for not giving her any warning. She must have known this was likely to happen.

Had she left Mac in the dark on purpose in order to get more publicity? Even leaked her address to the press? He wouldn't put it past her, but he'd deal with her later.

First he needed to help Mackenna.

Maybe he should go public straight away with the fact that he was quitting the band? He'd agreed to wait until after the new album had launched, but it would make for a much more salacious story and could divert attention from Mac. No. Better to wait and see if he could hide her away first. But how to get her out of there?

A quick hit-and-run, he decided. He had a couple of fast cars, but the best thing of all would be one of his motorcycles. With the Ducati, he would be able to weave in and out of traffic so that anyone giving chase by car would be left behind. And even if the paparazzi had bikes too, his was faster and more powerful than most. Plus he'd be wearing a helmet with a dark visor so no one would know who had picked her up, whereas if he arrived by car he would be spotted. That would only add to their frenzied attempts to dig up a story.

He texted her his plan, adding that she should pack her stuff in a rucksack so she could jump onto the back of his bike quickly, before anyone could react. *Just run outside and hop on. I'll stop as soon as I can for you to put on a helmet.*

He received a thumbs-up in return, and then she added, *I have a helmet. Long story, but boyfriend before last gave me one.*

That was great. He didn't like having a passenger without protective gear.

I'll text you when I'm round the corner. Give it two minutes and then sprint out the door.

He put on black leather trousers and a matching jacket, as well as gloves and the dark helmet. Making sure his house was securely locked and the alarm on – he'd had a break-in at a previous home and didn't want a repeat – he headed for his garage. It was situated in a converted stable block that still looked like stables but with garage doors at either end. His Ducati and a Harley were kept in the middle, accessed via a proper stable door, albeit one with secure locks and yet another alarm.

As he drove towards Bath, the realisation that he was going to have Mackenna in his house hit him. Mac, in a room near his, pottering around his kitchen, sharing meals with him . . . It seemed too good to be true. He hadn't heard from her in over a week, which had started to worry him. There had been no reply to his text message and calls, and he'd contemplated going to her place to check that things were OK between them. Now he had an excuse to see her. *Excellent.*

He'd actually dreamed of her the previous night. They'd been camping, snuggled together under warm blankets, his arm draped around her slim waist. His forearm had touched the underside of her breasts, sending a frisson of awareness through him, but he'd been content to hold her, nothing more. When he woke up, the sensation of having her in his arms had lingered, and his body had been on full alert. He couldn't let on that he thought of her that way, though. It might scare her away, and he wanted her to stay. He would have to tamp down any such longings and treat her like a good friend, nothing more.

A block away from her flat, he stopped and pulled his mobile out to text her that he was almost there.

I'm ready, came the reply, and he gunned the bike, pulling up behind the group of people milling around outside the front door of her building. Some of them turned around, peering at him with curiosity, but they didn't have a chance to ask who he was or why he was there. Mac came tearing out the door and virtually flew down the few steps, shoving aside anyone standing in her way. She was wearing a black helmet and had sensibly tucked all her hair inside so that it wouldn't become tangled in the wind, but there was no mistaking the rest of her. The journalists caught on immediately, but had no time to react as she gripped his shoulders and threw a leg across the saddle behind him.

'*Go!*' she shouted, winding her arms securely around his waist.

He didn't hesitate, and they shot away, the people behind them starting to snap photos. They flew down the street, tearing round a corner at a precarious angle. Luckily, she seemed to know that she had to lean with him, or the bike would have overbalanced. He gathered she'd been on the back of a motorcycle before, which was good. Hopefully she wasn't afraid of going fast either.

No one followed them, or at least not anyone who could keep up with his pace. Soon they were on the outskirts of Bath, and he made a couple of extra turns to confuse any would-be pursuers. He'd been out on quite a few rides during the last weeks, learning the area, and he was grateful for that now. Eventually they pulled up outside the automatic gates to his place. He extracted the remote control from his pocket and opened them, then drove through and made sure they were closed again. Making his way slowly up the drive towards the stable block, he felt Mac sit up straight behind him, taking in the view. He hoped she liked it as much as he did.

The house was Victorian Gothic, built out of Bath sandstone, complete with a turret in one corner and a massive conservatory to one side. The windows were huge and pointy at the top, some with stained-glass panels in the upper part, and there were lots of ornate details. The inside was even more over-the-top, but he loved it. Quirky, the estate agent had called it, and it definitely was.

He parked the bike and Mac climbed off, removing her helmet. Her hair, which was in a thick plait again, tumbled down her back, little wisps clinging to her cheeks and forehead. She brushed those off and looked towards the house again. 'Wow, Jonah, that's fabulous!'

He had taken off his own helmet and hung it on the handlebars, pushing his fingers through his hair and smiling at her. 'You like?'

She widened her eyes at him. 'Like? Are you kidding? I *love* it! It's like a fairy-tale house, and was that a pool I glimpsed out the back?'

'Yes. The water's a bit cold most days, but if you work out first, it's refreshing. I'll give you a tour later. Let me just put the bike away and we can go inside and have some lunch.'

He took her helmet and placed it on the other handlebar, then wheeled the Ducati into the garage. Mac followed him inside and scanned the large space and its contents, but she didn't gush about his car collection or the Harley. He supposed she was used to such things, as Blue had quite a few vehicles. His former bandmate wasn't into bikes, but they shared a love of sleek sports cars.

They walked over to the house and he unlocked the front door and turned off the alarm. The entrance hall was double height and octagonal, with a domed skylight and a glittering chandelier. A wide staircase with cast-iron banisters rose in front of them, and doors with intricately carved lintels led off the hall in different directions. The mosaic floor looked like something out of a Roman villa, depicting the figure of Neptune surrounded by mermaids and fish of various kinds. A round table with a precious vase stood in the middle on top of a Persian rug. That was a leftover from the previous owner, but he quite liked it now.

'Let me take you to your room first, then I'll show you where the kitchen is,' he said.

Mac appeared to be speechless, gazing around with eyes like saucers, and she ascended the stairs behind him without protest. He led her to a door on the right, which opened into a stunning bedroom with a large bay window overlooking the front garden and drive. A king-size bed with wooden carvings painted antique silver took up most of one wall, and there was a matching wardrobe, chest of drawers and vanity table, plus a couple of silk-upholstered slipper chairs. The walls were painted a soft duck-egg blue, and a pale-blue Chinese rug covered the varnished floorboards.

'Jonah! This is amazing!' Mac wandered over to the window and gazed out at the garden. 'Are you sure this is a guest room and that it's OK for me to stay in here? I promise I'll get out of your hair as soon as possible. In fact I can probably call my dad and have him pick me up this evening, so I won't need to bother you for long.'

He laughed. 'You're not bothering me at all. And yes, this is a guest room. My room is about the same size but on the other side of the landing.' Shrugging, he added, 'I live in this house alone, so it's not like I need all the bedrooms for myself. You're welcome to stay for as long as you need.'

She turned with a frown. 'I don't want to step on anyone's toes. Won't Rachel mind me being here?'

'Rachel?' He couldn't keep the astonishment out of his voice. 'What's she got to do with anything?'

'I thought . . . well, you seemed close the other day.' Her cheeks flushed and she wouldn't look him in the eye.

'No! Absolutely not! You've got that totally wrong.' He was horrified at the conclusion she'd drawn, although it explained why she hadn't returned his calls. 'She's an ex of mine who doesn't know how to take no for an answer. I was trying to get rid of her; the last thing I wanted was for her to find out you and I are friends. Trust me, her stalkerish behaviour knows no bounds and she would have latched on to you in seconds. You were only saved from that fate by the fact that she thought we met you by chance.'

'Oh, I see. Sorry.'

'Nothing for *you* to be sorry about. I should have realised you'd think we were a couple.' He shuddered. 'Never again! I'll tell you more later, but I honestly think she's bordering on mentally unstable.'

Mackenna's stance relaxed and she pushed her rucksack off her shoulders, dumping it on the floor. 'OK then, I won't worry about her any more.' She walked over and put her arms round his middle, leaning her head on his chest. Squeezing him hard, she murmured, 'Thank you so much! You're a lifesaver and I don't know how I'm going to repay you. But I really do promise to leave as soon as possible. I don't want to put you out any more than I already have.'

His arms went around her back and he pulled her closer, revelling in the sensation of having her there at last. In his arms and in his home. 'No repayment necessary, and please stay as long as you need,' he muttered gruffly. 'It will be fun to hang out. It can get a bit lonely around here, rattling around in a place like this. And if you fancy doing any cooking while you're here, that would be a definite bonus.'

'What, you don't cook?' She leaned back to look up at him, a teasing glint in her eyes.

'Let's just say I try, but more often than not a TV dinner and the microwave are involved.'

She smiled, the ordeal of the paparazzi obviously fading. 'Then I'm going to make it my mission to teach you. As long as you don't mind a bit of Swedish home cooking.'

He grinned back. 'I eat anything except snails.'

She wrinkled her nose. 'Yeah, let's steer clear of those.'

Jonah's kitchen was as awesome as the rest of his house. Mac shouldn't have been surprised. The members of Valhalla Storm had made piles of money from their records after all, and Blue's London penthouse flat was extravagant, to say the least. But she hadn't expected Jonah to live in a place this old, with exactly the kind of decor and style she herself loved. She would have pegged him more as the modernist type, wanting an architecturally designed glass-and-chrome type of home. Although come to think of it, his warehouse conversion flat in London had been decorated in a fusion of antique and modern that was stylish and tasteful, so perhaps he had the best of both.

The kitchen had white-painted cabinets, and most had glass panes tapering to a point at the top to match the Gothic feel of the place. He didn't seem to have much in the way of china and glassware yet, but perhaps he hadn't lived here for very long. She found him peering into the fridge with a frown, but he looked up when he heard her approaching.

'Ham and cheese sarnies OK for lunch?' He shrugged. 'Like I said, I don't cook much.'

'I think we can do better than that. Do you have eggs?'

'Yes. Probably?' He rooted around a bit and found a carton behind a couple of packs of beer. 'Here.'

'Excellent. Then I'll make us a *croque madame*. Will that do?'

'Sounds fab! Can you make me at least two?' He looked so hopeful it made her laugh.

It wasn't long before she'd plated up the grilled ham and cheese sandwiches with fried eggs on top. Jonah offered her a cold beer to go with it, and they sat down at his kitchen table to eat. The whole experience was a bit surreal, and Mac almost pinched herself to make sure she wasn't dreaming.

'Mm, this is so good! Can I hire you as my personal chef?' He smiled at her, and that dimple in his left cheek appeared again. It did funny things to her insides, but she tamped that down. They had established that he wasn't dating Rachel, but that didn't mean he wasn't seeing other women. Thankfully there didn't seem to be anyone permanent, at least, otherwise Mac would have felt uncomfortable staying here.

'Don't know about that,' she replied. 'You'll soon get bored, as my repertoire isn't that big. But I'll do my best while I'm here.' She took a bite of her own food and had to acknowledge it was good. Having lived on tinned soup and toasted stale bread for a few days now, it was nice to have something a bit more sophisticated.

'Well, just let me know what ingredients you need and I'll order them. I usually get a food delivery every week,' he told her.

'Will do. For now, I'll use whatever I can find in your fridge and freezer.' She suddenly realised she had the rest of the day with nothing to do and he was probably itching to get back to his songwriting. 'You'd better carry on with your work. I'll see to the dishes and then I'll explore the garden, if that's OK?'

'Sure, but I promised I'd take you on a tour of the house first. Then feel free to use the pool and the gym if you like. And if you're ever in the mood for some gardening, my gardener quit a couple of weeks ago and the weeds are growing rampant.' When she opened her mouth to say she'd be happy to do that, he shook his head with another smile. 'Nah, just kidding. I'm not expecting you to work while you're here. Just relax.'

'But I'd love to work in the garden. I find that very therapeutic. My Swedish grandmother and I used to always do weeding together before she had to go into a nursing home and her house was sold.'

'Really?' He looked dubious. 'Well, only if you absolutely want to. Not my idea of fun, but I won't stop you.' He finished his last mouthful of grilled cheese and sighed with pleasure. 'That was so good, thank you.'

'My pleasure. Thank you again for rescuing me. I had no idea the album was out today. Congratulations, by the way! I know it's awesome. All your songs are.'

'Thanks.' He grinned, but his smile faded as he added, 'I'm definitely having words with Harriet, though. Don't know what she was thinking, throwing you under the bus without warning. That is unacceptable. She's a professional PR person, for Christ's sake. She must have known they'd go after you.'

Mac shrugged. 'Maybe she wanted them to. Great publicity, presumably, even if I didn't engage with them.' She made a face. 'I bet there'll be loads of photos in the gutter press tonight or tomorrow of me looking like a deer in headlights. And "poor little dumped girlfriend" stories to go with them. Ugh!'

Jonah reached across the table and grabbed her hand, rubbing his thumb across the top of it. This sent inappropriate tingles up her arm. 'Ignore them. We know the truth and you have nothing to be ashamed of. It's that wanker Blue who should be hounded, and he probably will be too. Although knowing him, he'll lie through his teeth and blame you for being too sensitive or some such shit. He's such an arse.'

She surreptitiously pulled her hand from his. There was no point reading anything into the gesture. He was just being kind again. Besides, hadn't she sworn off rock gods for life? She tried to concentrate on their conversation instead of the gorgeous man on the opposite side of the table.

'Yes, it'll be interesting to see what he comes up with. You're right, though. No point worrying about it. They'll soon lose interest and I'll be forgotten. They shouted something about him dating some actress. She'll want the limelight to focus on her, I bet.'

He peered at her, a concerned expression on his face. 'Do you mind? I mean . . .'

'Who he's dating? No, of course not.' She grinned. 'I only hope he gets a dose of his own medicine one of these days. When he falls really hard for someone and they two-time him, I'm going to do a little happy dance.'

Jonah grinned back. '*Schadenfreude*, eh? I like it. And yeah, his time will come. Plus, very soon he won't have a band to front. With me and Owen both out of the picture, he'll have to scramble together a new line-up for Valhalla Storm.'

Mac had suspected that Owen, the drummer, would walk if Jonah did, as they were best mates going way back. 'Can he do that, though? Doesn't the name of the group belong to all of you?'

'Technically, but neither of us cares. That part of our lives is over. Owen's already got an invitation to join another band, and I'm staying in the background from now on.' Jonah shrugged. 'Blue will never be able to replicate what we had, and without my songs, the sound won't ever be the same.'

'True.' Mac smiled. 'Should be very interesting to watch him fail.'

It wasn't like her to be so vindictive, but in this case, she felt she was justified.

Chapter Fifteen

Southern Britannia, June AD *80*

As they walked back to their lodgings, Duro held out his hand. 'Look what I found at the bottom of the *natatio*.' On his palm lay two small oval gemstones, one lilac and the other a reddish colour. Both had miniature carvings on one side, and they shone in the late-afternoon sunlight.

'How pretty!' Gisel picked them up one by one at his urging and held them up to the light. 'Is that a goddess? And two serpents on the other one. The carving is very fine, is it not?'

'Indeed. Someone must be sorry to have lost them.' Duro accepted them back from her and stowed them in his pouch.

Gisel frowned. 'Aren't you going to give them back to their owners?'

He shrugged. 'I've no idea who they belong to. I did ask one of the attendants if anyone had come looking for lost jewels, but he said no. Apparently it's quite common for smaller items like these to become lost at the baths. Most end up in the drains and are never seen again. I was lucky these hadn't gone that far. I feel as though the goddess wanted us to have them, so I'm taking them with us. They might give us good luck.'

Gisel certainly hoped so, but she couldn't help but feel sorry for whoever had lost them. Still, if they hadn't come looking for them, where was the harm in keeping them?

They spent one more night at the *mansio*, then rode north the following morning. Duro had purchased a second horse so that Gisel would have her own mount. Not because he thought his steed couldn't handle the extra weight, but because having her so close, holding on to him all day, drove him insane with wanting.

He was already able to picture her vividly without clothes any time he closed his eyes, the sight of her on the auction platform etched into his mind. After their interlude in the baths, he now also knew what that nubile body felt like when plastered to his. It made it a lot more difficult to keep his promise to himself that he wouldn't touch her unless she wanted him to. For his own sanity, he had to put some distance between them, at least during the day. At night, he still slept with his arms around her, even though it took for ever to fall asleep that way.

'You can ride on your own, I take it?' he asked as he boosted her onto the horse's back.

'Of course. I was riding almost before I could walk. Father saw to that.' She gathered the reins in one hand. 'I can drive a cart too. I told you I often accompanied him to the nearest market. That is how I learned the Roman tongue.'

'Good. Follow me then, please.'

The next few days were a monotonous repeat of ride, eat, ride some more, sleep, wake up and do it all again. They followed another straight Roman road north to Corinium Dobunnorum.

'This apparently used to be the *civitas* of the Dobunni tribe,' Duro told Gisel as they guided their mounts along the main street.

Their tribal capital, in fact, but the Dobunni hadn't fought for their holdings. He'd heard tell that they had submitted to the Romans without putting up any resistance. Since the occupation, this particular settlement seemed to have been turned into an unfortified Roman town, with the usual street grid, and public stone buildings. Some, like the large *basilica*, were still under construction. Although Gisel looked impressed by the latter, he barely noticed it. He was used to such sights from his time in Pompeii.

They passed two different marketplaces in the town – one solely for cattle, by the looks of it – and various shops and houses. He was only interested in finding an inn where they could eat, rest and wash the dust off their weary bodies. When he asked a passer-by, they were recommended an establishment on the western side of town, which proved to offer everything they needed.

'I can't wait to sleep in a real bed,' Gisel murmured with a yawn. She hadn't complained about bedding down on the hard ground every night, but Duro agreed – it wasn't exactly comfortable.

'Me too.' Although it was easier to keep his hands to himself when he wasn't lying on something soft, and he knew sleeping in a bed with her wasn't wise. He still didn't quite trust her not to run away, though, despite the fact that she had relaxed more in his company each day. If he didn't have his body wrapped around her at night, he'd never get any sleep himself.

When he woke up the following morning, she had managed to turn in the narrow bed and her arms encircled his chest. They were both wearing nothing but their undergarments – short-sleeved linen tunics and loincloths – and her breasts were pillowed against him in the most delicious way. He drew in a sharp breath, which woke her. As she blinked up at him in the dawn light, he saw the exact moment she realised what she was doing. Her eyes opened wide and she started to pull back.

'Don't,' he whispered, his voice gruff with sleep. 'I like holding you this way as well.' He tightened his own grip on her and kept her in place, although not so hard that she couldn't have freed herself if she'd wanted to.

'I . . .' Her eyes flickered, peering into his as if searching for something, but she didn't push him away.

'Shh. Let me enjoy it for just a moment longer.' He raised one hand to move a strand of hair out of the way and kissed her forehead.

'Duro . . .' She sounded unsure and small, and he sighed.

'I know. You're not ready. I'm sorry.' Dropping another kiss on the top of her head, he let her go and sat up abruptly, swinging his legs over the side of the bed with his back towards her. To his surprise, her hand stroked down his spine in a soft flutter.

'I like it too, but I'm scared,' she admitted. 'I'm . . . afraid of trusting anyone.'

He nodded. It was understandable. Her rejected suitor had abducted her, she'd been attacked and captured by Romans, then sold to a man who had nearly raped her. Of course she was wary. He had to be patient and wait until she learned to trust him fully. If she ever would.

'It's fine. We'd better get ready. We have another long day's ride ahead of us today.'

And hopefully he could keep his thoughts away from how sweet it had been to wake up in her embrace.

Gisel's thoughts were not on the countryside they were passing through, but the man riding in front of her. He'd been very quiet today, and she knew why. Waking up in his arms like that had been a shock, but at the same time wonderful and reassuring. The sensation of security that always enveloped her when they slept next to each other had lingered, joined by another one – that of being cherished. He had kissed her as if she was something precious. Something he wanted to protect and never let go of.

Was that what she wanted? She didn't know.

A part of her was determined to make her way back to her homeland. Her father and brother must be frantic with worry, thinking the worst had happened to her. As it almost had. But thanks to Duro, she was safe and could potentially go home. Would anyone there believe her if she claimed to be physically unharmed? A maiden still? After being away for so long, it seemed unlikely.

The alternative was to stay with Duro. It was tempting, she had to admit. The problem was whether she dared to entrust herself to him fully. Her body wanted to, there was no doubt about it. Even if she hadn't seen him in all his glory in the baths – and the image of that wasn't something she'd forget in a hurry – she would desire him. He took care of her, saw to her comfort as much as possible and never treated her as an inferior being. That, more than anything, made her like him immensely.

However, if she gave herself to him, that was tantamount to a declaration that she would stay in Britannia for ever. She didn't think Duro would let her go home unless he tired of her, and she'd never see her family again. She sighed. It was a conundrum she'd leave for another day.

To distract them both, she rode up next to him and asked him a question.

'You spoke of the great queen your parents followed into rebellion. Do you remember her at all, or were you too young?' Even she had heard the tales of the fearless female leader who had dared to oppose the Romans. Her fame had spread far and wide, and bards sang her praises when they had the right kind of anti-Roman audience.

'Boudica? Vaguely. My father was kin to her on her mother's side, I believe, so we visited the settlement where the royal family lived a few times. It wasn't far from ours, although apparently it's gone now, the land appropriated by the Romans. Later, I remember standing with my parents and sister as our queen incited her warriors. She was quite tall for a woman, her countenance forbidding, with a fierce and penetrating gaze. Like my own mother, she had long fair hair in two thick plaits. I think I was mostly impressed by the massive gold torc she wore round her neck, though. Flashing in the sunlight as she moved, it seemed magnificent to me. Riches befitting a queen.' He smiled. 'I was too young to understand most of what she was saying. Something about the greedy tyranny of the usurpers, no doubt. I was told afterwards that she and her daughters had been violated by Romans, all their possessions confiscated.' He shook his head. 'It was a bad business. Brutal times.'

'She must have been quite a sight,' Gisel murmured. She could picture it in her mind. A proud woman standing up for her people. Any good leader would do the same. 'A shame she didn't succeed.'

'Indeed.'

'Have you or your kin ever thought of following in her footsteps?' She couldn't help but picture him as a powerful leader. He had the physique and proud bearing of a warrior. A king even.

'No, although my brother muttered a lot about the perfidy of the conquerors when last I saw him. If you ask me, it would be idiocy, and completely pointless. I would rather live in peace and try to have a good life, working within the Roman system to improve our lot.' He sighed. 'To tell you the truth, I had more than my fair share of bloodshed in the arenas of Campania. From now on, I will only fight if absolutely necessary.'

She could understand and sympathise with that. As a gladiator, he must have seen some horrific sights while being forced to kill for the entertainment of others.

'Then once you finish this quest, you will return home?' He'd mentioned something about bringing her with him, but she wasn't sure if he'd meant it.

'Yes. I aim to build my own house as part of my family's settlement.' He grinned. 'Actually, I recently bought the land, so they can't really refuse me permission. But I'm not going to be just a farmer. My friend Raedwald and I have started a trading business together. He lives near the coast and we're setting up a network of contacts here in Britannia as well as in Gaul and Frisia, his homeland. We'll gather trade goods during the winter, ready to sail across the sea from the *kalends* of the month of Martius to the end of October.'

'Won't you have a lot of competition?' Gisel knew goods were exchanged all over the Empire. Duro and his friend would by no means be the first to wish to join in the lucrative trade.

'Of course, but we have the advantage of being well versed in how things work in the Roman world. And we are fluent in their language, as well as our own. We've decided to concentrate on importing luxury goods, such as amber, fine glassware and silk. Perhaps spices and even sought-after gemstones. In return, we'll sell hides, silver, iron and tin from here. If you know how to haggle, there are always opportunities to be had.'

'Sounds good.' And she believed he would be successful at anything he set his mind to.

They continued north-west on yet another immaculate Roman road until they reached Glevum. This was a Roman fort with a *vicus* – a civilian settlement – surrounding it, containing among other things a bath house, as well as various craftsmen and traders supplying the legionaries with their services. The fort itself was situated not far from a wide river the Romans called Sabrina. There was a busy harbour, with quays and wharves. Ships came and went downriver towards the sea, and there was also a bridge to cross to the other side.

Gisel hung back while Duro chatted to an old man who'd been

sitting in the sun watching the hustle and bustle. A silver coin changed hands, and the man became very loquacious. As they walked away from him in search of a place to spend the night, Duro told her what he had learned.

'The fort was built by the Legio XX, but they were replaced by the Legio Secunda some fifteen winters ago.'

'Isn't that the one you're looking for?' Gisel asked.

'Yes, but most of their men were moved yet again five or six years back, to Isca. I will need to go out to a tavern this evening to try and find out whether the legionary I seek is here. Can you stay in our room, please, if I obtain a place for us at the local *mansio*? I doubt anyone will talk freely if I bring my wife along. I'll need to get them drinking and relaxing if they're to gossip about their superiors.'

'Very well.' She could see his point.

The word 'wife' sent a tremor through her, but she refused to dwell on it. They weren't married, even if it felt like it at times. She wasn't even sure that was what he wanted from her. He could merely be in the market for a concubine, even though he'd jokingly said he'd marry her in an instant. It wasn't as though she'd be bringing him either a dowry or social connections if they were joined in matrimony.

He put his hands on her shoulders and gazed into her eyes, his expression stern. 'You promise? No running away, please. You know it's not safe, and I wouldn't have a moment's peace thinking of you all alone and vulnerable somewhere.'

Gisel could see that he was genuinely worried, although he had no cause to be. She'd meant it when she said she was better off travelling with him than on her own. She wasn't stupid. But he clearly needed reassurance.

'I give you my oath I won't step outside the room.' To make absolutely sure he understood she was telling the truth, she stood on tiptoes and touched her mouth to his, as if sealing the pact.

His eyes went wide in shock, but he recovered remarkably quickly. In a flash, he had moved his hands to her waist and pulled her closer, kissing her back. She hadn't reckoned with that and wasn't prepared for it, which was probably why she allowed his warm lips to linger for quite a while. When he gently bit her lower lip, she opened her mouth in surprise and he slipped his tongue inside, exploring. Gisel almost swooned on the spot. It was such an intimate thing to do, so unexpected, she couldn't help but gasp. That made him even bolder, and somehow she found herself reciprocating, her tongue tentatively playing with his. She was in such a haze, she swayed when he stopped and just looked at her.

A grin spread over his features. 'Very well, I believe you. And thank you. That was all I'd hoped it would be.'

With that, he turned and gathered up the reins of their horses and set off in search of the *mansio*. It took Gisel a few moments to collect herself before she could follow on unsteady legs.

If that was what it felt like to be kissed, she was in serious trouble, because she'd never wanted it to end.

Aulus Julius Felix definitely wasn't in Glevum. Duro had chatted to various groups of legionaries at different taverns to make absolutely certain, but no one had heard of him here. If he was still alive, he ought to be fairly high-ranking by now. And he was ruthless and unpleasant enough that he would have left an impression on anyone who came into contact with him. Plus he had a rather memorable scar running down one side of his face that was hard to miss.

'He has to be at Isca then,' Gisel commented when he shared what he had learned.

He sighed and sat down next to her on the bed, where she'd been dozing while waiting for his return. 'Not necessarily. His legion is there, but as far as I understand it, the men don't all need to remain now that the region they're guarding is more peaceful. Some of the units, called *vexillationes*, have been marched off to help fight somewhere else. I pray the goddess has made Julius Felix stay put, otherwise we'll have to go north.'

'Why north?' She scooted herself upright and leaned against the wall.

'The new Roman governor of Britannia, Gnaeus Julius Agricola, has apparently decided to subdue the northern tribes, and he's taken some of the Legio Secunda troops with him. With a bit of luck, however, Julius Felix isn't one of them. But there's only one way to find out. We'll leave for Isca in the morning.'

They set off once again, heading over the bridge to follow the River Sabrina south-westwards for a spell. Although it meandered, there was a well-worn track that kept a straighter line. Eventually this turned into a new Roman road that took them to Venta Silurum. This was another market town, close to the Sabrina estuary, from where the Romans governed over the recently defeated Silures tribe.

They didn't stop for longer than it took to eat a hearty meal, as from there it wasn't far to Isca along yet another paved road. They crossed a wooden bridge over a river with the same name as the town and saw the Roman fort up ahead of them. It was surrounded by a ditch and ramparts consisting of an earth bank topped by a timber palisade with wooden watchtowers at regular intervals. Inside would be the barrack blocks and other buildings, but all they could see was the smoke from various hearths rising into the air.

'I was told this is a permanent base for the Legio Secunda Augusta now,' Duro commented. 'Although it's of fairly recent date, as it's only been here some five or six winters.'

'It must have grown quickly then,' Gisel replied, taking in the civilian *vicus* that sprawled to one side of the fort, next to a bend in the river.

'Yes, I expect it did. The Romans are nothing if not efficient when building their forts. Apparently this site was chosen because it's not too far from the mouth of the river, which means it can be reached by ship from the sea. That way supplies and reinforcements can easily be brought here.'

The *vicus* wasn't all laid out in a grid pattern with straight angles and regular streets, but it still contained some of the usual Roman components. A bathing complex built of stone had been constructed not far from the fort. It was almost on a par with the one near the sacred spring in size. There were other buildings with tiled roofs in the Roman manner, but they were mixed with native constructions of timber and wattle-and-daub, roofed with thatch.

'Let us find somewhere to stay, then we can make plans,' Duro suggested. 'Perhaps later, or tomorrow, we can avail ourselves of the bathing facilities.'

Gisel sent him a dubious glance, but nodded acquiescence. He guessed she was remembering their last interlude in a pool, and so was he. It would be wonderful to feel truly clean, however, and they both needed to loosen up their cramped muscles after so many days of riding.

As it turned out, they didn't need to worry about being in unclothed proximity, as they found out that men and women bathed separately here, and at different times of the day. Duro was disappointed, but also relieved. Right now, he needed to keep his wits about him and concentrate on the task in hand. He'd come here for revenge, not dalliance. Once Julius Felix had been dealt with, he could allow himself to think of other matters, but not before.

Over supper at a small tavern that evening, Gisel raised the question of what would happen next. 'What is our plan?'

He was pleased to hear the word 'our', as if she saw herself as his partner in this endeavour. It showed that she was coming to trust him, and that she considered them a team. That made him rejoice, although he kept his expression neutral. No need to spook her, or there wouldn't be any more of those wonderful kisses forthcoming.

He bit into the excellent roasted pork they'd been served and finished chewing before he answered. 'First, reconnaissance. We need to find out whether our quarry is here, and if so, where exactly. Once we have that information, we can lure him out. It is imperative that we get him alone. Legionaries are like brothers, their units tight. I want the man on his own so that I can challenge him to a fair fight. That has to be done outside the fort, preferably somewhere well away from any habitation. I don't want Roman officialdom to get involved or ever find out anything about it.'

'That sounds sensible.' Gisel appeared to be enjoying her meal as much as he was, and he was pleased to see that she looked healthy and full of vitality. It was a far cry from the pale, withdrawn creature she'd been when he had first come across her. Her lovely hair shone in the light of a nearby oil lamp, and her sea-coloured eyes sparkled. He had to force himself to concentrate on the matter at hand, and not on the almost magnetic pull she exerted on him.

'He's not the only person we're looking for, though, as I think I mentioned. I need to find my brother, Caratius, who's supposed to be with this legion too. If he's stationed here, he'll know whether Julius Felix is as well, and he could help me trick the man. It would be best if I could locate him first.'

Gisel frowned. 'But if your brother is aware that that evil Roman is here, why hasn't he killed him already?'

'I don't think he knows anything about the matter. Caratius was only a toddler when the uprising occurred and was probably never told exactly what happened. He and my other brother, Commios, were kept at home, whereas my sister Rufilia and I were brought along by our parents. We weren't old enough to take part in the actual fighting, but we watched from a distance each time the queen attacked a settlement. I still remember the flames shooting high into the sky at both Camulodunum and Londinium as the buildings were burned to the ground. But then came that final day when our queen and her army lost the battle . . .'

The memories were still painful, even after all this time, and clear in his mind. He hadn't allowed himself to forget, and he wouldn't until he'd had his revenge.

'Anyway,' he continued, 'Commios and Caratius never knew the name of the man who murdered our mother, or even that she had died in the manner she did rather than in battle. I was the only other person present. As I was enslaved and taken away soon afterwards, I never had a chance to tell my kin about Julius Felix until recently.'

'I see.' Gisel sipped her beer and regarded him with a thoughtful look on her face. 'And your sister? Didn't you say you were looking for her as well?'

'Indeed. As I told you, after he violated her and killed my mother, Julius Felix boasted that he was going to keep Rufilia as his personal slave for the rest of her life. He said it was what a little Iceni bitch like her deserved, and he wasn't ever going to let her go. I'm sure he meant it, so he'd have kept her out of sheer spite.' He paused, pushing down the anger that swirled inside him every time he thought about it. 'The life of a slave is hard, as you know, and it's doubtful that she'll still be alive. She'll have seen thirty-three winters, if so. But I remember her as tough and fierce, so there is a possibility she's not dead yet. I'd like her to be allowed to live out the rest of her days in peace and comfort at home, if I can find her.'

Gisel nodded. 'If she were my sister, I'd want the same.'

Her words warmed him. They showed her to be compassionate and kind, two traits that were essential to him. 'As the slave of a legionary, she'll be living in the *vicus* if she's here. I doubt there's room in the barracks for her. There must be thousands of people in this place, though, so searching every single dwelling would take too long.'

'Then what are we going to do?' Gisel polished off the last of her food, wiping the plate clean with a piece of bread.

'Ah, that's where you come in.'

'Me?'

'Would you be willing to do me a favour?' He took a sip of his beer and regarded her over the rim of the ceramic beaker.

She paused, the piece of bread halfway to her mouth. 'What kind?'

He smiled at her. 'Take a bath and gossip for a while.'

Her eyebrows rose. 'That's a favour to you?'

'It is if you can get chatting to some of the local women. Not the Roman matrons, the Britannic ladies, I mean. Mention that you've heard one of your husband's kinswomen is here, but you don't know how to find her. See if anyone recognises Rufilia's name. Perhaps they can help spread the word that we're looking for her.'

'Right. I'd be happy to. It's not exactly a hardship, spending time at the baths. You were right about that.' She smiled back. 'That sort of favour I'll do any time.'

'Glad to hear it. Then tomorrow, while you're enjoying yourself,' he sent her a teasing glance, 'I'll search for Caratius. It would be wonderful if I could get a message to him to see if he could meet me when he's off duty.'

'Why can't you just go to the fort and ask for him? Aren't kin allowed to visit?'

'To be honest, I have no idea, but I would rather not show myself to anyone who might remember me.' He gestured to himself. 'I'm afraid I do rather stand out, as I'm taller than most men. The training I did as a gladiator also made me larger than average. If anything happens to Julius Felix, questions might be asked about suspicious strangers entering the fort recently. The guards could point me out.'

She looked him over, her cheeks going a trifle pink. 'You are rather . . . memorable. Perhaps I should do it. I owe you.'

Alarm flared through him. 'No, Gisel!' He reached across the table and took her hand in his. 'You're not going anywhere near the fort. If anyone is memorable, it's you. Your beauty is such that I doubt any man would forget you in a hurry. Besides, there are no debts between us. If you do anything, it is of your own free will because you want to help me right a wrong. You owe me nothing, you hear?'

Her turquoise eyes widened and her fingers tightened around his. 'Very well. I do want to. I wish to help you avenge your mother and sister, because I know how they must have felt and because this is important to you.'

'Good.' He raised her hand and kissed each finger in turn. 'And thank you.'

Chapter Sixteen

Near Bath, June, present day

Jonah took Mac on a tour of his house, and she was enthralled. Each room was better than the last, and her absolute favourite was the conservatory, or orangery as he called it. This could be reached via either the kitchen or the living room, the latter having wide French doors in two places that opened into it. It was an enormous space. Two of the walls were made entirely out of glass panes, interspersed with ornate ironwork, while the other two consisted of the outside walls of the house, which formed an L-shape. The roof was also iron and glass, with large blinds that could be pulled across if the weather was too sunny. A mosaic floor and a disparate collection of rattan furniture completed the picture, and Mac felt as if she'd stepped back in time.

'This is incredible,' she breathed, staring around her in awe. 'Like a Victorian lady's paradise. I could see myself sitting here with a good book and a glass of ice-cold home-made lemonade. And wouldn't it be the perfect place for a summer garden party? Or afternoon tea.'

'True, but I've never invited anyone here, so that's not going to happen.' Jonah looked around as if he was trying to see it through her eyes.

Mac turned to face him. 'What, no one? Not even your bandmates?'

'No. You're the first person to set foot here, except for the cleaning lady and my mum and sister.' He looked a bit sheepish as he admitted this. 'And the decorators, of course, when I had a few things done after I first bought the place.'

'Wow, I'm honoured.' Although she had kind of foisted herself on him.

He gave her shoulder a teasing push. 'And so you should be. But no inviting friends over to party, OK?'

'Hah! It's not like I know hordes of people around here, and even if I did, I would never do something like that to you. You know that, right? I respect your privacy.'

He turned serious and nodded. 'Yes, I trust you. Wouldn't have invited you over otherwise. Now come and have a look at the pool.'

'OK, but wait, why don't you have any plants in here? That's what an orangery is for, isn't it? Oranges and lemons?' There wasn't a single plant in the whole room, although she spied a couple of massive Chinese pots that must once have held vegetation.

Jonah made a face. 'Black thumbs. Anything I try to grow withers and dies within a week at most. I can't even keep a cactus alive.'

Mac spluttered out a laugh. 'Did you perhaps forget to water them?'

Slashes of colour appeared on his cheeks. 'Um, maybe?'

It was her turn to shove him playfully, although he was so solid he didn't move an inch. 'Well, we can go buy some and I'll show you how to look after them, OK? Or you can get the cleaning lady to do the watering. This room would be even more fabulous with some little palm trees or something. There's got to be a garden centre nearby. How about I buy them for you as a thank you for having me to stay?'

'You don't have to do that. I told you, I like having you here. But sure, we can visit a garden centre. How about later this afternoon?'

Mac had been heading for a door that led to the garden, but she stopped to frown at him. 'Don't you have work to do? I didn't mean to distract you.'

He winked at her. 'You can distract me any time. And no, I wasn't planning on doing any more work today. Let me show you the pool, then we'll go plant shopping.'

Jonah had known Mac would be enchanted by the pool, as he had been himself the first time he'd seen it. From a distance it was nothing special, although each corner sported an old-fashioned stone urn that held trailing plants, ivy and some sort of tiny purple flowers that cascaded over the edges. The bottom of the pool, however, was a fabulous mosaic of fish and other sea creatures, as well as mermaids and mermen. It was similar to the floor in the entrance hall of the house. He'd been told it was a copy of an original Roman mosaic that had been found somewhere in Italy, and it must have taken ages to put together. All the colours of the rainbow were incorporated, but predominantly there were a lot of blue hues, making the water seem fresh and inviting.

'Wow!' Mac exclaimed. 'I seem to be saying that a lot, but honestly, there's no other way to describe it. How utterly gorgeous!'

Jonah smiled and ushered her towards a little house at one end. 'I know. I did the same when I first came here, although I tried not to say it out loud. Didn't want the seller to up the price.'

That made her laugh, and he loved that sound. It hit him right in the solar plexus, and he unconsciously rubbed at that spot while he pointed to the door with his other hand. 'In there is a little changing room and bathroom. I had it renovated and added a shower. Like I said, the water in the pool is pretty cold, so it's nice to come in here afterwards to warm up and get dry.' He led the way inside.

'Sounds perfect. I like that you stuck with the Roman decor.' She indicated the floor, which was also mosaic, but in a plain geometric pattern that was echoed on the walls of the shower. The tiny tiles incorporated some that were shiny and metallic, making everything gleam like a treasure cave.

'Seemed fitting somehow.' He had no idea why he'd chosen that. It had simply appealed to him at the time. 'You ready for some shopping then?'

They left the pool area and headed back to the house. 'You don't think the journalists will spot us there? Maybe we shouldn't go anywhere today.' There was an adorable little frown between Mac's eyebrows that he had the urge to smooth out with his thumb.

'They don't know where I live, and we'll be quick. If I see anyone suspicious, we can leave.'

'OK then. Let me just go and get my wallet.'

'You are *not* paying,' he told her sternly. No way was he permitting that, when he knew she was probably struggling on a student loan.

She sent him a cheeky grin. 'Maybe not for your plants, but I might see something I like for myself.'

She darted up the stairs before he could comment further, but he was determined not to let her pay for a single damned thing.

Half an hour later, he found himself wandering the aisles of the local garden centre. He hadn't been to one since he was a kid, and he was amazed at the sheer variety of plants on offer. He also loved the smell – fresh vegetation and soil mingled with flower scents – and breathed in deeply.

'You choose,' he told Mac. 'I'm totally out of my depth here. Buy whatever you like. I'll just push the trolley.'

They had a large trolley with a flatbed, and it was soon full, but it still didn't look like enough to fill his enormous orangery. 'Let me go and leave this by the till and fetch another one.'

'Are you sure?' Mac looked dubious. 'This is going to cost a fortune.'

'It's fine. I've been meaning to do stuff to the house now that I've got time. This is nowhere near enough. Go on, pick out some pretty flowers too. All we've got so far are green things.'

That cracked her up, and she shook her head at him. 'Yeah, green things. Like plants.'

The back of his SUV was chock-full by the time they were finished, but before they left, Mac spied a car boot sale going on in a field nearby. 'Can we take a quick look? Please? Pretty please?'

'Sure.' He couldn't have resisted that turquoise gaze if he'd tried, and ambled after her. He'd never been to a boot sale, and was soon fascinated with the odd jumble of stuff on offer.

'Hey, look, there's a couple more Chinese pots like the ones in your orangery. Should we get them?' Mac pointed at two dusty porcelain pots. Underneath the grime, the colours were pretty, with a pattern of red koi carp.

'Well spotted. I like them. Let's go haggle.' He was amazed when the owner let them each go for a couple of pounds.

'No room in our house for those. They came from my mother-in-law,' the man said, wrinkling his nose. There was clearly no love lost there.

'Our gain,' Mac whispered, as Jonah hefted one under each arm. 'We'd better leave now, or we won't fit in your car.'

They managed to squeeze in the pots, but it was tight. Jonah had never envisaged transporting such things in his SUV, but it was oddly satisfying. He drove home with a smile on his face that widened when Mac turned on the radio and started singing along to some pop song. It was goofy and not always tuneful, but he joined in and loved every moment.

'You were right. That's made such a huge difference, I can't believe it!'

'Told you.' Mac stood with her hands on her hips, surveying the veritable forest of greenery that now surrounded them in the orangery. A feeling of satisfaction suffused her, and happiness fizzed in her veins. This afternoon had been such fun, and with Jonah willing to spend obscene amounts of money on anything she suggested, the end result was sumptuous, to say the least.

All the Chinese pots held miniature palm trees. They stood at intervals, and in between were large terracotta pots with other plants and herbs that scented the air. The extra pots they'd found at the boot sale were perfect, once they'd washed the grime off them. On the windowsills stood smaller planters containing orchids of various colours, and they had bought a lemon tree that had pride of place in the corner where the two house walls met.

The weather had turned very sultry, and with the blinds only half rolled down, the orangery was stiflingly hot and humid. A single ray of sunshine reflected off Mac's intaglio ring, making it light up in a quick flash. She moved into a shaded part of the room and breathed in, feeling the moisture coating the inside of her lungs. The air stilled, and when she looked at the mosaic floor, it flickered before her gaze, the pattern shifting into a different one. Dimly, she heard voices and saw movement out of the corner of her eye.

Women giggling, chatting, gossiping. Some naked, others drying themselves with long linen towels. There was a slick sound coming from nearby, and when she turned to look, a masseuse was kneading and rubbing a woman's back while she lay on a high table. Some scented oil was drizzled onto her skin before the massage continued, and the perfume teased Mac's nose, herbal and a little sharp. Permeating the air were other smells – sulphur and sweat. And she could hear the sounds of bathing: water splashing and sloshing against stone, people shrieking with laughter . . .

Jonah's voice brought her back to the present, and she blinked at her surroundings. What the hell just happened? Was she suffering from heatstroke? Or just so hot she was having hallucinations? She shivered and tried to calm her racing heartbeat. No, her mind was playing tricks on her again. It was worrying how often this seemed to be happening lately. Had the paint fumes really messed with her brain? It was a scary thought.

'Now we've just got to remember to water them,' he was saying. They each had an old-fashioned watering can, which he'd unearthed from a shed that contained all sorts of gardening tools. Mac gripped hers tighter and tried to concentrate on the here and now. She told herself that she was merely overheated and if she went outside for a moment she would stop imagining things.

'Easy. Just set an alarm on your phone.' She held hers up and put it in her calendar for the next week. Though as she probably wasn't staying here that long, it was better if he had it in his.

'Good point.' He dusted off his hands on his jeans and put the watering can behind the largest Chinese pot. 'I don't know about you, but I need a shower now. Actually, I was going to get a quick workout in and then a swim. Want to join me? Then we can order a takeaway and chill for the rest of the evening.'

It all sounded very domestic and couple-like, but Mac buried that thought. He was just being a good host, keeping her occupied so she wouldn't think about what had happened that morning. Hadn't it been longer ago than that? It was like she'd been here with him for ages. It felt so right, spending time with him. *As if she'd done it before . . .* Pulling herself out of her strange imaginings, she smiled at him. A swim would definitely cool her down and she'd stop seeing things that weren't there. Or hearing and smelling them . . . She resolutely buried that thought. It wasn't real.

'Sounds like a plan. I'll go get changed. See you in the gym.'

The moment Mackenna stepped into his home gym, Jonah regretted suggesting this activity immensely. She was wearing those tight cycling shorts again, and a skimpy sports bra that didn't appear to be as supportive as it ought to be when she got on the treadmill. He was lifting weights and almost dropped one on his toe. He'd have to concentrate or he'd do himself a serious injury.

'So you work out a lot, huh?' she huffed, after running silently for a while. She looked to be in good shape herself, as she was going quite fast and wasn't perspiring much.

'I guess.' He didn't think he worked out more than the average guy, but it had been a way of getting some time to himself during tours while his bandmates nursed hangovers. He'd grown tired of feeling like shit every time he woke up, and had stopped partying so much quite early on. Most of the hotels they stayed at had gyms, and they'd been his sanctuary.

When he looked over at Mac again, he caught her checking him out, although she quickly turned away. Her face was already a bit red from the exercise, but he could have sworn she was blushing. That made him want to smile, but he held it back. Could it be that she liked what she saw? He wasn't vain, but he knew he didn't look bad. He'd always been a big guy, and he was fit. Still, he wasn't handsome like Blue, and that had clearly been her type. Did girls change that way? He knew most guys didn't. Once you had a preference, you usually stuck with it. Like Blue and his leggy blondes. The man was a walking cliché.

So what does that make you? He ignored the annoying inner voice. Sure, he didn't mind leggy blondes either, but it was only

Mackenna who really drew him, and not just for her looks. He'd come to know her over the months she'd spent touring with them, and he liked everything about her. Her ready smile, her helpfulness, her occasional shyness, and the fact that she was so unassuming. The nerdy side she kept hidden from most people, only letting it out in discussions with him, which made him feel special. And the natural way she acted, never bitchy or mean, even when some of the groupies were rude to her. She'd had all the bodyguards doting on her too, always a kind word for them. Never above stopping to chat and ask about them and their families. Blue had never noticed, but Jonah had.

She was, quite simply, adorable.

He averted his gaze when she picked up a skipping rope and started bouncing up and down. That was more than he could take. Concentrating on the rowing machine, he gave it his all for a while, then decided he couldn't handle any more. 'I'm going in the pool,' he called out. 'Join me when you're ready.'

She gave him the thumbs-up and he sprinted out of there, hoping she hadn't seen the evidence of what she did to him when he watched her lithe body bend down and touch her toes.

He jumped straight into the water, after shucking off his shoes, socks and T-shirt, and swam a couple of laps to wind down. Floating on his back, he stared up at the blue summer sky, which was turning pink now dusk was approaching. His whole body felt languid, and he realised that he was truly happy for the first time in ages. There was no pressure to go out and perform in front of thousands of fans, and he'd never have to do it again unless he wanted to. No need to assume a calm demeanour for his bandmates, or put up with their childish antics. He didn't even have to rescue Owen from himself, as the guy had finally found a decent girlfriend who kept him away from excesses. And he himself was being left alone to do what he loved most – songwriting.

Spending a carefree afternoon with Mac, messing around with plants, had been a bonus. The icing on the cake. Who knew indoor gardening could be fun? And now they had a whole evening to be together . . .

A huge splash brought him out of his trance, and he spat water, wiping his eyes with one hand. 'Why you little . . . I'll get you for that!' He took off after Mac, who squealed and swam as fast as she could towards the steps at the end of the pool. He caught her halfway there, hauling her back against his chest. She was laughing and squirming against him, and he clamped his arms around her to hold her still.

'You going to do that again?' he asked, trying and failing to sound menacing.

'Any chance I get,' she shot back.

'Well then, you'll be punished.' He put his hands on her waist and threw her up into the air, letting go and launching her into the water with another big splash.

She came up, spluttering and laughing even more. 'I'm not scared of you. Catch me if you can.' Again she took off, but this time with proper strokes that cut elegantly through the water.

Jonah had to admit she was fast, but the pool wasn't all that long and he caught her once more. 'You'll never be able to get away from me,' he murmured, and although they were talking about swimming, he had another thought in mind. He couldn't resist putting his mouth on the soft junction between her neck and her shoulder. If felt familiar, instinctive, as if he'd done it many times before. As if she belonged to him.

And if he could help it, he wasn't ever going to let her go.

Chapter Seventeen

Isca, south-west Britannia, June AD 80

Duro took Gisel back to the place they were staying at and left her there with strict instructions to bar the door. For the rest of the evening, he went from one tavern to the next, gaming and pretending to drink large quantities of watered-down wine. He spent freely, lubricating those off-duty legionaries who weren't averse to socialising with a native. When he was about ready to give up, he found a group who were Britons themselves, part of one of the auxiliary units, and finally struck gold.

'You have a kinsman in the Legio Secunda?' one of his drinking companions said. 'Then he'll likely be in the *alae* – the cavalry units. Most of the men in those are non-Roman citizens like us. What tribe are you from?'

'Iceni.' Duro wasn't too keen on revealing this. His kind were still viewed with suspicion by the Romans since their queen had started the infamous rebellion. If it helped him to find Caratius, however, it would be worth the risk. 'And yes, I believe he's in the cavalry.'

'Makes sense. You lot are well known for your skill in horsemanship. Not that us Atrebates are less proficient.' The man grinned broadly and saluted Duro with his mug.

'Of course not. We're all very capable,' Duro agreed, although secretly he thought the man's tribe inferior to his own. Epona, goddess of horses and cavalry, had always blessed the Iceni with amazing equine skills, which was why she featured on quite a few of the coins struck by the tribe's kings in the past.

'Hold on. Sulinus!' the man yelled, waving someone over. 'Say, aren't you in the cavalry? Got a comrade by the name of . . . what was it again?' He squinted at Duro.

'Caratius,' he supplied.

Sulinus, who was more than a little the worse for wear, swayed as he nodded. 'Aye, I do. Good man. Excellent at handling a spear and second to none with his *spatha*. Not to mention great horsemanship.'

The latter weapon was a type of long slashing sword used by the Britons. They needed these as the shorter *gladius* used by infantrymen wouldn't have had the required reach for a man fighting on horseback. Duro himself had started learning to use it as a child, but while living with the Romans he'd become used to the *gladius*. Not that he couldn't wield either, if the occasion called for it. His gladiator training had given him skills with any weapon available.

'You know him? Excellent!' Duro was immensely relieved to hear that his brother was here, and not in the north with Governor Julius Agricola. That was indeed a stroke of luck. 'I'm only here for a few days but would love to see him, even if briefly. How do I get word to him?' He could ask this Sulinus, but the man didn't look like he'd remember his own name come morning, never mind a message.

Sulinus shrugged. 'Write him a letter and send an urchin into the fort. There are quite a few outside, always ready to run errands for a small coin. Shouldn't be too hard to locate your kinsman in the cavalry barracks. There's only a hundred and twenty of us.

We're billeted three to a pair of rooms, next to our horses.' He took a sip of his wine, frowning as if he was trying to remember what they were talking about, then nodded. 'Might have been sent out on a scouting expedition,' he slurred. 'Be back soon, though.'

'Thank you. I'll do that.' Duro stood up and clapped the man on the back. 'Why don't you sit down and join us? Plenty of wine left in this pitcher, but I'll buy some more.'

The following morning, he obtained the necessary materials – a sliver of birch wood, a quill pen and some ink – to write Caratius a short message. He deliberated what to say and decided to keep it short.

To Caratius

Greetings, brother. I am in Isca. If you are free, please meet me outside the baths at a time of your choosing. Tell the messenger.

He signed it *Commios*, as Caratius would probably think it a joke if he gave his own name, that of a brother he thought was dead. He only hoped Caratius was literate, otherwise he'd have to find someone to read the message out to him. The fewer people who saw it, the better.

He loitered near one of the main entrances of the rectangular fort – there were four altogether – but not close enough that he could be seen by the guards. Row upon neat row of barracks could be glimpsed inside the ramparts. Duro had been told they housed somewhere between three and five thousand men, although some of them might be elsewhere as so-called *vexillationes*. These units were often sent off on special missions or to assist other legions, perhaps to help put down rebellions. Either way, it was a considerable force, but apparently necessary in order to keep the local Silures tribe in order.

A plaque bearing the legend *LEGIO II AVGVSTA* and a depiction of a ram with a fishtail proclaimed who the fort belonged to, should anyone have any doubts about it. Duro wondered why they'd chosen such a strange emblem. He knew it was called a *capricornus*, and presumably it had something to do with the emperor Augustus, who had founded this legion, but it was still odd.

Outside the walls, on a field just to his left, groups of legionaries were being put through physical exercise drills. Some were attacking a wooden post with training weapons, while others were running around the perimeter to improve their stamina. Watching them brought back memories of the daily training sessions he and Raedwald had taken part in as gladiators. The exercise regimen had been relentless, but neither of them had minded much. By being in the best shape possible, they had given themselves a better chance of survival. He supposed it was the same for the legionaries here.

Eventually he hailed a small boy whose quick movements and intelligent gaze had impressed him, and asked him to deliver the message.

'It has to be put into the hands of Caratius himself, no one else, mind,' he told the boy sternly. 'If he's not there, just find out when he's due to return and say you'll come back.'

The sight of the brass *sestertius* coin Duro promised him had the boy sprinting off eagerly. It wasn't long before he returned, empty-handed and smiling. 'I found him. He said to tell you he'll be there within the next hour.'

'Perfect, thank you! Here you go.' The boy's eyes gleamed when he was given the coin, as if he hadn't believed Duro would keep his word. It was probably more than he usually earned for errands.

'Any time you need another message delivered, I'm here.' He darted off, presumably afraid Duro would change his mind and take the payment back. That made Duro smile as he wandered off in the direction of the baths.

Excitement rose within him. In a short space of time, he'd be meeting a brother he hadn't thought he'd ever see again. The gods were definitely favouring him today.

Gisel entered the bath complex with some trepidation. Although she had the necessary coin to pay the entrance fee, it felt strange to be going on her own. She was an outsider here, and didn't fit in, which made her self-conscious. As well, there was no Duro to tell her what to do and how to act this time, and she missed that. Missed his company, truth to tell. No point being a coward, though. He needed her assistance and she was determined to help him in any way she could. Consequently, she straightened her shoulders and told herself not to be so silly, striding through the doors with her head held high.

'You can't rely on a man for everything,' she muttered to herself. She was a strong woman. She could cope very well without him.

The Isca baths were huge, with a vaulted roof that soared higher than all the other nearby dwellings, and beautifully painted walls. There was an indoor hall where men apparently practised various sports, and three other large rooms – the *tepidarium*, *caldarium* and *frigidarium*. There was also an outside exercise yard covered in sand, the *palaestra*, surrounded by a colonnaded walkway, and an outdoor swimming pool.

Since there were no men present at this time, Gisel dared to stroll into the first room naked, bringing only the items she needed for washing. Using a sponge Duro had obtained for her, she cleaned herself all over before proceeding into the next room, which was warmer. She again wished she had some wooden-soled sandals, instead of having to almost skip across the floor in order not to burn her feet.

If she'd been a man, she would perhaps have wrestled with her friends first, or exercised in some other way, then washed, swum in the *natatio* and finally played games or discussed politics while snacking on meats and olives. She guessed most of the patrons here were off-duty soldiers and their families. The females, however, were like the ones she'd seen in Bath in one respect – content to merely sit around and gossip, during and after their ablutions. They were clustered in groups here too, and by listening to them surreptitiously, she figured out which ones were not Roman. Fortunately, local women appeared to be in the majority here in Isca.

She sidled closer to three ladies who were talking about a friend whose name was definitely native. '*Ave*. May I sit with you, please? I'm visiting Isca for a while, but I don't know anyone here so I'm feeling a little lonely.' She spoke to them in Latin, even though she could probably have made herself understood in her own language. Best not to let on where she was from, though.

'Of course, do!' They made room for her on the bench they were occupying, instantly curious about the newcomer. 'What brings you here?'

'My husband is in Isca looking for trading opportunities,' Gisel lied glibly. It was the story they'd agreed upon this morning before Duro left her outside the baths. 'He brought me along because we are newly married.' The thought that she wished this was true actually made her blush, and the three women congratulated her, wreathed in knowing smiles.

They asked for details about Duro, and she had no trouble describing him favourably. In fact, she waxed so lyrical about him, she had to rein herself in.

'Aww, a love match. How wonderful!' one of the ladies said. 'You are so lucky.'

They proceeded to regale Gisel with tales of their own husbands and their various shortcomings. It made her realise just how fortunate she'd been to be rescued by Duro, of all men, and how unusual the way he treated her was. He'd acted with kindness and understanding at all times, never pushing her to do anything she didn't want to. It made her like him all the more.

Eventually, after the women had progressed to the outside pool together, which was quite a lot colder than the one by the sacred spring, she managed to bring the subject around to Duro's sister.

'Actually, my husband believes he might have kin here at Isca. A woman by the name of Rufilia. Perhaps you know her?' Gisel dipped her hair under the water briefly, trying to act as if the question was casual.

'No, the name doesn't sound familiar,' one lady replied, while the others also shook their heads.

'Well, to be honest, we're not sure she's actually still alive.' Gisel sighed and attempted a tragic expression. 'She was stolen away by a Roman legionary and enslaved. My husband only recently found out where she might have gone, and he thinks now that she was brought here.'

'Abducted? That's outrageous!'

'Yes, isn't it? Quite shocking. We'd love to find her and make sure that she is well, possibly even try to buy her freedom.'

'That's understandable.' The chattiest of the ladies frowned. 'The name is unusual, though, so we ought to have heard it if she was here. I would assume that as a slave to a legionary, she'd be living in the *vicus* with us. We know most people there, as we're all married to men who are attached to the fort in one way or another.'

Gisel shrugged. 'I'll ask around some more, but perhaps, if you wouldn't mind, you could spread the word that we are looking for a woman by that name.' She told them which tavern she was staying at. 'If you have any news, ask for Ivonerca. I can be found there most of the time, as my husband is busy during the day.'

She and Duro had decided not to give her real name, and he'd come up with the fake one.

'My father was Ivonercus, so if Rufilia is here and she's told someone called Ivonerca is looking for her, she might be intrigued and more inclined to come forward,' he'd said.

That made sense to Gisel.

'Of course we will,' the women promised. 'You can count on us. We'll get the word out, never fear.'

She hoped it was enough. Gossip travelled fast in a settlement such as this, and the women looked eager to be the ones to spread this titbit. If Rufilia was here, hopefully she'd soon be found. If these locals had never heard the name, though, chances were she'd perished a long time ago, as Duro feared. By the sound of it, Julius Felix was not the type of man to treat his slaves with any consideration. Perhaps it was as well if she was no longer alive.

Duro paced back and forth in front of the bath complex until a man came striding along the street, gazing around as if he was looking for someone. He was dressed in a similar fashion to the auxiliaries Duro had met the night before, in a pale-blue long-sleeved tunic with a fairly plain military belt, and *braccae* – the Roman-style trousers. Cavalrymen obviously didn't go around bare-legged, the way most legionaries did during the summer, as it was more practical to wear trousers for riding. Duro was glad of it. To him, the legionaries looked ridiculous and undignified. Caratius – if it was him – also wore hobnailed boots that made a tapping noise as he walked along the pavement. A baldric containing the longsword the men at the tavern had mentioned was slung across his chest. And a *pugio*, or dagger, was suspended from his belt. Duro had seen the decorative helmets worn by cavalry units when on a mission, with cheek, nose and neck guards, but the man approaching was bare-headed. He was also clean-shaven, and his golden curls were cut short, but Duro was pleased to see they were of a similar colour to his own.

He stepped forward. 'Caratius?'

The man halted and looked him up and down with a frown. 'Yes? Who's asking? I was told my brother was here.'

'He is.' Duro smiled. 'You probably don't remember me, but I'm Durobelinos. I'm sorry I signed the message with Commios's name, but I didn't think you'd come if I gave you my own.'

Caratius's mouth fell open. 'Durobelinos? No! That's impossible. You . . . you're dead!'

Spreading his hands, Duro shrugged and grinned. 'As you can see, I'm very much alive. If you look closely, you should notice the family resemblance, but in case you still doubt me, here is an amulet I borrowed from Commios. He said you'd recognise it as his.'

He pulled the amulet from his pouch and held it out. It was made of silver in the shape of a horse, in the distinctive style of their tribe. Apparently their mother had left it behind to protect her younger sons from evil when she rode off to accompany their father during the rebellion.

'If you lose it, I'll never speak to you again,' Commios had told him sternly. Duro had no intention of misplacing something that was so precious to his brother, but it had been necessary to bring it.

Caratius took the little horse and studied it carefully, before nodding. 'I do.' He blinked at his older brother. 'You're really Durobelinos? I can't believe it! Where have you been? When did you get back?'

'It's a long story, but if you have time to share a meal with me, I'll tell you. And I usually go by just Duro these days. What say you?'

'I can't stay long as I don't officially have time off, but lead the way. I can't wait to hear this. Duro! By Taranis, I couldn't be more surprised if the god himself had greeted me.'

Chuckling, Duro ushered Caratius towards the nearest eatery, where they procured some victuals. 'Let's take this and go and sit down by the river so that we can talk undisturbed,' he suggested. The things he had to tell his brother were best not shared with all and sundry.

While they consumed the roast lamb and bread, washed down with local beer, Duro told his tale. Caratius listened wide-eyed but silent, until it came to the part about their mother and sister. Then his eyebrows drew down into a ferocious scowl.

'Do you mean to say I've shared a fort with the murdering son of a bitch all this time? I'd have killed him if I'd known. And that our sister might be hereabouts as well, his slave woman? Unbearable!'

'Well, I don't know whether either of them is still alive. I've been trying to find out, but so far without success.'

'Oh, Julius Felix is alive all right. The mean cur is a centurion, ruling over one of the cohorts. Luckily not mine.'

'He's a centurion? Curse him!' Although he'd expected this, as the man was ruthless enough to have risen through the ranks, it still stuck in Duro's craw. Julius Felix did not deserve to be in charge of anything, let alone a troop of legionaries.

Caratius shrugged. 'He must have served with the legion for over sixteen years. Men who have survived that long are usually given a promotion. And I assume he's from a fairly prominent family of the so-called equestrian class, second only to the senatorial clans if I've understood correctly.'

'Still, I can't bear to think of the man in any position of power. He's bound to abuse it.'

'So I've heard. There are certainly rumours about the unusually fierce discipline in that particular cohort. He puts his vine rod to good use. Where other centurions order men to do extra chores or dock their pay, Julius Felix inflicts pain. I'd guess he enjoys it, the scurvy dog. In fact, a while back he beat a man to death for falling asleep on guard duty. Admittedly, that's a terrible crime, but it still seemed like excessive punishment. As for Rufilia, it's never crossed my mind to wonder about the man's slaves. Nor would I have recognised her if I'd seen her. I doubt she'd know who I was either.'

Duro laughed. 'No, you've changed somewhat from the three-year-old we last saw.'

'Aye, I suppose I have at that.' Caratius joined in the laughter. 'I can see the family resemblance, but you've grown a bit yourself. I suppose you had to do a lot of training as a gladiator, right?'

'Every day, but it wasn't so bad. I had my friend Raedwald to spar with, and we had a lot of free time as well to plan our eventual escape. Not that we ever dreamed the gods would help us the way they did, by making an entire mountain explode. That wasn't something we'd imagined in our wildest dreams. It did make things a lot easier, though, as no one was left alive who knew we were slaves. I'm a freedman now, and who's to say differently?'

'Indeed. And I'm glad.' Caratius shook his head. 'To tell you the truth, I'm still in a daze. This is a lot to take in all at once. Anyway, I must go. I made up an excuse about needing to purchase more leather for harness repairs, but I don't want to arouse suspicion if I'm away for too long. Got me out of the fort, but I'm on guard duty this afternoon so I'd better hurry. I'll try to sneak out again soon.'

'Yes, we'll have to meet up and make plans. Tell me when you can get away next and I'll try to come up with something. But for the love of all the gods, don't let on to Julius Felix that you know who he is!'

'I won't, you have my oath.'

Before he went back to his duties at the fort, Caratius gave Duro a bear hug, holding on for a while as if savouring the moment. 'I'm so happy the gods spared you. Welcome back, brother.'

Duro could only nod and hug him back just as hard.

Chapter Eighteen

Near Bath, June, present day

They shared a huge pizza, as they'd wanted the same toppings, and watched a couple of films on Netflix. Jonah allowed Mackenna to choose first and patiently sat through a romcom. To make things fair, she let him put on *Gladiator* next. It wasn't one of her favourites, as it had such a sad ending, but she found herself mesmerised. A lot of the Roman settings and costumes seemed awfully familiar somehow, but she put it down to the fact that she'd seen the film before. Jonah, for his part, appeared glued to the screen, and at one point he muttered an unfamiliar word.

'What was that?' She elbowed him to get his attention. They were sitting next to each other on his couch, but not too close.

'Huh? Oh, I was expecting them to call for *mitte* – that's mercy in Latin.' At her puzzled glance, he added, 'It's something I've heard about.'

Eventually they went to their respective beds. For some reason, Mac hadn't been able to fully relax and had felt on edge the entire evening. Although Jonah was the perfect gentleman, their childish antics in the pool had awakened something inside her. She could have sworn he'd kissed her shoulder in the water, although the contact had been fleeting. Yet he hadn't touched her since. What was that about?

Her unsettled thoughts must have carried on in her sleep, as she had one of the worst nightmares she'd ever experienced. Waking herself up with a whimper, she sat up in bed and tried to physically still her frantically beating heart by putting a hand on her chest. She was panting and disorientated, while details of the dream were etched into her mind, still clear as day. She shuddered as she recalled what had been happening.

She was being held down by two stony-faced men who gripped her wrists and legs firmly. No matter how much she thrashed, fought or even bit them, they didn't let go, and they seemed impervious to her plight. The terror and sheer panic she felt was making her heart beat so fast it hurt. Another man, middle-aged and florid, was giving orders while unclasping his belt. He was dressed strangely in some sort of dress or tunic whose braided edging shimmered with metallic thread in the light from half a dozen oil lamps. The whole scene appeared to be taking place inside a tent of some sort, although there was furniture, including the bed she was being restrained on, and rugs. A fourth man was watching with a smirk, his white-blond hair shining in the light. His dark-blue eyes showed a mixture of hatred, jealousy and satisfaction that made no sense. When the man in front of her began to pull up his tunic and undo the loincloth she glimpsed underneath, she knew he was going to rape her and there wasn't a single thing she could do about it. She screamed at the top of her lungs . . .

And that noise had translated into the whimper that woke her.

Restless and tense, she headed for the en suite bathroom that faced the back garden. After doing her business and washing her hands and face in cool water, she stared out the window while drying herself. There was some moonlight filtering through the clouds, and she jumped when she saw movement at the far end of the garden. A small wood bordered the lawn, and her eyes widened as she spied a figure standing there, staring at the house. The shape seemed insubstantial and unreal, but there was no mistaking the fact that it was a man. A rather robust one, wearing a knee-length garment. A coat?

Or a tunic, like the man in her dream . . .

She jerked back and put a hand over her mouth to stop a scream from escaping.

'Don't be silly. He's not a dream,' she muttered. If there was a man in the garden, he had to be real. A journalist perhaps? She wouldn't put it past them. Or a stalker? That wasn't unheard of for famous people like Jonah.

Without thinking, she raced into the bedroom and out the door onto the landing. After knocking on Jonah's door just a couple of times, she pushed it open and ran inside.

'Jonah, come quick! There's someone in the garden. He . . . he's staring at the house.'

It sounded stupid when put like that, as if looking was a crime, but that might not be all the intruder was intending. Too late she realised that she shouldn't have barged into his bedroom like that. He had shot up into a sitting position, the sheet he'd been sleeping under falling down to show that he was naked. His curtains had been left open and the moonlight gilded his toned torso and abs, the sheet only covering the most essential parts of him, and barely that. Mac gasped.

'Shit! I'm sorry. I . . . But the man . . .' She turned away, trying to blink away the image of a tousled Jonah with no clothes on. Sure, she'd seen him in board shorts earlier in the pool, but knowing he wasn't wearing anything at all now somehow made things worse.

'Hang on.' His voice was gravelly, and she heard rustling

behind her. Footsteps padded over towards his own en suite, and she dared to turn around again. 'I can't see anyone,' he was saying.

She trailed after him and into his bathroom, which mirrored hers and also faced the back garden. She stared out the window towards the trees, but the figure was gone. Nothing moved. 'I swear, there was a guy standing there,' she whispered. 'He was looking right at me.' She shivered, rubbing her arms, belatedly realising that she was only wearing pants and an oversized T-shirt.

Jonah, who had apparently pulled on some tracksuit bottoms, turned to study her. 'Are you sure it wasn't just a bad dream?' He didn't look angry at having been woken in such an abrupt fashion, merely curious.

'No! I mean, I did have a horrible nightmare, but . . . No, he was there.' She swallowed hard. It sounded feeble, and now she felt really silly. 'I'm so sorry. I shouldn't have barged in like that. I didn't think . . .'

'Shh, it's OK. I believe you.' He put his arms around her and drew her into a hug. His bare chest was warm against her cheek and he smelled wonderful. Clean soap, a touch of chlorine from the pool, and man. She allowed herself to breathe in his scent for a moment, before pulling away.

'Thanks. I'd better go back to bed.'

'Mm-hmm. Don't worry, we'll check it out in the morning.' He stroked her arms, then took her hands in his bigger ones. 'Even if someone's managed to get into the garden, they can't enter the house. The alarm is on and it's connected directly to the nearest police station.'

'OK. That's good to know. Sorry again for disturbing you.'

'No problem. Any time.'

As she fled back to her own room, the unsettling thoughts

about near rape, florid men and intruders had been replaced by something else. She fell asleep again reliving the sensation of leaning on Jonah's warm chest. She'd wanted to stay there for ever.

When Mac woke the following morning, she cringed as she remembered her night-time dash into Jonah's bedroom. What must he think of her? She hoped he didn't think she'd done it on purpose as some kind of attempt at seduction. That was too embarrassing for words. He must have had women try all sorts of things to get close to him – she'd met a few truly desperate groupies during the tour and had heard some stories – but she'd never do anything like that. Hopefully he knew that. She sighed and went to have a shower.

The horrid journalists had actually done her a huge favour in forcing her to be rescued by Jonah, but she mustn't outstay her welcome or make things weird between them. From now on, she'd keep at a safe distance and not intrude in any way. Although she knew she ought to make plans to leave as soon as possible, she wanted to enjoy it for just a little while longer. He'd said she could stay for as long as she liked, and she believed he meant it. Perhaps he really was lonely. It had to be difficult for someone like him to find people to hang out with that he could truly trust. He was a commodity, a famous person others wanted to be seen with, and he was rich.

In that situation, how would you know whether you were liked for yourself or merely for what you could do for others?

She dressed in leggings and a T-shirt, seeing no point in wearing anything fancy as she wasn't planning on going anywhere today. Possibly the garden, to have a go at the weeds growing rampant in the flower beds. She knew Jonah hadn't meant it when he said she could garden, but she wanted to and had nothing better to do. It was therapeutic, and she loved it.

Walking into the kitchen, she was ambushed by what could only be described as a meatball on legs, barking in short bursts interspersed with snorts. She stopped short at the sight of the French bulldog. 'What the . . .?'

'*Fred!* Leave her alone,' Jonah ordered sternly. 'She lives here.' He hurried towards her looking harassed, but Mac's gaze focused on the tiny creature nestled against his chest. It was a miniature version of the meatball, who was still barking and dancing around their legs.

'Oh my God! That is the most adorable thing I've ever seen! What . . . How . . . Did you buy dogs?'

She bent down to allow Fred to sniff her hand, then scratched him behind his big bat-like ears. His fur was short and shiny, but very soft, especially on top of his head. She couldn't take her eyes off Jonah and the puppy in his arms, though. It was a sight guaranteed to melt even the sternest heart. Definitely cuteness overload.

He sighed. 'Long story. Fred is my sister Gemma's dog, but she said she didn't want him any more and he's lived with my mum ever since Gems went off to uni. He was an impulse buy a couple of years ago, which I would have put a stop to if I'd been at home. Mum decided to keep him for a while in case Gemma changed her mind, but she hasn't. I'd promised to look after him, as Mum is going on holiday for two weeks, and she dropped him off this morning, but she'd never said anything about a puppy.'

He shook his head. 'I can't quite believe this, but apparently Gemma just bought this little guy because she thought Fred needed a friend. She didn't even check with Mum first! Who does that? And Mum doesn't want either of them really. But honestly, if I'd known she was bringing two of them, I would have told her to get a dog-sitter. Fred is one thing, but what do I know about puppies?' He scowled, but at the same time he was rubbing the puppy's head with one finger.

Mac tried to absorb this convoluted story. Jonah's sister sounded incredibly irresponsible. 'I didn't hear the doorbell. I must have been very deeply asleep.'

'No, I intercepted Mum before she got that far. I saw her car on the gate monitor.' He nodded towards a console on the wall that showed a grainy picture of the area outside the front gate.

'I see.' Mac leaned forward and held out her hand to the puppy. 'Aww, you are so precious!' As if he'd heard her, he answered with the smallest bark she'd ever heard. It was more like the sound a cat would make, a little miaow, and she laughed in delight. 'Yes you are! Unbelievably gorgeous.' She glanced at Jonah. 'Please may I hold him? Her?'

'Be my guest. Whenever I put him down, he tries to hassle Fred, who gets all grumpy. His name is Bagel.'

'Bagel?' Mac giggled. 'I guess he is kind of round, isn't he.'

'They're both ridiculous-looking,' Jonah groused. 'Don't know why she couldn't at least have bought a proper dog, like an Alsatian or something.'

Mac cradled the small, warm body against her chest and closed her eyes. This was bliss. She adored dogs and had always wanted one, but it had never been practical. Her mother worked full-time, and her father and stepmother didn't want their fancy home ruined by a pet. As for herself, she couldn't look after one if she was studying or working full-time either.

'So does this sort of thing happen often?' She was curious about Jonah's relationship with his family, as he'd never talked about them.

'No. Well, it hasn't in the past, as I've been busy. I guess Mum figured that now I'm around more, she can dump them on me.' He pottered around taking out cereal boxes, milk, bowls and spoons to put on the table, as well as bread, butter, jam and marmalade. 'I'm going to have to put a stop to it.'

'Why? You don't like dogs?' Fred had stopped barking now, and Bagel was snoring softly in Mac's arms.

'Sure I do, but I don't mean just this, today. It's everything really. I hate being taken advantage of, you know? And not only as a dog-sitter. When I started making a lot of money with Valhalla Storm, it was like my whole family suddenly took it for granted I'd buy them whatever they wanted. I mean, of course I was happy to spoil them at first. I love them. Ever since I was a kid, Mum's been a single mother working two jobs to try and make ends meet. I wanted life to be easier for her and bought her a house. I gave her an allowance each month too, a new car and whatever else she needed. And I got my sister all the things we'd both gone without.'

He took a deep breath. 'They were happy and grateful, but then something changed when I became really famous. Mum demanded a new house – not asked, mind you, but demanded it as if it was her right. She wanted bigger and swankier, even though the one I'd bought her was perfectly fine and way larger than she needed. And my sister wanted all sorts of things too. The list was endless. However much I bought, it felt like it was never enough. Even my dad crawled out of the woodwork. The bastard left us when I was four and never sent so much as a birthday card. I told him to go take a hike. Of course, he sold his story to the tabloids, making me sound like a stingy, ungrateful brat. I'm definitely not, but there are others who need my help more. I'm actually involved with several charities helping underprivileged kids, among other things.'

He poured Frosties into his bowl with some force and added milk, setting the carton down with a thump.

Mac felt for him. His father asking for handouts after ditching the family early on was unbelievable. And his mother and sister didn't seem much better. She sat down and placed Bagel on her lap, then helped herself to cereal. The puppy seemed oblivious. 'Hey, you don't have to talk about it if you don't want to. Sounds like a shitshow.'

He snorted and managed a small smile and a shrug. 'You could say that. I don't mind telling you. I know *you* won't run to the papers. There must be a lot of dirt you could spill about Blue, yet you never took revenge that way. As I said, I trust you.'

Warmth spread inside her at his words. His trust was something she cherished, and she would definitely never betray him that way.

'So what do you do now? With all their demands, I mean.'

He pushed his spoon around without actually eating anything. 'I did buy my mum a new house, a horrible mansion-type thing in a posh gated community. I figured I still owed her for raising me and looking after me. And I took my sister on a shopping spree, but after that I made it clear I wasn't their cash cow and enough was enough. They sulked for a while, and occasionally try to get me to pay for unnecessary stuff, but I think they mostly got the message. I'm protective of my sister, obviously, but I told her to stop being an entitled brat and that she had to get a job and support herself. I'm not her keeper. She's nineteen, so a lot younger than me, and has always been the baby of the family, but she needs to grow up and become independent.' He speared his fingers through his hair, making it stand on end. 'Does that sound heartless? I mean, in an emergency, of course I'd help, and I spoil them at Christmas and birthdays, but I live a pretty simple life myself, apart from indulging in a few luxuries now and then.'

'No, not at all.' Mac knew all about entitled girls from her half-sister. Savannah took it to new heights. It sounded as though Jonah's sister wasn't far behind, although in her case it probably had more to do with immaturity than spite. 'So Gemma's at university now?'

'Well, she's supposed to be studying, but as far as I can make out, all she does is party. It's only her first year, so maybe she'll calm down, but I wouldn't bet on it. I pay for her tuition but made her take out a student loan for the rest. She's got to learn to stand on her own two feet, right?'

'Absolutely.' Mac told him about Savannah, and how she'd been spoilt rotten all her life. 'It's made her unbearable, so I think you're doing the right thing.'

He nodded and sent her a grateful look. 'Thank you for saying that.' He gestured towards Fred, who was begging with soulful eyes. 'As for these guys, I'm tempted to keep them. Mum clearly doesn't want them, and Gemma's not responsible enough to be a dog owner. You can't just buy pets and expect others to look after them for you.'

Mac went to put some bread in the toaster, carrying Bagel in the crook of her arm like a baby. 'I agree. You *should* keep them. If you're sure *you* want the responsibility?'

'Yes, I think I do. They deserve to be loved and looked after properly. I'll make sure they are from now on.'

Jonah worked in his studio all morning, putting the finishing touches to a track he'd started after the picnic with Mac. It was a dreamy ballad, inspired by the way she made him feel, but he wouldn't be playing it to her any time soon. There was no way she'd fail to notice the yearning he had for her, nor the fact that the song was about her. Maybe one day he'd share, but not now. Not yet.

He'd had a recording studio built in the attics, which were huge and sprawling and must once have contained the servant's quarters. The dormer windows were smaller than the ones on the other floors, but still not insubstantial. With soundproofing, the sloping walls made for a cosy environment that was perfect for him. He'd had comfy sofas and chairs scattered around the place, as well as all the musical instruments that could possibly be needed. He played the guitar and keyboard himself, and could manage drums if he had to, but he knew Owen would be happy to come and help out with that any time he asked. Hopefully, in the future, other artists would come here to collaborate with him. For now, he was happy to work on his own, although he'd had little Bagel with him today, as he didn't want to inflict him on Mac. She wasn't here to babysit his family's dogs, although she'd said she was happy to keep an eye on Fred.

Around lunchtime, he picked up the puppy, who'd slept for most of the morning, and wandered downstairs to see whether Mackenna was cooking anything tempting. She wasn't indoors, so he walked through the now vegetation-scented orangery and out into the garden, and heard barking in the distance. Shading his eyes against the glare of the sun, he spotted Mac and Fred down at the far end of the lawn, near where she'd claimed to have seen an intruder last night. He had checked first thing, but hadn't found anything. There were no footprints or trampled grass. No signs of anyone. He was inclined to think she'd been half asleep and imagining things, but since it had earned him a late-night hug, he wasn't complaining.

She came walking towards him carrying a large basket of what must be weeds. Fred waddled along behind her, his tongue hanging out. Jonah noticed that she'd made progress tidying up one of the flower beds, and smiled at her.

'I told you, you don't have to do that. I'll hire a new gardener. Let's swap.' He handed her Bagel and picked up the basket, then headed for the compost heap behind the stables.

'It's fine, I enjoy it. And just look what I found! It came up with one particularly stubborn root.' She held out her hand, and on her palm lay a tiny gold coin, about the size of his fingernail.

It looked to be in amazingly good condition, the gold almost as new.

He threw the weeds onto the compost heap and put the basket on the ground before reaching for the coin. 'Whoa, nice! This was in my flower bed?'

He turned it this way and that, the metal shining in the sunlight. On the front was the face of some long-dead king, a fat man with double chins and some kind of wreath on his bald or short-haired pate. The reverse had the figure of a man holding a spear, with another figure next to him holding out something else. A palm leaf? When he studied it more closely, he noticed writing around the rim and squinted to make it out.

'Let's see who this might be. IMPC,' he read. 'Not sure what the next letters are, but after that I think it's VESPA something?' He frowned. 'Never heard of a British king called that, have you?'

'Hold on, I'll google it.' Mac pulled her phone out of her pocket. 'So gold coin, IMPC and VESPA.' She keyed in the information, then drew in a sharp breath. 'No way!'

'What? Who is it?' He went to stand next to her to glance over her shoulder at the screen. 'Emperor Vespasian?'

She turned to give him a beaming smile. 'It's Roman! How cool is that?' Checking the information on the screen, she added, 'A gold *aureus*, and he was emperor from AD 69 to 79. It's almost two thousand years old!'

'Awesome,' he agreed, peering at the coin once again. A frisson of awareness slithered down his back, making him frown. He had the strange sensation of having seen it before. That sense of déjà vu he'd felt when they'd visited the Roman baths, where some of the objects had seemed awfully familiar. The same thing had happened when they'd watched *Gladiator* the night before too. He'd felt as if *he* was in that arena, with thousands of people shouting at him to kill someone. It had been seriously unsettling. Now it was as though the coin was giving off a weird vibe that reverberated through him. He almost didn't want to keep touching it.

'Do you think it's real?' Mac asked, her expression sceptical. 'Maybe it's a fake. Something Victorian, since your house is from that period. It wouldn't be surprising to find a coin they'd dropped in the garden.'

'Hmm, I don't know. If it's a fake, it's a really good one, since it looks just like the coin in the photo.' He pointed at her phone.

'Yes. You'll have to take it to someone who knows about these things. There's an antique dealer in Bath who specialises in coins, at that centre where we bumped into each other. I think his name is Edward. You should go and see him.'

'I will. And I'll give you a finder's fee if it's worth anything.' He slipped it into his jeans pocket, making sure there wasn't a hole in the material so he wouldn't lose the coin.

'Not necessary. And it's your garden.'

A distant bark made Mac turn back and start walking towards the lawn again. 'We'd better get Fred. He's been busy "helping" me.' She emphasised the word and made a face. 'That consisted of digging up several plants that didn't need extracting.'

Jonah laughed. 'Sounds about right. Mum says he buries things in her garden and then digs them up again. Maybe he's confused.'

But the little dog wasn't where they'd thought he'd be, and Mac frowned. 'Fred! *Fred!* Come here, boy!' she called. They could hear him barking again nearby, but he was nowhere in sight. 'Where's he gone? I should have put him on a long lead.'

'This way, I think.' Jonah led the way into the wooded area, following the sound of excited yapping.

Little Bagel was struggling in Mac's arms, obviously wanting to get down and be part of the action. She held tight. 'No you don't. One lost dog is enough,' she muttered.

They found Fred in a small clearing, digging enthusiastically next to a couple of large boulders, with clods of earth sailing out behind him. He barked again and picked something up, holding it proudly between his teeth as he trotted over to show them his find. Jonah felt his eyes open wide, and he hissed out a breath. 'What the . . .? Is that what I think it is? Drop it, Fred. *Drop it!*'

For once, the dog obeyed, and sat down panting happily. Jonah and Mac stared at his prize, then exchanged a glance. 'Not that I'm an expert or anything, but it, um, looks a lot like a human bone.' Mac squatted down for a better look, and Jonah followed suit.

'Shit,' he said. 'It really does.' He peered over at the hole Fred had been working on. There was something else white at the edge of it. 'And I think there might be more.'

Mac had gone pale, and she cradled Bagel to her chest as if he offered protection from evil spirits or something. 'Should we check?'

'No. I think I'd better call the cops.' Jonah picked Fred up. The dog whined and struggled to grab the bone first, but there was no way he could be allowed to keep it. Even if it was only that of a dead sheep, Jonah wasn't having it in the house. 'Sorry, little guy. I'll buy you a better one, I promise. Come on. Let's go back to the house.'

The police came an hour later, and Mac watched through the windows of the orangery as Jonah took them into the woods. Fred stood next to her barking at the intruders, and Bagel tried to follow suit. She couldn't help but laugh at his attempts, which sounded nothing like his older companion, but she grew serious again as she contemplated their potentially gruesome find.

Had someone been murdered in this house? The thought gave her the heebie-jeebies.

Soon afterwards, men and women dressed in forensic suits

traipsed through the garden, and a white tent could be glimpsed being erected among the trees. She didn't envy them wearing those outfits in this heat, but knew that if it was a case of murder, they couldn't risk contaminating the area. Although presumably she, Jonah and Fred had already done that.

She shivered at the thought of there being a dead person at the end of the garden. Was it his ghost she'd seen the previous night? But no, ghosts weren't real. And why would he have been staring at her in that eerie fashion? She had nothing to do with whoever it was.

In order to forget what was happening outside, she busied herself in the kitchen preparing dinner. She'd found some mince in the freezer that morning and had left it out to defrost. Now she set about making Swedish meatloaf with mashed potatoes and gravy. It wasn't difficult, just a bit time-consuming. Ultimately, it also proved very satisfying when Jonah came into the kitchen with a look of delight spreading over his features.

'What *is* that?' he asked. 'It smells incredible.'

'Meatloaf. It'll be ready soon. Have they gone?' It was six o'clock by now, and although it wasn't dark outside, she assumed even forensics teams had to eat at some point.

'Yes. We're not to touch anything, but it's not a murder case.'

Mac stopped mashing potatoes and stared at him. 'It's not? You mean it wasn't human remains?'

He shook his head. 'The bones are human, all right, but not recent. More like a couple of thousand years old.' He took out plates and cutlery and began to set the table. 'The police told me they're calling in the local archaeologists instead. They found some artefacts that are definitely very old, so even if the person *was* murdered, it was a long time ago.'

'Wow! That's . . . I was going to say exciting, but it's kind of creepy at the same time.'

She gave the potatoes one last stir, then put them on the table, followed by the meatloaf and gravy, as well as a pot of cranberry sauce.

'What's that for? You have that with meatloaf?' Jonah regarded it with a bemused expression.

'In Sweden, we'd have lingonberries, but cranberries are similar, so we'll have to make do. Trust me, they go really well together.'

Jonah sat down at the table. 'Lingonberries? Don't think I've ever had those, but I'll try anything once. This looks amazing!'

'Well, dig in.' Mac glanced at Fred and Bagel, who were both sitting next to Jonah giving him puppy-dog eyes. 'And don't let them fool you. They've both been fed – I found your mother's written instructions and the dog food – and they've had several treats too. They're not the poor starving creatures they're attempting to portray.'

Jonah laughed and took a big mouthful of food, then closed his eyes and moaned. 'Mm, this is insanely good. Please stay here for ever.'

Mac pretended nonchalance, as she knew he wasn't serious, but a part of her wished she could.

Chapter Nineteen

Isca, south-west Britannia, June AD 80

'I'm sorry, but the ladies I spoke to didn't know anyone called Rufilia.' Gisel threw herself down onto the narrow cot she shared with Duro. The mattress and webbing sagged, thus making it impossible to do anything other than lie very close together, but she didn't mind. She was beginning to think she'd never sleep peacefully again unless his big body was wrapped around hers.

And to think I've only known him a matter of weeks! She must be mad to contemplate spending the rest of her life with him – if indeed that was what he wanted – but she could no longer deny she had fallen in love with the man. She was in deep.

'Well, it was worth a try.' He stretched out next to her and pulled her against his broad chest. Her arms went around him automatically, as if that was where they were meant to be, and she relaxed into his embrace.

'I could go again tomorrow,' she offered. 'There may be others there who can help.'

'No, I don't want to risk drawing too much attention to us. Leave it for now.'

'Very well. Although the ladies did promise to spread the

word. I'm guessing there is a formidable network of gossip in a town such as this. If Rufilia is here, surely she must hear that we're looking for her.'

'Let's hope so. At least I found my brother. I can't tell you how pleased I am about that!' Duro was clearly in a buoyant mood. He had already told her about being reunited with Caratius, and it warmed Gisel the way he'd beamed as he described it.

'I'm glad. And thank the gods he believed you! Although you did say you resemble your other brother, did you not?'

'Indeed. There's no mistaking the fact that Caratius is my kin as well. You'll see when you meet him.'

She felt him stroke her hair, which was loose at the moment. It was a soothing motion, making her snuggle against him.

'Lie still, my sweet, or I won't be answerable for the consequences,' he warned in a husky voice that sent a shiver down her back.

'And what are those?' she couldn't resist asking, leaning back slightly to look him in the eyes.

They narrowed, and those blue orbs smouldered. 'You're playing with fire. You know exactly what will happen – I'll make you mine in every way. And trust me, once I do, I'll never let you go.'

'So I'm to be your concubine for the rest of my life, is that it?'

'What? *No!* I want you for my wife, woman! Have I not made that clear?' The scowl he directed at her made her reach up a hand to smooth out the crease between his eyebrows.

She smiled. 'You've not actually made me a proposal, you know. Only given me vague hints.'

He hauled her against him so tightly that not a single hair could have been inserted between them. 'Very well then – Gisel, will you do me the honour of becoming my wife? I swear by the god Cernunnos I'll want no one but you for the rest of my life.

And I'll treat you well, I promise. We will be equal partners in marriage, and I will listen to you and seek your counsel.'

It was exactly what she'd wanted to hear, and yet she hesitated. 'I would like that very much, but do you think we should wait until this . . . quest is over? I mean, what if something were to happen to you?'

He sighed and loosened his grip on her a fraction. 'You're right. I can't take the chance that I'll leave you alone and with child. I'll not make you entirely mine until such time as I've dealt with Julius Felix, but can I at least have your promise that you want me for your husband?'

'Yes, you have my oath. I'm yours, now and for ever. And perhaps you can just kiss me for now?' She had enjoyed that so much, she wanted to repeat the experience.

'That I can.'

He proceeded to demonstrate this very thoroughly to both their satisfaction, and showed her a few other things they could do besides, without risk of getting her with child. Gisel knew she'd be embarrassed when thinking about it in the light of day, but for now, she was very happy to go along with whatever he wanted.

Duro was jerked awake the following day by someone banging on their door. Instinctively he reached for the knife he'd placed by the side of the bed.

'Yes? Who is it?'

'A visitor for you, downstairs.' It was the voice of the owner of this establishment. 'Leastways, I think it's you they want. I don't have any other patrons at the moment.'

'What kind of visitor?' Duro asked suspiciously, sitting up and pulling on his trousers and tunic. It couldn't be Caratius, as he'd said he was on duty this morning. And surely his own brother hadn't betrayed him to the Romans? Yet no one else knew he was here.

'A lady, asking for a blonde woman by the name of Ivonerca. Is that your wife?'

'Ah, yes.'

'Well, don't keep her waiting,' came the grumpy reply.

'It could be one of my new friends,' Gisel murmured from behind him. 'I told them I could be found here. Shall I go and see?' She emerged from under the blanket, yawning and tousled. A surge of love for her swept through him, so strong it made him almost gasp. She was so beautiful it hurt, and she was all his. She had promised. But that meant he had to protect her at all costs.

'No. Please stay here while I ascertain whether there is any danger or treachery. If I'm not back very soon, take our things and creep down the back stairs. You'll find enough coin in my pack to take you wherever you want to go.'

She glared at him. 'I'm not going anywhere without you. I'll wait for your return.'

He could see the determination in her eyes and didn't bother arguing, but pulled on his half-boots and strapped the knife to his belt. 'Bolt the door behind me then, please.'

Gliding down the stairs on silent feet, he peeked around the corner into the main room of the tavern, which was empty of customers this time of day. A lone woman stood by the door, gazing around furtively. She was dressed in a short-sleeved tunic of shabby material, with a Roman-style *palla* covering her head and the lower half of her face. This was a sort of rectangular mantle worn by Roman matrons when they went outside their home. Yet despite her attire, something about her told him she was a Briton.

As no one else appeared to be present and no danger threatened, he strode over to her. 'Were you looking for my wife, lady?'

She raised blue eyes to his, and he drew in a sharp breath. '*Rufilia?* Is it really—'

'Shh.' She shook her head and darted another suspicious glance around the room. 'My name is Felicia. Is there somewhere we can speak in private?'

He frowned at her, but nodded when he noticed the proprietor sending them curious looks from the doorway. 'My room. Please follow me.'

At his knock and murmured reassurance, Gisel opened the door, and he ushered the woman inside and barred it once more. When he turned to her, she had removed the *palla*, revealing thick hair that had once been as golden as his own but was now threaded with grey. It was tied up with woollen bands in the Roman fashion, with untidy wisps sticking out in places. But it was her gaze that held his attention. He'd recognise those eyes anywhere. She was staring at him as if she beheld a spectre, and shook her head in amazement.

'You're Durobelinos, aren't you? Not Commios or Caratius? How . . .? I mean . . . they took you, and you were so small, and I thought . . .' She appeared lost for words, and Duro did the only thing he could think of – he pulled her into his arms for a fierce hug.

'Yes, I'm Duro. I've but recently returned to these shores. It's a long story, but by all the gods, am I glad to see you, Rufilia!' There was a lump in his throat that he had to swallow down, and when he glanced over the top of his sister's head, he saw tears gliding silently down Gisel's cheeks. At the same time, she was smiling.

'I can hardly believe it,' Rufilia whispered. When he let her go, she stared up at him with misty eyes. 'I go by the name Felicia here, so please call me that for now. There are a few people who know my real name, but when I heard that a stranger had been asking for me, I had to come and see who it could be. The name Ivonerca intrigued me. I thought perhaps Commios, but . . .'

Duro shook his head. 'He had no idea where you might be. In fact, he believed you were dead. I was the only one still alive who knew what had become of you, and I've not set foot in Britannia these past nineteen years.' He put a hand on his sister's shoulder and turned her slightly. 'Before we speak further, may I introduce to you my wife, Gisel?' They'd said they would wait to make it official, but in his mind, she was already his spouse. 'She only pretended to be called Ivonerca because I knew you'd recognise the name.'

Gisel gave Rufilia a wide smile and took her hands. 'I can't tell you how pleased I am to meet you. Duro has told me so much about you.'

'Oh! Well, I'm very happy to meet you too. Duro has done well for himself, I see.'

'Haven't I just? I'm a very lucky man,' he agreed with a grin. 'And I have Gisel to thank for spreading the rumour that we were looking for you. She's a treasure, and no mistake.'

Gisel swatted him on the arm, blushing, but he pulled her in for a one-armed hug and smacked a kiss on her cheek.

'Shall we sit down? I'm sure we both have a lot to tell each other.' There was a stool in a corner of the room, which he pulled up to perch on, while the women sank down onto the bed.

'I daren't stay very long,' Rufilia warned. 'I can't risk word getting back to my master that I've been here, but I simply couldn't resist coming to see who was looking for me. We can meet up again after dark, perhaps.'

'Very well. Please fill us in. Are you . . . do you still belong to Julius Felix?'

'Yes.' When Duro swore under his breath, Rufilia raised a hand. 'It's not so bad now. He very rarely comes to see me. I believe he . . . er, finds satisfaction elsewhere, now that I'm old. And he knows that if he mistreats me, he'll have Marcus to deal with.'

'Marcus?'

A proud smile spread over her features. 'My son.'

'Oh, of course. I should have realised you might have offspring. Just the one?' Duro hadn't thought further than finding his sister. He hadn't contemplated the fact that she might have children, although he should have done.

'Yes.' She lowered her voice. 'Don't ever tell anyone, but I found ways of ridding myself of any others.' At Gisel's scandalised gasp, she hurried to add, 'It wasn't that I didn't want children, but *he* didn't deserve any more. Bad enough I had to give birth to Marcus when I was hardly more than a child myself. There was no way I'd be bringing any more into the world so long as Julius Felix was the father.'

'Understandable,' Duro said, and Gisel nodded. 'So he's seen, what – seventeen, eighteen winters, my nephew?'

'Eighteen,' Rufilia confirmed. 'Julius wanted him to follow in his footsteps and become a legionary, but he refused. He's working as a blacksmith's apprentice at the fort, but he lives with me. It's hard work that's given him plenty of strength, and these days he's able to protect me from Julius's attentions. It's a relief, I can tell you!'

'I'm glad.' It was bad enough having to imagine a very young Rufilia in Julius Felix's clutches, forced to give birth to his child when she was barely fifteen. Bile rose in Duro's throat, and he swore that vengeance would be forthcoming, one way or another.

'Anyway, your turn,' Rufilia said. 'Where on earth have you been?'

Duro gave her a short summary of his years abroad. 'I can tell you more later. For now, I'd better escort you home.' When she opened her mouth to protest, he added, 'I'll hang back. No one will know we're together. I merely need to know where you live so that I can find you again.'

'Right. Good thinking.' Rufilia frowned. 'Did you come here expressly to search for me?'

'No, I hardly dared to hope that you were still alive, and finding you has been a bonus. Mainly I came for vengeance. You and I both know what Julius Felix did, and I made a vow to the gods that day that he would suffer for it. I'm here to see that justice is done. It has to be in secret, though, so please don't tell anyone you've seen us.'

Rufilia's face had gone pale, but her hands clenched in her lap. 'Anything I can do to help, just let me know. I've dreamed of this for years. And Marcus will assist us too. There's no love lost between him and his father. He loathes the man.'

'Good. We'll be aided by Caratius as well.'

'Our little brother? You brought him?' At Rufilia's cry of surprise, he smiled.

'No. He's a cavalryman in the Legio Secunda. Would you believe he's lived here near you for years? And neither of you knew. I'll bring him to see you this evening.'

'Well I never!'

He followed her back to her dwelling, a ramshackle little house that had to be very cold in winter, and told her he'd bring Gisel and Caratius after dark.

'I can't wait!'

Duro couldn't either. Virtually the whole family together again, with the addition of Gisel. It was almost too good to be true.

It was nearly fully dark when Gisel followed Duro to his sister's house. She stayed close to him, scanning their surroundings. There were still people out and about, and some of them appeared sinister to her. In truth, they were probably merely inebriated, but she was feeling anxious and jittery, and the slightest sound spooked her. When Duro took her hand in his and plaited their fingers together, she didn't resist. She needed the reassurance. With everyone found, this quest was becoming real and terrifying. There was the distinct possibility that blood would be spilled, and she very much hoped it wouldn't be his. Nor that of his relatives.

Caratius was lurking near the baths, waiting for them. After a startled look at Gisel, he fell in on her other side, but neither man spoke for now. The town wasn't large, and it didn't take long before they were knocking on a sturdy door.

'Who is it?' came a woman's voice from inside.

'Your brothers,' Duro whispered. He ducked inside as soon as the bar was lifted. Gisel and Caratius followed, and Rufilia shut the door behind them.

There was but the one room, with a hearth in the centre that had a cauldron suspended above it on a tripod. The house had an earthen floor, but it was well swept and clean, as were the sparse pieces of furniture dotted around the walls. A bed, a table, a couple of stools and a bench, the latter items having been arranged around the hearth in a semicircle. A young man had been sitting on one of the stools, and he stood up as soon as they entered. He studied the visitors with a serious expression, as if trying to see whether they were a threat. He had the same golden hair as Duro and his brother, but his eyes were darker, as was his complexion. Although a youth still, he had broad shoulders and clearly developed muscles, presumably from his work as a blacksmith.

'This is Marcus, my son,' Rufilia said, then gestured to the others for his benefit. 'Your uncles, my older brother, Duro, and my youngest one, Caratius. Oh, and Duro's wife, Gisel.'

Rufilia took a moment to look Caratius over, then went forward to give him a long hug. 'I never thought I'd see you again, little one,' she whispered hoarsely. 'Well, neither of you, to be honest. Yet here you are. I can scarce believe it!'

He hugged her back, then held her at arm's length with a

quizzical smile. 'Me neither, but "little one"? Perhaps when standing next to our big brother, but I'll have you know I'm one of the tallest men in my unit.'

That made her laugh, and Gisel saw Marcus's mouth twitch as well. The banter served to break the ice to some degree, and the tension in the room lessened noticeably.

'Please, sit down, all of you.' Rufilia indicated the bench and stools. 'I've made some honey cakes, and Marcus will serve you beer.'

The young man nodded and busied himself with finding beakers for them all, filling them with beer from a pitcher. The whole time he was casting them surreptitious glances, as if he didn't quite trust them.

'You can relax, nephew,' Duro told him with a smile. 'We're not here to harm your mother, nor take her away unless she wishes it. Our purpose in coming here was twofold – to ascertain whether she was still alive and well, and to take our vengeance on your father. I gather you've no objection to that?'

'None.' Marcus made a face. 'He's scum, and the world would be well rid of him.'

'Yes, that's what we're hoping to accomplish. If you'd like to lend us assistance, we'd be most grateful, but if you'd rather not be involved, we'll understand.'

'Believe me, I'll do anything to achieve that. I've been hoping for years he'd be killed in a skirmish, but he's too much of a coward and always sends the newer troops in first. Doesn't ever get a scratch on him.' Marcus handed out the beakers, while Rufilia passed around a plate of cakes. 'And the way he's treated Mother over the years . . .' The youth shook his head, eyes dark with fury as his grievances came pouring out. 'He could have married her and made her a freedwoman as soon as he became a centurion. They're allowed to have an official wife, unlike the other ranks. We could have lived comfortably in his quarters at the barracks, but no, he preferred to hide us away in this hovel. It's not as though he's short of coin either. Centurions earn about sixty times more than ordinary legionaries. Plus he's picked up more than his fair share of loot over the years.'

Rufilia put a hand on his arm as if to restrain him from violence. 'We've not gone hungry at least,' she murmured. 'And now that you're working, we don't need him.'

'He'll get what he deserves,' Duro promised, and his steady gaze and serious tone seemed to calm his nephew more than Rufilia's words.

The latter urged everyone to help themselves to another honey cake.

'Thank you,' Gisel said. 'They're delicious.' She'd already had supper, but couldn't resist the sweet treat.

When Rufilia had sat down as well, she looked at Duro. 'Tell us what you've planned, brother.'

He was sitting very close to Gisel on the bench, and she felt him take a deep breath. 'Well, we need to find a way to lure Julius Felix out of the fort. For obvious reasons, I can't simply go in there and challenge him. Much as we might resent it, he was fully within his rights to take you as his slave after our tribe was defeated in battle. As for the rest of what he did . . . that was unnecessary, to say the least. Anyway, I need to get him alone. Although I'd like him to be held accountable for his actions in public, it's better if he simply disappears. I've been thinking, and I believe that with Marcus's help we might manage it.'

'How so?' A worried look entered Rufilia's eyes. 'I don't want my son hurt.'

'You can't stop me being part of this, Mother,' Marcus protested. 'For years I had to watch that pig abuse you until I was old enough to stop him. I want vengeance as much as my uncles here.'

His fists clenched. 'I'd have killed him myself before now if I thought I could get away with it.'

'Be that as it may,' Duro intervened, 'all I need you to do, Marcus, is to bring your father a message to lure him out of the fort. If you tell him your mother is hurt, do you reckon he'd come?'

Marcus scowled. 'I don't know. Depends, I suppose.'

'Say you tell him she's slipped down by the river and broken her leg, and that you need his help to move her. Would that work?'

'Aye, perhaps. I could point out she'd need to be put on a board to be carried, and that needs two men to handle it.'

'Wouldn't he wonder why you're asking him, of all people?' Gisel speculated out loud. 'Presumably you could have called on a friend or neighbour.'

'True.' Marcus rubbed his temples. 'But I'd need Father to pay for a bonesetter. I don't earn much beyond my board as an apprentice. I haven't the coin for such things.'

'It could work.' Duro glanced at his brother. 'What say you, Caratius?'

He shrugged. 'It's worth a try. I'm assuming the rest of us are to hide nearby and encircle him once he arrives?'

'Exactly. However, I'll challenge him to single combat. This is not to be an execution, but a just action for revenge.'

Both Marcus and Caratius protested against this, but Duro held up his hand. 'Listen! I know you both feel entitled to retribution on Rufilia's behalf, but it's doubly so for me. I'm the one who spent nineteen years as a slave of the Romans because of Julius Felix. And I'm the one who was forced to watch what he did to my mother and sister. If I fail to punish the man, by all means feel free to step in, but I really believe it's my right to have the first try.'

Gisel hooked her arm around his elbow and squeezed, giving him silent support, and he put his big hand on top of hers.

'It is my opinion we should do it the other way round,' Rufilia said.

'How do you mean?' The others all threw her puzzled looks.

'Julius Felix would be much more likely to come and help if he thought it was Marcus who was hurt. I doubt he'd believe that Marcus couldn't carry me by himself, whereas he knows very well I could never lift our son. Therefore it would be better if I go to the fort to fetch him, while Marcus pretends to have broken his leg.'

The others pondered her suggestion, then Duro nodded. 'That makes sense, but will you be safe? And are you allowed to go and seek him out there?'

'Yes. I bring his laundry every week. Most of the guards know me by sight.' Rufilia's mouth was set in a grim line, and Gisel recognised the woman's determination to protect her son at all costs.

'I'll go with her,' she said impulsively. 'If there are two of us, looking distraught, they'll be more likely to buy our story. And we can protect each other.'

Duro's eyebrows came down in a ferocious scowl. 'No! I don't want you going anywhere near the fort!'

'But you'll let your sister do so alone?' she challenged, crossing her arms over her chest.

'That's different. She's his slave woman. She has a right to be there.'

'And I could be her neighbour, lending her my support when she's distressed.'

'It could work,' Marcus put in. 'She can say she's a friend of Mother's who was there when the accident happened. If there's a stranger present, Father is more likely to be persuaded. And he'll want to appear caring towards his slave woman in front of others. He only ever mistreats her at home.'

'Over my dead body!' Duro pronounced, but Gisel shook his arm.

'I can do it,' she insisted. 'And nothing will happen to me if I'm with Rufilia.'

Duro glared first at her, then at the others. 'I don't like it. I wouldn't want any woman of mine within ten feet of the man. No offence, nephew.'

'None taken. But if there's any trouble, Mother can involve my master, the blacksmith. He's as big as a house and most men are reluctant to tangle with him. His forge is but a stone's throw away from Father's lodgings, and I can tell him beforehand to keep an eye out, just in case.'

Duro grumbled some more, but in the end it was decided that Rufilia would enter the fort with Gisel the following day, towards dusk. The stage would be set at a point further up the river, round the bend, where they weren't likely to have an audience. At that time of day, most people would be at home eating their supper and relaxing.

Their plans agreed, talk became more general, and Gisel listened in fascination as each of the siblings told their tale. When it was Caratius's turn, Rufilia asked him rather abruptly why on earth he'd signed up to serve the Romans in their army. Her hatred of them was understandable.

He shrugged. 'I'm a younger son, with no real say in matters at home in our settlement. I preferred to make my own way in the world. The Romans pay well, not to mention regularly. Two hundred and fifty *denarii* a year is not to be sniffed at. There's not much to spend it on, unless you're a gambling man, which I'm not, so I've amassed quite a nice sum already. And at the end of my service there will be a fat bonus as well as guaranteed Roman citizenship and all the privileges that apparently entails. Everyone in the legion is well fed, albeit we have to pay for our own victuals. It's not a bad life. Certainly no worse than at home.'

'But you had to sign on for what – twenty-five years?' Duro interjected. 'And you're so far from your tribe.'

'Yes, that's true.' Caratius smiled. 'It would be stupid of them to station us Britons anywhere near our kin, wouldn't it? That's asking for trouble. I'm happy with my lot and I don't regret it. Fighting is what I do best, and I'm a skilled horseman.'

'What about all the other backbreaking tasks they have you do? Building work and such?'

'I'm excused from most of them as I'm a skilled leatherworker and my services in that regard are needed more.' Caratius gave Duro a playful shove. 'I'm not as stupid as you think, brother. Why would I exchange one life of hard labour for another? No, toiling in the fields all day every day wasn't for me. Especially not with Commios ruling the roost. He's not the easiest man to get along with, it has to be said.'

Duro laughed at that. 'Ah, so it's not just me he likes to order around?'

Caratius rolled his eyes. 'Our brother is very fond of his own consequence.' He grinned. 'I would imagine your reappearance has put his nose firmly out of joint. He used to tell me he had every right to be chieftain because he was older than me, and I wasn't to quibble about it. I wonder if he'll apply that advice to himself, now you're back.'

'Doubtful, from what I've seen so far.' Duro chuckled. 'But I'll deal with him later. First we have more pressing matters to attend to.'

Gisel couldn't help a shiver of apprehension from slithering through her, and she hugged Duro's arm tight. He bent down to kiss her cheek and whispered, 'Fear not, little wife-to-be. You won't be rid of me so easily.'

She hoped to all the gods he was right.

Chapter Twenty

Near Bath, June, present day

A warm, muscular arm was slung around her middle, holding her against a hard chest. The steady thumping of someone's heart behind her was soothing, reassuring, and she snuggled against it. She had never felt so at peace, yet at the same time, a frisson of foreboding shot through her. The man behind her – the one she loved – was in danger. Not right this minute, but it was coming. Evil was near. And she needed to protect him, to keep him safe, but how?

Mackenna jerked awake and blinked against the sharp rays of the afternoon sun. She'd fallen asleep on a sunlounger next to the pool – a rookie mistake. Thank goodness she'd slathered on suncream before lying down. And she had tethered Fred and Bagel under a parasol with a huge bowl of water next to them. When she glanced over, they were both dozing as well. Little Bagel was snuggled up to his older companion, and Fred appeared to have accepted him at last. The two of them had actually played earlier, Fred good-naturedly allowing Bagel to chew on his ears and generally make a nuisance of himself. It was very sweet, but seeing them sleeping together was even better.

She'd had to keep them on a leash so that Fred wouldn't

rush over to 'help' the archaeologists, who had turned up that morning. Their presence made her feel vaguely uneasy, but she couldn't understand why. She loved history and often watched archaeology programmes on TV, so she ought to be excited about the skeleton in Jonah's back garden. And yet she wasn't. It was as if its mere presence threatened them somehow, which was ridiculous.

'I need to get a grip,' she muttered. It wasn't even her house. Whatever was found here had nothing to do with her.

Still, she couldn't shake the niggle of apprehension that lingered from the dream. Something wasn't right. But what?

Jonah wandered outside late afternoon and found Mackenna talking to the head archaeologist, Roderick, or Rod as he'd told them to call him. He was a slightly scruffy-looking guy, but handsome in the way Blue was – all sharp cheekbones, pretty eyes and long hair tied into a man bun. Jonah had disliked him on sight, even though he'd been nothing but friendly and professional when they'd first met the previous day. He didn't like the way he surreptitiously checked out Mac's legs and curves. She'd covered her bikini with cut-off jeans shorts and a T-shirt, but there was still a lot of sun-kissed skin on display. And there was no denying she'd look beautiful even wearing a dirty sack. No wonder the guy couldn't keep his eyes from straying.

Unclenching his fists, Jonah took a deep breath and bent to greet Fred and Bagel first. They seemed pleased to see him, and he gathered they were fed up with being contained.

'You can have a run soon,' he murmured to them, while scratching their soft ears. They might look like little meatballs on legs, but they were growing on him. The more he thought about it, the more he was determined to keep them. His mother never paid them much attention anyway, and his sister had stated categorically that she didn't want them when he'd texted her earlier. So why shouldn't they stay here? It would be best for everyone.

'Did you hear the exciting news, Jonah?' Mac was asking.

He stood up and brushed dog hairs off his hands. 'No, what's happened?'

'The skeleton is that of a Roman,' Rod told him. 'And he was buried with some valuable artefacts. There's a multitude of coins – both gold and silver, as well as some that might be brass or copper – and a belt buckle and a dagger. All in pretty good condition.'

'That's cool.' He meant it, although he hoped this didn't mean there were more dead people buried in his garden. Briefly he considered showing Rod the gold coin Mac had found the other day, but for some reason he didn't want to part with it yet. He hoped she hadn't mentioned it either. Instead, he asked, 'So is it a formal grave, then, part of a Roman cemetery?'

Rod shook his head. 'No, I don't think so. Geophys haven't found anything else nearby and the burial is unusual.'

'In what way?' Jonah glanced at Mac and didn't like the way she was hanging on the man's every word, her aqua eyes shining with excitement. He wanted her to look at *him* that way, not this stranger. He ground his molars together and tried to get a grip. She wasn't his and he had no right to be jealous.

'We think the man might have been murdered. He was buried face-down, as if someone had just thrown him into the grave, and his possessions were chucked in after him. The coins were underneath him, presumably having been in a pouch or something, but the belt buckle and dagger were on top of his back. That's not where they should have been in a regular burial. We can't see any marks on him, like a blow to the head or something, but he could have had his throat slit or died of a stab wound.'

Mac made a little sound and turned pale. Rod held up his

hands. 'Sorry, sorry, I get a bit carried away. Didn't mean to give you the gory details.'

'No, it's fine.' She swallowed hard, but still looked distressed. Jonah took this opportunity to grab her hand and twine his fingers with hers, a move that made her blink at him in surprise. She didn't pull away, though, and he squeezed her hand as if in reassurance. The fact that he was claiming her like some sort of caveman, and that Rod was frowning, was something he ignored.

'Any idea as to why?' he asked calmly.

'No, but anti-Roman sentiment ran high sometimes. If this man was killed during the early years of the conquest, he could have just been caught unawares by some locals who resented his presence. Other such murder victims have been found – two in Kent that I know of – but we'll never know for sure.'

'Well, I'm glad you don't think there are any more hidden surprises here,' Jonah said. 'Fred likes to dig, and I'd rather not be brought human bones every day.'

Rod chuckled at that. 'No, I'm pretty sure you're safe. We've surveyed the entire garden and there's nothing unusual, except maybe an old well and possibly the remains of a Victorian ice house.'

'Ice house? Awesome. I'll have to dig that out.' It sounded much more appealing than a grave.

'You do that.' Rod threw one last longing look in Mac's direction – or at least that was how Jonah interpreted it – and scowled briefly at their joined hands. 'I'd better get going. We'll come back tomorrow to do a final check, but we've taken everything away for now. We'll be in touch about the value of the items found, as you're entitled to claim half of it.'

'OK, thanks.'

Jonah didn't let go of Mac's hand until Rod was out of sight, and even then he was reluctant to. Pretending to focus on the dogs, he forced himself to pull away from her. 'Should we let these guys run around for a bit before dinner?'

'You take them, and I'll get started on the cooking.' Mac was gathering up her book, sunglasses and other paraphernalia, and didn't look his way.

'Maybe we should just get takeaway? Fish and chips? I feel bad about you cooking for me all the time.' He hadn't brought her here to be his kitchen slave.

She turned to smile at him. 'It's fine. I enjoy it, honestly. If I get bored with it, I'll let you know. Fish with white wine sauce sound good?'

'Absolutely!' In fact he'd probably eat anything she put in front of him, as long as she didn't leave.

He had it bad.

'I'll need to pop over to Caerleon tomorrow to see Owen. Fancy coming along?'

Jonah was leaning back in his chair, one hand absently rubbing his flat stomach as if he'd eaten too much but was supremely satisfied anyway. Mac tried her best not to stare when his movements made his shirt ride up to show a sliver of toned abs, but it was difficult to tear her gaze away. She wanted to see more.

'Caerleon? Is that where he lives?'

Mac didn't know much about Owen, as he was a quiet guy except for when he was drunk. He'd taken full advantage of the rock-star lifestyle and the women who went with it, but to her he had always been distantly polite. She wasn't sure if that was because he didn't like her, hadn't approved of girlfriends going on tour with the band, or didn't want to annoy Blue by interacting with her. Either way, he'd kept out of her way for the most part.

'Yes. Well, just upriver from there. He's got this awesome guitar that he's decided to sell, and he gave me first dibs. We could take the Harley. The weather is supposed to be good, so it'll be a nice day for a ride. And you'll get to meet his girlfriend. He tells me she's moved in with him.' Jonah shook his head with an amused smirk. 'Never thought I'd see the day he'd settle down, but he didn't hang around. They only just met a couple of months ago and he kept her a secret even from us, the sneaky bastard.'

'Um, sure, that would be nice.' Mac loved motorcycles, and a bike ride with Jonah sounded perfect. She wasn't as excited about seeing Owen again, though. He might resent her for breaking up the band, as she'd gathered she was sort of the catalyst for Jonah's decision to leave even if he said she wasn't to blame. Another thought struck her. 'What about the dogs?'

'I can ask Mrs Llewellyn, the cleaning lady, to come and stay with them for the day. She's usually happy to do whatever extra things I need help with. What do you say?'

'OK, why not?'

'Great, I'll go and call her now.'

They set out at around eleven the following morning, Mac dressed in a black leather outfit consisting of trousers, jacket and gloves. Jonah had produced it without explaining who it belonged to, and she thought it best not to ask. It was practical and would keep her warm, as well as being safer if there was an accident. The helmet she'd brought was also black, as was Jonah's entire get-up, and the Harley-Davidson he wheeled out of the garage was black and chrome.

'We look very heavy metal,' she joked as she climbed on behind him and settled her booted feet on the foot rests.

Jonah laughed. 'Yes, I should buy you some turquoise leathers instead. It would match your eyes and look great with your hair.'

Mac felt her cheeks heat up and was grateful for the visor that hid her blush from view. She knew Jonah liked her hair, but she hadn't realised that he had noticed her eye colour. His own baby blues twinkled at her as he sent her a glance over his shoulder before lowering his own visor.

'Ready?'

She nodded, and they were off. Sitting behind Jonah on the comfortable pillion seat of the Harley-Davidson was pure bliss. The big bike purred and rumbled underneath them, and it was like floating along the roads. Mac held on to Jonah's waist, lightly at first, until he increased the speed, taking the corners at a precarious angle. Then she wound her arms tightly across his stomach and leaned her chin on his right shoulder. He drove fast, but not recklessly so, and she had every confidence in him. She trusted him not to do anything stupid or show off, the way Blue had sometimes done when they'd been out for a drive in one of his many sports cars.

They took the smaller roads through Wiltshire and up to the M4 motorway, then headed west past Bristol and across the Prince of Wales Bridge. A couple of junctions later, Jonah turned off onto a smaller B road towards Caerleon. They entered the town from the south across a bridge that spanned the River Usk. The view was familiar somehow, although Mac had never been here before. Something about the curve of the river stirred images at the back of her mind. Fleeting memories of mud, grunts and the clash of steel . . . She shook her head. That *Gladiator* film had messed with her head, or maybe she'd watched too many YouTube videos about Romans lately. After the find in Jonah's garden, she had wanted to learn more about them.

Navigating the winding high street, they carried on through to the other side of town, where they turned right to continue on smaller roads. After a while, they took another right, looping back towards the river. Jonah seemed to know where he was going and stopped by a pair of old gates between gateposts topped with stone eagles. There was a modern intercom button set into one of them, and he pressed it. When the gates glided apart, they sped through them and down a long winding drive that ended in a circle outside a small manor house. It was built of some sort of local grey stone and covered in honeysuckle, wisteria and Virginia creeper.

'Oh, this is lovely!' Mac exclaimed, climbing off the bike and pushing up her visor to get a better look.

Jonah narrowed his eyes at her as he hoisted the Harley onto its kickstand. 'You like this better than my house?' He seemed so offended, it made her laugh and punch him lightly on the shoulder.

'No, of course not. Yours is absolutely perfect, but this is nice too, don't you think?'

'I suppose so,' he muttered, pulling his helmet off and taking hers to hang on the handlebars.

The front door creaked open and Owen came out, followed by a girl with caramel-coloured hair. 'You made it. New bike? Nice.' He tipped his chin at Mac. 'Hey. Good to see you.'

She wasn't sure he meant it, but answered with a smile. 'You too.'

Owen gestured to his girlfriend. 'This is Helle. Helle – you know Jonah, and this is Mackenna.'

'Lovely to meet you! I've heard a lot about you, Mackenna.'

'Just Mac is fine,' she answered in Swedish. She'd detected a strong Danish accent the moment Helle opened her mouth, and her name was a bit of a giveaway in any case. Owen had pronounced it correctly: Hel-leh.

Helle's eyes opened wide. 'Oh, you're Swedish? Excellent! There aren't many fellow Scandinavians around here. Come inside, please. You must be ready for a drink and some lunch.'

'Sounds perfect, thank you.' Mac smiled and followed her into the house.

Their conversation had taken place in Swedish and Danish, Helle kindly speaking slowly so that Mac would understand. She obviously knew that some Swedes found it harder to follow Danish than vice versa. When she looked back, Mac saw Jonah and Owen exchange a puzzled glance, then grin at each other.

The four of them went through to the back of the house and out onto a patio. 'Hope you're hungry,' Owen said. 'Helle's been preparing all sorts of goodies. No idea what, as most of them have unpronounceable names. All tastes great, though.'

'I could definitely eat.' Jonah ushered Mac towards a table set for lunch under a large parasol. The feel of his warm hand on her back made a shiver snake through her, but she tried not to let on that she was so affected by such a small touch.

'When can't you?' she shot back jokingly.

'Hey, it's not my fault you're a fab cook,' he protested with a smile, while holding out a chair for her like a gentleman. It struck her that Blue had never done anything so considerate, whereas Jonah was always attentive. How had she not noticed that?

They helped themselves to the delicious spread, which included home-made bread, pâté, quiche and several salads, as well as cold meats. Conversation was lively, and Mac found herself liking Helle immensely. It wasn't just that they were both Scandinavians – or half of one in her case – but the other girl was easy to talk to, very down-to-earth and with no airs and graces. Some women might become stuck up when dating a famous rock star, but Helle treated Owen as if he was a regular guy, nothing special. Mac could see that the pair were deeply in love. Owen was more talkative than she'd ever seen him, and happiness radiated from him. It was great to observe and she was pleased for him.

The fact that she was jealous of the couple was something she buried deep inside.

* * *

'You should do some sightseeing while you're here,' Helle said, when they were all stuffed and enjoying coffee and cake. 'Caerleon has a couple of Roman museums and an amphitheatre that's well worth seeing. And the remnants of a fort.'

Jonah shivered. Was it just him, or were they stumbling on a lot of references to Roman stuff lately? 'That's weird. We just found a Roman skeleton in my garden.'

'A what? When? You didn't tell me that!' Owen punched him on the shoulder. 'I would have come over to have a look.'

'Really? It's not that exciting, man. Just some guy who got himself murdered by the locals, probably.' Although there was nothing 'probable' about it – somehow he was sure it was true. He felt it in his own bones.

Last night he'd had a very vivid dream about fighting with a corpulent Roman, one who'd been hell-bent on raping Mac. It had made him so furious he'd seen red and stuck a long dagger into the man's chest. In the dream, he'd known exactly where to place the blade in order to pierce the heart, as if he was an expert in killing, then he'd watched with satisfaction as the bastard crumpled to the ground, his eyes rolling up into his head. It had been both exhilarating and terrifying at the same time.

'Still, would have been exciting to watch the excavation,' Owen was saying. 'I take it you didn't get to be part of that?'

'No, a local archaeology team came to do it and we weren't allowed to help. They're finished now. I'll let you know if they allow us to look at the finds. You could come along.'

'That would be great. I love old stuff!'

Jonah wasn't surprised. Owen had been studying archaeology when Valhalla Storm was first formed, but he'd left his studies after his first year at uni, when the band were lucky enough to find almost instant success. Maybe now he'd go back to it.

He turned to Mac. 'Want to stop in town then and have a quick look around before we head home?'

It wasn't until the words were out of his mouth that he realised what he'd said. 'Home', as if Mac belonged there with him. He saw Owen glance at him with his eyebrows raised, but pretended not to notice. There was unfortunately nothing going on between him and Mac, although he was hoping there would be one day. Perhaps it was time to test the waters. Had he been too cautious?

She nodded enthusiastically. 'Yes, please, I'd love that!' She turned to their hosts. 'And thank you so much for this amazing lunch. The poor Harley will be groaning on the way back.'

Helle said something to her in Danish, and the two women exchanged phone numbers. Jonah was pleased they'd hit it off, although he didn't yet dare to hope it meant Mac wanted to stick around with him and his friends. She might just be lonely and in need of female company.

'Right, well, we'd better go then. Mac, are you sure you're OK riding with the guitar on your back?' When he had suggested the outing, he'd forgotten its original purpose – for him to buy the guitar Owen had picked up at auction. Now Mac had to wear it slung across her back, unless he came to fetch it another time. 'Or I could come back for it?'

'No, no, it's fine. Let's go.'

They parked in the car park outside one of the museums in the high street, and Jonah took the guitar and slung it across his own back. 'I'll carry it for now,' he told Mac, and she was relieved. It was fine while she was sitting still on the bike, but it would get heavy if she had to cart it around.

She had more pressing concerns, though. The moment they'd entered the town, she'd again had the impression she had been here before, but that was impossible. She was sure she'd never gone further west than Bristol. Yet her head buzzed with long-forgotten memories, fleeting images that flickered in and out of her mind. Nothing tangible, and not a single one fully formed, but teasing and tantalising, as if they wanted to surface but didn't know how. Or were waiting for the right moment. It was unsettling and, quite frankly, a bit worrying. She tried to tell herself her imagination was just running away with her. Caerleon was clearly an old place, and it gave off a certain vibe. She'd been too caught up with Roman stuff recently, so her brain was playing tricks on her.

Jonah insisted they immerse themselves in all the town's Roman experiences, starting with the Fortress Baths museum. There was a simulation of the former swimming pool, or *natatio*, as it was apparently called, which was interesting. They goofed around with a Roman helmet that was available for visitors to try on, and took photos of each other wearing it. With big red plumes on top, it made Jonah look regal, while Mac more or less disappeared inside it. For some reason, though, it seemed totally wrong on him – almost like sacrilege – and she wanted to rip it off him. She had a brief vision of him wearing a clunky bronze helmet instead, his long golden hair sticking out around the rim, but it was gone in an instant. It made her frown, but as her face was covered by the rim of the helmet she had on, Jonah didn't notice.

'I think you need a smaller size, babe,' he chuckled. 'I can barely see your eyes, and that's a shame.'

Was he flirting with her? She threw him a furtive glance as she put the heavy helmet back on its stand. He appeared not to notice that he'd called her 'babe' again and complimented her eyes. Again. She followed him to look at the other exhibits, and he absently took her hand in his to tug her along. Perhaps it was just his way of being friendly.

There was another museum further up the street, and they had a quick look around in there as well. While gazing at some of the exhibits, Mac had that strange sense of déjà vu again, as if she'd handled the items personally and knew exactly what they were for. *There's a strigil. I had my skin scraped with that. And look at that glass vial full of oil. It smelled divine, like lavender and something else, when massaged into my skin* . . . She shook it off. Her mind was merely playing tricks on her, using the information she'd gleaned at the Bath museum. But she was pleased to escape from the place and back out into the late-afternoon sunlight.

'The amphitheatre is this way,' Jonah commented, pointing at the signs. They exchanged glances and grinned at each other as if they were on some grand adventure. Happiness bubbled up inside Mac. He hadn't let go of her hand the whole time, and had interwoven his fingers with hers. It felt so right, she didn't want to pull away. When his grip tightened, a swarm of butterflies danced in her stomach. He was acting like they were a couple. Was he aware of what he was doing? She wished she knew, but he didn't say anything.

He led the way along a narrow street, past old houses and high stone walls, until they came to an open space on one side and turf walls on the other. The turf turned out to be covering an impressive oval stone structure, and walking in between two mounds they emerged into the former amphitheatre arena.

'Wow, this is a lot bigger than I thought.' Jonah swept the place with his gaze and Mac followed suit. 'Imagine being a gladiator here, fighting while an audience of thousands cheer you on.'

'Great if you win. Not so much when they're calling for your blood,' she commented drily. 'Remember how that film ended.' She shuddered. Poor Russell Crowe – or Maximus, as he'd been called in the movie.

'Don't diss my fantasies.' He shoulder-checked her playfully, then turned serious as he contemplated the arena once more, swivelling round to take it all in. 'Actually, I dreamed about being a gladiator after watching that film, and I won. It was amazing. The adoration of the crowd felt just like being on stage at a rock concert. Total adrenaline rush.'

He fell silent, clearly remembering that sensation as his gaze became unfocused. He'd moved to stand right in front of her, and she had to look up to see his expression, which was unusually tense and sort of faraway, even though he was looking right at her now. It was as if he was there in body but not in spirit. Eerie. Mackenna shivered. The sounds of cars passing on the street outside and voices from the nearby park faded, and she began to feel light-headed. As she stared back at Jonah, something passed between them, like an electric current, and his handsome face seemed to shimmer in the sunlight. Those piercing blue eyes became more intense, and for a moment she thought his golden hair was long again, waving in the breeze. She blinked in confusion.

Was she having more hallucinations?

He put up a hand to cup her cheek and murmured something that sounded like 'Gisel, *amata mea . . .*'

Because his words sounded similar to both Spanish and French, she had no trouble understanding them, even though they weren't in either language. They were familiar too, as if she'd heard him say the same thing many times before. But how could that be? Before she had a chance to react, he'd dipped his head to cover her lips with his own. His mouth was soft and tentative, the stubble surrounding it adding a rougher touch. At first, she was so surprised she just stood there and let him kiss her, neither pushing him away nor reciprocating. Then she started to kiss him back, their lips moving in perfect sync. His mouth on hers was so familiar, so welcome, but at the same time not. It was like inhabiting two different bodies at the same time, and her mind recoiled at that thought, jolting her out of her trance. Then the first word he'd said registered, and she wrenched away, frowning up at him.

'Who's Gisel?' Her brain had grasped the fact that it was a female name, although not one she'd heard previously, but it wasn't hers. And he'd called this Gisel 'my love'. Was he spending time with Mackenna while pining for some other woman?

'What?' He stared down at her, his expression thoroughly puzzled as his eyes focused on her with some difficulty. What was wrong with him?

'You called me Gisel just now.' *And then you kissed me.* But she didn't add that, because he must know what he'd done.

'I did? Shit, sorry. I . . . I don't know what the hell just happened.' He ran a hand through his hair and looked up at the sky, as though he'd find the answers there. He shook his head. 'I must have been out in the sun for too long. Honestly, I don't know what that was, and I've never met anyone called Gisel. Did I really say that?'

'You did. It sounds kind of German. Maybe someone you met in Europe?'

'Doesn't ring a bell.' He put his hands on her shoulders and peered at her. 'Are you OK?'

'Yes, I'm fine.' But she wasn't, not really. Jonah had kissed her thinking she was someone else. That was very far from OK, because she desperately wanted him to do it to her, Mackenna. She couldn't say that, though. It would be too embarrassing for words.

He opened his mouth as if he was going to try to explain more, but then closed it and shook his head again. 'Seriously, I'm sorry. I didn't mean to just pounce on you like that. I should have . . . No, never mind. Let's go see the fort, then we'd better get back to the dogs.'

He turned away and walked towards one of the openings between what had once been seating areas.

Mac stood frozen in place for a moment, then hurried after him. She didn't know what to think, her emotions tumbling all over themselves inside her chest. Was that all he had to say on the subject? What was going on? And why had she felt so strange. Like she'd had some sort of out-of-body experience. Perhaps it had been the same for him. Were they possessed? If there even was such a thing. No, that was impossible.

So many questions, and no answers.

She clenched her fists as she strode after him. They'd have to talk about it later, because something weird was going on and she wanted to get to the bottom of it. And if he wasn't willing to discuss this, it was probably time for her to go home. Surely the journalists must have tired of hanging around her place by now.

And perhaps she had outstayed her welcome.

Chapter Twenty-One

Isca, south-west Britannia, June AD 80

Entering the fort proved a little more difficult than predicted, as none of the guards on duty were men who knew Rufilia. The two women had checked all four gates without any luck.

'Never mind, we'll just have to do it the hard way,' Rufilia muttered, and marched up to the nearest one. 'Oh please, let us through! I must see my master urgently. There's been an accident! Our son . . . his leg is broken. The gods help me! My poor boy!'

Her acting skills were impressive, and she managed to produce real tears to accompany her loud wailing. Gisel hovered behind her, keeping her expression grim and full of fake concern, and watched as the guards by the gate exchanged shrugs. Two women were not a threat to the fort. They would have no reason not to let them in if it was an emergency.

'Who is it you're seeking?' one of them asked.

'Aulus Julius Felix, my master and the father of my son. Please, there's no time to lose. The boy is in absolute agony!'

Rufilia was wringing her hands and dabbing her eyes with the corner of her *palla*. Gisel was wearing her Britannic clothing, but had made sure to tie her plaits up with *vittae*, the woollen bands

Duro's sister used for her hair. He had told her that her blonde tresses were much too pretty and made her stand out; this way they were covered in dull-coloured cloth.

'Try not to look at anyone or they'll be enthralled by your eyes,' he had added. Gisel had never thought her eyes extraordinary in any way and suspected he was merely biased and worrying for nothing, but she had promised to do as he asked.

'Felix? Then by all means hurry,' the guard said. The name of the hated centurion appeared to have more effect than the words of a distraught mother.

'Thank you. Thank you so much.'

As they rushed inside, Gisel followed close behind Rufilia, who appeared to know where she was going. 'It's easy to find your way around, as every fort is laid out more or less the same way,' she whispered.

Gisel glanced around apprehensively. It seemed to her that there were Roman legionaries everywhere, some patrolling the walkways along the outer walls, others standing vigilant in the watchtowers. A few of them were accompanied by ferocious guard dogs, who barked intermittently. Rufilia glanced their way and shuddered.

'Molossian hounds,' she muttered. 'You don't want to go anywhere near them, trust me.'

Gisel had no intention of doing so if she could help it, as they were large, heavily muscled beasts with jaws that looked as though they could snap a person's arm off in one bite.

They hurried along what appeared to be a main street that ran in a straight line between two of the gates. The workshops they passed were hives of activity, and there were also men scurrying from one end of the fort to the other, all intent on whatever task they'd been assigned. A few sent the two women curious looks, but most strode past without a glance.

'See that workshop at the end? That's where Marcus works with the master blacksmith, Vassinus.' Rufilia pointed to a building whose double doors were thrown open. The noise of a hammer on a metal anvil came from inside, and a glowing hearth could be glimpsed in the background. An enormous man wearing a leather apron raised a hand in acknowledgement, and the women nodded a greeting.

'Marcus warned him we were coming,' Rufilia said. 'He'll listen out for any trouble. Not that I think he can hear much over the din he's making, but still . . .'

There was row upon row of barrack blocks; long, low whitewashed buildings.

'The centurions' quarters are at one end of each block,' Rufilia continued. 'Julius Felix doesn't have to share his accommodation with anyone, which is lucky for us, as we'll hopefully catch him alone.'

As it turned out, they were not that fortunate. His door stood open, and when they peeked inside, they could see him sitting at a low table playing a board game with three other men. All four were dressed in off-duty clothing: thigh-length short-sleeved tunics that might once have been white but were now an indistinct grey colour. These were cinched at the waist with a military belt – a *cingulum*. When going into battle, the men would wear body armour covering their chests. Gisel had been told this was called *lorica segmentata*, and it consisted of strips of overlapping metal on top of leather straps held together with hinges, giving good protection from blows to the upper body. It wasn't necessary for everyday tasks, so none of them wore it at the moment. Neither did they have on the heavy metal helmets they'd wear when heading off for a skirmish. They were, however, all armed with a dagger and a sword, while a couple of javelins and four shields were leaning against the nearest wall.

'Who are the other three men?' Gisel murmured as they took in the scene before them. 'They weren't part of the plan. Should we go back and wait for another opportunity?' She wasn't sure if Duro would be able to carry out his challenge with three of Julius Felix's comrades present. They'd be certain to report the matter to the authorities.

Rufilia made a noise of frustration. 'Curse it! These men are Felix's closest friends. They were there helping him the day he killed my mother. If Duro recognises them, he'll want to kill them as well.'

Very likely, but he couldn't fight four men at once. Gisel swallowed hard and wondered how this would play out. Then she remembered that he wouldn't be alone – Caratius and Marcus would be present, and they'd have to fight if Felix's friends came along. There was no way she'd stand by and watch either. 'Your son and his brother will help him, and so will I,' she muttered.

'Me too. It's past time they all paid for what they did. Let us carry on.' Rufilia's eyes shone with determination as she knocked on the door frame, bursting into the room as if she'd arrived in haste.

'Felicia! What in the name of Jupiter are you doing here?' Julius Felix didn't look pleased to see her. Judging by the pile of coins next to him on the table, he was winning, and the two women had interrupted a good game.

Gisel hung back as Rufilia started up with the wailing again. In between sobs and hand-wringing, she told her tale and urged him to come and help her.

'I simply cannot move him on my own and none of the neighbours were willing to help. Well, except for Alicia here, but what use are two women? Marcus is a strapping young man, as you know. It's beyond us to lift him.'

During this impassioned speech, Gisel had had time to

surreptitiously study the man who had inspired such hatred in both Duro and his sister. He must have seen at least forty winters by now, and what was left of his hair was grizzled. His visage was lined and weathered, clean-shaven but sporting a quantity of greying stubble, and his eyes shone with malice. In his youth, he must have been tall and well built, but the years had taken their toll and he looked older than his age, with deep grooves either side of his mouth. Dark circles and bags under his eyes bore witness to a life lived in excess. An ugly puckered scar ran the length of one side of his face, giving him a sinister appearance.

His eyes narrowed as he watched Rufilia's theatrics. Gisel wasn't sure he was buying it, but there was enough doubt in his mind to make him at least consider her words. He stood up abruptly and gathered up his winnings, scooping them into a leather pouch.

'What exactly happened?' he demanded.

'Marcus came to talk to me as I was doing the washing down by the river. The blacksmith had given him leave to visit me, but after all the rain last night, the banks were slippery. One moment he was chatting away, and the next thing I knew, he was lying at the water's edge, his leg at a horrible angle.' Rufilia managed some more of her convincing crying. 'My poor boy! I didn't know what to do. He's in so much pain, and—'

'He's not a boy,' Julius Felix snapped. 'He's a man grown, and he'd better not be making a fuss.'

This callous statement was met with further sobs from Rufilia, and Gisel grabbed her arm to lend silent support while Felix rolled his eyes.

'Fine, we'll come and take a look.' He bent to pick up his swagger stick, which had been lying on the floor next to his chair, and glanced at his three companions, who had remained silent. They were of an age with him, and their demeanour was no less cruel. 'You'll all help, aye?'

'Of course,' one of them replied, smirking at Rufilia. 'Always happy to assist a *lady*.' His emphasis on the last word showed clearly that he thought her no such thing. She didn't react to this taunt, but kept her gaze firmly on her master.

The man's lascivious tone of voice made Gisel snort and throw him a disgusted glare, forgetting for a moment that she was supposed to stay in the background. She was only here to lend credence to Rufilia's story. Unfortunately, Felix noticed her reaction, and he stepped towards her, reaching out to grab her chin. Hard fingers gripped her and forced her to stare him in the face.

'Well, well, what have we here?' He smirked. 'Perhaps you should leave your little friend behind, Felicia. We could do with some entertainment on our return, and this one's a rare gem and no mistake.'

The way he devoured her with his eyes made bile rise in Gisel's throat. She realised that Duro's apprehension had been warranted. He was right – she shouldn't have come. She stepped back to free herself from his grip. 'I'm married,' she hissed. 'My husband won't take kindly to you manhandling me.'

'By the time he finds out, it will be too late,' Felix stated confidently, and a shiver of apprehension streaked through her. Duro had told her that some of the Roman soldiers acted with casual brutality towards the locals. Extortion, theft and rape were not uncommon, and most of the time they got away with it, as the authorities were on their side. She hadn't thought she'd be in danger here in the fort, surrounded by so many people, but clearly she'd been wrong. She tried to get her breathing under control while her heart began to beat uncomfortably fast.

'Or two of us could remain here to keep her company,' one of his companions suggested, reaching for her.

His leer was uncannily similar to the looks she'd received when standing naked on the slave market's auction block. Although she was fully clothed this time, it still made her feel undressed. Skin crawling, she ducked out of the way and took a step towards Rufilia, trying to hide behind her. If only she'd listened to Duro – this situation was getting out of hand.

'Leave her be!' Rufilia cried. 'There's no time for your games.'

'Not now, perhaps, but definitely later.' Felix moved faster than Gisel had thought him capable of, and in a flash he had her pinned to the wall with his hand around her throat. 'What? You thought you could escape me, did you?' He smirked and slammed her head back so hard she saw stars as it connected with wood. 'I'll be seeing you soon.' He nodded at one of his friends and shoved her towards him. 'Lock her in the back room.'

'No! You can't take someone else's wife,' Rufilia protested. 'She's a free woman, not a slave. The authorities—'

'Will turn a blind eye to anything I do, as you well know,' Felix interrupted, while his henchman caught hold of Gisel and tugged her towards a door in the back wall.

'Don't touch me!' she snarled, trying to fight him off, but it was no use. He had her arms in a vice, thus depriving her of any chance to reach for the knife at her belt. Before she knew it, she'd been shoved into the other room. The last thing she saw before the door slammed shut was Rufilia's anguished glance. In the next instant, she heard a bar drop into place, locking her in.

'Disgusting pig!' she yelled. 'My husband is going to kill the lot of you! Just you wait.'

For now, she was trapped. Her only hope was that Duro succeeded in his mission and came to find her before someone else did.

Duro waited behind a stand of trees with Caratius, impatience fizzing through his veins. Now that this day had finally arrived, he couldn't wait to get it over with. He had the rest of his life to live and wanted this shadow gone. There were better things to strive for than vengeance. Happier times hopefully ahead, with Gisel by his side. As soon as this matter had been dealt with satisfactorily.

'What's taking them so long?' he muttered, but received only a smirk from Caratius.

'You're just worried about that woman of yours. She'll be fine. There's a quiet strength to her and she won't let anyone get the better of her. Germanae women are fierce, everyone knows that. Besides, Rufilia promised to protect her. If the worst came to the worst, she'd see to it that Gisel can run away.'

'Curse you! Of course I'm worried about her. I love her!' He hadn't said it out loud to her yet, and it was perhaps unfair to tell his brother first, but he couldn't keep the words inside. He did love her, and couldn't bear to think of anything or anyone harming her.

'That's fairly obvious, brother.' Caratius laughed. 'I don't think I've ever seen any man more smitten. Are you sure she's not a magical creature of some sort? A forest sprite? She's certainly ensnared you.'

'Shut up. You have eyes in your head, but I love her for more than her looks. She's exactly the kind of woman I've always wanted for a wife.'

Caratius clapped him on the back. 'Indeed, I have seen her. And very lucky you are to have found such a treasure. Even more fortunate is that she gazes at you exactly the same way. She doesn't have eyes for anyone else. I wish you both all the happiness in the world.'

'She does? Thank you.' When Caratius only laughed again, he gave him a shove. 'Yes, yes, I know I'm being ridiculous. I just don't want to lose her before we've even begun our life together.'

'You won't. Shh, I think I hear something. Marcus! Start groaning.'

Marcus was lying in the mud near the shore, one leg twisted up beneath him. He began to groan realistically and hiss in laboured breaths. A group of people descended the steep riverbank, and Duro swore under his breath. 'Curse it! He's brought reinforcements. Now what?'

'We'll have to fight them together. Can't be helped. They're unfortunate collateral, but look, they're all much older than us. That's to our advantage.'

'Perhaps not so unfortunate after all,' Duro gritted out from between clenched teeth. 'I think I recognise them. They were there too that day! Now they can all pay for what they did.'

'Even better,' Caratius murmured.

'But hold on, where's Gisel?' An icy sensation shot through Duro and twisted his insides as he took in the group approaching the scene. His wife was nowhere in sight. 'By Teutatis, if he's harmed so much as a hair on her head, I'll . . .' His blood began to boil and his heart pumped out a fierce beat. 'I have to go and find her. *Now!*'

'No, wait! Calm down.' His brother placed a restraining hand on his arm. 'He's not had time to do anything to her. Perhaps she had the good sense to stay outside the fort after all. She'll be here soon.' He gave Duro's arm a shake. 'You can't lose focus now. There's too much at stake. Concentrate! We'll find Gisel after this is over.'

Logically Duro knew his brother was right, but suddenly revenge seemed much less important than the whereabouts of the woman he loved. Although the rational part of his brain agreed that the priority was to deal with Julius Felix, he couldn't do it while worrying about Gisel. She was his everything now.

'I can't. I'm sorry.' He gripped the sword in his hand so hard his knuckles went white, then sheathed it. 'You do it. They're your mother and sister too. I entrust this vengeance to you, brother.'

'What? But . . .' Caratius must have seen that he was deadly serious, because his expression grew grim and his mouth tightened as he nodded. 'Very well. Do what you have to.'

'Thank you.' Duro clapped his brother on the back, and was about to slip off through the trees to double back towards the fort when there was a commotion behind the approaching group of men. Someone was shouting, 'Wait!' in a loud and booming voice.

Julius Felix and his cohorts turned to stare as a man came running towards them. He was tall and built like a bull, with massive arms and shoulders and a neck as wide as his head. Behind him ran a smaller figure, and Duro felt an enormous weight drop from his own shoulders.

'Gisel!' he whispered, a grin spreading across his features. She was safe and she was here. *Thank the gods!*

'Told you,' Caratius muttered.

'I'm guessing that's the smith, by the size of him and that huge hammer he's gripping.'

'Yes indeed.'

'Vassinus? What are you doing here?' Julius Felix addressed the man, clearly perplexed. 'And why is *she* here? I thought we . . .'

Vassinus ignored the latter question and strode forward. 'I heard that my apprentice was wounded. Are you all right, boy?' he called out.

Marcus had said he trusted the master blacksmith with his life and would share their plans with him beforehand. The fact that the man was here now must mean he wanted to be part of the venture. So be it.

'Time to begin,' Duro whispered to Caratius.

Just as the group of Romans had almost reached Marcus, Duro and his brother sauntered out from behind the trees. 'Well, well, if it isn't the cowards who raped two defenceless women and killed a mother in front of her children,' Duro spat, coming to a halt not far from his nemesis. 'Julius Felix, I challenge you to single combat to avenge the death of my mother and the enslavement and rape of my sister.'

Rufilia and Gisel had retreated to a spot higher up the bank, out of reach of Julius Felix and his men, who were gaping at Duro. 'Who are you?' snapped the centurion, frowning mightily as his son jumped to his feet, his supposedly broken leg absolutely fine. 'Why you little . . .'

'Surprise, Father! May I introduce my uncles? They appear to have a bone to pick with you.' Marcus smiled, but it wasn't a nice smile. He pulled out a *spatha* from behind his back and watched as all four legionaries unsheathed their own swords.

'I'm Rufilia's – sorry, *Felicia's* – brother, the little boy you sent to Rome,' Duro confirmed. 'Remember? I swore vengeance that day, and by all the gods, I'll have it.' When Julius Felix blanched, he added, 'Didn't think I'd make it back, eh?' He shook his head. 'You should never underestimate an Iceni. Now fight me like a man, one on one, if you dare, or are you going to hide behind your friends like the coward you are?'

'Of course I dare, but you're not worth the effort.' The man glanced at his three companions. 'Let's annihilate these stupid *Brittunculi*.' He glanced at Marcus. 'Including you, you little traitor. You've never been a worthy son.'

'*Brittunculi*' was a derogatory term meaning roughly 'wretched little Britons', but Duro only smiled, as that epithet definitely didn't describe any of them. Even Marcus was taller than their opponents, although he wasn't as stocky.

The four Romans attacked as one. Legionaries were used to working in groups and formations, and it probably came naturally to them. Duro concentrated on Julius Felix, however, leaving the others for Caratius and Marcus. He didn't know how much weapons training his nephew had had, but he trusted his brother to kill at least one of their foes. Vassinus, meanwhile, held back, as if he was contemplating whether his assistance was needed.

Using his own *gladius*, Duro managed to separate Julius Felix from the other three by driving him backwards with ferocious thrusts. They were both slipping in the mud, but Duro was used to fighting in sand, which was what covered the gladiatorial arenas, and kept his balance well.

'Not so easy to fight a grown man as a small boy, is it? How does it feel to be an old man on the verge of death?' he taunted. 'I hope the gods of the afterlife punish you for all eternity.'

'Shut up,' Felix panted. His eyes were flickering wildly, as if searching for a way out of this predicament, but Duro would make sure there was none. He slashed and feinted, more or less toying with the man, inflicting small wounds here and there. If this was over too quickly, he'd feel cheated after waiting so long. He saw the moment Felix realised what he was doing, the man's eyes widening in consternation and fear. That made him smile.

A cry went up behind him, distracting him momentarily. As he glanced over his shoulder, he could see that Marcus was having trouble fighting two trained legionaries on his own. Caratius was not yet finished with his own opponent and couldn't help. Duro contemplated killing Felix swiftly. It wasn't worth sacrificing his nephew for the sake of satisfaction. But in the next instant he heard war cries in three different dialects rising into the air – one Iceni, one Treverii and one possibly Dumnoni. Rufilia and Gisel both charged down the hill, brandishing daggers, and Vassinus finally joined the fray, swinging his hammer. Duro didn't know why the man had waited so long, but perhaps he'd been reluctant to take part in a fight that wasn't really his. Gisel jumped onto one legionary's back, stabbing him wherever she could reach, while Rufilia attacked him from the front. This left Marcus with only one man, and with Vassinus at his side, the odds were more than evened out.

Duro laughed out loud. The Romans hadn't expected to have to deal with women, and their expressions of consternation were a sight to see. Presumably they'd also taken their blacksmith's allegiance for granted, but the man appeared to despise them. Felix had grabbed the opportunity to launch his own attack on Duro, but the latter turned back in time to defend himself. Their swords clashed, but he was two decades younger, strong and agile, his strikes lightning-fast and precise. He also had the advantage of years of gladiatorial combat, where he'd honed his skills to perfection fighting foes much scarier than this pathetic middle-aged man. This stood him in good stead, and he was able to continue his onslaught, backing Felix towards the river.

'Perhaps we'll shove your corpse into the water,' he mused, while parrying the weakening blows of his enemy. 'If it floats out to sea, no one will ever know what became of you. No doubt you expected a handsome memorial to be raised in your honour when you died. "To the spirit of the departed, Aulus Julius Felix, who lived forty-odd years, having died while fighting the Silures; Felicia and Marcus set this up beside his tomb." Is that roughly what you thought it would say? A shame they don't care one whit for you, isn't it? And neither does anyone else, from what I've heard. You'll die in the knowledge that you are universally disliked, old man, and your name will soon be forgotten, never to be spoken again. There will be no tomb for you, no carving to remind posterity of your existence.'

'Accursed barbarian! I'm not sorry for what I did to your mother and sister. They deserved it! Rebel bitches—'

'Shut your foul mouth!' Duro cut the words off with an unexpected punch to the side of Felix's head. It snapped back, and the man blinked as he realised he was staring certain death in the face.

Tired of playing games, Duro sank his sword between the man's fourth and fifth ribs on the left-hand side, where he knew the heart was located. 'May you be for ever cursed, and may the gods punish you even more severely. I leave it in their hands.'

Julius Felix sank to the ground, his eyes glazing over. Duro didn't waste time, but hurried across to see how the others were faring. It would be as well to get this over with as quickly as possible so that they could bury the evidence. Thankfully, they were far enough away from the *vicus* that no one would hear the fracas. Caratius had just killed his opponent, and was standing bent over with his hands on his knees, breathing heavily. Duro watched as the third man toppled over, receiving one final slash to the throat from Marcus's long sword and a cracked skull courtesy of Vassinus's hammer. At the same time, the fourth one crumpled, his eyes rolling up to show only the whites. Gisel jumped nimbly off his back and landed next to Duro, who pulled her into his arms.

'Are you hurt, my little warrior?'

She buried her face in his chest. 'No. You?'

'A few scratches, that's all.' He let out a deep sigh of relief. 'It's over. Thank the gods! But why did you arrive with the smith? You scared the life out of me! I was about to come looking for you.'

'That pig locked me in, but Vassinus was keeping watch as he'd promised. He noticed I was missing as the others left, and immediately went looking for me. I told him I could find my own way here, but he insisted on coming along.'

'I'm glad. I owe him.' Duro would speak to the man later and express his profound gratitude.

Rufilia was turning Marcus this way and that, while the youth tried to push her away. 'I'm fine, Mother. Stop fussing! It's embarrassing.'

Duro and Caratius shared a look, and both hid a smile. 'You

can check him over later, sister,' Caratius said. 'We need to dispose of these bodies first. Let's go.'

They had a small boat moored nearby, and with help from Vassinus, they loaded the four legionaries into it.

'It's probably best if I go back now,' the smith said, dusting off his hands. 'The less I know about their whereabouts the better, then I won't have to lie.'

'Makes sense. Come and have a meal with us tomorrow,' Duro told him. 'We'll meet at Rufilia's . . . sorry, Felicia's home.'

'Will do.'

The women set about erasing all the footprints in the mud with twig brooms, while Duro, Caratius and Marcus rowed upstream. They stopped at some dense woodland, where they buried the bodies deep in the soil, hiding the grave with moss, leaves and a couple of boulders. They'd stripped them first, and placed the Romans' clothing and weapons into a couple of sacks, together with some heavy stones. Rowing into the middle of the river, they allowed these to sink to the bottom, where hopefully they would remain.

Finally, the three of them undressed and bathed in the river before putting on clean clothing for the return journey to Isca. Their dirty garments were placed in yet another sack, to be washed by Rufilia another day.

It was almost fully dark by the time the five of them convened back at Rufilia's house to share a quiet meal. There was no need for words. Relief that it was all over permeated the room, and Duro felt a quiet satisfaction sink into his bones.

He had kept his oath. Vengeance was done.

Chapter Twenty-Two

Near Bath, July, present day

Jonah hadn't said anything more about the kiss, and things felt awkward between them back at his house. Mackenna tried to raise the subject, but he shrugged it off, merely saying that he'd had too much sun and had been a bit out of it. He seemed embarrassed to have pounced on her without warning, as if he regretted it, and she wasn't sure what to make of that. If she told him she'd liked it and wanted more but he didn't, that would be even worse. In the end, she decided to just drop it. When she tried to tell him she ought to be going home to her flat, however, he wouldn't hear of it.

'No, please, don't go yet! I'm sorry, I didn't mean to scare you off. I just . . . Stay! At least until we've had the party in London to launch the album. After that, things will die down and the journos will move on to other stories. Please? You know I hate events like that, but I can't get out of this one. I need you there to help me get through it.'

He looked so earnest, Mackenna gave in. The party was the following week and she'd been dreading it, not least because she'd have to see Blue again. Unfortunately, there had been a clause in the release document for the photos saying she was obligated to attend the album launch. Since she'd signed it – and cashed in that huge cheque – she had no choice but to go. Earlier in the week she'd thought it wouldn't be so bad with Jonah there as her friend. But the easy camaraderie between them had gone, and their interactions became stilted.

The following day he spent most of his time in his attic studio, and Mac worked in the garden with the dogs for company. She tried not to show it, but she was feeling depressed and lonely, and furious with herself for having fallen for yet another rock star. It was something she'd sworn never to do again, but Jonah was so different. He was gorgeous, kind and caring, everything Blue hadn't been, and she was hopelessly in love.

But there was no way she could tell him that, since he obviously didn't feel the same way.

She was halfway down the stairs one morning when she heard the doorbell, quickly followed by Jonah's steps towards the front door and the dogs barking. It sounded as though they were outside, so he must have just let them out into the garden. Unwilling to show herself in case the paparazzi had somehow tracked her down again, she hung back. But the voice she heard was not that of a stranger.

'Hey, Jonah. How's things?'

'Blue? What are you doing here, man?' She heard the confusion in Jonah's voice, and it was obvious the band's singer hadn't been expected.

'I just, um . . . came to see if you had Mackenna's address in Bath by any chance. You weren't answering my text messages and Harriet won't give it to me. She said you'd told her not to and that I should text Mac, but she's blocked my number.' Blue sounded at once defensive and belligerent, a strange combination.

'What do you want it for?' Jonah's tone of voice was distinctly frosty now.

'I need to talk to her.' There was a gusty sigh from Blue. Mac could imagine him running his hands through his messy hair, the way he'd always done when he was uncomfortable. 'Look, I know I screwed up, OK? But some of the PR people – not Harriet, though – suggested I should date Mackenna for a while again, just until we've launched the album. Since everyone found out who the girl on the cover was, there's been a lot of speculation in the press. They dredged up the break-up and all that, which is fine – it happened and it's all good publicity, yada, yada – but it would make for an even greater story if we'd made up in time for the album's release party, you know? Having her there and in all the photos would give them lots more to write about. Excellent for sales. Plus, there's no denying she and I looked good together. We're both photogenic.'

Mac held her breath. The ego on this guy. How dare he? Did he seriously think she was going to take him back for his or the band's convenience? Or that she was stupid enough to fall for his dubious charms again? Jeez.

Jonah was apparently as sceptical. 'And how are you going to win her back? You really messed up royally. She's not like the other women you've dated. She actually has a brain, for one thing.'

'Yeah, yeah, I know, but I'll grovel as much as I have to. She'll buy it. She always was a softie and loved big romantic gestures. If I'm suitably contrite and maybe buy her flowers and a huge, swanky piece of jewellery or something, it'll be fine. Then once the album is properly launched and doing well, we can split up again. No hard feelings.'

Jonah snorted. 'Seriously? That's your plan? You really don't know her very well, do you?'

'What? And you do?'

Mac decided it was time to intervene. She glided down the last few steps and walked up to stand next to Jonah, linking her arm through his. 'Actually, yes, he does. Jonah is much better at listening than you ever were, and he's very observant.'

Blue's mouth fell open and he glanced between them, his confusion soon replaced by red-hot fury that seemed mostly directed at Jonah. 'You've shacked up with my girlfriend? What the hell, man? What happened to the bro code?'

Mac jumped in. 'I haven't been your girlfriend for months! What do you care? You just said you were going to use me for PR purposes and then dump me again. Who does that?'

Blue turned his angry gaze on her. 'So the minute I turned my back, you hopped into bed with *him*? Couldn't live without being attached to a famous rock star, huh? Well, you've definitely gone down in the world, haven't you – from lead singer to guitarist. Is it going to be the drummer next, or the bassist?'

She tried to stay calm, because losing your temper with someone like him never worked. As if he was trying to steady her, Jonah disentangled his arm from hers and slung it across her shoulders instead, pulling her into his side. Her cheeks flamed when she realised belatedly that he was shirtless, but it felt good. She couldn't resist putting her hand on his warm chest while leaning into his shoulder a tiny bit. The guy was rock solid. And ripped. And he smelled divine from a recent shower and . . . But that was neither here nor there at this moment.

He looked at her as if asking whether she wanted to answer this, or if he should. She nodded an 'I've got this' to him and speared Blue with a death glare.

'For your information, we didn't get together until recently, and I don't give a rat's arse how famous Jonah is. He's not even going to be a rock star any more, remember? What I *do* know is that he's a hundred times better than *you*. He's a real man, mature and sensible, with his shit together. Not a spoiled, petulant pretty-boy!'

Clenching his fists as if he wanted to hit someone, Blue opened and closed his mouth a few times, clearly at a loss for the right words. Finally he pointed at Jonah and snarled, 'You're dead to me, man. I'm never working with you again.'

Jonah shook his head and sighed. 'Like I care? I already told you I quit. Weren't you listening? I don't *want* to work with you. You're a fucking diva and I'm sick of it. Now go away. We'll see you at the launch party. Unfortunately.'

And with that, he slammed the front door shut in Blue's face.

Mac took a deep breath and ducked out from under Jonah's arm. Heading for the kitchen, she busied herself with filling the kettle, then stood with both hands gripping the counter and her head hanging down while she waited for it to boil. God, what a mess. What was she supposed to do now? She'd probably made things even more awkward between herself and Jonah. *Shit!* She'd better leave. Today.

'Hey, are you OK?' He was standing in the doorway, arms crossed over his bare chest. There was a strange look in his eyes – wary, with a dash of something else. She glanced his way, trying not to notice how that pose showed off the muscles in his tattooed arms, not to mention the acres of tanned skin and those toned abs. Why did he have to look so amazing? It wasn't fair. He scrambled her brains, but she couldn't tell him that.

She did, however, owe him an apology.

'Yes, I'm fine. I'm so sorry. I shouldn't have let him think that we . . . that we're a couple. I didn't mean to make more trouble for you. I know relations between you were already strained, but he made me so mad. Still, it was wrong of me to involve you.'

She swallowed down the lump in her throat. The threatening tears were pure anger. It had felt good to get some sort of revenge on Blue, but at the same time, she'd used Jonah, and he had been nothing but kind to her. Well, before that kiss, but still . . . he deserved better.

Right now, her mind was still fixated on Blue's words, though. She smacked a hand on the counter in frustration. 'How dare he assume I'd fall for his lies again? He must think I'm a complete moron. And fancy jewellery? When did I ever ask for anything like that?'

Jonah stared at the floor. 'Nah, he's the idiot. I'm sorry if you were hoping he had come to try and make up for real. Unrequited love sucks.'

Mac's head came up. 'What? You seriously think I'd want him back? Jonah, I'm not in love with Blue! I'm not sure I ever was, and definitely not after I found him in bed with the toxic twins.'

'You sure?' He blinked at her.

'Of course I am. Honestly, I haven't been carrying a torch for him all this time, I swear.' She threw up her hands. 'I can't believe you think I'm that stupid too. I thought you knew me better by now.' She grabbed a mug from the mug tree and opened the cupboard above to find a tea bag. Her hand shook as she dumped it in and picked up the kettle to pour water onto it.

While she was busy with this, Jonah had moved to stand behind her. He put one hand either side of her now, leaning into the counter. She stiffened as his warm chest came into contact with her back and the fresh scent of his shower gel enveloped her again.

'I think you're far from stupid, Mac, but I'm used to seeing most girls throw themselves at Blue because he has a pretty face. It's kind of . . . demoralising. Why would they want me when they could have him?'

She was almost afraid to breathe, because she didn't want him to move. Having him this close was heaven and hell at the same time, and she had no idea why he was boxing her in like this. 'I'm not most girls, and they should be so lucky,' she murmured.

'I see that now.' He lifted a hand and moved her hair away from one side of her neck, placing the heavy mass of it across her other shoulder. His warm breath was close to her ear as he spoke. 'So was it true, what you said? You think I'm a hundred times better than him?'

A shiver went through her and goosebumps broke out on her arms. 'You know you are, and you're good-looking too,' she whispered. 'Millions of fan girls tell you that every day.'

He placed a kiss on her neck, underneath her ear at the most sensitive spot. 'I'm not interested in what they think. I only want your opinion.' Another kiss, slightly further down.

'OK. You're stupidly hot and totally irresistible, and can you stop teasing me now, please?' She turned around, hoping to make her escape. The tea could wait. She couldn't take another second of this torture because she didn't understand what was happening here.

He didn't move so much as an inch. Instead, his arms banded around her and pulled her chest tight against his. 'What if I tell you that I find you irresistible too? That I've wanted you from the first time I met you, even though I knew you were taken?' He bent down slightly to look her straight in the eyes. 'Mackenna, you are the most beautiful, most wonderful girl I've ever met, and I'm totally gone for you.'

She blinked, completely at a loss for words, but he didn't need any because he must have seen the answer in her eyes. His mouth slammed into hers, kissing her with an urgency that made fireworks go off inside her instantly. And this time she was sure he was kissing her, Mackenna, not someone else. One of his hands came up to tangle in her hair, wrapping it around his fist to pull her head back to give him a better angle. At the same time, his tongue demanded entry, and she opened for him without hesitation. He tasted of minty toothpaste and something sensual that was all him, and she moaned deep in her throat. This was everything she'd dreamed of and more. She never wanted him to stop.

They had to come up for air eventually, but although he was breathing heavily, he started to drop kisses down her throat and onto her shoulder instead. He pushed the thin strap of her tank top out of the way with his teeth, and she trembled as his hands travelled down her back. One of them came round her side and up to cup her breast through her thin top, sending more shock waves through her. Heat gathered in her stomach and lower, and she kissed the underside of his chin. 'Jonah . . .'

She wanted to touch him as well, and allowed her fingers to trace the contours of his sculpted back and shoulders. His skin was velvet over the hard granite of his muscles, and he shivered too as her fingernails scraped them lightly. 'Christ, Mackenna, I want you so much,' he hissed, returning his mouth to hers.

'Mm, yes!' she got out, as he put both hands under her thighs and lifted her up. 'Sofa. Now!'

He didn't need to be told twice, and carried her through the door into the orangery. There was a rattan day bed in there, and he almost tossed her onto it, making it creak ominously. Neither of them cared as he crawled over her body to continue those hot kisses. Along the way, he pushed her top up, exposing her breasts. He hissed at the sight of them, his eyes going wide.

'Gorgeous,' he mumbled. 'Absolutely stunning.'

He stilled for a moment before tugging the top all the way off and diving down to lick and suck her nipples, one at a time. She was making needy noises, and couldn't stop her hips from bucking off the sofa cushions. 'Jonah, please . . .'

He appeared to know instinctively what she needed, and

moved down her body until he was pushing down her shorts and underwear, kissing her along the way.

'Oh my God, yes!'

'Like that, do you?' He sounded pleased with himself, but she didn't have it in her to protest, because he was melting her brain. A wave of pleasure rolled over her, so strong she cried out, and when it was finished, there was no time to think because he was moving up her body again. He kissed her deeply, then lifted himself up so he could stare into her eyes. 'I want to be inside you,' he whispered. 'Is that OK?'

Beyond words, she nodded.

'Do I need protection?'

'No, we're good,' she managed.

Somewhere along the way, he'd shed the sweatpants he'd been wearing, and he didn't waste any time surging inside her. 'God, you feel amazing!' he panted. 'This is going to be too quick, but I swear I'll make it up to you.'

Instead of replying, she brought his mouth down to hers and kissed him as if her life depended on it. He started moving and the old day bed creaked alarmingly again, but neither of them noticed. Luckily, it held, and it wasn't long before he groaned out his own release and she exploded again at the same time. Then he collapsed on top of her, both of them breathing hard. After a moment, he made to lift himself up, but she stopped him by clamping her arms around him.

'Don't move. I like the weight of you. So good,' she whispered.

He turned his head to kiss her shoulder, then the side of her neck and under her chin. 'Mm, incredible,' he murmured. 'I want to stay like this for ever.'

Mac relaxed and closed her eyes. That would be absolutely fine with her.

However, a bark and a plaintive whine outside the window,

following by a scratching sound, made them both look up. Fred and Bagel were staring at them accusingly, as if they'd been forgotten for years.

Huffing out a laugh, Jonah pushed himself off Mac and went to let them in. 'Maybe I need to rethink my decision to keep you two,' he told them mock-sternly. 'Talk about a mood killer.'

But he didn't let the dogs stop him from going back to lie down on top of Mac once more. 'They'll just have to watch,' he said as he kissed her again.

Chapter Twenty-Three

Isca, south-west Britannia, June AD *80*

'I hope you're not going to join the uprisings in the north, brother, or else I'll be forced to fight against you.' Caratius looked serious as they all shared one final meal at Rufilia's house before Duro and Gisel left Isca. Vassinus had joined them too, and Duro liked the quiet giant. He was glad his nephew had such a great mentor, and trusted that the blacksmith would look out for Marcus in the future too.

'No, I have more sense than that,' he replied. 'The time for resistance passed a long time ago. The Romans have such a grip on these lands now, there's no point rebelling. I hear tell they keep the largest number of garrisons ever here, compared to other conquered territories. There's no way they'd ease up. They're determined to hang on to Britannia.' He shook his head. 'They're not all bad, and in some ways they're brilliant, it has to be said. We can learn a lot from them and it's better to accept the inevitable and use their systems for our benefit. My friend Raedwald and I are establishing trading links with Gaul, Frisia and Germania. It should make our people rich and able to live in peace and comfort. There's no reason we can't continue our own traditions quietly in the background.'

Caratius nodded. 'That does sound sensible, and I'm glad. I'd never wish to go up against you, that's for certain.'

'Likewise. If you are ever given leave, do please come and visit. I'm sure Commios would love to see you, despite his grumpy tendencies.' Duro laughed. 'Mayhap I'll have come to an understanding with him by then.'

'Hah! I wish you luck with that.'

'As for you two,' he smiled at Rufilia and Marcus, 'if you ever wish to move back home, you'll be very welcome. There is always space for family, and once you've completed your apprenticeship, nephew, a blacksmith of our own would be useful. I noticed the settlement didn't have one when I visited recently.'

'We'll think about it,' Rufilia said. 'I have friends here, and so does Marcus, but it is tempting, I must say.'

'Good. You know where to find us.'

He'd make sure to leave her enough coin to travel back to Iceni lands if she so wished, and to pay for repairs and improvements to her little house. Caratius and Vassinus had both promised to make sure that she was given a share of Julius Felix's estate, once the fort's commanders realised he was missing and presumed lost. Rufilia had been questioned about his disappearance, but she told the soldiers she hadn't seen him for days. He and his companions had been seen leaving the fort, but no one had questioned him at the time. As a centurion, he was free to go into the *vicus* if he wished, and the other men were under his command.

Most men left instructions for their slaves to be freed upon their death, but they doubted Julius Felix would have been that benevolent. Caratius said he'd do his best to urge the authorities to give Rufilia her freedom so that she'd be able to live as she wished henceforth. Vassinus promised to buy her and grant her manumission if they refused.

'I'll tell them I want her as my wife,' he said, causing Rufilia's cheeks to heat up. 'Mine died two years ago.'

Duro had no objection to that plan, but it would be up to his sister.

Once the food was consumed, Duro took Gisel's hand and stood up. 'As we are all here together, Gisel and I would like to formalise our union in front of witnesses. It is not quite according to tradition, but we wish it to be known that from now on we are officially man and wife.' He gazed at the beautiful woman who had promised to be his for the rest of her life. 'I, Durobelinos, hereby pledge myself to you, Gisel, for as long as I shall live and beyond. I promise to honour and cherish you, provide for you, and protect you to the best of my ability. May the gods bear witness to this, my oath.' He extracted an arm ring from his pouch and held it out to her. It was fashioned in the Britannic style of thick, twisted gold strands that ended in two gaping animal heads facing each other. He held it out to her. 'Please accept this as a token of my love for you.'

'Thank you.' She took it and pushed it onto her arm, squeezing the two ends close to each other so that it fitted her wrist perfectly, then recited her own, similar vow.

The others all cheered as Duro swept her into his arms and kissed her soundly.

'Congratulations! May you live happily together for the rest of your days. To Gisel and Duro!' Caratius lifted his beaker of beer and everyone followed suit.

Duro was sure his heart would burst with happiness, and for the rest of the evening he didn't let go of Gisel's hand.

When they were finally alone, back at their lodgings, he pulled her into his arms and kissed her again, more urgently this time. 'I really do love you, you know,' he murmured in between kisses. 'More than I could ever say.'

She stood on tiptoes and wound her arms around his neck. 'And I love you, Duro. I'm so fortunate to have met you. The gods must have been looking out for me.'

'And me! Now I'm going to make you mine completely.'

Gisel didn't protest when Duro pulled her garments over her head and carried her to the narrow bed. He laid her down with infinite care while continuing his kisses and caresses. *My husband!* It still hadn't sunk in that she was truly his wife, and that he loved her as much as she loved him. And now she'd be his in every way.

He broke off to pull off his own clothing with impatient jerks, flinging the garments to the floor. She'd seen him naked before, but only through the waters of the sacred spring bath. Having him stand before her in all his glory was a different matter altogether. Quite simply breathtaking. He appeared to feel the same way about her.

'By Cernunnos, you're so beautiful!' he breathed, leaning over to trail kisses and little bites from her neck down across her chest and stomach. His fingers were dancing over her skin everywhere else, or so it seemed, and tingles rushed through her entire body.

'I don't want to hurt you,' he whispered, his fingers reaching the most secret parts of her. 'But it might sting a little at first. Can you cope, love?'

He was doing magical things, building a wave of pleasure that threatened to erupt inside her. He'd done this before with her, but not the next part. This time she didn't want him to stop.

'Yes, please. I want you, Duro, all of you.'

He was right, it did sting at first, but only very briefly. After that, he moved slowly to allow her to become accustomed to the feel of him inside her – and his not inconsiderable size – but she soon began to urge him to go faster. She was drowning in sensations that were overwhelming in the best possible way. When he added pressure to her secret place with his fingers, she came apart completely. He soon followed, groaning out his own release, and then gathered her into his arms while their breathing and heart rates recovered.

He caressed her cheek and turned her face up to his. 'Did I hurt you, my love?'

'No, not at all. Well, only a tiny bit at first, but then . . .' She felt her cheeks heat up. 'I . . . I enjoyed it immensely, husband.'

That made a huge grin spread across his features. 'I'm glad, and please keep calling me that until I actually believe it's not too good to be true.' He pulled her into the crook of his arm. 'If you wait a few moments, we can do it again. Trust me, it will be even better the second time. And the third. And—'

'Duro!' She swatted his shoulder. 'We have the rest of our lives.'

'And I have weeks of waiting to make up for.' He kissed her tenderly. 'And I'll never tire of you. Not in a million years.'

When he put it like that, how could she refuse?

They left Isca the following morning, having said their goodbyes the night before. Gisel was a bit sore after the night's activities, but Duro had anticipated that and bought a fleece to cover her saddle with. The softness helped, and he told her they'd stop any time she wanted.

Retracing their route, they rode to Venta Silurum, then on to Glevum and Corinium Dobunnorum. Instead of taking the southerly road towards Calleva Atrebatum, however, Duro planned to choose a north-easterly one that would eventually bring them to Verulamium.

'From there, we will continue cross-country towards the coast. My family's settlement is inland, but not too far from the sea,' he told Gisel.

While fetching supper for them to eat at their lodgings in

Glevum, he happened to run into one of the men he'd shared wine with last time he was here, when he'd been gleaning information about Julius Felix's whereabouts. The man hailed him like a long-lost friend.

'Duro! You have returned. Did you succeed in finding your brother?' That was the excuse he'd given, pretending that Caratius was part of Julius Felix's cohort.

'Indeed I did, thank you. He's alive and well. Thriving, in fact. It was good to see him.'

'Excellent! I'm glad.' His erstwhile drinking companion smiled. 'By the way, someone came asking about you after you left. Or at least I assumed it was you he meant. He didn't mention you by name, but he described you fairly accurately. I told him you'd probably gone to Isca, but I wasn't sure of your exact movements. Did he catch up with you?'

A tendril of unease sneaked down Duro's back. 'No, he didn't. Did he give his own name? I wasn't aware that anyone was following me.'

'Not that I recall. Fellow with hair the colour of bleached straw. I'd guess he was from foreign parts. Spoke the Roman language well enough, but with a strange accent, you know?'

'Oh yes, I know who that is.' Duro played along, while secretly clenching his fist. 'Thank you for letting me know. We'd best wait for him to catch up. I thought he'd given up on the idea of coming with us.'

As soon as the man had left, Duro rushed back to Gisel, relieved to find her exactly where he'd left her. There was only one man with blond hair who might be following them and asking after Duro – Eberulf. He'd not thought the man stupid enough to remain in Britannia, but it would appear he'd underestimated his desire to take Gisel back.

Curse it! He should have killed him when he had the chance, but it hadn't seemed honourable when he was knocked out and dead to the world.

'Here's some bread, cheese and roast pork,' he announced, setting out the food on a small table in their room while debating whether he should tell Gisel what he had learned.

In the end, he thought it best not to frighten her. Forewarned was forearmed, and now he knew the man was on their trail, he could keep an eye out surreptitiously. Or even set a trap for him . . .

Yes, that was a much better idea. Then he'd deal with the cur once and for all.

Duro was unusually quiet as they left Glevum, but Gisel didn't comment on it. She'd only known this husband of hers for a matter of weeks, even though it felt like a lot longer, and she still had much to learn about him and his moods. Perhaps he was brooding about the other brother who was waiting for them at the settlement. She'd gathered that one wasn't best pleased to have Duro back, but he'd have to accept it unless they went to live somewhere else. However, that wasn't likely.

'I'm really looking forward to living surrounded by kin from now on,' he'd told her. 'After so many years with only Raedwald to support me, I crave the sense of belonging that only a family can give you.' He'd stroked his knuckles down her cheek in a soft caress. 'Will you miss yours terribly? Would you rather we went to stay with them?'

'No, I'm content to remain with you.' And she was. Although it would have been wonderful to see her father and brother again, they might not be as pleased to have her return with a Briton for a husband. They had agreed with her that Eberulf wasn't suitable, but her father had promoted other matches with men from neighbouring tribes. He held a deep-seated mistrust of anyone not from the immediate region.

The weather was favourable, and they made camp in a clearing near the road that night, working in tandem as if they'd done this a thousand times. Gisel spread out their blankets and unpacked the food while Duro saw to the horses. When he'd finished, he picked up their water container.

'I'll go and fill this up,' he said, his voice loud in the stillness of the evening. 'I won't be long, love.'

Gisel frowned after him. Was it her imagination, or was he acting strangely?

She was bent over rummaging in one of the saddlebags when there was a rustling noise behind her. Before she had a chance to react, a muscular arm snaked round her waist from behind and a knife was pressed against her throat.

'Come with me quietly, or I'll hurt you,' a voice hissed into her ear.

Gisel stiffened. She knew that voice only too well and had hoped never to hear it again. Eberulf.

'Never,' she retorted. 'I'd rather die than go anywhere with you.'

'I thought you'd say that, you traitorous bitch, but you'll do as I say or that big man of yours will die too. Is that what you want? I've got men surrounding this place and he can't fight them all. If you obey me, we'll leave him alone. You just have to admit that I'm your rightful husband.'

Gisel was torn. Eberulf was right – she couldn't bear the thought of Duro being hurt for her sake. And perhaps if she went with her erstwhile suitor now, she could find an opportunity to escape later. Besides, Duro would come after them, she had no doubt about that.

She capitulated. 'Very well, I'll go with you.' As she straightened up slowly so that the sharp knife wouldn't nick her by mistake, she heard a crack behind her, and Eberulf's grip on her suddenly loosened.

Reacting quickly, Gisel pushed the hand holding the knife away from her and threw herself forward, scuttling out of the way. She turned to see Duro grappling with Eberulf. He must have circled round the clearing and attacked from behind, because the stream was in the other direction. There was no sign of anyone else, although Gisel kept a watchful eye out for movement among the trees. Duro punched Eberulf hard in the face, breaking his nose. The Germanus howled and stumbled backwards, his eyes wild with hatred and confusion.

'How did you . . .?'

'I heard you were looking for us, so I knew you were coming. Did you really think I'd let you take my wife away from me that easily?' Duro growled.

'She's mine, you Briton swine! She was always mine and no one else is going to have her!' Eberulf yelled, surging towards Duro while brandishing the knife.

Duro sidestepped and clouted him on the side of the head. 'Wrong. Gisel has promised herself to me and I'm not letting her go. Ever.'

The fight that followed was fierce and violent, neither man giving any quarter. Duro had the advantage of size and height, but Eberulf was almost unhinged with desperate fury and proved a slippery foe. Gisel could hardly bear to watch, her heart beating madly with fear. She wanted to intervene, to help somehow, but knew she had to trust her man to deal with this on his own. She would only get in the way and distract him if she tried anything.

Eventually Duro's calmer and more clinical approach paid dividends, the years of gladiator training obviously standing him in good stead. He managed to inflict several hard blows on his opponent's head and chin, and he swiped Eberulf with his long knife time and time again, leaving gashes that bled profusely. It looked as though he had him beaten, but Eberulf tried one last desperate trick. Instead of retaliating, he swivelled round and sprinted towards Gisel. She had been so intent on watching the fight, he took her by surprise. Before she had time to turn and duck out of the way, he had grabbed her tunic and raised his knife.

'If I can't have you, he won't either!' he shouted.

His dagger never reached its target. Before he had a chance to sink it into her heart, he jerked and cried out. Gisel had vaguely registered Duro throwing his own knife, and it must have hit Eberulf in the back. A well-aimed kick had the Germanus falling forwards onto his hands and knees. Arching his back, where a huge bloodstain was rapidly spreading, he stared up at Duro in disbelief.

'*No!* No, it wasn't supposed to end like this . . .' he mumbled. His gaze sought Gisel. 'You . . . I always wanted you no matter what . . . Why did you have to be so difficult?'

She stared down at him dispassionately. 'Because you weren't worthy of being my husband,' she snarled. She grabbed Duro's hand. 'This man is everything you're not – good and honourable. The love of my life. You could never compare.'

Blood was gushing out of Eberulf's wound and he was struggling to breathe, air rattling through his lungs. He shook his head, clearly still in denial. 'No, not true . . .'

Duro's hand tightened on hers as he addressed the man on the ground. 'I'm sorry, but you brought this on yourself. I gave you the chance to go home and live your life in peace, but you chose a different path. You should have taken no for an answer.'

Eberulf seemingly had no reply to that. His eyes closed, and after struggling on for a while longer, he stopped breathing and fell face-first into the grass.

It was over.

Chapter Twenty-Four

London, July, present day

'I don't care how much it costs. You're having it, and that's that.'

Mackenna stared at her reflection in the mirror of the exclusive shop in London's New Bond Street, and stopped herself from checking out the price tag of the dress she was wearing. It was a shimmering ocean-coloured blend of silk and chiffon, and according to Jonah it matched her eyes exactly. The appreciative look in his gaze as he saw her come out of the changing room had sent a tremor of delight through her, so how could she possibly refuse?

'It's obscene, spending so much on something I'll probably only wear once,' she protested half-heartedly.

He gave her a naughty smile. 'You can always wear it for me, just so I can take it off you,' he whispered.

Mac felt herself blush. Having him talk to her like that was very new, but she loved it. Every moment they'd spent together since Blue's visit had been utter bliss, and she never wanted this to end. She'd been so wrong: he hadn't been sorry about that weird kiss at Caerleon at all, only embarrassed at calling her by another woman's name and grabbing her without preamble like that.

'It was as if I was someone else for a moment,' he'd admitted.

'I honestly can't explain it any other way. I thought I was going insane.'

'No, I felt it too.' She'd reassured him and told him of the strange sensations that had assailed her. They'd discussed it at length, but couldn't find a sensible explanation for any of it, so in the end they'd decided to try and forget about it. Enjoying their time together seemed more important.

'OK, fine, we'll buy this,' she conceded now, 'but only because I don't want you to feel ashamed to have me with you at the party tonight.'

Jonah got out of the chair he'd been sitting in and reached her in two long strides. 'Never!' he murmured, taking her in his arms. 'I will be the proudest guy there, I swear.' The kiss he gave her added emphasis to his words, and they didn't break apart until the saleswoman cleared her throat behind them.

Carrying the large bag with a fancy logo, Jonah pulled her down the street, weaving in and out of all the people who thronged the pavement despite the humid July weather. 'Let's go check out Burlington Arcade,' he said. 'I love that place.'

Mac had nothing against this idea. She was just hoping no one stopped them and asked for selfies or autographs. Luckily Jonah wasn't recognised. Wearing his usual baseball cap and sunglasses, he blended in with the tourists. Or perhaps people could see that he wasn't in the mood to stop as he strode along purposefully, towing her in his wake.

As for the jealous looks she received from other women, she already knew she was the luckiest woman on earth.

Burlington Arcade was a covered walkway lined with quirky shops, leading from near New Bond Street to Piccadilly. It had apparently been there since at least the early eighteen hundreds, and Jonah had discovered it by mistake once when he was fleeing from paparazzi. All the stores sold exclusive and usually expensive items, but if you were looking for something out of the ordinary, there was nowhere better.

He was on a mission to buy Mac a piece of jewellery to wear with the spectacular dress tonight. Not that she needed adornment, but the caveman part of him wanted to show that he could afford to give his woman jewels. That thought made him smile. He'd never been this possessive of anyone in his life, but he was fathoms-deep in love and couldn't believe things had worked out this well. He stopped to study the items in the window of a tiny shop squeezed in between one that sold old clocks and another full of luxury cashmere sweaters. The display showed an eclectic array of antique pieces, and he spied the perfect item in one corner.

'Let's go in here,' he said, tugging Mac with him before she had time to protest.

'Why?' she hissed, sending him a suspicious glance. He'd never met a woman so averse to spending his money. It was both refreshing and frustrating at the same time.

'I just want to browse,' he replied, giving the elderly lady behind the counter his best smile. 'Hello! Could I please have a closer look at one of the necklaces in the window?'

He'd spotted an aquamarine teardrop-shaped pendant in a white gold and diamond setting. It was Victorian in style, something he knew Mac liked, and would be perfect for the deep neckline of her new dress. The saleswoman extracted it from the display and held it up to the light. 'Good choice,' she said. 'Is it for your lovely wife?'

He didn't bother to correct her, even though Mac's cheeks turned pink. 'Yes. Can you try this on, please, baby? I want to see what it looks like on you.'

She tried to tell him with her eyes that it was too expensive and he shouldn't be buying it, but he ignored her and just held it out. 'Fine,' she murmured.

As she was wearing a low-cut tank top, the pendant was showcased perfectly, hanging just above the valley between her breasts. Jonah nodded. 'I like it, but perhaps you'd prefer something else? See what you can find.'

Mac took off the necklace and gave it to the saleswoman before turning her back on them to study a display case to one side. Jonah nodded surreptitiously to indicate he'd be buying the pendant, then bent to study a tray full of rings. 'Can you tell me about these, please?'

The old lady proceeded to give a potted history of each ring. Jonah was barely listening, though, as one in particular had caught his attention. It was one of the plainer ones, of pure gold with an intaglio of two serpents carved into a reddish-coloured stone. For some reason, it seemed to be calling to him. He pounced on it and picked it up to study it in more detail. 'What about this one?'

'Oh yes, that's an interesting choice. Roman, I believe. The stone is a carnelian, and snakes were symbols of good fortune. It was an heirloom, not dug up illegally somewhere – not recently, anyway – so we're allowed to sell it. It came from the Duke of Essex's family, I believe.'

It was definitely made for a woman, as it was small in circumference and fairly dainty. Jonah knew he had to have it for Mac, but now was not the right time to give it to her. He checked that she was still preoccupied with the tiaras and whispered, 'I'll take it, but don't show my, um, wife.'

The woman gave him a conspiratorial smile and said loudly, 'So just the pendant then, sir? Thank you very much. I'll bag it up for you.'

'Let me just check. Mac? Did you find anything else you liked?'

Jonah went to peer over Mac's shoulder at the fancy tiaras she was studying. 'You want one of those?'

She laughed. 'No. When would I wear something like that?' She added in a whisper, 'You might be a rock god, but you're not royalty.'

He smiled back and wiggled his eyebrows at her. 'You think I'm a god, huh? Good to know.'

She gave him a playful shove. 'Don't get too big-headed, mister.'

He paid for the items and took the small bag that contained both of them, then grabbed Mac's hand. 'Let's go.'

Once outside, she turned more serious and shook her head at him. 'You shouldn't have bought that, Jonah, it's too much.'

He bent to give her a scorching kiss. 'No, it's not. It's perfect for you and I wanted you to have it so you can wear it tonight. Now let's go and get ready for that damned party.'

The album launch party was being held at a swanky hotel in central London and Mac felt like a princess even without a tiara. They arrived in a chauffeur-driven car and exited onto a red carpet. Flashes went off and there were shouted questions from the journalists lining the short route into the hotel. Jonah had told her to hold her head high and not try to hide.

'You'll be the most beautiful woman there by far, so just own it,' he'd said.

His words warmed her, even though she didn't believe them to be true. But he did, and that was all that mattered. For his sake, she would act confident, despite the fact that she hated being in the limelight.

Jonah held her hand and smiled at everyone as they walked slowly into the foyer. A large screen with the cover of *Blonde Revolution* had been set up as a backdrop for photos, and they paused in front of it. It felt weird to see herself blown up in high definition like that. Thank goodness the picture focused mostly on her hair and not her face. She was wearing it loose tonight, exactly like in the photo, as Jonah had asked her to.

They stood still long enough for everyone to get the pics they wanted, but just as she thought they were done, Blue came striding along the red carpet. He was dragging a pretty blonde, who stumbled slightly in her four-inch heels. Mac recognised her as Ashley Kenton, the actress he was supposedly dating at the moment.

'Blue, slow down!' the woman protested in an audible hiss, a flush of annoyance staining her cheeks.

He ignored her, his eyes fixed on Mac and Jonah. He came to a stop in front of them, studying her with a narrowed gaze as he took in her dress, the expensive pendant, and the possessive arm Jonah had draped over her bare shoulders.

'Nice,' he sneered, obviously meaning the opposite.

Jonah stared him down, a silent challenge that finally made Blue turn away. Without introducing Ashley or giving her a chance to say hello, he stepped to one side and lined up next to Mac, turning to fire off one of his signature smiles at the cameras that were avidly capturing this little exchange. Jonah immediately moved Mac to his other side, so that he was the one standing next to Blue instead. The journalists were eating this up, shouting questions.

'Are you all still friends?'

'What really happened?'

'How do you feel having swapped Blue for Jonah, Mackenna?'

'Yeah, isn't it awkward?'

'Ashley, do you and Mackenna get on well?'

None of the four replied. They just kept on smiling, until Jonah apparently decided he'd had enough.

'Come on, let's find our table.' He twined his fingers with Mac's and led her into the hotel's ballroom.

Thankfully they hadn't been seated next to Blue and his date, and the next few hours were more peaceful. Mac was happy to find Helle in the chair next to her, and she also chatted with Owen and their other bandmate, Steve. They all ignored Blue, who alternated between glowering at them across the table, drinking heavily, and schmoozing with whoever came up to talk to him. There was a manic air to him, and he was fidgety and loud, but he didn't attempt to talk to the rest of the band. Mac was grateful for that. Ashley was clearly a pro and kept her composure throughout, but Mac wondered what the poor woman was thinking. She probably hadn't reckoned on entering a battlefield.

Some time later, Mac made her way to the ladies' room while Jonah talked to a couple of people he'd said were important in the music industry. She hoped they'd be willing to work with him as a songwriter instead of a member of Valhalla Storm. He would need their support going forward, but she had every faith in him. Jonah really was exceptionally talented.

When she opened the door to go back to the ballroom, she was met with a snarl and a hand to her throat. Before she had time to react, her head had been slammed into the nearest wall and she blinked to clear her vision.

'Where do you think you're going, bitch?' Blue's eyes were hazy from whatever he'd imbibed – and possibly inhaled – but at the same time they shot bolts of pure hatred towards her. 'You really thought I was going to let you swan around pretending to be Jonah's girlfriend just to get back at me?' He shook his head. 'That's not how it works, babe.'

'Let go of me!' she croaked, trying to prise his fingers off her throat. His grip was tightening and she was having trouble breathing. '*Blue!* Stop it!'

'You've made a fool of me and that's not something I can tolerate,' he growled. 'You need to be punished and then I want you gone. Take the expensive jewellery and crawl back to whatever hole you came out of. You don't belong here with us. Never did.'

'Not everything is about you,' she managed to huff. She lashed out, scratching him on one perfect cheek and stomping on his foot with her high heel, but her head was swimming and she needed air. Now. 'Get away from me, you conceited bastard!'

She tried to knee him in the groin, but he was ready for her and bashed her head into the wall once more. Pain sliced through her, and she gasped for breath as black dots danced across her vision. Remembering something she'd read, she reached out and grabbed his balls instead, twisting as hard as she could. He hadn't anticipated that, and shrieked with pain, letting go of her throat a fraction. It was enough for her to draw in some much-needed air, but in the next second her whole body was pinned to the wall by his, her back connecting with the fancy panelling with an excruciating jolt.

'You'll pay for that!' Blue roared.

Suddenly his head snapped to the side, and he let go of her as a fist smashed into his temple.

'What the hell, man? Get your hands off her!'

Blue stumbled, then swivelled round to face a furious Jonah, who went after him with determination and white-hot rage burning in his gaze. Mac clutched her throat and concentrated on breathing, only glancing up when another person suddenly pushed Jonah out of the way with a shriek of outrage. Ashley had come rushing down the corridor, taking in the scene at a glance, and she didn't hesitate to join the fray.

'What's the matter with you? Are you insane?' She bashed Blue over the head with her designer handbag. It had sharp studs on it, some of which cut his forehead, and he cried out and put up his hands to shield himself from her attack.

A couple of flashes went off nearby, and Mac became aware

that they weren't alone any longer. People must have followed in Ashley's wake and witnessed the scene as well. They were murmuring amongst themselves, some of them with expressions of glee, cameras at the ready to film every second. This incident would be all over the papers tomorrow, no doubt, and by the looks they were throwing his way, Blue would not come out of it covered in glory. More likely his reputation would be in tatters, and she'd be surprised if anyone wanted to work with him in future. Served him right. With a bit of luck, he'd get a jail sentence too, as she was fully intending to report him to the police for assault.

'You're pathetic,' Ashley snarled. 'I can see why she broke up with you now.' She threw Mac a concerned look. 'Are you OK?'

Mac nodded weakly. 'Yes, thank you.' She leaned on Jonah, who had hurried over to put his arms around her. He flashed a death glare over his shoulder at Blue.

'You're a waste of space,' he huffed. 'Just stay away from my girlfriend from now on, you hear? If you so much as breathe in her direction, I won't hesitate to rearrange that pretty face of yours permanently. Then where will you be? It's the only thing you've got going for you. Now get lost!' That last sentence was superfluous, as security guards had already arrived and were preparing to haul Blue away. Jonah told them to keep hold of him and call the police, then glanced at the group of spectators and added through gritted teeth, 'We were supposed to be here to launch our album, dammit, not enact a soap opera.'

'Well, you can do it without me,' Ashley declared. 'I'm going home.' She pointed at Blue with a well-manicured talon and narrowed her eyes. 'And I don't want to ever hear from you again, understood? Bastard.'

Blue scowled at them all one more time. 'Whatever,' was all he had time to mutter before he was led away.

Jonah put gentle fingers under Mac's chin and lifted it to inspect her throat. 'Are you all right? Do you need to go to hospital to get checked out? That looks painful.'

'No, I'll be fine. I . . . I can breathe now.'

He pulled her close and hugged her tight. She was shaking with the shock of what had just happened, but being held by him calmed her.

'Jesus,' he muttered. 'I knew he was a crazy son of a bitch, but I didn't think he'd attack you physically. He's always been about snide comments and sulking when he doesn't get his way, but this . . . Christ! I thought he was going to kill you!'

She could feel his heart beating rapidly, and knew her own was only just slowing down after the ordeal. 'Me too,' she whispered. 'But you came in time. Thank you for saving me.' Rising on tiptoes, she placed a soft kiss on his lips.

'Always, baby, always,' he murmured, kissing her back. It was a gentle caress, as if he was afraid she would shatter if he didn't hold back. Mac felt cherished and safe, and knew he'd never again let Blue come anywhere near her.

That nightmare was over.

Chapter Twenty-Five

Eastern Britannia, July AD *80*

Night had fallen when they finally arrived at Duro's family settlement. They were soaked through, as the rain had been lashing them for the past few hours. The track was a virtual mud bath, and he was grateful the horses had managed to stay on their feet. Gisel was huddled inside her hooded cloak, just like him, but he knew it didn't make any difference. The water had found a way through, and they were both chilled to the bone. It was hard to believe it was summer. Where had this thunderstorm come from?

Getting off his horse to open the gate to the compound, he led the way through and closed it behind them. As they reached the main house, a figure came hurrying from the direction of the privy, and Duro grabbed hold of an arm. Bellicia's face lit up at the sight of him.

'Duro! You're back.'

'Yes, and wanting to go inside as soon as possible.' He turned to help Gisel off her horse. She was shivering so much, he had to prise her fingers off the reins. Setting her on her feet, he turned back to Bellicia. 'Please see to my guest immediately. I'm going to take the horses out of the rain.'

He grabbed the reins of both animals and trudged off. No matter how wet and tired he was, the horses would need to be rubbed down, fed and watered, or they wouldn't survive. They were too valuable to be left outside to catch cold.

He heard Bellicia say, 'This way,' before the darkness swallowed him up. He drew in a deep breath of relief. At least Gisel would be warm in a trice. He couldn't bear the thought of her becoming ill. She was his future, the woman he loved beyond reason, and he needed to keep her safe and well from now on.

Gisel stumbled after the young woman without looking where they were going. She was shaking so much it was a struggle just to keep upright. At least moving her legs brought a little bit of warmth back into her limbs, but she couldn't wait to be inside and out of the rain. She should have agreed to Duro's suggestion that they stop halfway through the afternoon, but he'd looked so eager to reach home. She hadn't had the heart to deny him the pleasure of getting there as soon as possible.

'In here,' the woman instructed, opening a door.

They entered a smallish roundhouse that was dark, damp and chilly. It didn't seem to have been occupied for some time, and the hearth looked as though it hadn't been lit in ages. It took a while for the woman to strike enough sparks to light a lamp. She put it on a shelf and gestured towards a bare bench that didn't have so much as a single sheepskin on it.

'Have a seat. I'll go and get someone to see to your needs. I've no idea why my husband brought you here, but I hope you're not staying long. I've been looking forward to having him back and all to myself.'

'Husband?' What did the woman's husband have to do with anything? Gisel sank down onto the hard bench and squinted at her, confusion clouding her mind. She was so tired, but something about this whole scenario seemed off.

'Yes, Durobelinos. I'm Bellicia, his wife. Did he not tell you?' The woman put her hands on her hips and scowled. 'If you believe he'll keep you, think again. I won't tolerate him bedding anyone but me. In fact, it might be best if you left straight away. I can give you some coin and find you a mule, then you can be on your way. Go and ply your trade elsewhere.'

Trade? Was she implying that Gisel was a prostitute? *What on earth . . .?*

Gisel stared at the woman, dumbfounded. Duro's wife? No, surely not. Had she really been so completely blinded by him that she'd fallen for a pack of lies? It was possible. They'd only known each other for a relatively short time, after all, and he was an incredibly charismatic man. One who knew what he wanted and went after it wholeheartedly. And yet . . . she'd never pegged him for a liar. He'd always seemed honest and straightforward. Could she have been so very wrong about him?

A lead weight settled in her stomach and she swallowed hard. A quiet fury began to ignite inside her. How dare he? And how dare Bellicia treat a visitor in this manner? That was plain rude. Either way, Gisel wasn't leaving without confronting Duro first. If he wanted her out of the way, he'd have to tell her to her face. She needed to look him in the eye when he admitted to his lies.

'I'm not going anywhere tonight,' she declared, raising her chin a notch to glare at Bellicia. 'Kindly fetch someone to bring me dry clothes, a blanket and some victuals. The least you can do is offer me hospitality, as is the custom.'

'Hoity-toity,' Bellicia huffed, but she headed for the door. 'It might take a while, and don't expect to be waited on hand and foot. We don't usually serve the likes of you here.'

The door closed behind her with a distinct bang.

Gisel was left shivering in her wet garments, but they were nothing compared to the cold spreading inside her.

Duro, what have you done?

Duro ducked inside the roundhouse, where Maerica was busy over by the hearth. She looked up as he entered, a smile spreading across her features. 'Duro, my boy, you're back! But oh, you poor thing. You're sopping wet!'

He took the linen cloth she offered and wiped his face, then scanned the room to make sure Gisel was being taken care of. She was nowhere in sight, and he frowned.

'Where's Gisel?' he asked.

'Who?' Maerica blinked in confusion. 'You brought someone with you?'

'Yes,' he bit out through gritted teeth, searching the room for Bellicia. She too appeared to be absent. 'Teutatis curse her,' he hissed. 'Where's she taken her?'

Throwing the cloth at Maerica, he ducked back outside and ran a circuit of the other huts, shouting Gisel's name. Just as he was about to turn back, he heard her call out. Her voice was faint and seemed to be coming from a small hut, which was odd, but he decided he'd better check. He flung the door open and stopped momentarily to blink at the scene before him. Gisel was sitting on a dirty bench, still in her wet garments, shivering uncontrollably. Her expression was the epitome of misery.

'What on earth . . .? Why are you in here?' He swept the interior of the hut with a glance, but there was no one else to be seen. It was dark and cold, a single lamp the only illumination.

To his surprise, she stumbled to her feet, eyes flashing with fury. 'That's what I'd like to know too. Perhaps you'd care to explain? And while you're at it, you can tell me all about your *wife*!'

When uttering that last word, she stabbed him in the chest with her finger. He got the impression she would have preferred it if it had been a dagger going straight into his heart.

He wondered if he was dreaming. The entire scenario was unreal, and for a moment all he could do was stare at her. Then her words registered. 'What wife?' he asked, blinking in confusion. 'You're here. What am I supposed to tell you?'

He put out a hand to feel her forehead to see if she'd developed a fever and was delirious. She jerked back. 'Not me. Your *real* wife. Bellicia?'

'Huh?' Duro's mouth fell open, but he closed it with a snap. Anger surged inside him as he finally understood what was going on here. He grabbed Gisel's shoulders and shook his head. 'She's *not* my wife. Never was. Never will be. What she is is a dead woman,' he snarled.

'What?' Gisel stared at him, her gaze wary as if she didn't believe him.

'She lied, my love. She's a stupid, wilful little girl who needs to be taught a lesson. I've no idea what she thought she'd achieve by stirring up trouble between you and me, but trust me, I wouldn't marry her if she was the last woman on earth.' He put his hands on either side of her face and looked her in the eyes. 'Gisel, I love you! Only you. Now and for all eternity. *You're* my wife. I would never lie to you or deceive you in any way, you have my oath.'

She searched his gaze for a moment longer, then sagged against him. 'Thank the gods,' she murmured. 'I was so scared. I . . . I thought perhaps I'd been duped. You are so very . . . Well, I love you so much.'

He hugged her tight, then bent to kiss her, but only briefly. 'We can talk more about this later, but for now we need to get out of these wet clothes. Come, my love, I'll take you to the main house. I don't want you catching a cold.' He added through clenched teeth, 'Bellicia is going to regret this, I swear.'

He picked her up and carried her back to the house, where Maerica hovered by the door, opening it for him to pass through.

'What happened? Is she hurt?'

'I need linen drying sheets and warm blankets, please. A basin of hot water and some dry clothes, if you have them.'

'Of course. Take her to your sleeping bench.' Maerica scurried off to fetch the items he'd asked for.

Duro headed for the space he'd occupied last time and set Gisel on her feet. He pulled a curtain closed behind them to give them some privacy, but waited until Maerica returned with the drying sheets before undressing Gisel. Her overtunic came off fairly easily, but he had some difficulty peeling her sodden undertunic over her head. She stood before him shivering, teeth chattering. He hurried to dry her before threading her into warm clothing. A linen shift and a thick woollen overtunic with long sleeves followed by a blanket wrapped around her shoulders lessened her trembling.

'Sit, *amata mea*.' He guided her to the sleeping bench while he kneeled to pull off her shoes and dry her feet. Maerica had provided new ones that were a little on the large side, but would have to do for now.

When he'd put those on her, he turned his attention to drying her hair.

'I can do that,' she murmured, grabbing the drying sheet. 'You need to get out of your wet things too. I'm not losing you to a congestion of the lungs now.'

He bent to give her a searing kiss and a smile. 'It will take more than rain to finish me off, but you're right. I should change.'

He did so as swiftly as he was able to, then sat down and pulled her onto his lap, holding her close. 'I hope you'll soon be warm enough. I don't want you becoming ill. If anything were to happen to you, I'd go out of my mind.'

Gisel was quiet for a moment, wrapping her arms around his torso to squeeze him hard. 'Likewise. What are you going to do about Bellicia? She took me to that disused hut deliberately and obviously wished me harm. She called me a prostitute and tried to bribe me to leave, but I refused. Then she said she was going to fetch me dry clothing and victuals, but she never came back.'

Duro felt a chill running down his spine. He sincerely hoped Gisel hadn't been out there for too long. 'I'll deal with her, never fear. In fact, let's do it now.' He lifted her off his lap. 'Come,' he said, and took her hand, marching into the main area of the roundhouse.

The others were sitting around the fire, Bellicia half hidden next to her father. She peered round him, but quickly averted her gaze. Duro wasn't fooled by this attempt at meekness.

'Good evening, everyone, this is my wife, Gisel,' he announced. 'And it would appear that someone here wished her ill.' Looks of consternation were thrown around, people peering at their neighbours as if to ascertain whom he was talking about. 'Bellicia, I will personally give you ten lashes tomorrow morning. What you did was despicable, and you'll be lucky if I allow you to stay in this settlement henceforth.'

Commios stood up. 'Now see here, I decide who stays or goes. What is going on?'

'You're wrong, boy.' Belcatus got to his feet too. 'Whether you like it or not, Duro is your older brother, and as such he has the right to lead this settlement. Besides, he owns it. Best you come to terms with that.' Before Commios could do more than open his mouth to protest, Belcatus fixed his gaze on Duro. 'What did my daughter do?'

'She deliberately took my very cold and very wet wife to a disused hut and left her there without so much as a drying sheet. This despite the fact that I told her specifically to see to my *guest.* Since when do we treat guests like that? And she also disrespected her, then lied and claimed to be married to me, trying to sow discord between us to make Gisel go away. Presumably so that she could attempt to seduce me at some point, even though I made it abundantly clear that I'm not interested in her.'

Belcatus glared down at his daughter. 'Is this true?'

Bellicia pouted but wouldn't look her father in the eye. 'How was I supposed to know she was Duro's wife? She looked like a bedraggled rat and it was dark.'

'Did he or did he not ask you to see to a guest?' her father growled.

'I suppose,' she muttered.

'You suppose?' Belcatus backhanded her, the blow snapping her head back. 'What is wrong with you, girl?'

'She's been going around saying she was to marry Duro when he returned,' Mina piped up helpfully.

'Has she, by Belenos.' Belcatus grabbed his daughter's arm and hauled her to her feet. 'Did I not tell you Duro wasn't for you? The man has better sense. Commios didn't want you, so why should his brother? You're nothing but trouble, and everyone knows it. The gods help me. I have no idea how I sired such a daughter.'

Bellicia began to cry, but Duro merely gave her a hard stare. 'Ten lashes,' he repeated. 'Perhaps your father will be so kind as to lock you in somewhere for the night. I'd suggest the disused hut you put Gisel in.'

'That I will,' Belcatus said through gritted teeth. He dragged a protesting Bellicia out the door and into the rain.

After they'd gone, appalled silence reigned for a moment. Duro went over to sit by the fire and again pulled Gisel down onto his lap. He was grateful to be snug indoors where the howling wind and pounding rain couldn't even be heard. They were both safe at last, thank the gods, and he'd make sure they stayed that way from now on.

'I'll introduce you to everyone tomorrow,' he told her, 'but for now, this is my brother Commios.' He indicated the man on his right. 'And the kind lady bringing us something to eat is Maerica, who helped raise me. Thank you,' he added, when a bowl of warm broth and a piece of bread was placed in his hands. Gisel was given the same.

'My pleasure. And welcome, Gisel, it's lovely to meet you.' Maerica beamed at them both.

'My thanks,' Gisel murmured. 'I look forward to getting to know you.'

'So you're staying?' Commios asked, scowling.

Duro sighed. 'Yes, we're staying. Whether you like it or not, this is my home, brother. I have spent nineteen years longing for my family, my kin, and there's nowhere else I'd rather be. I'm hoping we can live together in harmony. To that end, I'm willing to share the duties of chieftain with you, if you'll agree. I cannot say fairer than that. I understand your resentment, but it's not my fault I was taken captive, nor that I was born before you. I do not wish to fight you. Please, can we have peace between us?'

Commios bent his head and nodded, before looking up at Duro again. 'Aye, we can. I'll be happy to share with you. Come to think of it, you're the only family I have as well. Unless you're about to tell me you found the others?'

Duro felt his shoulders relax. He hadn't realised how tense he was, wanting his brother to accept his presence so much it hurt.

'Actually, I did. Or rather, *we* did, as Gisel helped me. But neither of them wished to come home at this point. Rufilia confided at the last moment that she is hoping to wed a blacksmith she's fond of, and her son is apprenticed to that very smith.' At his brother's look of astonishment, he smiled. 'Yes, she has a son, Marcus, who's seen eighteen winters already. And although he's the offspring of a man whose name I'll never mention again, he is nothing like him. He's one of us, honourable and brave. As for Caratius, he's alive and happy with his life for now. He said that when his term in the legion ends, he'll head this way, but who knows? That's many years hence. They all send their regards to everyone.'

'I'm glad to hear they are doing well. And a grown nephew? Who would have thought.' Commios smiled too.

Duro realised it was the first time he'd seen him do that. It made warmth spread inside him. 'Yes, makes me feel very old.'

Gisel, who had finished eating and handed her bowl back to Maerica, smacked him on the shoulder. 'You are not old, husband. I'll be enjoying you for many years yet.'

That made everyone laugh, and Duro prayed to all the gods she was right about that.

Chapter Twenty-Six

Wiltshire, July, present day

They were both rather quiet on the way home. It had been an eventful twenty-four hours and they were still reeling from what had happened the previous night. Mackenna's throat was sore and her head hurt, but her injuries weren't too serious. She had decided to press charges against Blue immediately, and had been interviewed by the police at length. Jonah had backed her up, of course, and there were quite a few witnesses as well as video recordings of the altercation. There was no way Blue could wriggle out of it, and he had been arrested.

Halfway along the M4, Mac received a surprise text message from her mother, Emelie, saying she was coming to the UK for a few days and asking if she could visit. She read it out to Jonah, thinking that perhaps it would be a good thing if they spent a few days apart. It would give him some space to calm down and come to terms with his former bandmate's behaviour. He'd been furious, wanting to beat the crap out of Blue when they didn't have an audience. This was uncharacteristic behaviour for Jonah, normally such a laid-back guy.

'He's not worth it,' she'd told him. 'He'll be more hurt if you ignore him. Besides, he's already in custody.'

'Yes. You're right. I'm sorry. I'm just so pissed off at him. Bastard!'

She turned to him now. 'My mum will want to stay with me, so I should probably go back to my flat for a couple of days. Would you mind dropping me off there, please?'

'Sure, but she'd be welcome at my place. You know that, right?'

She hesitated. 'Probably best if you don't meet her this time. She can get a little . . . overexcited, shall we say, about my boyfriends. What we have is so new, I kind of want to keep you to myself for a while longer. Is that OK?'

'Fine. You'll come back, though? I like having you with me.' The smile he gave her could have melted icebergs, and she reached over to caress his cheek.

'Of course. I'll be back as soon as I can.'

Mackenna was very happy to see her mother, and they spent an evening eating takeaway, sharing a bottle of wine and catching up. Apart from a brief description of events when Emelie exclaimed at the sight of Mac's bruised throat, she managed to forget the incident for a while. It felt so nice to just be her normal self, not a rock star's girlfriend caught up in a drama with her ex.

The following day, however, reality caught up with her in spectacular fashion. She and her mum had decided to go out and act as tourists in Bath, as Emelie had only been there once before. The weather was sultry, and they set off for the centre of town on foot, happy and carefree. That changed after only a few steps, when a group of journalists came rushing up to them, taking photos and shouting questions. Mac recoiled, instinctively burying her head in her mother's shoulder, while Emelie snarled at them and lifted a hand to shield her face.

'What on earth . . .?' she muttered.

'Shit, I should have realised they'd look for me here,' Mac muttered, but it was too late, and the eager group of paparazzi were blocking the way back to her flat. They must have been lying in wait around the corner this time, the sneaky bunch. There was nothing for it but to try and run in the other direction while the journalists continued to shout after them.

'Is it true you broke up the band?'

'Did you two-time Blue with Jonah? Is that why they had a fight?'

'Did you just make up the story about him cheating?'

'The fans are all blaming you for the band's break-up – how do you feel about that?'

'Blue's been arrested but he swears it's all your fault! Is it?'

The barrage of words washed over her like a foul tsunami. She wanted to put her hands over her ears so she wouldn't hear them, but she was too busy running, towing her mother along behind her. 'Run, Mamma, hurry! If we can get to the antiques place, Henry will help us get away.'

It was the only plan she could come up with. There wasn't enough time to stop and call Jonah, and she wasn't sure she wanted to involve him in any case. That would just excite the paps even more.

Somehow they made it to the antiques centre, and she and Emelie hurriedly fled upstairs and crouched down behind Henry's display counter, red-faced and panting. Panic was rising inside Mac, clawing at her insides. How could she have been so stupid? Of course they'd track her down after what had happened. But she'd been hoping they would concentrate on Blue and his arrest in London. She could see now she'd been incredibly naïve.

'Mackenna? What's going on?' Henry stared at them, eyes wide.

'Hide us, please! We're being pursued by journalists,' Mackenna hissed.

Henry looked startled, but he was a smart man and quickly grasped that his help was needed. 'Come this way,' he said, ushering them towards a small door that led to a back office. 'Stay in here until the coast is clear. I'll let you know.'

Soon afterwards, they heard a commotion outside, but Henry lied like a pro and claimed that he'd seen two women running past him but had no idea where they'd gone. A little while later, he came to tell them it was safe to emerge.

'But I think you'd better come back to my place, as they'll be bound to wait for you outside your flat,' he added. 'I doubt they're giving up that easily.'

While waiting, Mac had had ample time to scroll on her phone, and what she found made her feel sick to her stomach. Valhalla Storm's fans were divided in their opinions, but Blue had a huge, vociferous and sometimes rabid fan base, and they were all blaming Mackenna for the band's break-up. She was being called vile names and made out to be some kind of vicious man-eater who had lured Jonah away and caused all the issues between the two guys. She'd dealt with jealousy from fans before, when some of them had implied she wasn't good enough to be Blue's girlfriend, but she'd never taken them seriously. They would have disliked anyone who was lucky enough to be chosen by him.

This, however, was a whole other level of hatred.

She doesn't deserve to live. Die bitch! was only one of a long list of comments as the fans whipped each other into a hate-fuelled frenzy. Every aspect of Mackenna's life and appearance was picked apart, dissed and ridiculed. If she'd been low on self-confidence, reading these vile attacks would have floored her. As it was, it made her nauseous, but deep down she knew they would have done the same to anyone who threatened their beloved band or lead singer. It just happened to be her.

'Mac, darling, don't take it to heart.' Her mother had been reading over her shoulder, muttering imprecations at the online trolls. 'This will all blow over and none of it is your fault. You know that, right?'

She did, but at the same time there was a niggle of doubt. Jonah's decision to leave the band had been made after what happened between her and Blue. Although he'd told her that had nothing to do with it, and that he'd already made up his mind long before, Mac couldn't be completely sure. If, as he said, he'd wanted her right from the start, Blue's mistreatment of her might have pushed him into leaving sooner. No matter how she looked at it, she *was* the cause of dissention between the two. If she hadn't been in the picture, maybe they would have managed to make things work and kept the band together.

She sighed. 'Let's just go back to Henry's for now and then we'll decide what to do.'

'You should talk to Jonah,' her mum said.

'I know, but . . . not right now.' She couldn't face it. He'd definitely try to persuade her she wasn't at fault, and at the moment she wasn't sure she'd believe him. What she really needed was to escape from here altogether.

Jonah had mooched around the house for the rest of that day and evening, restless and unable to settle down to doing anything useful until Mackenna returned. He missed her like crazy. It was weird how quickly he'd become used to having her in his life and in his home, but he never wanted to be without her now. Also, he couldn't stop thinking about Blue's vicious attack on her. It made him want to spend every second of every day protecting her. That sort of thing could never be allowed to happen again.

When his doorbell rang the following morning, he ran to open it, hoping it would be her. He figured she might have had a change of heart and decided to introduce him to her mother after all. But his spirits sank as he found his sister outside instead. Not that he wasn't happy to see her, but he was disappointed it wasn't Mac.

'Gemma? What are you . . . *Oof!*'

She threw herself into his arms, hugging him tight. 'Oh my God, what a shitstorm! I thought I'd better come and make sure you're OK. You are, aren't you?' She leaned back to study his face, as if searching for confirmation.

He frowned. 'Of course. I wasn't hurt. It was my girlfriend Blue attacked. I just roughed him up a bit. Come in.' He opened the door wide and she stepped inside, dropping a backpack on the hall floor.

'I didn't mean that. Haven't you been online today? Your fans are up in arms, and there's a lot of hate, even death threats against your girlfriend. Blue's army are blaming her for everything.' Gemma scanned the hallway. 'Is she here? I think you need to hire some beefy security guys or something.'

'Death threats?' Jonah was horrified. 'What the hell?' Dread pooled in his stomach and the caveman instinct to protect Mackenna at all costs resurfaced with a vengeance. 'Show me!' he demanded, ushering Gemma into the kitchen.

Fred and Bagel came running and wanted to say hello, so it was a while before they were able to settle down at the table. Gemma scrolled on her phone, showing him the worst of the vitriol that was being hurled Mackenna's way. There was criticism of Jonah too – mixed with support from his own fans – but for the most part he was being portrayed as having been duped by Mac. For each comment he read, he became more and more upset. Fury rose within him, making him see red.

'What the fuck is wrong with these people? They're insane!

Blue attacked her. Actually tried to strangle her. Why aren't they mentioning that?' To be fair, a few of the fans had alluded to Blue's behaviour, but they were excusing it as justified jealousy towards a woman who had cheated on him. 'Unbelievable!'

Gemma slung an arm around his shoulder, giving him a sideways hug. 'I know, I know, but that's trolls for you. They love a good target, and like it or not, Blue has always been a big favourite with the women.' She hesitated. 'Look, I don't want to make you mad, but . . . is anything they're saying true? Did you leave the band because of Mackenna?' She held up a hand, as she must have seen the storm brewing in his gaze. 'I mean, I can see she's gorgeous, and she's probably totally worth it, but—'

'No! It had nothing to do with her. I had already decided to quit. Blue mistreating her was just a small part of it. Everything he did had started to annoy me, so I'd made up my mind to leave after our tour was done.' He gestured towards her phone. 'All this crap is lies. Mac and I didn't get together until two weeks ago. Before that, we were just friends. So how can she possibly be blamed? My beef was with Blue, always has been. And I'm not the only one. Owen felt the same.'

Gemma nodded. 'Well, then I guess you're going to have to set the record straight. Maybe talk to Mackenna first? And feed me, please. I haven't had any breakfast yet.'

He shook his head at her, but truth to tell, he was grateful to her for coming. They might not always agree on everything, but they had each other's back. 'Help yourself to anything in the fridge. And don't feed the dogs, they do *not* need any extra titbits. I'm going to go and call Mac.'

He headed for the orangery, a place he would always associate with her, but although he tried several times, she wasn't picking up. Perhaps she was busy doing stuff with her mother and hadn't seen any of the social media frenzy yet. He hoped so. He sent off a couple of messages asking her to call him urgently, but there was nothing he could do until she replied.

Even more restless now, he spent some time with Gemma, catching up on her news, then played with the dogs in the garden. Still nothing from Mac. He was just contemplating heading into Bath to find her when he finally received a text.

Hey, sorry for the silence. Had a bit of a crazy day being chased by paparazzi and hated on big-time. In hiding now but heading off to Sweden tomorrow to lie low for a bit. I need some time to think things over. Thanks for the last few weeks. They meant a lot, but I'm not sure I can do this. And I don't want to ruin things for you either. You deserve better. Xxx

His insides turned to ice and he felt as if he couldn't breathe. 'Nooo!' he whispered. Despair settled in his gut and he wanted to howl. How could things have gone so wrong so fast?

'*Fuck!*' he shouted, banging his fist on the nearest table.

Fred and Bagel came running, followed by Gemma. 'What's going on? Are you OK?'

'No!' he yelled, then buried his face in his hands. 'No, I'm not. Mac just texted. She's running away. Going to Sweden. And I think she just broke up with me. I . . . I don't know what to do! She won't talk to me.'

Gemma came over and put her arms around him, letting him lean against her. 'Hey, it'll be fine. You can't blame her for being scared right now. I'd run away too if I was her. Seriously, death threats? Just for dating someone? That's crazy. She'll calm down.'

'Yes, but how do I persuade her to come back to me? I've wanted her for so long, I can't lose her now, Gems. Not when I finally got her to be with me. What do I do?'

'Hmm, I don't know, but we'll come up with something, don't worry. Judging by the photos from the launch party, she's totally gone for you. She was looking at you like you were some kind of god.'

Jonah groaned, remembering the stupid joke he'd made. But Gemma was right – Mac had seemed as keen on him as he was on her. He just had to persuade her this madness would die down and he was worth all the media intrusion that came with being his girlfriend. And he needed to set the record straight – no way was he going to let Blue win. Because that was what the bastard was doing right now, and Jonah didn't doubt he had fed a few trusted fans a bunch of lies to make it seem like he was the victim here.

He wasn't going to get away with that. Never again.

Mackenna was lying in a hammock with one foot on the ground, listlessly rocking herself while staring at the blue sky. It had been three days since she'd arrived in Sweden, where her mother had taken her straight to her summer cottage by a lake. It was deep inside a huge forest somewhere in the southern part of the country and no one would find her here. Not unless she wanted them to.

Jonah had texted her a few times, but she hadn't replied. He'd pleaded with her to call him, to talk things through, but what would she even say? That although she was madly in love with him, she wasn't sure she could handle being harassed to the extent that people wanted her dead. They'd only just started dating, so wasn't it better to end things now, before they were in too deep?

You're already in too deep, idiot! But she silenced the little voice inside her head.

She'd indulged in a couple of long crying sessions, curled up on her bed, but she knew that was pointless. Tears achieved nothing. She had to decide what to do, but she was still feeling fragile after Blue's attack and the panic of that chase through Bath. Not to mention the vitriol on the internet. It wouldn't be a bad thing to cut herself some slack and try to heal before making up her mind.

In the meantime, she wasn't even going to look at social media. That way lay madness and despair.

The only person whose texts she had been responding to was Helle. The Danish girl had reached out to her almost immediately, saying that she and Owen were on her side.

Don't let the bastards get you down! This is going to be sorted out soon. Just hang tight, she'd said. Mac didn't know what they could do to help, but it was nice to have a friend.

The following day she woke up to a message from Helle with a link attached. *You need to watch this*, was all it said, and Mac sat up in bed to make herself comfortable against the pillows before clicking on the link. It was a video that had been uploaded to YouTube, and it appeared to have gone viral judging by the number of likes and views.

It turned out to be an episode of a daytime talk show, and the surprise guest of the day was none other than Jonah. Mac inhaled sharply, watching his beloved face as the host began to speak.

'Today we welcome Jonah Miller, lead guitarist of rock band Valhalla Storm. It's lovely to have you here today and I'm honoured – I know you've never done anything like this before. You're a pretty private guy, am I right?'

'Yeah, this isn't really my thing,' Jonah confirmed with a tight smile. 'I used to leave all that to Blue Daniels, the frontman of our band.'

'Right, right. But I understand that you've been having a bit of a disagreement with your bandmates recently, and you've chosen my programme to clarify a few things. Thank you for that.'

'No, thank you for having me. And it's only one band member who's been causing problems. Owen, Steve and I are tight. In fact, they came with me today.' Jonah glanced to the side of the TV studio, and as if on cue, the other two Valhalla Storm guys came ambling over and sat down next to him on the garish red sofa.

The host looked genuinely surprised, but recovered with aplomb. 'Oh wow, well, well! This is great. Welcome, guys!'

Owen and Steve nodded and mumbled their thanks. They too had always left TV appearances to Blue, as Mac well knew. Her ex-boyfriend had revelled in the limelight.

'So what was it you wanted to say?' the host prompted.

Jonah turned to face the camera head-on, his expression serious. 'We wanted to set the record straight once and for all. Recently there have been some rumours about the fact that the band is splitting up. My amazing girlfriend Mackenna Jackson has been blamed by fans for this break-up, but the fact is that I had decided to quit ages ago. Long before she and I started dating. I was just waiting for the band's latest tour to be over with and the new album to be released before going public.' He nodded towards his bandmates. 'Owen had decided to leave too, while Steve was going to stay and try to carry on with Blue and a couple of new guys.'

'Not any more,' Steve interjected, shaking his head.

'And why is that?' the host enquired, avidly watching the three rock stars.

'Because of what Blue did, of course,' Owen replied. 'I'm sure everyone's seen the footage from our launch party when he attacked Jonah's girlfriend. Totally unacceptable, man.'

'I'm guessing he didn't like it that she'd hooked up with Jonah behind his back,' the host said, smiling insincerely.

'She didn't!' Jonah practically growled. 'They broke up back in May because she found Blue in bed with two other women. She and I didn't start dating until recently. He has only himself to blame for losing her.' He looked into the camera again. 'And Mackenna, if you're watching this, I want you to know that I love you, and I'll move heaven and earth to keep that creep away from you from now on. And all the nosy journalists and trolls too. I mean it! Please trust me.'

His gaze was so earnest, that blue gaze piercing straight into her heart. Mackenna had to pause the video and take a deep breath. She found that there were tears running down her face, and she swiped at them impatiently. This was unbelievable. Jonah was on daytime TV confessing his love to her. How could she possibly resist that? She knew how much courage it must have taken him. He hated interviews and being the centre of attention. But he'd done this for her. Wow.

Swallowing down a sob, she hit 'play' again to watch the rest of the programme.

'So you're saying Miss Jackson is not to blame for anything? It's all the fault of Blue Daniels, who, I understand, is currently in custody facing serious assault charges?' The host sounded almost gleeful at mentioning this.

'Yeah, that's right. His fans have been trolling my girlfriend, but she's completely innocent,' Jonah confirmed.

'And he's been fired by our management,' Steve added. 'I'll never work with him again, and nor will anyone else if they've got any sense.'

'The fans should know what Blue is really like – self-centred, egotistical and a total narcissist,' Jonah continued. 'It's been great to have their support for Valhalla Storm all these years, but them sending my girlfriend death threats because of him is a step too far, and you'd better believe we'll prosecute anyone found doing it.'

'Absolutely. That's terrible,' the host agreed with a theatrical shudder, turning to the camera. 'Really, people, there's no need for anything like that. We're all civilised here.' He smiled smugly. 'And now that you've heard the truth right here on my show, everything should be crystal clear. Thank you so much, guys, for coming here today. We appreciate it and wish you all the best for the future, whatever that may hold.'

The host was obviously delighted with this coup, and Mac

could understand why. Those three guys had never before willingly appeared on a show like that. But they'd done it for her.

That thought galvanised her into action. She needed to go back to the UK now, this instant, to see Jonah. If he was willing to tell the whole world he loved her, she was surely brave enough to put up with the internet trolling. Interest would die down eventually, and they'd be left alone.

It was time to leave.

'Are you sure this is the right way?' Jonah glanced through the windscreen anxiously, while Owen calmly carried on driving. 'Looks like the back end of beyond.'

'Ever heard of satnav?' Owen teased.

'Yeah, yeah, smartass.' Jonah turned to look at Helle, who was in the back seat of their hire car. 'This is the address she gave you, though?'

'Yes.' Helle smiled and patted his shoulder. 'Relax. This is where she said she's been staying, so unless she's left suddenly, she'll be here.'

'And you forwarded the YouTube link?'

Jonah still couldn't believe he'd gone on TV to confess his love for Mac, but Gemma had urged him to make what she called 'a big romantic gesture'. It had seemed the only way to make Mackenna see that he was serious.

'Yes. She said she cried.'

'What? That doesn't sound good.' Jonah tried to quell the butterflies that had taken up semi-permanent residence in his stomach.

'Trust me, it is. Good tears.' Helle grinned and pointed ahead. 'Look, we're here.'

'Here' was in the middle of nowhere, as far as Jonah could make out. They were deep inside a massive forest that consisted mostly of huge Christmas trees and tall, straight pines. The road they'd been following had turned into nothing more than a small track, which ended near a lake that glittered in the summer sun. It was a beautiful setting for the tiny red-and-white-painted cottage that sat near the shore. But Jonah barely took it in. His eyes were scanning the scene in front of him looking for only one person – Mackenna.

He jumped out of the car the minute they stopped, not waiting for the other two, and sprinted towards the open door of the cottage. Just as he reached it, Mac stepped out, stopping dead at the sight of him. Her eyes opened wide, and she dropped the bag she'd been carrying. He vaguely registered that it was a small suitcase, but then his arms were suddenly full of warm, sweet-smelling woman and he forgot everything else.

'Jonah! You're here!'

He didn't reply at first, just kissed her as if his life depended on it. And maybe it did. He'd meant to just give her the one kiss before making sure she was really OK, and that she loved him as much as he loved her. But once their lips met, it ignited an inferno between them and he never wanted to stop.

Giggling and a throat being cleared loudly finally brought him back to his senses. He pulled away slightly, but didn't let her go entirely. Staring into her eyes, which were red-rimmed with dark circles underneath, emotion tore through him. He shook his head. 'Sweetheart, I would follow you anywhere. I'm crazy about you! Surely you know that?'

She smiled, her eyes brimming with tears, but he was fairly sure they were the good kind, like Helle had said. 'I do now. I mean, you kind of told the whole world.'

He laughed and hugged her tight. 'I did, didn't I. Do you mind?'

'Hell, no! In fact I was just leaving to go back to the UK. I had to see you, to tell you I feel the same way. I love you, Jonah! You have no idea how much.'

'Thank God for that!' He threw a glance over his shoulder at Owen and Helle, who'd been waiting patiently. 'See? I didn't make a prat of myself for nothing.'

'Never said you did. You're just a prat in general.' Owen chuckled, then yelped as Helle punched him on the arm. 'OK, OK, he's a great guy. I'm glad you're taking him back, Mac. He's been unbearable since you left. Hello, by the way.'

Mac peered around Jonah and waved at his two friends. 'Hi. Thank you for bringing him. I take it I have you to thank for this, Helle?'

'He would have found you one way or another. I made it faster, is all.'

'Ahem. Do I get to finally meet the famous Jonah?'

He looked over Mac's head to see a woman who had to be her mother grinning at him. He held out a hand to shake hers. 'That's me. Pleased to meet you, Mrs . . . Jackson?'

'Oh no, no. That's Mackenna's father's name, not mine. Just Emelie will do. Welcome! And you too,' she added to Owen and Helle. 'I think this calls for *fika*, don't you?'

'Um, sure?' Jonah glanced at Mac, hoping for clarification.

'Coffee and cake, or preferably cinnamon buns,' she explained. 'Yes, please, Mamma. Just give us a minute.' She towed Jonah into the little house and he gladly followed.

Once inside, she pulled him into a small room with an iron bedstead covered in an old-fashioned crocheted bedspread and shut the door. 'I wanted you to myself for a moment first. I can't believe you're here! I've missed you so much.'

He put his arms around her again and tugged her close. 'Same. I thought I'd go crazy without you. Please don't ever leave me again. Next time, talk to me, OK? Together we can sort anything out.'

'I promise. And I'm sorry. I overreacted and it won't happen again.'

'Good.' He kissed her deeply, then stared into her beautiful eyes. 'I'm not letting you out of my sight again for a long time,' he murmured, his voice husky with emotion. 'And I'm going to make up for all this crying you've been doing. As soon as we get home, we're staying in bed for at least a week.'

'Sounds like heaven to me.'

Jonah agreed. He kissed her some more, but tried not to get too carried away since there were people waiting for them outside. They had all the time in the world now, and he couldn't wait to get her back to his house. No, *their* house, because he was going to make sure she never left again.

She belonged with him, nowhere else.

Chapter Twenty-Seven

Eastern Britannia, July AD 81

Gisel hoisted her four-month-old son onto her shoulder and patted his back, smiling as she heard him belch. He was a voracious little thing, wanting to feed at all hours, and it showed in his robust physique.

'You're going to be as big as your father, aren't you, eh, Cunobelinos? And just as handsome.' She hoped he would also one day become a wise and great leader, since he was named after a king, or so she'd been told.

Duro ducked inside the roundhouse, his gaze immediately finding hers. The love that shone in the depth of those blue eyes made warmth spread inside her, as always. She was happier than she'd ever been, and it was all thanks to this man.

With the help of his kinsmen, he'd built them a dwelling of their own so that they didn't have to share with others. It wasn't as large as the one Commios still inhabited, but it was cosy and suited Gisel perfectly. He'd also insisted on hiring some Roman veterans to build a bath house, complete with underfloor heating supplied by a special furnace, and a fine mosaic floor in the changing room.

'I became used to almost daily bathing in Pompeii and I can't do without it now,' he'd explained. Gisel had no objection, especially when they got to spend time there alone while Maerica watched their son. Private moments with Duro were precious, and she cherished each and every one, as did he.

Things weren't always easy, and Duro still occasionally butted heads with his brother. He'd wanted to implement various new innovative techniques to guarantee better harvests, and try new crops, but Commios protested on principle. Duro had built drying ovens to stop the grain from going mouldy, and granaries to store it in rather than the pits his tribe had used for generations. Commios had grumbled, but finally admitted it made sense. The latter had also refused to use shears for clipping wool, rather than hand-plucking it, until he had realised how much they gained by doing so. Everything was a battle with him, but Duro was stubborn and usually got his way in the end, rarely losing his temper. Gisel was proud of him for that.

He walked over to her now and took their child from her, wedging him securely in the crook of his arm. Holding out the other hand to her, he nodded towards the door. 'Come, wife, we have visitors.'

'We do?' She stood up and tidied her clothing, smoothing out any creases, then picked up a beautiful, highly polished bronze mirror Duro had given her and made sure Cunobelinos hadn't brought up any milk on her shoulder. 'I thought you said Raedwald and Aemilia were too busy to come over at present. Did they change their minds?'

She'd met his friends many times now, and had formed a strong bond with the Roman woman Duro's fellow gladiator was married to. She and Aemilia had much in common and Gisel liked her immensely.

Duro shook his head. 'No, it's someone else.' Without giving her any clues, he headed for the door, murmuring to his son. Gisel smiled at the sight of her husband doting on their child. He was fair besotted, which was as it should be.

The July sunshine temporarily blinded her, but as she blinked to clear her vision, she gasped out loud. 'Father! And Lurio? I can't believe it!'

Her father and brother stood next to Commios and Maerica, with other inhabitants of the settlement crowding round them. Gisel fairly flew over to them and threw herself at her father, hugging him while tears of happiness flowed down her cheeks. He pulled her close, then relinquished her into a crushing embrace from her brother.

'Gisel, my dearest daughter! I never thought we'd see you again.' Her father was visibly moved, but managed to keep the tears at bay. He looked at Duro, who grinned back. 'We can't thank your husband enough for letting us know you were safe and well. And for making our travel arrangements.'

Gisel let go of her brother and stared between the two. 'Duro found you? And had you brought here?' She turned to her husband and pulled him down for a kiss. 'Thank you! You have no idea how much this means to me.'

He kissed her back. 'Oh, I think I have an inkling. I arranged for one of our trading partners in Gaul to bring them over. I'm only sorry it took so long to find them. It was more difficult than I'd expected, and then we had to wait for the summer weather before it was safe to cross the sea.'

'No matter. They're here now.' She beamed at her relatives. 'I'm so happy to see you both. Come inside and have some refreshment. You must be tired from your journey.'

'Thank you, but isn't there someone you should introduce us to first?' Her father sent a meaningful glance at the baby nestled against Duro's chest.

'Oh, of course. How could I forget?' Gisel laughed. 'This is our son, Cunobelinos. He's four months old and thriving, as you can see. In fact, he's a little glutton and will soon be as big as a house.'

'I'm pleased to make your acquaintance, young man. May I hold him?' He took the infant and held him up, smiling at the way the little boy studied him. 'Hmm, I believe he's still a bit suspicious of us, but he'll soon learn. I'm your grandfather, and we're going to be great friends.'

Once he'd handed the child to his mother, they all trooped inside, where Maerica took charge of dispensing refreshments. Gisel halted by the doorway and tugged on Duro's arm, looking up at her wonderful husband.

'Have I told you lately how much I love you?' she whispered. 'You're absolutely wonderful and I'm so lucky to be your wife.'

He bent to give her a tender kiss. 'Not as lucky as I am. I have everything I ever dreamed of, and more, and I love you more than words can express. I always will.'

She believed him, and as she followed him inside the roundhouse, she knew they would have a very long and happy life together.

Chapter Twenty-Eight

Wiltshire, September, present day

It was the perfect day for a celebration – sunny, but not too hot and humid, and with a perfect blue sky, the same colour as Jonah's eyes. Mac tore her gaze away from that of her husband and looked around the orangery with pride. They had transformed it for the occasion, and it was decked out with garlands and wreaths of yellow and white flowers, with accents of lilac. Little café-style Victorian tables with cast-iron legs and marble tops were dotted around the room, each with its own flower arrangement. And matching chairs seated the guests, who were few in number but had been selected with care.

'I love this room,' she murmured, opening her mouth for the forkful of cake that Jonah was holding up to her. 'Mm, and that's delicious!'

He leaned over to lick off a small blob of cream that had escaped to the corner of her lips. 'Yes, it is,' he murmured, his voice as always sending a ripple of desire through her body. 'Maybe we can take some of it to bed with us later. Then I can lick it off other parts of you.'

'I like how you think.' She smiled at him and gave him a

lingering kiss. It would have to be enough for now, as they still had a lot of partying to do.

They had been officially married the previous day at the local registry office, a secret event attended only by themselves and their two witnesses, Owen and Helle. Today they'd wanted to celebrate with all their loved ones, staging a pretend wedding ceremony in Jonah's garden that was merely an affirmation of their love, renewing the vows they had made the day before in front of everyone.

Their guests comprised both their families, as well as their closest friends. Helle was matron of honour, while Savannah and Gemma were Mac's bridesmaids. The latter two had been ecstatic at getting to choose dresses from a famous store in New Bond Street. Jonah had paid for everything, his only stipulations being that Mac had the final say. Mac's own dress had been designed by a very talented lady who had a shop in Bath, and the Victorian twist on a modern design fitted the wedding setting perfectly. She'd also loved seeing the appreciative look Jonah had given her when he'd first caught sight of her in it, walking down the aisle of the outdoor venue that had been set up on the lawn. It had consisted of just a few rows of chairs facing a flower-covered arch, underneath which they'd exchanged vows they'd written themselves.

Fred and Bagel had been the ring-bearers. The two French bulldogs wore little matching waistcoats and bow ties, and had had a ring each hanging in pouches around their necks. Savannah and Gemma had held on to their leads, as well as the long lacy veil Mac wore, while Helle had been in charge of the bridal bouquet. The sight of the two dogs had made everyone smile, and the canines had behaved impeccably for once.

Everything had been just perfect.

'Let's go outside and get some fresh air,' Jonah suggested, when the speeches and toasts were finished. 'I want you to myself for a little while before the dancing starts.'

They were having an eighties-style disco on the patio, which had been decorated with flowers and shrubs in planters and strung with fairy lights. It was starting to look beautiful now that dusk was falling.

Mac followed her new husband outside, and they held hands as they wandered down the lawn. She'd kicked off her high heels, which was just as well or she would have got stuck. Once they were out of sight of their guests, Jonah stopped and pulled her into his embrace. He looked down at her and pushed a tendril of her hair behind one ear.

'Have I told you that you look absolutely stunning, Mrs Miller? I'm definitely the luckiest man on earth.'

She smiled. 'And I'm the luckiest woman. You don't look so bad yourself, husband dearest.' Standing on tiptoes, she cupped his cheek with one hand and kissed him tenderly.

Her Roman ring flashed in the last rays of the sun, and it had now been given a companion in similar style. Jonah had surprised her by proposing during a recent visit to the Roman baths. He'd sunk down on one knee by the edge of the pool, pulling out another intaglio ring from his pocket.

'Please will you marry me, Mackenna? I love you and want to spend the rest of my life with you,' he'd said, his eyes shining with love.

She'd been absolutely gobsmacked, but ecstatic. To the accompaniment of cheers from other visitors to the attraction, she'd accepted, nearly catapulting the pair of them into the green water as she threw her arms around his neck.

Later, he'd told her, 'The ring reminded me of the one from your aunt, and I wanted you to have a matching one from me.' She was moved to tears by his thoughtfulness.

As he'd put it on her finger, for a moment it had felt as if it hummed against them, binding them together with an electric shock, but Mac was sure she'd imagined that.

Before the wedding, the shop owner in Burlington Arcade had helped them to hunt down some more antique Roman rings, one for each of them, and it had felt so very right. Mac knew that Jonah also carried the gold coin they'd found in the garden in his pocket. He had purposely forgotten to tell the archaeologist about that particular find. It was illegal, but they had tacitly agreed never to speak of it as Jonah said he felt as though it belonged with him.

The Roman rings all seemed to shine extra brightly today, and Mac glanced at hers. 'You know, I had the weirdest dream last night,' she said. 'You were in it and you had long golden hair and were wearing strange clothes. It was like an older incarnation of you, but I was in love with that version too.'

'Oh yeah? And did I adore you in your dream too? I feel like we were always meant to be. I knew the moment I saw you that you ought to be mine, even though you took a bit longer to notice.' He nudged her nose teasingly with his.

She smiled. 'Maybe we're soulmates all the way back from Roman times? Either way, I'm not letting you go in this lifetime. Perhaps not in future ones either.'

'That is absolutely fine with me, my beautiful wife. Now let's go and have our first dance and start our life together. I can't wait to share it with you.'

Mackenna couldn't wait either, and as she followed Jonah back across the lawn, she knew he was hers now and for ever.

Acknowledgements

This is the second book I've written set in Roman times and I really enjoyed returning to that era. I had already done a lot of the research about the Romans for the first book, but as this one takes place in Britain, I still needed to go on various trips to find out specific details. A massive thank you to my husband Richard for his patience in coming with me to places like Butser Ancient Farm, Caerleon's various Roman museums and sites, and to Bath. He definitely deserved that afternoon tea in the Pump Room!

I want to say a big thank you to my lovely editor Sophie Keefe and her team at Headline – you're such a joy to work with! I'm also very grateful to Caroline Hogg for her brilliant structural edit – she helped make the ending so much stronger. As always, many thanks to the cover designer Sarah Whittaker for the gorgeous cover, and to the narrator of all my books, Eilidh Beaton, who does such a great job whether the stories are about Vikings or Romans! Huge thanks also to Lina Langlee, my fabulous agent, for always encouraging and supporting me!

The hero in the present is in a rock band and I had quite a lot of trouble coming up with a suitable name – the best ones all seem to be taken already! But I'd like to thank my daughter

Jessamy for the many hours she spent brainstorming with me. Although I didn't end up using any of those names, I still appreciate all the effort she put into it. In the end, I asked my friends on Facebook for help too and their suggestions gave me inspiration. Some were brilliant but sadly also already used by real bands. I ended up with Valhalla Storm, which was half my own invention and half of the name Rebecca LaGrange McDonald came up with, so I owe Rebecca a free book for that – thank you!

A special thank you to my wonderful friend Alison Morton for answering random questions about the Romans – I really appreciate your assistance and patience, and I hope I haven't made any terrible *faux pas*!

As always, thank you to my lovely friends – Sue Moorcroft, Myra Kersner, Henriette Gyland, Gill Stewart, Tina Brown, Carol Dahlén, Nicola Cornick and the other Word Wenches: Anne Gracie, Andrea Penrose, Patricia Rice, Mary Jo Putney and Susan Fraser King. You're the best!

I wouldn't be able to carry on writing without the amazing readers, reviewers and book bloggers who support me – thank you so, so much! I am incredibly grateful and I hope you will enjoy returning to the Roman era with me again!

Christina x

PS. If you want to keep up with news, behind-the-scenes information and special deals, please sign up for my newsletter – you'll find the details here: https://tinyurl.com/mr3fu9ch

Bonus Material

The Perfect Spouse

Eastern Britannia, June AD 82

As Commios left his home settlement he felt as though he could finally breathe properly. An invisible weight was lifted off his shoulders the moment he exited the gate, and his entire body relaxed. He urged his horse into a canter, and the animal must have picked up on his improved mood as it set off eagerly.

'That's it, boy! Let's get away from here,' he murmured. If the road hadn't been so full of holes from a recent rain storm, he would have gone even faster.

Lately he'd been feeling suffocated and depressed, and yet he had no valid reason for that. He ought to have been happy. He liked and got on well with everyone in his extended kin group, and had come to love his older brother Duro since the latter's return two summers ago. Duro was the elder of the two of them and therefore had the right to be chieftain, but he'd graciously offered to share those duties. Since Commios had been the settlement's leader for several years before that, he'd been relieved not to be completely demoted. And on the whole, everything had worked out well.

They still butted heads occasionally, but what brothers didn't?

It was only to be expected. And Commios had to admit that Duro had some great ideas, even if he'd rather not acknowledge it straight away. Commios really had no reason to complain about his brother, so why did he still secretly resent him?

You're jealous, the little voice inside his head said. Nothing to do with the chieftain's duties, but more the fact that Duro was so happy. The man had everything he'd ever wanted – a beautiful wife who adored him, a son who was thriving, more riches than he needed, a business venture that was starting to go well, and a place among his kin. Commios knew Duro had earned all this. Fate had been unkind to his brother for nineteen years while he was enslaved by the Romans and was forced to be a gladiator, risking his life every time he fought. He'd made it through all those hardships and returned to Britannia, and he deserved all the happiness in the world.

Then why does that make me so miserable?

Commios wasn't unhappy exactly. He had everything he needed too, but he was alone. None of the women in their settlement tempted him to embark on matrimony, and in truth he was lonely. He'd like a family of his own too. Children. A loving wife to welcome him home of an evening, but he refused to settle for just anyone. Although marriage, for most people, was just a contract, he didn't see it that way. Like Duro, he wanted the perfect spouse. Someone who was perfect for him.

The two foremost candidates in their settlement, Bellicia and Mina, were not to his taste. Bellicia was a nasty piece of work, vain and perpetually dissatisfied, while Mina was so self-effacing she'd blend into the shadows if she wasn't careful. Neither was the kind of wife a chieftain needed. Commios sighed. He was on his way to a settlement almost a day's ride away to see if there was a suitable wife for him. He'd been told the chieftain had a daughter of marriageable age and a match had been proposed between them. She was said to be comely and well trained in all housewifely duties. That wasn't enough for him – looks weren't everything to his mind – so he wanted to meet her for himself before he agreed to anything.

He prayed to Cernunnos that she proved to be suitable in every way.

Commios arrived at dusk, just before supper. He was greeted by the chieftain Adminius who stood outside the largest of the settlement's roundhouses. On one side he was flanked by what was presumably his right-hand man, a heavy-set warrior with a forbidding countenance, and on the other stood a lady with a stony expression.

'Welcome, Commios. I trust you had a good journey? This is my wife, Verica.'

The lady nodded at him regally, looking down her nose at him despite the fact that she was at least a head shorter. Commios pretended not to notice even though she was being rude.

'A pleasure to meet you both,' he said, although he wasn't convinced this was an auspicious start.

Adminius moved slightly to the side to reveal a younger woman who'd been standing behind him. 'And this is our daughter Enica.'

She was indeed strikingly beautiful in an other-worldly sort of way. Small but perfectly formed, with a heart-shaped face that tapered into a determined little chin. Translucent skin, a perfect little nose, rosebud mouth, and enormous cornflower-blue eyes, surrounded by tresses of blonde hair confined in two plaits. She wore a costly tunic in varying shades of blue that matched her eyes, and a cloak loosely held together by an intricate silver brooch.

'I'm pleased to make your acquaintance as well,' Commios told her politely.

'And you.' She inclined her head, her expression cool and not particularly welcoming.

His heart sank. He had the immediate impression that he was being judged and so far she wasn't impressed, although he couldn't for the life of him figure out why. It was true that he wasn't as impressive in size as his brother, but he wasn't far off and had been told he wasn't bad-looking. He had the same golden hair as Duro, the same ice-blue eyes, and a good physique. Still, perhaps Enica was merely reserving judgement until she got to know him better. He resolved not to make a snap judgement either and he would give her the benefit of the doubt for now.

'Come inside, do. Supper will be ready in a trice.' Adminius ushered him into the roundhouse, and indicated that he should sit next to him on a chair that must have been placed there specially. Normally only the chieftain had a chair while everyone else made do with benches around the hearth.

The other inhabitants of the settlement filed in behind them. Commios had seen them gathering outside soon after his arrival. No doubt they were all curious about him, this possible suitor to their chief's daughter. He pretended not to notice and made small talk with his host while ale was served.

'Ivixa! Look what you're about. You spilled on my best tunic, you clumsy oaf!'

Commios turned to look in surprise at Enica, who'd been seated on a bench on his other side. A serving woman was attempting to mop up a minuscule amount of ale that had apparently dripped onto Enica's clothing while the latter glared daggers at her. To his surprise, the serving woman talked back.

'You can barely see it,' she retorted. 'Don't make such a fuss for nothing. There, all dry now.'

He blinked as he digested this strange interaction. The

woman – Ivixa he assumed – was dressed rather plainly, but decently. Her tunic was russet-coloured and well made, but of a sturdy everyday material. The sort of thing a housewife would wear while doing chores. She was obviously not a slave, or she wouldn't have spoken thus to her mistress, and yet Enica was clearly furious.

'Well, don't stand there. Go and fetch the food for our guest,' Enica ordered.

Ivixa didn't reply, merely turned on her heel and went to do as she was bid. Commios watched her as she moved over to the hearth, where an older woman was ladling food into bowls for her to pass round. She was taller than Enica, and her hair was a chestnut colour that glinted with red highlights in the light from the fire. When she'd regarded Enica, he'd noticed that her eyes were an unusually clear green, and although she wasn't as dainty as the other woman, she was no less comely. Something stirred inside him and he couldn't stop staring at her, although he did so surreptitiously. Her movements were sure and precise, and she carried herself like someone who knew her own worth. She looked strong and resilient too, and not at all meek.

Now he was even more intrigued, but dared not ask about her as he didn't want to offend his host. There was obviously some mystery here, but it wasn't any of his business.

Ivixa brought them each a bowl of stew that smelled divine, and he thanked her. She threw him a surprised glance, as if she wasn't used to that, but turned away hastily when he smiled at her. Chunks of the best kind of bread were served with the stew. It must have been baked specially for this occasion, and Commios wondered if his host treated all Enica's suitors thus. With her looks, he shouldn't have had any problems finding a suitable husband for her, but she had only just come of age so perhaps Adminius hadn't been trying for long.

'I hear tell you are second in command in your settlement, Commios,' Enica suddenly said, interrupting something her father was saying about this year's crops.

Commios regarded her with raised eyebrows, but her father didn't reprimand her for butting in. Instead he murmured with a smile, 'Enica, my dear, that's a little abrupt.'

It was more than abrupt, it was downright rude.

'Well, if I'm to wed someone I need to know more about them, don't I?' she replied, giving them a smile that was calculated to please and opening her eyes wide in feigned innocence. She added, 'I apologise. Perhaps I should have asked something inane first.'

'No need,' Commios said. 'I'm happy to answer any questions. And you're misinformed – I share the duties of chieftain with my older brother Duro. We are equals and both have a say in how our settlement is run.'

'That is . . . unusual.' Her perfectly shaped brows came down in a troubled frown. 'Does that mean your wife would have to share the role of chief woman with your brother's wife then?'

'Exactly. I'm hoping to find a wife who will take on half my sister-in-law's burden and work with her in harmony.'

'I was brought up to run a household on my own.' Enica's chin came up as she sent her father a look of challenge. 'I'm not used to sharing.'

'The gods can testify to that,' someone muttered behind Commios, but when he glanced over his shoulder, he only saw Ivixa standing there with a bland expression on her face as if she hadn't uttered a word. No one else appeared to have heard her so he returned his attention to Enica and her father.

'Now don't be hasty, daughter,' Adminius was saying. 'A burden shared is a burden halved. If you look at it like that, it means your duties would be less onerous and the responsibilities too.'

'Hmm, yes.' She turned those blue orbs on Commios again. 'Why have you not married before? You look to be well past the usual age.'

He didn't know whether to laugh or take offence. She made it sound as though he was ancient and not a man in his prime. Behind him a snort told him someone else found it amusing, but he dared not check this time. He was almost certain it was Ivixa who was still hovering in the background, holding a pitcher of ale at the ready in case anyone needed a refill.

'I have seen six-and-twenty winters, if that's what you want to know,' he informed Enica. 'And the reason I've not taken a wife yet is because I haven't found anyone to my liking.'

'I see. Well, that makes sense. One has to choose the best, after all.' Enica preened slightly and her mother, who'd been silent up until now, patted her arm.

'There, I told you he'd have a good reason.'

The conversation became more general after that, and Commios had the feeling he'd passed some sort of test. Enica didn't contribute any more, but sat quietly while he and Adminius discussed various topics. The older man hinted that his daughter came with a good dowry, which frankly wasn't important to Commios since his settlement was doing very well. He pretended he hadn't heard as he was now fairly certain he wasn't going to marry Enica. The girl was very attractive, but self-centred and rude. She was also so tiny she looked as if a gust of wind would blow her away. He doubted she'd have the strength – or inclination – to help Duro's wife Gisel much. Poor Gisel would be left to do most of the work herself.

After a while, he excused himself to use the privy and then stood outside in the dark breathing in the cool night air. He was reluctant to go back inside as he wasn't sure how to tell his host he wasn't interested in his daughter without offending him. With a sigh, he finally headed for the door, only to collide with someone who bounced off him and ended up on the ground with a thump.

'Ouch!'

He crouched down. 'I'm so sorry. I didn't see you there. Are you hurt?' He reached out to grab the person's upper arms to help them stand up.

'I'm fine. A little knock won't harm me. Really, you'd best be on your way. They're probably wondering where their prize has got to.'

'Ivixa?' Commios thought he recognised the voice.

'Er, yes. You know my name?' She was dusting off her backside and he had to force himself not to help. The moon had come out from behind a cloud and he could see her more clearly now.

'I heard it earlier. Tell me, how did you dare to answer back to the chieftain's daughter the way you did? I've been wondering about it all evening. Will you not be punished?'

She huffed out a laugh. 'Hardly! Enica is my sister and I talk to her how I please, no matter how important she thinks she is. I mean . . . not that she doesn't have every right to—'

Commios interrupted her. 'Sister? Adminius has more than one daughter?'

'Yes. I'm his daughter by his first wife, but my stepmother doesn't like it to be known by outsiders. She wants her precious child married off before they find me a husband. Enica is to have first choice. And by the looks of it, she's chosen you.'

'Has she, by Belenos.' He ground his teeth together. 'Despite me being so ancient?'

That made her giggle. 'Perhaps she won't mind so very much since you don't look it yet.'

'Thank you, you're too kind,' he retorted sarcastically, making her laugh again. 'Well, she won't be marrying me. Not if I have anything to say to it.'

Ivixa put a hand on his arm, instantly serious. 'I'm so sorry. I didn't mean to say anything detrimental. She'd make you a great wife. You'll be hard put to find anyone better. You've seen her – she's pure perfection. Everyone says so.'

'On the outside, perhaps, but that's not what I'm looking for in a wife. I need someone who is not afraid of hard work, who'll be a partner to me, and someone to share my sister-in-law's duties, as you probably heard me say earlier. Do you seriously believe Enica fits that description?'

'Um, I wouldn't like to say.'

'Ivixa, tell me the truth.' He gripped her shoulders so that she couldn't escape.

'Please don't make me,' she whispered, sounding torn. 'Enica is my sister, spoiled or not. I'll not ruin her chances. I can't.'

'And if I tell you she's already done that herself?' He wanted to shake her, but merely held her still instead.

'Then . . . no. Enica is not the right woman for you.' She took a step back and shook him off. 'Can I go now? I'll be missed.'

'Why? Are you at their beck and call at all times?' The thought made him supremely irritated. 'You're the older daughter. Shouldn't you sit with everyone else and relax? Your father has others to do the serving.'

'No, that's my task. I'm only allowed to stay here if I help out. My stepmother wanted me banished when she married Father. This was the compromise they agreed on.'

'Unbelievable,' Commios hissed. 'Right. We're going to do something about that.'

'Huh?'

He grabbed her hands and tugged her towards him. 'Ivixa, will you do me the honour of becoming my wife?'

'I beg your pardon? Have you run mad?'

It was his turn to laugh. 'No, on the contrary. I think I've finally found what I was looking for – you. From what I've seen so far, you fit all my requirements. There's only one thing we need to do to make sure we are compatible.'

'And what's that?' Ivixa sounded completely dazed and was staring at him as if she truly believed he'd lost his wits.

'This,' he said, and bent to kiss her.

He'd meant it to be a fairly chaste kiss, but once he started it took on a life of its own. Her mouth was luscious and inviting, with soft lips that fit his to perfection. After only a brief hesitation, she played along and copied his movements. When he nipped her bottom lip, she gasped in surprise and he took the opportunity to allow his tongue to delve inside. She soon caught on to this new game and followed his lead. He couldn't seem to stop and lost all sense of time and reason until they eventually had to come up for air.

He was breathing heavily, but his mind was made clear. 'I think that proves it beyond doubt,' he murmured, putting his arms around her and pulling her close. 'What say you?'

She was trembling and leaned her cheek against his chest. 'Are you seriously asking me to be your wife? This isn't a jest?'

He leaned back and placed one hand on her cheek, making her look up at him. 'I've never been more serious in my life, Ivixa. Please marry me? I want only you.'

She nodded. 'Then yes. Yes, I would love to be your wife.'

'Good. Let's go and ask your father's permission.'

They went back inside the roundhouse, Ivixa following a few steps behind him. He stopped in front of his host's chair and looked the man straight in the eyes.

'Adminius, I don't believe in beating around the bush so I will tell you the truth – I don't feel that Enica and I are suited to each other. I'm sorry. She is not the sort of wife I'm looking for.'

'What? But how can she not be? I'll have you know she's a prize and no mistake. Not to mention she comes with a substantial dowry, as I mentioned.'

Commios held up a hand. 'Indeed, she is beautiful beyond compare, but she is not for me. However, I would still like to make an alliance with you and marry your daughter, if you'll allow it.'

Adminius blinked, clearly flustered and confused. 'But you just said you didn't want her.'

'No, but I'd like your other daughter, please.' He turned slightly and held out his hand to Ivixa. 'This one. She's exactly what I've been looking for and I feel she'll make me an admirable wife. Hard-working and resilient, not spoiled and pampered.' A glance at Enica showed that she was turning bright red.

'I knew she'd ruin everything,' Enica burst out, surging to her feet and pointing angrily at Ivixa. 'You bitch! Father should have banished you at birth.'

'That's enough!' Adminius bellowed. 'If you didn't make a good impression on Commios, you have only yourself to blame.' He frowned at Commios. 'But are you sure? Ivixa isn't used to being in charge of a household.'

'Rubbish!' The older woman who'd been doing the cooking stomped over to stand before him with her hands on her hips. 'She's done all the work of running this settlement since you married for the second time and you know it. Your wife has concentrated all her efforts on bringing up her child. Much good that did her . . .'

Commios gathered the old woman was someone important in the settlement because the chieftain didn't admonish her for her audacity in speaking up. Instead he nodded. 'Yes, you're right.' He sighed and regarded his older daughter. 'Ivixa, I owe you an apology. You have been treated unfairly and it's my fault. But please, don't feel you have to marry this man in order to escape. I can promise you things will be different around here from now on if you'd rather stay.'

Commios was still holding out his hand to her and she stepped forward and took it. 'I want him,' she said simply. 'I believe we will deal well together.'

He squeezed her hand and sent her a small smile, as well as a heated glance that made her cheeks flush. 'That's settled then. Can we marry tomorrow? Then we'll travel back to my settlement the following day.'

'So soon? But we haven't discussed a dowry or bride-price. And Ivixa will need new clothing and such things.' He glanced at his wife, who looked as though she'd swallowed something sour. 'Perhaps some of Enica's items will be suitable?'

To prevent an all-out marital war, Commios intervened. 'No need. I'll provide everything Ivixa will ever need. We can discuss the rest over another mug of ale after the women have retired for the night.' He raised his eyebrows at Ivixa. 'Does that meet with your approval or am I being too hasty?'

'No, that sounds perfectly acceptable. Thank you.'

'Then that's settled.' He squeezed her hand one more time and let her go, checking to make sure she wasn't headed in the same direction as her half-sister. He had a feeling that could have ended in a bloodbath. Fortunately, Enica stomped off to a sleeping alcove, closely followed by her mother who was attempting to stop a full-blown temper tantrum. Commios shuddered. He'd definitely had a lucky escape there.

And he'd found his perfect match.

As he rode into his own settlement two days later, he had his arms around his wife who was seated in front of him on his horse. He halted just inside the gate and pulled her close, kissing her cheek and nuzzling the side of her neck. Although it was too soon to tell her, he was already in love with her and he hoped she would come to feel the same way about him. They'd had a most satisfactory first night together and he was a little worried she might be sore, but she hadn't complained. Just as he'd thought, she was strong and not one to whine. She'd revelled in his love-making, curious and unafraid. He was already looking forward to a repeat.

'I hope you'll be happy here,' he said. 'Let's go and find my kin.'

Duro and Gisel happened to be on their way to the largest roundhouse and they stopped to stare as Commios rode up to them. He jumped off then turned to lift Ivixa down. With a smile he took her hand and brought her forward.

'Duro, Gisel, may I introduce my wife, Ivixa. My love, this is my brother Duro and his wife. And the imp is Cunobelinos, their son.'

The little boy, carried by his father, struggled to escape and held out his arms to Commios. 'Easy, easy,' Duro muttered. 'I think he's missed his uncle.' He handed over the child and, for the first time, Commios didn't feel a pang of envy in his heart while hugging the little boy. If the gods were willing, he'd soon have his own child, and he couldn't wait. 'Welcome, Ivixa,' Duro continued. 'I see my brother has made a great choice.'

'Yes, welcome.' Gisel came forward and gave Ivixa a hug. 'I'm so glad Commios has finally found someone to share his life with. I hope we'll be the best of friends.' She added in a loud whisper, 'I was also an outsider here when I arrived, so I know what it's like.'

'Thank you. I look forward to getting to know everyone.' Ivixa's eyes were suspiciously shiny. Commios guessed she wasn't used to such consideration or being welcomed anywhere. He was very glad to have changed that. And he'd make sure she was loved and appreciated for the rest of her life.

'Come and meet the rest of our kin,' Duro said, indicating that they should enter the roundhouse.

'Give us a moment, brother. We'll be in shortly,' Commios replied, and received a knowing smile in return.

Duro and Gisel went inside, after he'd given them their son back, and he stopped Ivixa from following them. 'First, though, I need a proper kiss,' he whispered. 'Something to keep me until it's time for bed.'

His wife blushed rosily, but didn't hesitate. Throwing her arms around his neck, she stood on tip-toe to meet his mouth with hers, eagerly, passionately. 'Any time,' she murmured.

Commios closed his eyes and lost himself in pure joy.

He had found his perfect spouse.

Discover Christina Courtenay's Runes novels!

Available now!